IT GLITTERS.

"The amulet looked to be real gold. Rachel brought the chain close to her eyes, searching for the clasp. She touched it lightly with her fingers, and to her great surprise, the catch flew open, and the necklace came apart. She lifted it around her neck and it snapped shut, mysteriously . . ."

IT CHARMS.

"The pendant fell over Rachel's breast, and she considered, as she looked into the mirror, that it became her marvelously. She caught the reflection of the clock behind her, and realized that she ought to be downstairs getting supper. She reached around to take the amulet off but could not find the catch."

IT KILLS.

"Suddenly, from down the hall, several small voices began to argue over a toy; the dog barked, the television set was turned on, and the baby began to cry. Normally, this sudden onslaught of noise would not have bothered her. But tonight it irked her horribly. Pressing on her were the responsibilities the noises represented: the house, the children, the husband. Her whole life had been subsumed by these six loathesome creatures. She wondered darkly how she was going to get even. . . ."

The following morning, the house was a low pile of moldering cinders, black and wet, stinking of fire and waste. The terrifying toll had begun.

THE AMULET

MICHAEL McDOWELL

AVON
PUBLISHERS OF BARD, CAMELOT AND DISCUS BOOKS

THE AMULET is an original publication of Avon Books.
This work has never before appeared in book form.

AVON BOOKS
A division of
The Hearst Corporation
959 Eighth Avenue
New York, New York 10019
Copyright © 1979 by Michael McDowell.
Published by arrangement with the author.
Library of Congress Catalog Card Number: 79-50327
ISBN: 0-380-40584-9

First Avon Printing, April, 1979

AVON TRADEMARK REG. U.S. PAT. OFF. AND IN
OTHER COUNTRIES, MARCA REGISTRADA, HECHO EN
U.S.A.

Printed in the U.S.A.

TO DAVID AND JANE

Had I but all of them, thee and thy treasures,
What a wild crowd of invisible pleasures!
To carry pure death in an earring, a casket,
A signet, a fan-mount, a fillagree-basket!

Robert Browning
"The Laboratory"

Prologue

━━

In March 1965, Fort Rucca—in the southeastern corner of the state of Alabama—was a busy, crowded area. Here new army recruits underwent basic training, and were further instructed in helicopter piloting and helicopter maintenance. It had become known what a terrible war was being fought in the jungles of Vietnam, and how little prepared our soldiers were against that tropical foliage, where thousands of men, and whole factories of machinery and weapons could be moved along supply trails that were invisible from the air. The earliest veterans of the war had come back, and were frantically training more men, with the terrain of Vietnam in mind. The Chattahoochee River is not far from Fort Rucca, and the basin of that slow-moving, wide stream is very similar in density and quality of vegetation, and was the ideal proving ground for those men who would soon see combat.

Fort Rucca is located in the most unfriendly section of Alabama, a flat, featureless landscape, that seems always hot, always menacing, always indignant when farmers try to scratch their meager livings out of the hard soil. The vegetation is coarse, and sharp, and not much good for anything. The only plants that seem to grow well are trees whose lumber is worthless, and shrubs with thorns and briars. The four kinds of poisonous snakes indigenous to the continental United States are found together in only one place: the Wiregrass area of Alabama. That seems only natural to the people who live there.

In one corner of the crowded camp, "wiregrass," the coarse ground cover that gives the area its nickname, had been shorn close, and an extensive firing range constructed for the rifle instruction and practice of army inductees from all over the country. One very hot Friday morning, shortly before noon, and underneath a blazing, cloudless sky, about seventy-five men, in three equal groups, were shooting at targets cut in the shape of men, with yellow faces and slanted eye-slits.

Well behind the line of prone, firing privates were the other fifty who were waiting their turn. Two men, not much different from the others, leaned against the wire fence that separated the camp from the dusty peanut fields belonging to an Alabama state senator. The senator had made a fortune out of this soil, obtaining government subsidies for not raising cotton and corn, and taking a tax loss on his income each year, because somehow or other, the peanut crop always failed. He was one of the very few who could make money off the land of the wiregrass.

The two privates could not have cared less about the senator's peanut fields. One of the men was of middle height, coarsely handsome, and in extraordinary health; from his thick accent it was apparent that he was very much at home in this part of the country. His companion was somewhat taller, but more delicate; his features had a distinctly Jewish cast to them.

The first man, whose name was Dean Howell, said to his companion, "You look here at this, Si." Dean held up the rifle he carried, and thrust the butt of it before Simon's eyes. "You see that pinecone?"

Si nodded. He had already noticed the small pinecone embossed in the lowest corner of the butt of every rifle on the firing range.

Dean continued: "This rifle was made—start to finish—in Pine Cone, Alabama, and my wife Sarah is right there on that 'ssembly line. She had her hands on this piece 'fore I did. It's like it was blessed, in a way."

Si nodded. "How far is Pine Cone from here?"

"Oh," said Dean, "if you was to stand on my shoulders, you could see it. It's about thirty miles." He pointed

2

vaguely over the senator's peanut fields. "We got pine trees and cotton fields and the Pine Cone Munitions Factory and that's about all." He waited a moment, while the line of men fired at the targets again, and then continued, "But the pine trees get burned down, and the cotton gets eaten up, and so there's the rifle plant that's left. Ever'body I know works in that place. You know why?"

Si shook his head, and asked, "Why?"

Dean Howell spoke harshly now. "I tell you why." The rifles fired once more.

"Why?" Si repeated his question. Dean Howell was being deliberately mysterious.

Dean's strange smile turned sour. " 'Cause," he said, with unexpected bitterness, "you get a job there, and you get a deferment—'Services necessary to the National Welfare and Security.' Ever'body I know works in that place," he repeated, with angered significance.

"And you wanted a job there too?" said Si, who had begun to understand Dean's apparent disgust with the Pine Cone Munitions Factory.

"You're right, you're exactly right," said Dean, "and I ought to be there right now myself. I ought to have a good job there, *inside*, not out in the sun like this, building these damn things, or carrying 'em from one place to another. *Not* firing 'em off. I *ought* to be there, 'cause I know the man who's in charge of hiring there, I know him real good, 'cause we used to go after the quail together ever' year."

"Why didn't he hire you then?"

"Well, he said he didn't have no place for me, and that he just had to wait until something opened up, but goddamn I'd have taken anything, I tell you, not to have to go to goddamn Asia. I love this country, but goddamn, I want to have both my legs this time come three years. Well, he was 'waiting for something to open up' when I got drafted, and here I am."

"But your wife had a job there, you said."

"Yeah," said Dean Howell, "Larry thought he could make ever'thing all right by putting Sarah on the line. That's what they call the 'ssembly line in Pine Cone—the 'line' and ever'body knows what you're talking about. But Sarah being on the line didn't make nothing all right.

3

Sarah and I hadn't been married more than a year when I got drafted. Even the people down at the draft board said it was a shame I was getting taken away like that, but they said there wasn't nothing they could do about it, either."

"Dean," said Si, "it sounds like you got the wrong end of the stick."

"Listen, Si, you listen to me—we both did." The two men shook their heads, for neither of them was happy to be in Fort Rucca, with only the prospect of jungle combat before them. There were many rumors just then going around the camp, about tortures that the Vietnamese had designed just to prolong the deaths of captured American soldiers, of the terrible things they could do to a man that would make him beg for immediate execution. Dean pulled a handkerchief out of his back pocket and wiped his forehead and his hands of the sweat there, and then handed it to Si, who did the same. They were being called forward by the platoon sergeant to take their places on the firing line.

They moved quickly through the crowd of shifting men, and dropped to the ground beside one another. Once again, Dean silently pointed out to Si the pinecone on the butt of the rifle, smiled, and winked; he evidently considered the pinecone insignia a kind of good luck charm.

At the other end of the range, the spent targets had been replaced with fresh ones, and the sergeant took his place at the end of the row of prone, expectant men. "Ready!" he called out. "Aim! Fire!"

Briefly the noise was deafening to Si, but the sound continued longer than was usual; then he realized it was not a firing rifle, but a man screaming that he heard. Si turned instinctively to his friend.

Dean Howell was struggling slowly to his feet, both hands clapped over his face. Blood spurted out between his fingers, and poured down over his sweat-stained khaki fatigues. He reeled with the injury, and still screaming, fell back into the stiff brown grass. The Pine Cone rifle lay blown in pieces beneath his writhing body.

Si moved closer, and pulled Dean's hands away from his face, to try to quiet him and determine the extent of the injury. But when he saw the corrugated, bloody mess that

4

was hardly recognizable as a face, with one of the eyeballs dangling by the distended optic nerve, Si staggered backward with unconquerable disgust, and Dean continued his inarticulate screams until he gagged on his own blood.

He was on his feet again, and reeled blindly into a group of men who had watched all this in shocked immobility. They scattered as he fell over into their midst.

Chapter 1

Pine Cone, Alabama, is located on the western edge of the Wiregrass region, tantalizingly near the border of the pine barrens, which are more lonely perhaps, but infinitely more profitable. Another town had been settled in the same spot about 1820, and called by another name that no one remembers, but it was burned down by three Union soldiers, not because it was a rebel stronghold, but because they were drunk. It was not built up again until late in the nineteenth century, and no one knows why.

The town is not on a railroad line, and in fact, after the munitions factory became a place of importance to military leaders, it was necessary to build a spur from the L&N tracks, which run about ten miles east of Pine Cone. Burnt Corn Creek, which meanders through the town and much of the adjoining countryside, is not navigable, even by Boy Scouts in their canoes, who for boating exercise must go many miles south to the junction of Burnt Corn with Murder Creek. (Both were named after certain common practices of settlers in an earlier period of Alabama history.) The water is filled with rapids, and interrupted by trees that fall across the breadth of the narrow watercourse after every heavy rain. It is not even good for swimming, for the margins of the river breed leeches and water moccasins in staggering numbers.

Nor is Pine Cone the center of extensive farming lands.

The Amulet

The tracts and small farms around produce few substantial cash crops, though cotton, peanuts, soy, potatoes, corn, and pecans are in moderate favor with farmers who, with pitiful regularity, fall one by one into insolvency and bankruptcy. Occasionally one of these hard-pressed men will relieve his financial troubles by suicide.

At one time there was a chenille mill in the town, but it folded during the Depression. Now there is the Pine Cone Munitions Factory, and that keeps the town going. Other than this, the principal industry of Pine Cone is said to be three crippled black women who spend their days constructing patchwork quilts which are sold in the North for fabulous sums.

The town is proud of its population of two thousand, and it might well be, since there is nothing to keep them there except stubborn civic pride, overwhelming inertia, or a perverse moral self-discipline bordering on masochism. Eleven churches minister to the needs of unregenerate souls in Pine Cone, and nearly two dozen retail establishments vend articles that the inhabitants of the town may or may not require. There is a public library, not much used, which was set up and maintained by a spinster in the 'twenties. Now it is run by her first cousin once removed, also a spinster, and even nastier to the few children who go there than the first woman had been. The only building that survives from the burning of the town during the Civil War is the jail, a shell of a brick building, with bars on the front windows. It is now almost hidden by vines, and cannot boast of a roof. It is located on property belonging to the hard-shell Baptists, and is supposed to be haunted by the ghost of a slave who starved to death in it.

The police force is limited, but there is not much belligerent crime in Pine Cone, though it must be admitted that what there is, is usually of a violent and often fatal nature. The town has more murders than robberies. This is because most homicides arise out of quarrels among family and friends, and are crimes of passion. A robbery is cold-blooded, and the citizen of Pine Cone, though he will not hesitate to plunge a butcher knife into his wife's heart when he discovers her in bed with his domino crony, is at heart a law-abiding man.

7

MICHAEL MCDOWELL

Sheriff Phelon Garrett has been head of the police force for twelve years; under him is Deputy Ray Barnes. Garrett is often heard to complain that Barnes has a bad aim and a thick head. Officer James Shirley is reliable, though he does not lead a happy domestic existence. Two more policemen spend the greatest part of their time on duty in a cafe near the train tracks which is known more for the friendliness of the two waitresses than for the quality of the food.

Downtown Pine Cone is three blocks of dilapidated storefronts, with the usual complement of a bank, a dime store, three clothing stores, a shoe store, a supermarket (part of the Piggly Wiggly chain), a smaller grocery, a movie theater (closed for thirteen years now), a store that distributes greeting cards and fundamentalist religious literature, two auto-parts supply stores, four gas stations, three restaurants, two 9-to-11 convenience stores, a furniture store, the city hall, and a gift shop that makes all its money on wedding gifts and graduation presents. This area is not so crowded that there is not space for a couple of vacant lots, grown up with weeds, where buildings have been burned and not rebuilt. A go-getting mayor some years back thought to upgrade the image of Pine Cone by putting in three sets of traffic lights in the three intersections in the commercial district. He was not reelected, largely because of this move, and his successor disconnected the lights, though they remain in place.

There is no motel or hotel, but a rooming house can be reached by sidling through the alley that runs between the bank and the more prosperous auto parts store. No one in Pine Cone has any idea what sort of people stop there, or indeed, even of who runs it. Traveling salesmen come only for the day, and stay in the towns to the south of Pine Cone: Andalusia, Opp, Florala—where there are bars.

The street that goes through the center of Pine Cone was optimistically christened Commercial Boulevard, and is distinguished by an archipelago of narrow, neglected traffic islands, which support occasional palm trees. These plants do well enough in the climate of Pine Cone, but would look much more at home a little farther to the south, in Florida. But during the week, shoppers on Com-

8

mercial Boulevard are few, and all appear to have their cash in the pocket of the pants that are still hanging in the closet at home.

But the merchants, in a single flash of financial wizardry, conceived a scheme to draw great numbers of people to shop in Pine Cone. A ticket is given for each dollar's worth of merchandise purchased in every store in the downtown area, and the customer fills out his name and address on the scrap of cardboard, and then deposits it in a great barrel that stands out in front of the city hall, in a specially constructed shelter which is locked up every night. Each Saturday afternoon at three o'clock, the drum is spun around by the head majorette of the county high school, and a ticket is drawn. The winner receives a few hundred dollars, and six months of congratulations and stale jokes and slant-eyed envy from his friends.

The scheme works. This drawing, as the lottery was called, was and continues to be an enormous success in the small rural town—in the entire county in fact—where gambling is something that people did in Nevada and on television and nowhere else. For the first time in their lives, the people of Pine Cone were being offered something for nothing. The town is mobbed all day on Saturday, so that it is difficult to drive a car those three blocks through the center of Pine Cone. Farmers and their wives and their eight children who before had gone to one of the larger towns nearby now come to Pine Cone, do their shopping, carefully (and laboriously) fill out the tickets, deposit them in the rusting drum, and desperately pray for the few hundred dollars that, in truth, would make a substantial difference in the quality of their lives for many months to come.

On Saturday morning, the stores are crowded with people who spend money with glad hearts, knowing that they may have the chance to make it all back in the afternoon. All day there is a line in front of the city hall, everyone in town sticking his few or many tickets through the narrow slot in the top of the barrel. Everyone likes to give it a "lucky" spin, in hopes that the motion will increase the chance that their own ticket will be pulled out by the pretty blond girl in the high white boots, and the gold tassels on her stovepipe hat.

9

The few hundred dollars would mean much to almost anyone living in Pine Cone, for it is not a prosperous community. The richest men in town are the two lawyers, the president of the bank, the dentist, the three general practitioners, and the chiropractor. The richest—the dentist—makes in his best years, with half the eighth grade class going into braces, no more than thirty-two thousand dollars. Certain people stand to inherit money someday, but their kin are hanging stubbornly on to their sorry lives; others have wealthy relatives in other parts of the state, but a rich relative, everyone knows, has a tighter fist than a three-day-old corpse. And everyone, no matter his income, has the same trouble with mortgages and overdrafts.

The residential area that lies to the north of Commercial Boulevard can not exactly be called fashionable, but it is the most desirable area of the town. Here live the professionals, the store owners, and the schoolteachers. Factory workers live in less substantial housing south of Commercial Boulevard. The black section of Pine Cone is on the eastern edge of the town, geographically separated by Burnt Corn Creek. Here the people are often very poor indeed.

The oldest houses in Pine Cone stretch along the highway leading out of the town to the west: they are pleasant, well-constructed buildings, though not to the modern taste. The people who live in them are old, proud, impoverished, and not much thought about. The grammar school is located north of Commercial Boulevard; the junior high school to the south of it. Older students have to take the bus every day to the county high school in Elba. The munitions factory had been constructed just to the west of the town, but recently the town expanded its boundaries so as to include it. It is screened from the highway by heavily wooded vacant lots. Cheap housing for workers had been recently erected up to the parking lot of the plant, and for many people, the Pine Cone Munitions Factory, in the very corner of Pine Cone, is its center.

The people of Pine Cone recognize one principal division of themselves: black and white. Other divisions can be seen, but they don't matter as much. All the black people in the town, about thirty per cent of the population, are descended from slaves who had worked the plantations in the Black Belt, only a few miles to the north. Many of them bear the peculiar last names that facetious white masters had bestowed upon them at the time of their emancipation: Shakespeare and Hiawatha, and Canteloupe. Some of the black women are employed as maids, and some of the black men work at the plant. Other men and women are hired for seasonal work in the fields and some businesses are operated by blacks specifically for their own community, for there is still rigid segregation in many areas of commerce in the deepest portions of the South. The blacks live their own lives on the other side of Burnt Corn Creek.

The white people of Pine Cone are for the most part the great-grandsons and -daughters of the sharecroppers and petty landowners who tried, with no more success than their descendants, to work the soil of this region. The white inhabitants of Pine Cone are not overly educated, they are not overly refined, and they are not overly civil to one another. The community is so homogeneous it seems like an extended family, but it is a family that feuds with itself constantly. The Wiregrass is not a region that breeds tolerance or friendliness, and the more genial of human attributes seem to exist in that place by chance and neglect rather than by cultivation. Neighbors distrust one another as a matter of course, and a brother is very careful when he turns his back on his sister. "To give the benefit of the doubt" is a phrase that is not even understood, much less put into practice, in Pine Cone.

Religion is a great occupation in this part of the country, and there are many factions among the Presbyterians, Methodists, Baptists, Seventh-day Adventists, Congregationalists, and Church of Christ-ers. And many of these denominations are further split up: the Baptists, for instance, came in both the hard-shell and soft-shell variety. Hard-shell Baptists sing their hymns a capella, for they consider bringing a piano or an organ into a sanctuary is no better than turning it into a dance hall. They do not cross their legs, for that is thought to be a form of dancing, and dancing is a sinful abomination. Soft-shell Baptist women cross their legs, but leave the

dancing to the Presbyterians and the Methodists and
cheerfully damn them to hell for it. Three families of
Catholics live in Pine Cone, all of them employed at
the factory. Two of the families go every week for
services in Andalusia; the third is apostate. There are
no Jews in Pine Cone, and no one could be found who
would admit to atheism.

Religion is often hard in Pine Cone but life is not
particularly easy itself, and it gets appreciably sterner once
you cross the city limits out into the countryside. Many
people can see the cotton and peanut fields from their
houses, and some plots are never situated within the
boundaries of the town. People in the country live in un-
painted wooden houses, still without indoor plumbing,
with only fireplaces to heat them through the few bitter
months of the southern winter. They haven't a dollar to
spare for any luxury. The school board had to rescind its
order that no student come to school barefoot, when too
many children from the country were being kept home because no shoes could be afforded.

Country people think that the inhabitants of Pine Cone
are all rich and wicked, and perhaps by comparison, they
are; but people in Pine Cone say that *country* people are
meaner—and they may be right. In any case, the people
who live in the country don't like to go into town any
more than is necessary, probably once a week for most
of them. They have their own little establishments on the
highways which serve their midweek needs admirably—
Morris Emmons' store, for instance, about five miles to the
west of town. It is no bigger than the auto supply store
in Pine Cone, but Morris Emmons sells gas and diesel
fuel (at cheaper prices than in town), provides all manner of canned goods and fresh vegetables, long under-
wear, firearms, spinning tops, bed linen, certain tractor
attachments, scratch feed, calico, domestic hardware, and
fishing bait. And there is even a slaughterhouse in the
back.

In the countryside surrounding it, and in Pine Cone itself, morality is rampant. When a boy playfully filched a
pencil from his best friend, it was universally predicted
that he would end up in the state penitentiary, if he recovered from the whipping that his father adminis-

tered. And among adults, adultery is an unmentionable thing, which only occurs in the Bible and in Mobile. But this morality is that of the hard face: it is scandalous to mow your lawn on Sunday, for that shows disrespect for God, who likes long grass on the seventh day. On the other hand, it is perfectly natural—because it is legal by the laws of the United States—for the president of the bank to foreclose on a piece of property adjoining his own, so that he could purchase it for the price of a dead dog, tear down an old woman's house, and build a swimming pool for himself. The old woman died in a nursing home in Andalusia before the pool could be filled with unchlorinated water.

But it could be said also that there is a great vitality in the mean-spiritedness of the town's inhabitants. Sometimes they are creatively cruel to one another, and there were seasons in which Pine Cone was an exciting place to live—if you were a spectator, and not a victim.

Chapter 2

THE Pine Cone Munitions Factory is made up of half a
dozen large, single-story, clapboard buildings set on piles
of concrete blocks. These unsightly structures were built
during World War II for the emergency production of exploding shells. Pine Cone was selected for the location of
this facility precisely because it was small, insignificant,
and remote—though not so very far from the important
base at Fort Rucca, then technically only a camp—and
because a congressional representative from Alabama on
the Armed Services Committee had a nephew who owned
a tract of land in Pine Cone which, because it was good
for nothing at all, *screamed* out to be purchased at a fabulous sum by the wartime government.

The plant during the war employed a great number of
people, and these lucky ones, many of whom had not
known employment since the beginning of the Depression,
actually dreaded the end of the great conflict in Europe
and the Pacific, because that would also mean the cessa-
tion of their weekly pay envelopes which, if not generous,
were at least regular. They were right, for directly after
Japan surrendered, the railway stopped bringing into Pine
Cone the carloads of parts that had been so easily assembled into the bullet-shaped instruments of destruction.
The people who worked at the factory were let go, and
they wandered disconsolately about the town, making

trouble late in the night, consuming great amounts of bootleg whiskey (an industry that was not affected by the end of World War II), and wondering what they were going to do next.

Unknown to them, however, the buildings had been sold privately, without bidding, and at a scandalously low sum, to the first cousin of the Alabama congressional representtative who had got the plant located there in the first place. When questioned regarding the propriety of this, the Alabama congressman replied that the family had a sentimental attachment to the acres in Pine Cone, and wished to retain them in the family. He wasn't sure, but he thought that his great-grandmother might be buried in the vicinity.

The machinery that had put together exploding shells was quickly converted for the assembly of a kind of rifle then much in favor with the army. Modifications, suggested by a Pentagon general who was rabid on the subject of repeating rifles, were incorporated and before long a large government contract had been awarded to the Pine Cone Munitions Factory, though as yet it had only its physical facilities as capital, half a dozen menial office workers, as many more incompetent executives, and no stock whatsoever. The workers were hired back as fast as they could sober up, and since that time the Pine Cone Munitions Factory has turned out many millions of firearms, which have been employed in training camps mostly, but also in Korea and, more recently, in Vietnam.

The factory employs nearly five hundred workers, a full quarter of Pine Cone's population; that works out to a much heftier percentage of the town's adult, ambulatory, sane population. The executives are hometown men who are not very bright, but can be trusted by the owners of the plant to do exactly what they are told. All the girls who go away to college or to vocational school can be sure to find a place in the offices of the plant when they return to Pine Cone to support their mothers, or wait on their fathers, or humor their husbands. They are secretaries and file clerks.

The white men in the town work the heavy machinery, and are trained in a specific skill that is sufficient to earn them their weekly check and to keep them busy for forty hours a week, but does not have much meaning or application outside the factory. But it is the women of Pine Cone —at least the white women—who keep the place going, for they are put to work on the assembly line, setting in screws and adjusting the sites and locking in the barrel of every rifle that lurches past the conveyer belt. The management of the factory has found that it is best to have women in these boring jobs, because they are more patient than their husbands and brothers, less likely to complain of low wages, and they do not scurry about for promotions. Without these wives, and daughters, and sisters of Pine Cone, the family of the Alabama congressional representative (he has never been defeated for reelection) would have a great deal less money than it does possess at this time.

The black men are put to work on maintenance crews about the factory, and it is their responsibility to see that the buildings are kept in repair, that no damage comes to the machinery through grime or sabotage, and that the parking lot is kept free of liquor bottles. Black women are put to work after hours in the buildings, sweeping the place clean every night of candy wrappers, spent shells, and iron filings that are spewed out of the die presses.

The management of the plant even contrives in summer to find menial positions for the sullen teenagers of Pine Cone; having them endlessly restack empty crates, or spray letters and complicated directions onto the sides of boxes that are to be burned, or destroy the raccoons and skunks that make their homes, in great numbers, beneath the buildings. In addition to these, several high school senior boys are employed year-round for a few hours each day after school. Their job is to test the rifles. They stand out in a clearing a few hundred yards from the factory buildings and fire again and again at targets several dozen yards away or sometimes, for variety, at birds that fly overhead. The rifles are loaded for them by two senior boys from the county high school for blacks, for the management is nervous seeing young black men holding rifles. The white boys become quite proficient in the course of the year, and when they subsequently enter the army, by choice or by ill fortune, it is not infrequently that they are awarded medals and commendations for sharpshooting. Dean Howell had been one of these. He had been very familiar with the kind of rifle that destroyed his face and a large part of his brain.

The Pine Cone Munitions Factory was like the town of Pine Cone itself, insofar as both were small and mean. The owners of the plant made a good deal of money off the place, and it caused them not a whit of trouble. The plant made one kind of rifle, that is, it assembled one kind of rifle: the parts were manufactured in other places—in Detroit, and in Des Moines—then shipped to Alabama. A few special pieces that could not be obtained elsewhere were stamped out in Pine Cone, but the metal plates were forged in Pennsylvania, and brought in once a month on the L&N spur. A more aggressive owner would have expanded the capacity of the plant, diversified the manufacture, upgraded and streamlined the facilities, but really, what need was there? The family members of the congressman were lazier than they were greedy, and they liked to spend all their time in their houses on the Florida Gulf coast. They got checks every month, which were very handsome, and once a year they threw away the annual report without even looking at it. Once in a while they worried vaguely about a union coming in and making trouble, or fretted that the minimum wage was going to be raised again, or they dreaded being sued for negligence in the event of an industrial accident; but they didn't concern themselves so much that their tans faded, and they invariably decided against reinvesting profits to increase the safety precautions in the plant buildings.

The Alabama congressional representative had a grand-nephew who went to business school somewhere in the North, and came to his great-uncle with all sorts of ideas on how to "maximize long-term profit" for the Pine Cone Munitions Factory, which he had never laid eyes on. The Alabama congressional representative explained carefully to the young man, that until he got rid of such ideas entirely, he was not to go near the place. "It made money for your mama, and your grandmama. It made money for me, and it sent you through eight years of school in the goddamn North. You don't touch it, and maybe it'll get you through the rest of your life, so that

you can afford to have all the crazy ideas that you want."
The Alabama congressional representative was a savvy
man, though you wouldn't have known it to hear what the
grand-nephew had to say about him after this interview.

Chapter 3

DEAN Howell's young wife Sarah sat at the assembly line from eight to twelve in the morning, and then again from one to five in the afternoon, five days a week. She set three screws into the butt of the Pine Cone rifle. The woman next to her—her best friend and next-door neighbor—flipped the rifle over, and set in another three screws. Becca Blair thought that she had the more interesting task, because on her side was the embossed pinecone that was the emblem of the company, while Sarah Howell's side was smooth and unadorned.

Becca explained, "The reason you got this job at all is because Marie Larkin died—she had a brain tumor, and I suffered with her through ever' damn day of it—and she had this place on the line, where I am right now. I had your place, then they brought you in, but they moved me up to Marie's place, because I had the seniority. I had been here for eight years, so they handed me the side with the pinecone on it. It wouldn't have been fair to give it to you, coming in fresh like you did, you know . . . you probably wouldn't have appreciated it the way I do . . . it would have caused unrest . . ."

Sarah said she understood and that it was only fair that Becca should get to look at the pinecone all day.

Everything in the factory was new to Sarah, and strangest of all was the very notion of work, for she had

19

never before been able to find employment in the depressed economy of Pine Cone. She was sure that the factory was going to ruin what good looks she had left after three months of living with her mother-in-law. The girl was slender, above average height, with thick dark hair that she had always arranged as simply as possible. Her smile was arch, and many people objected that it was mocking, but this was not so. Sarah's eyes were black, moved about ceaselessly, and seemed altogether too intelligent to be wasted in Pine Cone; but wasted they were, and there were times that Sarah thought she had rather have them put out entirely rather than to have them staring—for forty hours a week—at three little screws being worked into the butt of a military rifle.

But Sarah Howell was not responsible only for herself; she had two other people to think of now. She had just turned twenty, but girls in Alabama—those without money, whose parents work in shops or are farmers—grow up quickly. She had been married to Dean Howell almost a year before he went off into the army. They had known one another in high school, though Dean was a couple of years older, had dated once or twice, and then, for no very good reason, had decided to get married as soon as Sarah had graduated. Perhaps it was that Sarah's parents had both died, of different kinds of cancer, within six months of one another and Dean felt sorry for the girl, thus left all alone; perhaps it was just that Dean wanted to spite his mother.

Sarah and Dean had lived for a while in a trailer camp just outside the city limits of Pine Cone, but Dean lost his job at the Piggly Wiggly supermarket because of a fight he had with one of the stock boys. Dean broke the boy's arm, and the boy was the son of the manager's first cousin. During the depressing season of his employment, Dean fell behind in the payments on the trailer, and it was repossessed; he and Sarah were forced to move into town, and share the house inhabited by Dean's widowed mother. Sarah was displeased with this setup, because Josephine Howell had never liked her daughter-in-law, and had tried to persuade her son not to marry at all. Now the woman maintained only that her son had made the wrong choice. She would be completely happy now, she claimed, if Dean had only married Jackie Madden, when she was still available, because *she* had a sweet temper, could cook, and would stand to come into money when her grandmother died.

Dean was not successful in obtaining work, because his temper was known, and there were few jobs anyway; but when a place opened up on the assembly line at the plant, Dean's old hunting buddy, who was in charge of hiring at the plant, gave Sarah the job, and this eased their financial condition somewhat.

Before he was able to find himself work, however, Dean was drafted into the army. He was sent to train at Fort Rucca. Because he had shown considerable mechanical aptitude on the intelligence tests that the army routinely administered, he was being trained in helicopter maintenance. It was virtually certain that he would be sent to Vietnam, for this was 1965, during the first great buildup of American forces in that part of Asia.

Sarah lived alone with her mother-in-law now, and every day she thanked her stars that so good and kind a woman as Becca Blair lived next door, so close that they could wave to one another out their kitchen windows while they were washing dishes.

It was not a happy life that Sarah Howell led, but she had resigned herself to it as being no worse than she had ever imagined life would be, though certainly it was no better.

Becca Blair was about forty, with harsh good looks. Her husband had run away more than ten years before, and since that time Becca had lived alone, finishing off the payments on their house, and raising their daughter. Margaret Blair was now sixteen, and in her junior year of high school. But in this time of her grass widowhood, for she had legally divorced her husband, Becca had not lacked for male companionship. Jo Howell despised her next-door neighbor and said at least twice a week, that "Becca Blair is no better than she has to be, and sometimes she's not even as good as that!" But Becca Blair was a good friend to Sarah Howell, and with her good humor and unfailing spirit, had pretty much talked Sarah out of her depression about being left alone with Dean's mother. Becca said all the things about Jo Howell that Sarah thought but did not dare say herself. "That old woman," Becca Blair would exclaim to Sarah on their way to work every morning, "mean as the hell that's prepared for her, with a rear end like the side of a Mack diesel, making you *wait* on her. Sarah, I don't see how you put up with it, making you wait on her like you was paid forty dollars a week to do it, and she don't do a thing all day long while you and me are twisting our fingers off at the plant. I see you at night, and I know you do the laundry, I see you hanging out your sheets by the light of the moon, and I tell you, I don't see why you put up with it! She's not your mama, she's Dean's mama, and that's not the same thing at all "

"Well," said Sarah, "she does let me live there rent free."

"Honey," replied Becca, "besides the fact that you buy all the food, she'd have to *pay* me to live in that house with her. Don't seem like I have ever seen her standing on them two fat ankles of hers."

Sarah laughed and felt better about her lot.

Becca Blair was religious, but hers was a strange religion of fear and superstition; she wore charms about her neck, and was afraid to step out of the house on certain days, and lay shivering in bed at night with the fear of evil spirits in the pantry. There were partitions, about shoulder high, that separated the women on the assembly line. This was to keep them from talking to one another, supposedly; though sustained conversation was impossible anyway, because of the noise of the machinery and the conveyer belt. But on these partitions Becca had placed, with pins and thumbtacks and nails, numerous Catholic artifacts: lithographed cards, a couple of rosaries, and even a tiny vitrine with a figure of the Pietà surmounting a crude copy of Da Vinci's "The Last Supper." "I tell you, Sarah, I tell you something," Becca would sometimes whisper to her friend, "I'm scared as hell of going to hell." But she was never strong enough to give up her men or her weekend six-pack of beer for that fear, and she listened gratefully when Sarah would try to convince her that there were worse things than men and beer: "Like being mean, like being mean at the heart, like Jo Howell."

Chapter 4

SARAH Howell had no car, which is a considerable hardship in a place like Alabama, which sets great store by automobiles, and where the possession of one is not deemed a luxury, but an absolute necessity. The supermarket does not make deliveries in Pine Cone, there is no public transit system, and no taxi service since 1937 (and it had been a failure and a joke even then). In the newer parts of town, the municipal government had not even bothered to put in sidewalks, for who walked? Schoolchildren, perhaps, when they lived not more than a block or so from the school, and even then only in the finest weather.

Dean and Sarah had had a car when they married, of course, and they had ridden in it down to Panama City, Florida, for their honeymoon. They stayed in a miserable little cottage in a complex of many such small run-down buildings collectively called the Bide-A-Wee Inn. The Bide-A-Wee was not very expensive, and it was just across the highway from the Gulf of Mexico and Dean and Sarah had enjoyed themselves very much, walking up and down the beach and fishing off the great pier. At night, they played carpet golf or lost themselves in an arcade that boasted over a hundred and fifty pinball machines. A mechanized gypsy in a glass case had pointed to

23

the jack of clubs with a broken finger and then promised Sarah a long life, ample fortune, and many friends.

The 1959 Ford Country Squire station wagon got them to Florida and it got them back to Pine Cone; it lasted through the first ten months of their marriage and would probably have seen Sarah through the three years that Dean was scheduled to be away from her had he not smashed it to junk the night before he was to leave for Fort Rucca. He was drunk, in the company of two young men who were not going into the army, and, driving without headlights, had plowed into a fence post about eight miles outside of town, on property belonging to Jack Weaver, a not-very-prosperous pig farmer. Mr. Weaver was understanding when he learned that Dean was to go into the army the next morning, and his wife Merle bound up the foreheads of Dean's two companions with much sympathy. Then all three men rode back into Pine Cone in the back of Mr. Weaver's pickup truck, but the Country Squire was left in a drainage ditch, until it was taken away about two months later by someone who wanted the parts.

Dean left for Fort Rucca, before dawn, without telling Sarah about the accident. She was very surprised not to see the car in front of the house the next morning when she needed to get to work, but supposed that one of Dean's companions had had to drive her husband home the night before, and had kept the automobile overnight. She learned the truth when she talked to the wife of one of these men at the plant on morning coffee-break. If there had been any way of getting in touch with Dean right then, Sarah thought she would have yelled at him for not having told her. An accident was an accident, it was even excusable that he had been drunk, but there was no justification for his cowardice in keeping the news from her. But when she wrote to him that night she could only think how depressed Dean had been about going off to Fort Rucca, and of course there was the possibility that he might not come home alive from Vietnam. Sarah had not had the heart to bring the car up to him, except in passing, asking what she should do about the insurance.

No insurance money was forthcoming, for Dean had not carried collision coverage. All of Sarah's money went into the household expenses, and she had none to spare, especially not the kind of money that is needed for car payments. Dean's checks from the army were meager; he kept half for his incidental expenses, and the other half went directly to his mother. Sarah saw not a penny of these funds, and Jo explained to her daughter-in-law, "I told Dean you didn't need the money, and you don't. You make lot more than him. You got your mama and daddy's insurance money laid up somewhere, and if you really wanted a Cadillac Eldorado, I know you could take the bus down to Mobile, and walk right into the Cadillac showroom, and drive that thing right off the floor. There is not a reason in this world for Dean to send you money when you don't need it, and I can't work and I'm not going to be getting Social Security for another eight years and four months, unless I go blind first, and then I'll get it sooner . . ."

Sarah had explained to her mother-in-law many times that her parents had left only enough money to pay for their funerals, and to discharge their debts. There had been nothing left over for Sarah herself. Jo had always told Sarah in return that she didn't believe a word of this. Sarah had stopped trying to convince her, and when Jo now demanded, every other day, that Sarah go out and buy them a Cadillac Eldorado, Sarah merely said, "Jo, I couldn't afford a glove to put in the glove compartment . . ."

Sarah was again fortunate in living next door to Becca Blair, for Becca was always pleased to take Sarah wherever she needed to go, and if she wasn't available, Becca's daughter Margaret had strict instructions to make the purple Pontiac available to Sarah at any time. This was no great hardship on Becca, however, for the two women maintained schedules that were quite similar. They went to work and left it at the same time, needed to shop at the grocery store as often (and had just as soon do it together anyway), and whenever Jo bore down particularly hard on Sarah (usually every weekend when Jo and Sarah were in the house together for many uninterrupted hours) Becca was more than happy to drive Sarah around out in the country until she had recovered herself. Sarah grew to think of the front passenger seat as her own, and learned how to open the glove compartment of the car without all the little statues of the Virgin Mary and Saint Christopher tumbling out onto the floorboards.

Most days, after work, Sarah would ask Becca to drive around Pine Cone once before they went home. Sarah always said it was because she wanted a little fresh air after having been cooped up in the factory all day, and Becca every day agreed cheerfully, exclaiming, "What a good idea! Let's do it!"—as if it were the first time that Sarah had asked such a thing of her. Becca was sure, in her own mind, that Sarah simply didn't want to have to return directly to the house where Josephine Howell was waiting for her.

Chapter 5

JOSEPHINE Howell's parents had lived in a small house halfway between the Weavers' farm and Morris Emmons' store, but that was long before either of those latter places existed. The house burned down, with Jo's parents in it, when Jo was eight years old. The child, already stout, which was remarkable in an area where children of farmers more commonly suffered from malnutrition, was out picking pecans off the ground in a neighboring orchard at the time. Pecans sold for five cents a pound in Pine Cone, but they were proved much more valuable to little Josephine in that they preserved her life.

The cause of the fire was never known, though it must be admitted that it was never really looked into either. After this accident little Josephine went to live with her only surviving relative, Bama, a second cousin (twice removed), who was old, infirm, and most people said, insane. Jo was sixteen when the old woman drowned in Burnt Corn Creek, in her eighty-seventh year. No one could ever determine what the old woman had been doing down there on the bank, since she had always maintained to anybody who would listen how much she hated and feared running water. No one however much regretted her passing, and many were even relieved, for Josephine's cousin had been a spiteful woman who kept grudges against the third generation of a family that had wronged her. She was poor, physically almost helpless, and had possessed no real influence in the scattered community of farmsteads, yet it was thought very bad luck to be on the wrong side of her. This bad luck was a very corporeal thing, and would manifest itself in loathsome boils and ulcerations of the skin, at the best, and at the worst was evidenced in sudden violent death. But Alabama was a backward place then, where loathsome skin diseases and sudden violent deaths were not uncommon phenomena anyway.

Before the meager wooden headstone had been raised on the old woman's grave, Jo had married Jimmy Howell, a young dirt farmer, who didn't know what he wanted out of life, and wasn't smart enough to realize that what he most certainly didn't want was a wife like Josephine. Even when she was young, and she married when she was no more than seventeen, Josephine Howell was both large-boned and fat. It is a shape ill-suited for the hard life of the spouse of a dirt farmer. Jimmy Howell had raised cotton while a bachelor, but Josephine complained so much of the difficulty in stooping to work with the plants, that he had switched over to corn, though it was a less profitable concern.

Josephine would have refused to work the farm altogether had she not realized that her effort was absolutely necessary for their economic survival. She had not wanted children, had no wish for the bother of raising and caring for them; but after seventeen years of marriage, she gave her husband a son—not to please Jimmy Howell, but to provide a worker for the farm. Jo raised Dean with one object in mind: that he should take her place in the fields, and before five years had elapsed, Dean had proved himself already a better, more valuable worker than his mother. Jo retired in triumph to her kitchen, with her radio, until Jimmy Howell died. Then she took the insurance money and the scant proceeds from the sale of their forty-acre farm (it had increased from thirty acres in their thirty-five years of marriage), and purchased a small house in Pine Cone, one that was old but still in fair condition. It had been one of the first to be built south of Commercial Boulevard. Jo had wanted a new house, but could not afford it. The whole of her life, she grumbled, had been like that.

It was sometimes said, in the places where farmers gather, that Josephine Howell had driven her husband to an early grave with her sullen temper, her constant complaining, and her intractable laziness, just so that when he was dead she could sell the farm and move into Pine Cone, where she wouldn't have anything to do but grow fatter than she already was, if that was possible. The problem was, that she had had to wait until Dean was old enough to support her, so that she wouldn't have to do any work at all. The wives of these farmers whispered that her means of disposing of her husband had not been of the legal variety, but this has to be discounted as malicious gossip. It was well known that Jimmy Howell had died of a snakebite, though the doctor couldn't tell exactly what kind it had been, and no one had seen the reptile. Two fang marks were found on the dead man's leg just above the ankle, and it was very likely that he had been bitten in the field. Mal Homans was a farmer who owned acreage immediately adjoining that of Jimmy Howell, and whenever this story was repeated, Mal invariably said: "I'd think it was Jo Howell put them marks on Jimmy's legs with her own teeth, and it was poison out of her own mouth that killed him, except that she's too fat to bend down that far . . ."

Jo Howell paid no attention to what people said; she and her teenaged son lived quietly together in the small house, and much the greatest portion of Dean's minuscule salary went to keep them in food. At this time, Dean was much oppressed by his mother and wanted desperately to leave her, though he knew that if he did, she would be forced to go on welfare.

Dean wed Sarah Bascom much against his mother's wishes, but this attempt to be free of Jo was a failure. Sarah was not fond of her mother-in-law, but she insisted that Dean not abandon the woman altogether. When he lost his job, and the trailer was seized by the bank, Dean with his bride reluctantly returned to the house that belonged to his mother.

To Jo's credit, she ignored the fact that he had treated her shabbily in the previous few months. On the other hand, she did not treat Sarah any more kindly though she knew that her daughter-in-law had stood up for her cause with Dean. Dean and Sarah had been living in the second bedroom of the house at the time that he was drafted, and now Jo was alone with Sarah.

It was common knowledge that Jo Howell did not get along with her daughter-in-law, and that the household was not a cheerful one. It was Sarah who was invariably pitied, and in fact admired for putting up with Jo Howell's harsh ways. Not only did Sarah work very hard to bring money into the household, had for a time supported both her husband and his mother, but she waited on Jo Howell as well, performed all sorts of little services for that fat, lazy woman, who sat around the house all day long, watching television and eating Ritz crackers.

Every afternoon at five-thirty, when Sarah Howell returned from the Pine Cone Munitions Factory, she found Jo Howell sitting in a rocking chair in their simply furnished, dusky living room. The sun was going down on the other side of the house, and the principal light in the room was from the television set. Jo usually pretended to be absorbed in the late afternoon movie, or whatever actress happened to be talking to Mike Douglas, so that she wouldn't have to speak to her daughter-in-law. But on one afternoon late in March Jo Howell, with the remote control, turned off the set as soon as Sarah came in the back door.

Sarah knew something was up, when she could not hear the television. She put the groceries down on the counter, and went directly in to Jo. The woman sat in her accustomed chair, grimly smiling. Sarah distrusted the woman, had never had any liking for her, and actually hated the way that she looked: oily and gross, with streaked, greasy hair pulled hard back from her face. Jo's eyes were small and black, and loose flesh almost closed over them, especially when she looked hard at you.

"Hey, Jo," said Sarah, and tried not to let show the apprehension that she felt. But there was no sense in antagonizing Jo before she even knew what the matter was. Their argument would come soon enough, but sometimes, when Sarah put a cheerful face before it all, she was allowed to get through an entire evening easily enough—and these days, with Dean gone, she really didn't ask for much more than that.

Jo replied nothing at all, but stared hard at her daughter-in-law. Sarah sighed then, a small sigh, and fell into the very corner of the couch with a mixture of fatigue, curiosity, and impatience.

"Sarah . . ." began Jo, very slowly. Sarah was glad that she didn't own a dog, because Jo looked as if she were about to inform her that it had just been run down in the road.

"What, Jo?"

"Army called, Sarah . . ." Jo was holding on to every word.

"What'd the army want with you?" said Sarah trying, but not able to match her mother-in-law's sullen deliberateness of tone.

"Wasn't me they wanted. They wanted to talk to you . . ."

"What'd they want, Jo? I got to go put up the groceries." Sarah wanted Jo to get on with this; it wasn't that she was worried about anything that Jo might have to say, she just didn't want to give Jo the satisfaction of keeping her guessing, keeping her in suspense. It was one of Jo's favorite games, and one of the most exasperating.

"Dean's coming home . . ."

"Why," said Sarah, involuntarily, in her surprise. "Why's he coming home now? He got leave three weeks ago, and I didn't think he could get it again so soon. He said—"

Jo interrupted her. "Dean's coming home for good."

Sarah moved her hand in a slight protest, and she gazed on Josephine Howell with annoyance and apprehension.

Chapter 6

SUMMER comes early to south Alabama. Less than two
months later, when Sarah Howell returned home from
work a little after five, the air was stifling hot, and water
from a late-afternoon shower burned off the driveway in
a slowly dissipating fog.

Jo Howell hated the heat because it reminded her of
the years in the fields with Jimmy. In summer, all the curtains of her house were kept closed from early morning to
sundown. This kept out only a little of the seasonal
warmth, and all of the cooling breezes and cheering light.
Sarah Howell moved directly through the kitchen, into
the dim, close living room, paused a moment, and then
resolutely entered her own bedroom.

Double drapes were drawn close here, and the venetian blinds behind them lowered; the room was almost
wholly dark, and Sarah could see nothing until her eyes
became accustomed to the lack of light. In those moments,
when she stood with her hand behind her, on the knob of
the door, she could hear the soft whirr of an oscillating
fan, and beneath that, somewhere, the irregular breathing
of two people.

"Home late," said Josephine Howell.

Sarah could just make out the figure of her mother-in-
law. She sat in an overstuffed chair that had been drawn
out of its usual place in the corner to stand at the foot of

the bed. "No, I'm not," Sarah said, and glanced at the clock on the dresser: its luminous dial read 5:20.

"Clock's wrong," said Josephine.

Sarah did not bother to contradict her mother-in-law. There was something monumentally immobile about that great woman's bulk oozed, for all the afternoon Sarah was sure, into the soft faded plush of that chair. Sarah had brought that chair from her parents' house, one of the few pieces that survived the paying of the debts after their deaths. "So," said Sarah, "you took over that chair too."

"You're just lucky I'm here to take care of him during the day," said Jo, with quiet malice.

For the first time since she had entered the room, Sarah glanced down at the bed. In it lay her husband, his face and neck completely swathed in white bandages. His flat, tight stomach was bare, and below the waist he was covered with loose pajama pants that had belonged to his father. The bed had been turned down but he rested, completely still and breathing just perceptibly, on top of the sheets. Dean's eyes were wrapped over, and the bandages were parted over the mouth, a simple black slit that widened and contracted with the man's breathing.

Sarah stared a few seconds at the figure, refusing to admit to herself that she still couldn't even recognize it as her husband. It was difficult to feel anything but revulsion for that anonymous body that responded to nothing, that only breathed and swallowed, and filled bedpans.

Sarah glanced back to her mother-in-law. For the first time she saw that Jo had been sewing in the almost non-existent light, putting a new hem on one of her vast shapeless dresses.

Jo nodded in the direction of her son. "Asleep," she said briefly.

"How can you tell?" asked Sarah. Since he had returned, Sarah had been unable to make out any changes or variations in her husband's movements or reactions.

"His wife ought to know," said Jo.

Sarah shook her head with fatigue mixed with despair, and sat in a straight chair beside the bed. She sighed despite herself and wearily removed her shoes. "Well," she said, "I don't. I can't tell when he's awake. I can't tell when he's asleep. I don't know if he's hungry, or wants to—"

"You ought to *feel* them things, a wife ought to know her husband like she knows her own kitchen."

"He just lies there, though," sighed Sarah. For the past week she had been relying on Jo to tell her what to do for Dean. She wondered if he ever heard them talking about him; Sarah didn't like to address him directly, because it was like talking to a corpse.

Sarah stood up out of the chair, and removed her dress. After putting it on a hanger back in the closet, she took a paper fan on a stick from the little rickety bedside table, and sat down again in her slip.

Sarah fanned herself wearily, wondering how long she would be able just to sit still here without Jo lighting into her about something or other, something she had done, something she hadn't done. There was bound to be something.

She thought suddenly how much she disliked the doctors at Fort Rucca—with the single exception of the one who had proved himself of so much assistance to her with the government forms—the doctors who had taken care of Dean after the accident on the firing range. They weren't good men, she thought, and it wasn't just because they had strange accents and came from different parts of the country; it was that they hadn't seemed to realize that Dean's life was ruined—probably just as she hadn't realized at first that hers was ruined along with it.

Becca had driven her over to Fort Rucca as soon as the news came, that very night. She had even offered to let Jo go along as well, but Dean's mother only said, "He'll be home soon enough. I'll have plenty of time to be with him then. Besides, I ought to stay here and get things ready for him coming back, coming home for good." Becca said nothing to this little speech, and if Sarah had not been almost beside herself with worry over Dean's condition, she would have made a couple of little digs regarding the probable extent of Jo's preparations for Dean's homecoming.

They had arrived past visiting hours, but Dean's condition was so bad that it was thought that Sarah ought to be allowed to see her husband, while she still had the chance. It was really not known at first whether he would survive or, surviving, whether his wife would want him. He had already been wrapped in the bandages that he still wore. He made no special movement when she entered the room, when she came nearer his bedside, when she turned in tears and left. Kindly, the nurse had told Sarah that her husband was asleep, but Sarah had known better than that.

They kept him seven weeks more. He was no longer in danger of dying, but there didn't appear to be much life in him either. The doctors talked hopefully of the surface wounds healing more or less quickly, but they were more vague when they spoke of the good that could be accomplished by a plastic surgeon in ameliorating his ravaged features, and could not be brought to speak a word of any operation that might help to restore the part of his brain that had been seared away in the blast of the exploding rifle. They told Sarah, in quiet voices, that they could not even know the extent of the damage until Dean had rested himself for some time, till he had got over the physiological shock of the injury to his head. That didn't make sense to Sarah, but she must suppose that they knew more about what was wrong with Dean than she did. Yet she had never got over the notion that something they knew about Dean they were not telling her.

The doctors allowed Dean to return to Pine Cone because they said there was very little that constant care at the hospital could do for him that could not be done better, or to more effect, with Sarah and his mother at home. It would have been a different case, the doctors continued, if they had not been assured that Dean's mother was in the house all day to make sure that he was all right. But as things stood, he would probably recover quicker in familiar, congenial surroundings. He was to return to Fort Rucca once a week for a checkup, but when Sarah explained that she had no car in which to transport her husband, one of the doctors suggested that since he lived in Opp, it was no great hardship for him to go through Pine Cone once a week and check on Dean in his own home before he came to work at Rucca. Sarah said that she was thankful for this, as indeed she was; she would not have wanted to take too much advantage of

Becca's good nature to the extent of a weekly trip with Dean—though she was sure that Becca would readily have agreed to the inconvenience, and would never have admitted that it was a burden.

This doctor, who lived in Opp, had taken a liking to Sarah, and one afternoon, had talked to her for a good half hour, advising her about veterans' benefits for those disabled in the line of duty, even going so far as to secure for her the proper forms to be filled out, and promising to do what he could to expedite the matters. Of course there were to be no present charges for Dean's medical care, nor would there be so long as he continued to see the doctors at Fort Rucca. But Sarah was warned that there might be—there would doubtless be—problems in the years to come, and she ought to be cognizant of what was Dean's due in these things.

Sarah and Becca spent several evenings filling out the forms as carefully as possible, for Becca, who was superstitious in things small and great, had warned Sarah that a single mistake would negate the entire claim. If she misspelled a word, Dean would never get a penny out of the government for what had happened to him. Now the forms had been submitted, and Sarah awaited the government's decision on how many dollars a week Dean's injury had been worth. It was these thoughts that went around and around in Sarah's mind, while she stared at Dean— and saw little more than he did, with the bandages over his eyes—when Jo, looking up suddenly from her sewing, said harshly, "How much do you think we'll get?"

Sarah shook herself slightly to dissipate the melancholy reveries, and said, "I don't know. I don't have any idea, Jo. I asked the doctor, but he didn't tell me, he said it was best to say nothing at all, because you never knew what the government was going to say about these things—"

"I sure hope it's enough to buy a air conditioner for this room," said Jo, impatiently trammeling the end of Sarah's response, "I sure hope we can get a two-ton job in here, because it sure is hot, and Dean is suffering. Look how he's just laying there, burning in hell on the top of the covers—"

Dutifully, Sarah looked at the figure on the bed. "He's

36

not sweating," she said, and wondered if it was really her husband beneath the bandages.

" 'Course you can't see the sweat," said Jo, "it's under the bandages. Hot as hell under them bandages. The bandages soak that sweat up, and you can't see it, but I know it's there, and Dean is suffering, like you and I don't suffer. We got to have at least two-tons in here, I've got the place marked in the Sears catalogue, so that Dean won't suffer so—"

"We also got to buy a lot of medicine with that money when it comes. I can get it at the PX over at Rucca, but it's still expensive, Jo, and the doctor says that Dean has to have that medicine."

"A two-ton air conditioner would do Dean a world of good more than a whole handful of pills taken every hour on the hour. I know it would and you ought to know it too."

"Well," said Sarah placidly, "we have to do what the doctor says do, or else I guess they'll take Dean back to Rucca—"

"Nope!" cried Jo. "They won't take him back. I got him, and he's not getting out of my sight again. He left me once, and he married you. He left me again and they blew his face off . . ."

Sarah determined that she would not take offense. She smiled at her mother-in-law, though that was possibly the last thing in the world she felt like doing at that moment, and said, "You do a good job, Jo. I'm glad that you can be here during the day with him. We wouldn't have him here at all if it weren't for you. He's taken care of, and he's not so lonely."

Jo nodded with reluctant satisfaction. She didn't like to agree with Sarah on any subject at all.

"Larry Coppage said he was coming by after the plant was closed," said Sarah. "He said he wanted to see Dean, see how he was."

"I know," nodded Jo, with a malignant smile. "He called me up earlier from the plant. Dean and I have been getting ready for him."

"Do you talk to him?" said Sarah curiously. It was not idle questioning, she wanted to know. Dean never moved, Dean never showed recognition of anything in Sarah's presence, and she found it impossible to address a remark directly to him. When she was alone with Dean, she was completely silent. When Jo was with them (which was most of the time) Sarah directed all her remarks to her mother-in-law.

Jo evaded the question. "I know what Dean wants, and I know when he wants it."

"I don't see how you can tell. He doesn't talk, he doesn't say a word. They won't even tell me if he's got a voice or not."

"Don't matter if he says anything or he don't," snapped Jo. "*I* know it. And you ought to know it—you're his wife."

They had been through it more than once, and Sarah didn't want to pursue the argument. She was bound to lose, and for all she knew, it was possible that such bickering might have an adverse effect on Dean's recovery. She shrugged and said, "Wake him up. Larry's on his way."

"He weren't never asleep," said Jo quietly, but with an unmistakable smirk of triumph.

With a little shock, Sarah stared down at the figure of her husband still motionless on the bed. While she was trying to figure out which time her mother-in-law had lied to her, telling her that Dean was asleep, or that he had been awake all the time, the doorbell rang.

Chapter 7

SARAH pulled a robe quickly around her and went to the front door. She opened it to a man about thirty, with a good-natured but not handsome face. Though he was clumsily dressed, it was apparent that he had a great deal more money than the Howells. His current-model Buick Riviera was parked in front of the house.

"Hey, Sarah," said the man shyly, with lowered eyes.

"Larry," Sarah replied with a warm smile, generously trying to relieve the man of his obvious embarrassment.

"I didn't see you at the plant today," he said hesitantly.

"I don't usually see you there," replied Sarah, with a small laugh. Sarah after all was on the line, and Larry was an executive in the building farthest from hers. But she knew he was only trying to be friendly, and felt warm toward him for it.

Larry Coppage was Dean Howell's oldest friend, and had been best man at the wedding. He was a number of years older than Dean, but their common interest in quail hunting had drawn them together when Dean was no more than twelve or so, and Larry was graduating from high school. Jimmy Howell's farm had the best quail in the county, and the farmer didn't allow anybody but his son and Larry Coppage to go after them.

Larry went to the University of Alabama, where he performed only indifferently, but this was of no consequence. He was a distant cousin of the Alabama representative to Congress, but since he was one of the very few of that multitudinous family to reside in Pine Cone, a job—and a good job—was assured him in the factory. He had only recently graduated from the university, only recently joined the personnel department of the Pine Cone Munitions Factory.

It was just at the time that Dean was looking for a job in the factory in order to escape the draft that Larry had taken on the responsibilities of hiring the assembly line workers. He had wanted very much to find something for Dean, but he was unfamiliar with the rules, and did not yet know between which paragraphs they could be broken so as to allow entrance for a good friend who was in need.

Larry was so ashamed of himself when he heard that Dean had been drafted that he found it difficult even to go up to his friend, to tell him how sorry he was that it had all turned out this way. He said nothing, but hoped he could overcome Dean's increasing coldness toward him by offering Sarah the first job on the assembly line that had come available, even though she had not applied for it.

"Is it okay if I see Dean now?" asked Larry Coppage at the door. "I mean . . ."

Sarah nodded. It was an uncomfortable situation now, and likely to become more so. "In the bedroom. His mama says he's awake."

Larry did not understand this remark, and looked at Sarah with a puzzled expression. She did not attempt to explain herself, but preceded Larry into the bedroom. She stepped quickly inside, and moved over into the corner by the closet door.

When Larry Coppage first entered the dimly illumined bedroom, he saw only Josephine Howell. She had put her sewing aside, and sat with her hands folded in her lap.

"Hey, Miz Howell. How you?" Larry asked in a low voice.

Jo dropped her sewing into her lap, looked up with a small smile and said briefly, "Hey, Larry. Glad you came by to see Dean . . ."

This surprised Sarah greatly, for Jo had many times

told her that she blamed Larry Coppage for Dean's being drafted, and she had said only the day before that it was because of Larry Coppage that Dean was smothering in his bandages.

Then Larry glanced down at the bed beside him, and was shocked by the appearance of his friend there. He could not recognize Dean beneath the bandages; it could have been anyone. His stomach sank when the thought crossed his mind that Dean had just died, and that he was staring now at a corpse. But then he recalled that Sarah had said that Dean was awake, and so he asked, "He know I'm here?" He turned to Sarah for an answer.

"I don't know," said Sarah grimly. "Ask her." She inclined her head toward her mother-in-law.

Larry Coppage was growing ever more uncomfortable. He had known of course that Jo and Sarah Howell were not on the best of terms, but he had not imagined that there was this much hostility, or that they would let it show to such an extent in the room where the man that they held in common lay helpless and unmoving.

Larry wished that he had not come to this house at all, but now that he was here, he felt he must go through with the visit. "Can he talk?" he asked Jo.

She shook her head slowly, but said nothing.

"Oh!" cried Larry in genuine despair. "I told you. I just wanted to see how Dean was doing, Miz Howell. Dean and I was *good* friends, you know that. They said he was bad cut up, Miz Howell, but they didn't say nothing like this." He glanced down again at the bed, which he had been avoiding with his eyes and whispered then, in dismay, "Can he hear me?"

Larry's question went unanswered.

Jo Howell put forth another. "You still in charge of hiring at the plant?" Sarah detected a note of slyness in Jo's voice, though she had evidently tried to make it sound merely conversational, but Coppage seemed not to notice. He nodded abstractedly, for he was absorbed now in trying to catch some movement in the figure on the bed. He could detect none. "Terr'ble thing," he whispered. He turned then to Jo Howell (Sarah thought that he was about to cry), and in conciliatory deference, he

MICHAEL MCDOWELL

said, "Oh, Miz Howell, I look at him, and I could think it was almost my fault . . ."

Jo said nothing, but Sarah knew what the woman was thinking just then.

Larry continued, in the fullness of his heart, "I just wish I could have done something for Dean so that he didn't have to go off. But it wasn't up to me, because there wasn't no place for him in the plant, there wasn't no position. He could have got that job at the end of the line when old Mr. Evers died if he hadn't have got drafted just when he did. Sometimes we can keep 'em out of the army, Miz Howell, but we can't get 'em out once they gone in. And I took on Sarah. I'd have done it, Miz Howell, you know that, I'd have given him a job, if there'd have been a job to give him. Dean was my *friend*." He stopped in some embarrassment, when he realized that he was talking about Dean as if he were dead.

Sarah continued to stand in the corner of the darkened room, expressionless and silent, with her arms folded. But she was earnestly praying that Jo would say nothing to Larry Coppage, that she would not try to make him feel worse than he already did.

Jo looked away from Larry, and seemed about to speak, but at last she shook her head briefly, and said nothing at all. It was apparent that Larry's excuses would not compensate for the loss of her son, and sharp words would not even help her for the moment.

"Gotta go, Sarah," said Larry weakly.

Sarah moved away toward the door into the living room, intending to accompany Dean's friend to the front door.

"Larry Coppage, you come here," said Jo peremptorily.

Surprised, Larry turned his face toward Jo, but did not advance.

"I got something for your wife," said Jo. Her voice was hard-edged but civil, and it was evident to Sarah that Jo was making a great effort to be pleasant to the man.

Larry and Sarah were both puzzled, and wondered what on earth Jo would have for Rachel Coppage.

"What you got, Miz Howell? A recipe or something?"

Jo unclasped her hands and slowly held up a gold chain. It was delicate, of small linkage, entirely fabricated of gold, and if it had a clasp in its length, it was so small and delicate that Sarah could not readily locate it. From this chain was heavily depended a simple, flat circular disc about three inches in diameter. Its center was a circle of blackest jet, two inches across, bordered with the same gold of which the chain was fashioned, and there was finally a slightly wider border of jet outside that. The attractive combination of black and gold concentric circles constituted a stark, striking abstract design. Jo dangled the necklace before Larry and Sarah. Sarah glanced down at the figure of Dean briefly, because she thought she detected a heavier breathing than usual, but staring at his chest a moment, she could not be sure.

When she looked up again, Jo was smiling and rocking her head slightly in the same rhythm as the swinging chain.

"Where'd that come from?" Sarah asked involuntarily. She was sure that she had never seen it before.

"It's for Rachel," said Jo quickly. That was not an answer to Sarah's question.

"I can't take that for Rachel, Miz Howell," said Larry. "Why you giving anything to Rachel, Miz Howell?"

There was a slight pause before Jo answered. "Dean said he wanted her to have it." Sarah was sure that Jo was lying, and yet, since she could think of no other plausible explanation (not that this one was very likely), she had to accept it.

Jo reached forward a little, and handed the necklace to Sarah. Scarcely glancing at it, Sarah handed it over to Larry. There was something about the piece that she did not like, but imagined her distaste arose from its being Jo's. Larry stared at it a moment with contracted brows, and then slipped it into his pocket.

"Well, I know she'll just love it," said Larry to Jo, but without much conviction or enthusiasm. Jo did not reply, but smiled strangely.

Larry and Sarah stood beside one another at Dean's bedside, and stared down at the strange, motionless body, the head and neck wrapped tightly in yards of tape and bandages.

Sarah saw Larry to the front door. He had stepped over the threshold and already said his good-byes, when he turned suddenly back to Sarah, and said glumly, "You don't think it was really my fault, do you? You don't blame me for that, do you, Sarah?"

"No," she replied, with her hand still on the knob of the door, "I don't blame you, Larry. But Jo Howell blames you, and Jo Howell blames me. It wasn't nobody's fault, what happened to Dean. You didn't hire him, and like Jo says, I had my hands on that gun when it went down the 'ssembly line, and she would blame the draft board that sent him away, and she would blame the man that sent him out to rifle practice, but Larry, you know and I know, it was just a accident."

"Well, you know," said Larry, "we hadn't sent any rifles down to Fort Rucca in six months, and that was 'fore you started working at the plant, so you *didn't* have your hands on the one that . . . that hurt Dean so bad."

"Well, wouldn't matter if I had, Larry. And it's not gone change Jo's mind, even if I was to tell her that."

"This is hard on you," said Larry pitifully.

"Yes," she agreed quietly, "it's hard on me."

"I hope it gets better."

"I'm sure it will, and I 'preciate your thinking about me, thinking about Dean and me." But that comfort was more for Larry's benefit, to make him feel a little easier, than it was conviction on Sarah's part.

Larry turned and went down the sidewalk toward his car, and Sarah went back into the house. She moved into the kitchen to start supper, though she was weary after a long day. But anything was better than returning to the bedroom and the sullen silent company of Jo and Dean. She wondered how much of the rest of her life was going to be this harsh, this comfortless. There had been times before Dean had gone away that she had thought herself trapped by her marriage to him, trapped into a long existence without much reward for constant backbreaking work, in which even peace of mind was made impossible by the presence of Jo Howell. But now she was worse off, with an unresponding invalid on her hands—a husband who could not earn money, a husband who was no companion. It was possible of course he would recover, but it would be folly to imagine that he would be the same. There might be brain damage, there was surely great disfiguration. In this part of the country it was easier to get a job if you were missing an arm, than if your face had been mangled. She could understand how people felt about that, and though Dean was a great deal of trouble to her now, she dreaded the day when the bandages came off.

Chapter 8

❧❧❧❧❧❧❧❧❧❧❧❧❧❧❧❧❧❧❧❧❧❧❧❧❧❧❧❧❧❧❧❧❧❧❧❧❧❧

Larry Coppage had never been sure why he was Dean
Howell's friend—he wasn't really certain he liked the
man, or had *ever* liked him. Dean's temper frightened
him, and he didn't like Dean's laugh when he frequently
talked about people getting hurt and dying in peculiar and
painful ways, as if it were all a joke got up specially for
his entertainment. Why had he never given Dean up, even
though Rachel had objected to their companionship? Well,
he told himself, for one thing, Dean didn't have anybody
else, and Larry would have felt terrible leaving him
friendless. But also, he was reluctant to become one of
Dean's enemies, and Larry knew that was what would happen if he ever showed any coolness toward him. Dean
wasn't so bad, if you kept him in check, and Larry had
managed to do that when nobody else could. And even
though Larry regretted that he had been unable to get
Dean a job at the factory, he had found that he was not
sorry that Dean had broken off their friendship because of
it. It was as much a relief to him as to Rachel—she particularly had not liked to see Dean around the children,
though she never said why.

Today was the first time Larry had seen Dean since
long before he had left for Fort Rucca. Larry sighed
heavily on the slow drive home: Dean Howell might just
as well be dead. *I never worked on a farm,* he told him-

self ruefully, *but I think I know a vegetable when I see one.*

Larry Coppage's house was a two-story frame structure about a mile away from the Howell home, in the very best two blocks north of Commercial Boulevard. Situated on a large corner lot, the building was neat but not imposing. It had been a wedding gift from his father, when he returned from the University of Alabama with his young bride.

When Larry Coppage returned home after visiting Dean Howell, he walked distractedly up the sidewalk to his front door. Several small children, most of them his own, were playing about the front steps, and he saw his wife glance at him out the living room window. He was late, and she was waiting for his return. Larry had not told Rachel that he would be stopping at Dean and Sarah's. His going there had been an act of courage and that morning, before he had left the house for work, he had not been certain that he would go through with it.

Thrusting his car keys into his pocket, his fingers knocked against the strange gift that Jo Howell had given him for his wife. He pulled the necklace out and examined it briefly in the light of the declining sun. Two of the children, one of them his youngest girl, the other a little boy totally unfamiliar to him, noisily grabbed for the swinging, shiny metal, but he lifted it out of their reach.

Rachel Coppage opened the wooden front door to her husband, and talked to him through the screen. "What you got, Larry?"

Standing a few feet away from her, he held the piece up for her to see. She opened the screen a little, so as not to let in flies, reached round, and snatched the necklace from his grasp. "Where'd you get it?" she asked.

"Present for you," he smiled.

Rachel looked at Larry sarcastically. "Where'd you get it?" she repeated.

"Dean Howell's mama gave it to me."

Rachel said, "Larry, you can't wear a necklace, look like a hippie. You and me and all five kids would be laughed right out of town."

"Rachel," said Larry patiently, "I said this was for you. A present for you. Miz Howell said for me to give it to you." Rachel was a good wife in many respects, but she had a habit of chafing her husband. She looked closely at the pendant, traced her finger round the circle of gold. "Jo Howell hasn't spoke to me since 1958 when my daddy bought their farm when old man Howell died so funny."

"Well," said Larry, "I don't know about that, but she and Dean wanted you to have it." Then, as an afterthought, he added, "It wasn't funny. It was just a snake, some old snake out in the corn, bit him on the ankle . . ."

Rachel disregarded her husband's remark. "I don't know why she would have gotten mad at me, 'cause it was Daddy that bought the farm, not me. I didn't have anything to do with it, and besides, she hated the place and was just dying to get off it. And you say Jo Howell give this to you to give to me?"

Larry nodded.

"Will wonders never cease," Rachel commented, and shook her head pensively. "Next thing you know she'll start coming to Sunday school and choir practice."

Rachel opened the screen door, and allowed her husband entrance. A couple of their five children also asked to be let into the house, but she shouted, "No, no! You stay out here till I call you in to supper! I don't clean this house so you kids can trample all over the floors!"

Larry followed Rachel into the kitchen, where she examined the necklace under the fluorescent light. There was no manufacturer's mark.

"Wonder why they wanted to get rid of it?" mused Rachel acidly.

Larry repeated his remark. "Jo Howell said Dean wanted you to have it. He's real bad, just real bad, Rachel. I don't even like to think about it. I didn't even recognize him. All them bandages over his face. I don't even know if they feed him with a spoon or a tube."

"Dean never liked me either," said Rachel.

Larry did not dispute this. "Dean was funny, sometimes, in some ways."

"Real funny," said Rachel, with distaste, "but if he's bad off like you say, then I feel sorry for him. I sure would hate to be laid-up in a house with Jo Howell keeping me company solid eight-to-five. And I really do feel sorry for

Sarah, 'cause this wasn't her fault and now she's stuck with it."

Her husband nodded solemnly. He felt very sorry for Sarah, sorrier for her in a way than for Dean himself. It was impossible to feel sympathy for that thing in the bed, with the pulsating black slit in the bandages, that really wasn't like a mouth at all.

"Did he lose anything?" asked Rachel. "Like a arm, or eye or something?"

"He may have lost an eye, I think, but he looked like he was all there."

"D'you count his fingers?" asked Rachel, and Larry shook his head.

"That would have been rude," he said.

Rachel weighed the necklace in her hand. "There's something funny about all of this," she said and stared at her husband out of the corner of her eye. "This thing didn't come from Woolworth's."

Chapter 9

THE sun had sunk behind the screen of diseased pines that backed the scanty property owned by Jo Howell, and the room where Dean lay was now in complete darkness. Jo had been too lazy to get up and switch on a lamp, so that she might have continued with her sewing.

Presently, Sarah's figure appeared in the doorway, a black shadow interrupting the dim light that struggled across the dark living room from the kitchen on the other side of the house. "Jo, will you get the light so I don't fall with this tray?" Sarah had prepared Dean's supper, several bowls of soft, mashed foods.

"Can't see a thing, Sarah. If I was to get up. I might knock you down."

Sarah knew better than to argue with her mother-in-law, though it was patently impossible that Jo would come in contact with her if she attempted only to switch on the bulb that was not three feet away from her. Sarah moved into the room very carefully, but still nearly tripped on the edge of the threadbare oval carpet beneath the foot of the bed. She set the tray down on the night table, turned on the small lamp that was there and then moved the straight chair to the bedside, just at Dean's head.

Spooning the food into the narrow black slit that represented Dean's mouth was an odious task to Sarah and she wished to heaven that Jo would do it. The old woman claimed that she felt no repugnance at all when she looked on her son, "but," she said to Sarah, "you're his wife, and you ought to feed him. It's not for me to come between a man and a woman. I won't be accused of that!"

Sarah set the tray in her lap and took up the spoon. Conversation even with Jo, she thought, might distract her from this tedious, unpleasant ritual. "Bad at the plant too," she said, referring to the heat, which was still very much in evidence in the room, though the sun had gone down.

"I hope they rot in hell! Hell won't be hot enough for 'em!" exclaimed Jo, with sudden bitterness.

"Who?" said Sarah automatically.

"Ever'body in that whole damn place, that's who!"

Sarah had heard Jo Howell go on before; it was always in the same tone, and always to the same effect. Sarah composed herself to listen, and was actually thankful for the distraction.

"Dean," said his mother in a low voice, with her sewing not yet picked up off the floor beside her chair, "Dean was the only good man in Pine Cone, in this whole damn town of layabouts and whores, and he was the only one of 'em to go in the army. They was all in that plant, ever' one of 'em got a job and they ever' one of 'em stayed at home, niggers and white people too. And it was a Pine Cone rifle that liked to tore off his head!"

Sarah sighed, she rubbed her forehead with the back of her hand. How was she supposed to tell if that black hole wanted more, how would she know when it was satisfied?

"D'you make that rifle, Sarah?" said Jo, viciously. "D'you put your hands on it? That rifle that put out one of his eyes, and we don't even know what he's gone look like now? D'you touch it, Sarah? Got the whole damn town's fingerprints on it . . ."

"Don't blame me, Jo," said Sarah calmly. "Wasn't my doing, what happened to Dean." She stuck the spoon into the black hole. "You might just as well blame me for the whole Vietnam War."

Bitterly, Jo Howell continued, "Them women down at the plant, on the 'ssembly line, they got silver dollars rolling out their ears, and they got their boys and their men

51

at home. They get cane sugar from the niggers down the river, and they make cookies and send 'em to Saigon. And you just know them cookies go stale 'fore they're halfway there! I hate them women!"

Sarah knew that Jo Howell could go on for a good half hour with such speeches. It was better to have her talking, but she wished that she would speak of other things. As soon as Jo had paused to draw in a short breath, Sarah said, "Jo, where'd you get that thing?" The necklace, which she had almost forgotten about, suddenly occurred to her as a convenient change of subject.

Evidently feigning ignorance, Jo inquired testily, "What thing, Sarah?"

"That thing you gave Larry Coppage. That necklace. You know what I'm talking about." Sarah pushed the spoon through the hole in the bandages and pulled it out clean.

"Not no necklace," said Jo, after a moment's consideration. "Called a *amulet*."

Sarah looked up briefly. Why had Jo's response been so reluctant? Another spoonful. There was no motion in the body, but the spoon always came out clean. Sarah didn't think that she would ever grow used to this disgusting operation.

"Where'd you get it though?" Sarah asked.

"Always had it," said Jo. Jo watched the feeding carefully and smiled grimly, though at what Sarah had no idea.

"Well, *I* never saw it before. I never saw it around here."

"Well," said Jo, "there's lots you never saw. My cousin Bama gave me that thing one week to the day 'fore she drowned herself in Burnt Corn Creek. I used to wear it a lot when Dean's daddy was still alive. I had it on the day Jimmy got bit by that water moccasin in the creek on the farm. I sure do wisht we was still out there," she said dreamily, and Sarah glanced up at the sudden change in tone. "Dean used to kill them snakes with a hoe, when they was still in the water. He never missed. After they killed his daddy, he used to go out in a little boat, with a hoe and a gun, 'cept he never used the gun, 'cause he could always get 'em with a hoe. I don't hardly see how he done it, killing snakes in the water with a hoe. But he said it was even better than blasting a covey of quail. Dean was happy out on the farm, 'cause there was the creek, and there was all the quail in the county, and I wisht we was still out there." Jo sighed nostalgically.

"You hated the farm, Jo. You told me you couldn't wait to get off that farm. You told everybody in town that. You also told everybody in town that Dean's daddy got bit in the cornfield. I have never heard anybody say a word about a water moccasin when they was talking about Dean's daddy dying like he did. How come you start to say now that you wish you was back on the farm?" Sarah demanded, and started on the mashed carrots.

"I was talking about for Dean. I wisht we was out there for Dean's sake. If I knew he would be happy there, I'd go back out there in a minute. I'd do anything for that boy."

Everything, Sarah thought, *except feed him.* Suddenly, Sarah realized how Jo had turned the subject away from the amulet that she had given to Larry Coppage, as if she were hesitant to speak of it. Sarah didn't believe that Jo had always had it, for she was positive that, in that case, she would have seen the thing before. It was a small house, and Jo didn't have much anyway. It was Sarah that cleaned her room, and Sarah had never seen anything among her mother-in-law's belongings that resembled the amulet.

She turned to ask Jo about the amulet again, but just at that moment, the spoon got somehow caught in Dean's mouth, and she had difficulty withdrawing it. Finally, after some seconds of pulling, it jerked out, and Sarah upset the last of the bowls of food onto the floor.

By the time she had returned from the kitchen with towels to clean the spill up, she had forgot the question that she had intended to ask.

The Amulet

much worse than any other. She didn't think so badly of her existence in Pine Cone. What she did like, however, —thought sweetly—and she knew that she loved

Chapter 10

Making supper for her husband and five children, who ranged in age from eight months to seven years, was a task that Rachel Coppage had grown used to. She had married Larry in the course of their sophomore year at the university, much against her parents' wishes, but her parents had not known just how much money there was in Larry's family. Other married student couples might have had a rough go of it, but Larry's father had pushed Larry into college, and wanted to make sure that he came out the other end, diploma in hand. Larry's father sent Rachel a substantial check every month and told her he didn't want his boy worried about financial matters. Rachel had seen to it that he was not.

But Larry grew weary of school, and in an effort to escape the intellectual rigors of the University of Alabama for a space, he enlisted in the air force. With the first two of their children still in her arms, Rachel had followed Larry first to Texas for his basic training, then to Virginia for a year and a half. At the end of that time, Larry declared he was still not yet ready to return to school, so they spent a further two years at the air station in Panama City, Florida, in which place they were blessed with two more infants. The fifth—and Rachel hoped the last—was born sometime after they settled in Pine Cone.

No place that Rachel had lived was much better or

much worse than any other. She didn't think so badly of
her existence in Pine Cone. What she did like, however,
was financial security, and she knew that as long as she
remained with Larry, money would never be lacking.
Rachel was not so interested in having *things*—a big
house or a motorboat, or anything like that—she just
didn't want to be bothered by bills, and debts, and
monthly payments. If Rachel went to Montgomery and
saw a pair of green shoes that she wanted, she bought
them; if she felt like getting away from Pine Cone in
June, then she asked Larry to rent a house in Pensacola,
and she knew he wouldn't complain of the expense. Rachel's parents had worried about money, and fought about
money, and yelled at her about how much money she cost
them, and Rachel hadn't liked it a bit; life with Larry
was decidedly a change for the better.

Rachel knew many women who would complain of having to raise five children, but she didn't mind so much.
There was a maid hired to help seven days a week, and
there was no problem about getting clothes for them, or
braces or whatever it was that they needed. Rachel took
a great deal of care with her children, though she didn't
coddle them. She took pains with her house, and though
she often was sharp with Larry—that was her nature,
which probably would never change—she loved him, and
did what she could to make things go easily for him.
Larry's relationship with his father was strained, for Larry
was not so ambitious as he might be, the old man considered. But it was Rachel who dealt with the senior Mr.
Coppage when that man wanted Larry to do this or that
for him in Pine Cone. Rachel knew how to mollify the
old man with a short visit from her and the grandchild of
his who seemed most likely to be quiet and respectful for
a couple of hours.

But even with a maid, the running of so large a household was an arduous undertaking, and Rachel Coppage
thought herself entitled to half an hour's rest each afternoon before she began preparations for supper for the
seven of them. This was always a major business because
the children were sometimes finicky—one wouldn't touch
collard greens, another couldn't abide fish—and Larry
himself almost gagged at the smell of baked sweet pota-

toes. And of course the baby had to be fed separately. The children, who were noisy enough at other times, seemed hardly to breathe between six-thirty and seven, when their mother's bedroom door was closed and locked. Even the baby slept peacefully in its wicker basinette at the foot of the bed for that half hour, and after taking the phone off its hook, Larry sat in the den to read the *Birmingham News* front to back.

When Rachel woke this early Wednesday evening, she rose from the bed, straightened the covers placidly and kissed the baby, which woke softly at the touch of its mother's lips. Then she sat before her dresser, and stared at herself in the mirror. This was not mere vanity, but a part of her routine which she considered absolutely necessary for waking up; for Rachel Coppage, it was the most delicious two minutes of the day.

While she sat on the little wicker bench, with her hands folded in her lap, thinking only that she felt very pleasant indeed after her short nap, she noticed the necklace that Larry had brought back to her from the Howells'. He had laid it atop her jewelry case. She stared at it, still wondering what could have possessed Jo Howell to send it over to her. Usually when Rachel got a piece of jewelry as a gift, it was a rhinestone clip in the shape of a poodle or something like that; this piece seemed very stylish, but also very peculiar. She was almost positive she had never seen another like it.

It occurred to Rachel suddenly that maybe it was really Sarah that had given it to her and that Larry had misunderstood. Rachel liked Sarah, but because Rachel couldn't stand Dean it had not been possible for the two women to become close. Sarah realized this and had not pushed the relationship. But why would Sarah send her a present out of the blue—unless it was to thank her for the two casseroles that she had carried over on the day after Dean got back from the Fort Rucca infirmary. It was the kind of thing that Rachel would have done for almost anybody in town, but maybe no one else had done it and Sarah felt grateful to her. Rachel felt better about the gift when she allowed herself to think that Sarah had sent it over. Rachel liked the necklace and wanted to keep it.

She picked it up, and weighed it in her hand. It was

heavier than she had remembered. It looked to be real gold, but that was impossible of course; the Howells didn't have money, and there was no reason for Rachel to think that even if they did have any they would be spending it on gifts for her. They ought to be buying themselves a car first, for instance.

Rachel brought the chain close to her eyes, looking for the clasp, for it was very small and she had trouble locating it. It seemed just another two links, and she couldn't figure out at first how it worked: there was no pin or spring or screw. She touched it lightly with her finger, and to her great surprise, the catch—or whatever it was—flew open, and the necklace came apart in her hands. She lifted it around her neck, wondering how she was going to get it back together, when it suddenly snapped shut, just as mysteriously. *Well,* she said to herself, *I sure do wish every piece of jewelry I had went on and came off this easy . . .*

The pendant felt just a little heavier than was entirely comfortable over Rachel's breast but she considered, as she looked into the mirror, that it became her marvelously. She sighed, and thought the unexpected acquisition a very happy one. In the mirror she caught the reflection of the clock behind her, and realized that she was a little past her time and that she ought to be downstairs already, getting supper together. She reached back around her neck, intending to take the amulet off, but could not find the catch. She pulled the chain all the way around looking for it, but the thing appeared to be made of uninterrupted links. She could not pull it over her head. She laughed at herself, blaming her slight grogginess for her momentary blindness and told herself that she would take it off after supper.

She opened the bedroom door, and the whole house seemed to sigh in relief. Suddenly, from down the hall, several small voices began to argue over a toy; the dog barked downstairs, the television set was turned on, and behind Rachel, the baby began to cry.

Normally, this sudden onslaught of noise would not have bothered her. It happened every night; she had grown used to it, and even found it a reassuring bother. But tonight there was something about the noise that irked

her horribly. It pressed in on her, but even more
wretchedly pressing were the responsibilities that the
noises represented: the house, the children, the husband.
Her whole life had been subsumed by these six loathsome
creatures. She told herself that she had only chosen one
of them—Larry—and he had been a mistake. The others
had been foisted on her. They had taken everything away
from her, and left her with nothing; she wondered that
she had got through so many years of it, and wondered
even more darkly how she was going to get through another night.

Rachel screamed out for the children to shut up, she
slammed the bedroom door on the crying baby, stormed
down the stairs and kicked the dog out the front door.
She turned off the television set in the middle of the
sports report, and didn't reply at all when Larry in great
surprise asked what the matter was.

She pulled the kitchen door to behind her, and locked
it. This had never been done before. Larry wondered
greatly at it, and feared for the rest of the evening. Half
an hour later, Rachel unhooked the door and commanded
them all inside for supper. Larry and the four children
who were walking came in meekly and sat down without
a word; there was not the shadow of incipient bickering
to be found among them. Their mother was upset, and
though they didn't know why, it was obviously best at
these times (and she had never seemed so bad as this)
not to cross her.

Not even her husband ventured to say anything, for he
feared that he was somehow the cause of this anger. He
didn't want to get into a fight with Rachel at all, and
especially not in front of the children. Rachel told them
all to get on with it, and then she left the room. While
she was gone, Larry questioned the children in whispers:
had they done anything to bother their mother that day,
or did they know of anything that might have happened
to upset her? The children shook their heads with
troubled mystification. In a few moments, Rachel returned
with the infant in her arms, sat down huffily at the end of
the table, and began to feed the baby with a bottle of
warm milk.

It was the quietest and most wretched meal that had

ever been consumed in that household. Whenever one of the children looked about to speak, Rachel stared him down so hard he choked on his food. They hardly dared to ask for the salt, and pointed out to one another which bowls and platters were to be passed. The children were so unused to this extremity of ill treatment from their mother, this unwholesome sternness directed at them altogether, that they began to feel sick. And even Larry suffered a queasiness in his lower intestines.

As soon as the food could be bolted down, the children asked to be excused, and Larry indicated that he wouldn't have any coffee, but might watch television for a little while. "That is," he said quietly, "if you don't think the noise will bother you."

"Do what you want," she said briefly, and cast over him a chilling glance of absolute loathing.

One of the children, the eldest girl, bravely ventured to tell her mother that she felt ill. "It's my stomach," she said. The other children nodded vigorously. The baby spit up its milk.

"Go upstairs and lie down," said their mother, without any apparent concern. "When I finish here, I'll come up and see how you're doing."

"Rachel," said Larry hesitantly, "I feel funny too. You think there might have been something wrong with the pork chops?"

"Nothing wrong with the pork chops. I had one a while ago, and I feel fine. Go watch television."

Larry sighed. At least she had spoken to them. Maybe she would get over whatever it was that had her on edge. Maybe, he ventured to hope, there wouldn't be any fight at all.

The four children left the kitchen quietly; they went upstairs, following their mother's directions, and lay in their beds. In a few minutes, Larry turned off the television and went upstairs after them. He passed their bedrooms, and heard their muffled groans through the closed doors. He would have stopped to see about them, but was in too much pain himself. He pushed open the door of the guest room and fell across the bed—he had not been certain that he would make it to his own bedroom at the end of the hall.

Chapter 11

LESS than an hour later that evening, Sarah Howell was alone in her kitchen. The room was dark but for a single fixture above the sink. Here Sarah stood, washing the day's dishes, and staring with a small smile out into the yard that separated Jo Howell's house from that of Becca Blair.

This was the first time in the entire day that Sarah had been wholly alone, and she was enjoying the restfulness of it. The noises of the plant had been left behind, and the hundred women and men all trying to chatter and gossip over a staggering number of decibels. Jo and Dean were in the far part of the house, and it was with some relish that Sarah calculated the number of steps that lay between her and them. She imagined the dark kitchen behind her, how she would have to move slowly across that tiled floor, to keep from knocking into the table. And the living room was dark as well, and cluttered, so that she would have had to proceed even more cautiously. At last she would reach the little hall, which would have to be crossed, and that was at least a couple more steps, and then, even standing at the closed door of the room in which Jo watched over her son, Sarah could have chosen not to knock at all, could have decided that it was best not to turn the knob.

And in front of Sarah, out the window, was a flat piece

of grassy ground, empty and still. Two fingers of concrete pointed up from the street and Becca's two-door purple Pontiac rested just within Sarah's sight. The moon was out, and full, and the empty yard was illumined with a dim, gray light that was peaceful and chill.

Becca Blair's house was dark, but Sarah could see only her kitchen and dining room windows, and it was probable that there were lights in rooms on the other side. But while Sarah looked out the window, Becca's kitchen light was switched on, and in only another moment, the back porch light. Becca Blair flung herself out the back door; a rosary swung and glinted in her hands. The screen door slammed sharply behind her.

Sarah leaned forward over the sink and put her face near the screen of the open window. Becca ran up to the house and looked up at her friend. Excitedly, she cried, "Coppage house gone up in flames! Larry and Rachel and ever' one of them five kids still inside! You come out here, Sarah, and you can see the smoke!"

Quickly, Sarah stepped outside and joined her friend. They moved together to the street in front of the houses and gazed in the direction of the Coppage house. A siren started up to their left, where the fire station was located a few blocks away. The house was too distant for them to see flames, but frighteningly, the stars in a large section of sky, in the direction of the Coppage house, were obscured beneath a veil of smoke that was black as the night.

Sarah turned when she heard Becca's car being cranked-up in the driveway. Margaret leaned out the window and cried, "Get in! We'll go on over there!"

"We'd be fire chasers," said Sarah doubtfully. "Ought not chase fires."

"Oh, come on," said Becca, "let's go. It's not like we don't know who the people are, not like we won't try to do ever'thing we can to help 'em—if they's any of 'em that's left alive by the time we get there. Come on, Sarah!" She opened the door of the car, and slipped into the backseat. "Get in, honey! And Margaret," she said to her daughter, "you watch out for that fire engine! We don't want to get into no accidental collision on our way over there! You hear me?"

"I hear you, Mama," said Margaret, and when Sarah had pulled the door shut, the car screeched out into the street and away they flew to where the Coppage house was burning to the ground.

"How'd you hear?" asked Sarah, "I mean, how'd you know it was the Coppage house that was burning? We didn't even hear the sirens until we got out in the yard!"

"No, it was me that heard, Sarah," said Margaret, with a little pride. "The Nelsons live right next door to 'em, in that little green house with the dogwoods right out in front—you know the place I mean—and Mary-Louise is a good friend of mine, and she called me up just as soon as she saw the flames. She didn't really call me up, 'cause we were already on the phone, but when she saw the flames she told me what was happening and then hung up to call the fire department and I told Mama!"

On the drive over to the Coppage house—and half the population of Pine Cone that lived below Commercial Boulevard seemed on its way to the other side—Sarah told Becca and Margaret, in a hushed whisper, that just that afternoon, not two hours before, Larry Coppage had come over to the house to see Dean.

"Well," said Becca, "it's probably a good thing he come over when he did, 'cause it'd be just awful if Larry or Rachel or one of them kids got burned the way Dean did at Rucca. Larry and Dean used to be such good friends, and if something happened to Larry, I'm glad he and Dean had the chance to make it up between 'em . . ."

"They didn't exactly make it up," Sarah had to admit. "Dean didn't do much talking."

"Well," said Becca, "he come over, and that's what's important. I sure do hope we find him all right when we get over there, him and Rachel and all them kids . . ."

Sarah was on the verge of telling her friend about the strange gift of the amulet, but they turned the corner, and the Coppage house came into view.

Chapter 12

◈◈◈◈◈◈◈◈◈◈◈◈◈◈◈◈◈◈◈◈◈◈◈◈◈◈◈◈◈◈◈

SILENT, searing flames consumed three walls of Larry and Rachel Coppage's bedroom. It was a fire that was sure of itself. All the glass in the room—the window-panes, the mirrors, the light bulbs, the jars of perfume on the dresser—had broken in the intense heat. A fur jacket that had been thrown across the back of a chair, to be put up for summer storage the following day, ig-nited suddenly, and was devoured in a moment with a pervasive forest smell that for a few seconds conquered the overwhelming odor of burning wood. All the fabric in the center of the room—the carpet, the coverings of the bed, the contents of the open cedar chest—had begun to smoke.

Rachel Coppage sat on the edge of the bed in an atti-tude that was completely relaxed. She was bouncing her youngest child up and down on her knee, smiling at it, plying it with a soft voice to stop its crying. The baby wailed abysmally from the discomfort of the heat and the smoke.

Larry's voice crested a moment over the buzzing, un-definable noise that a house makes when it is on fire, calling Rachel's name, and those of their children. But Rachel did not respond. She looked up briefly when their seven-year-old daughter, Beverly, ran past the bedroom door, screaming. The child's pajamas, of a synthetic ma-

63

terial, had melted onto her skin, and her curly blond hair had been completely singed away.

Beverly's four-year-old sister lay dead of smoke inhalation in the hallway. The two boys were beating against their locked bedroom door, screaming in fright that was even greater than their intense abdominal pain. But the noise gradually subsided beneath the crying roar of the flame.

Larry lay on the floor of the guest room, unable to raise himself for the intestinal cramps. He would have gladly given over the struggle if he had not been able to hear the frantic cries of his two boys in the next room. He wept for his helplessness to preserve their lives.

The fourth wall of Rachel's bedroom caught fire, and a ceiling beam collapsing into the middle of the room ignited the bedclothes and the contents of the cedar chest. The infant on Rachel's knee fainted, overcome by the smoke. Rachel lifted it to her breast, cradling its head against her shoulder as if it were asleep, and walked it across the room, carefully avoiding the little patches of fire on the carpet, as if they had been toys left by the other children. She laid the child in the burning wicker basinette, tucking it lovingly between smoldering sheets.

She turned around then with a small smile, and picked up a fragment of the full length mirror that had exploded a little time before. Holding it before her, she admired in it the handsome, becoming, stylish amulet that Larry had brought her that afternoon.

Again, Larry called her name, but his voice was very weak.

"What do you want, honey?" she called back, still looking into the piece of glass. "I'm in the bedroom!"

Chapter 13

THE two fire engines of Pine Cone were driven onto the lawn of the Coppage house, and the hoses were hooked up as quickly as possible; but it was impossible to save the building. It was not known at first whether the Coppages were still inside or if they had escaped and were at a neighbor's or somewhere in the gathering crowd. Their names were called continuously. Then the eldest boy, only six, jumped from his bedroom window. He caught his foot in the gutter, twisted round, and dropped headfirst onto the brick steps. He died in a fireman's arms.

A perimeter of neighbors and friends gathered round the house on all sides, trampling the flower beds, gently swinging in the hammocks set up between the trees. Some had brought out pieces of chicken, having been interrupted at supper; others were already in their pajamas. Small children played games of catch among the legs of the adults. There was nothing to do but watch the house burn.

The Baptist preacher's wife thought she heard someone yelling from inside the house, and a cry of "Shhh!" shot around the circle, but nothing more could be heard, nothing but the sound of falling timbers, collapsing walls, and breaking glass.

A fireman tried to get to the second floor, but the

staircase inside was itself burning, and by the time that ladders had been set against the second-floor windows, the floors had broken through, and the whole structure—and whoever was inside—was lost.

"Let's leave," sighed Sarah, "there's nothing that we can do. I don't want to see the bodies, I don't want to see them brought out."

"Honey," whispered Becca, so that Margaret could not hear her, "there's not going to be nothing to bring out of there!"

Becca and Sarah moved back to the car. Margaret came after them and said, "Mama, I want to know if it's all right if I stay over tonight with Mary-Louise. Miz Nelson said it was all right."

Becca shook her head. "You're not gone do that, Margaret. You and Mary-Louise—I know you two—you'd be up half the night just looking at them smoking embers out her bedroom window. We don't know how long this is gone go on, and what if the Nelsons' house was to catch? You think I want you to be getting hit in the face with them hoses? Water like that would break your nose in two!"

When Sarah returned home, she went into her bedroom to tell Jo what had happened, and why she had left the house suddenly and without explanation.

Jo still was at the foot of Dean's bed, but all the blinds in the room had been raised, and Dean's bandages were lighted faintly but eerily by the moonlight shining obliquely through the rear window.

"Well," said Jo, "it wouldn't have happened if Larry Coppage had given Dean a job, like he wanted, like he needed, like he asked him for, making guns to blow up in *other* people's faces . . ."

This reaction of Jo's distressed Sarah. "How can you say something like that?" she demanded. "They're ever' one of 'em lying dead and burned on the other side of town. Larry Coppage was standing right where I am now, not four hours ago, being nice to you and Dean—"

"You think I care about Larry Coppage being *nice!*" cried Jo. "I look at Dean in that bed, can't see, don't talk, and it was Larry Coppage that put him there. You think Larry Coppage saying he's sorry what happened is gone make Dean see again? You think Rachel Coppage's casseroles are gone put the flesh back in Dean's face?"

Sarah did not reply to this. Instead she asked, "Why do you say this wouldn't have happened if he had given Dean the job? That didn't have nothing to do with the Coppage house burning down—it couldn't have . . ."

Jo paused a moment, and then said carefully, "If Larry Coppage had given Dean a job, then things would be different, that's all. Things would be a lot different . . ."

"Jo, you listen to me," said Sarah, still in the heat of her anger, "Dean lying there don't do me a bit of good either. I hate it worse than hell what happened to him, he's my husband, but the blame for it don't go to Larry Coppage, it don't go to nobody at all. There's nobody to point your finger at."

Jo glared at Sarah but said nothing.

"But," said Sarah in a low voice, "if you are bound and determined to blame somebody, go ahead and blame it on Larry Coppage, 'cause the poor man is dead now, him and Rachel and ever' one of them five kids. Go ahead and blame him, because it cain't hurt him—"

"Wasn't just Larry Coppage," said Jo slowly, "it's the whole damn town—layabouts and whores—the draft board, and the factory, and—"

"You talking crazy, Jo! You talking crazy!" cried Sarah, and fled the room. It was only Dean who heard the list of those responsible for his injury—if he could hear anything at all.

Chapter 14

THE following morning, the Coppage house was a low pile of moldering cinders, black and wet, stinking of fire and waste. The carefully tended lawn had been torn up by vehicles, which left deep tracks in the turf. A few of the neighbors stood about in robes and pajamas, and others came by for a quick look before going off to work. A woman in a housecoat knelt in one of the flower beds next to the street, digging up bulbs and dropping them one by one into a paper sack. The Coppages were dead and would not miss the plants. No one tried to stop her.

On the official side of things, two men in shirtsleeves were picking carefully through the wreckage. They avoided going near the few timbers that were still upright, though heavily charred. Officer James Shirley, in uniform, stood on the brick steps that now led nowhere, as if he were guarding the soggy refuse behind him. He was talking to Sarah Howell and Becca Blair, who had dropped by before work to get the latest news on what had happened.

A small girl, about nine years old and possessing a thin face with features too sharp to be entirely pleasant, was moving round the edges of the burnt house, gingerly touching pieces of charred wood here and there, wondering perhaps if the pieces were still hot, hoping more likely to find something of value.

"James Shirley," said Becca Blair, interrupting him, "your little girl's gone get a splinter if she don't watch what she's doing!"

The policeman turned, and saw the little girl. He called out to her, "Mary, you be careful! They's still nails in them things! Mary, you get away from there! I don't want you touching any part of that house!" He shook his head, and turned back to Sarah and Becca. "Don't know what might not fall down, fall through. They didn't have no basement, that I know of, but if they had a cesspool or something, why little Mary could drop right through and drown 'fore I could get to her, and Thelma would beat my head if anything happened to little Mary."

Thelma was James Shirley's wife, and not known in town for her generous disposition or the control of her temper.

"Gosh-damn," he sighed. "It was terrible what happened here last night. Five children, two grownups!"

"Not much left," commented Becca, without sarcasm.

"Don't really matter much," replied the officer, "they's all dead. The family'll get the insurance money, and they don't need it."

"Four of them five kids was walking," said Sarah, "and not one of 'em got out—"

"The oldest boy . . ." Becca reminded her.

"He was bad burned already, though," said Officer Shirley, "might not have survived anyway."

"They was all walking," Sarah repeated, "so why didn't none of 'em get out? And I can't understand what happened to Larry and Rachel."

"Maybe," said Becca, "they was trying to protect the kids, maybe they was asleep . . ."

"Too early to be asleep," argued James Shirley.

Becca shrugged. "Well, *something* happened, even if we can't guess what it was."

"They have plots, Mr. Shirley?" Sarah asked.

"Don't know, Sarah, don't know. Probably had family plots, since they got such family, but I don't know which cemetery. Ya'll 'scuse me." The two men in shirtsleeves had beckoned the policeman over to where they were standing.

69

Becca and Sarah glanced at one another, sadly, and then walked together back to the purple Pontiac.

"What time that fire start?" asked Sarah, when they drove off toward the plant. Sarah stared out the window, at the now-empty corner lot, and thought how desolate a place that whole section of town appeared now.

"Don't know. Why? About eight o'clock, eight-thirty, I guess," she added after a moment. "Why?"

"I was just thinking about Larry coming over last night," Sarah said in a low voice.

Becca nodded, and whistled. "That's right. You was probably the last one to see him alive . . ." she intoned with melodramatic emphasis.

Sarah nodded.

"I meant to ask you all about that," Becca said, "but I didn't want to say anything in front of Margaret. Margaret's got a bigger mouth than the Mississippi River. Say the fire started at eight-thirty—what time was Larry over to see Dean?"

"He got there about a quarter of six, I think, didn't stay more than twenty minutes. He was in and out," said Sarah. She wrinkled her brow, and said, more to herself than to her friend, "It almost seemed like there was some sort of connection . . ."

"What do you mean?" demanded Becca. "Some sort of connection between his coming to see Dean and then his house burning down two hours later?"

Sarah nodded. "That's crazy, isn't it?" She wanted reassurance.

"Sure is," Becca replied. "D'you say anything to him?" she asked doubtfully. "I mean, were you ugly to him or something? I thought you liked Larry."

"I do like Larry," Sarah protested. "I liked him a lot," she said more softly, recalling that the man was dead. "But Jo was being Jo. She didn't say anything to him direct—and I'm real glad that she didn't—but she was real mad at Larry for not giving Dean a job back 'fore he went in the army." She paused, and then added, "She thinks it was Larry's fault that Dean was—" She stopped, and tried to think of a way to complete the sentence. "Larry's fault that Dean was covered up in white like he is."

78

Becca's eyes widened. "Well," she said, "it's Jo that's gone have to live with herself for talking mean to the man two hours 'fore he went up in smoke."

"You know what she said to me last night when we got back from the fire, and I told her what happened?"

"What?" said Becca, and it was obvious she was expecting, and probably would relish, the worst.

"Jo said she wished she could have got her licks in on him 'fore he died."

Becca whistled again. "That woman sure knows how to be mean. She must take a correspondence course, filling out all them forms, and answering all them questions on how to be ugly to people, doing it all while you're away at work, and practicing on ever'body that comes to see her." Becca Blair experienced a sudden wave of pity for her friend, a sudden blast of revulsion against the lazy fat woman who was making Sarah's life miserable.

Becca Blair said the things about Jo Howell that the woman's daughter-in-law could not allow herself to speak. Sarah Howell knew that she would have no peace at all in her life if she permitted her animosities against her husband's mother to become a common part of her speech, or even her thoughts. It was because of this cautious resolve on her part that Becca's periodic flare-ups against Jo—periodic being almost any time that the woman's name was mentioned in her presence—were a source of comfort and relief to Sarah. To these scathing speeches of Becca's, Sarah would sometimes add a tag of defense for the woman. That became Sarah as a daughter-in-law, but it did not go far to mitigate the accusations that Becca had put forth. This strange, but genuinely kind collaboration was one of the more subtle ways in which Becca Blair showed her great affection for Sarah Howell.

Sarah felt better after Becca's little blowup about Jo Howell, and when they reached the great asphalt-and-packed-red-dirt parking lot of the Pine Cone Munitions Factory, Sarah held her friend back for a few moments, and told her about Jo's gift of the amulet to Larry Coppage.

Becca listened thoughtfully, and with some puzzlement. "That's real peculiar . . ." she said, when some comment seem to be required of her.

71

MICHAEL MCDOWELL

Sarah nodded.

"Why does it bother you?" asked Becca: "I mean, do you think it was worth something, and now it's burned up? Or you think Jo's been out spending money that ought to go to buy Dean's medicine, or what?"

"No," said Sarah, "None of that. I don't know what bothers me about it . . ." She paused, and then added, "You don't think that there's any connection, do you, between Jo giving him that thing, and then the house burning up . . . ?"

"You mean you think it was a bomb or something?" cried Becca. "You said it was just a necklace!"

"Oh!" Sarah replied quickly. "It was . . . just a necklace. I saw it close up. I don't know, it's crazy. I just couldn't figure it out . . . those peculiar things happening. The house burning down, everybody trapped inside when they shouldn't have been . . . and then just two hours before, Jo giving Larry that necklace. She called it a *amulet*."

Becca shrugged. "What connection can there be, Sarah? I cain't see none. D'you ask her about it?"

Sarah nodded. "She doesn't answer me. But then she doesn't ever really tell me what I want to get out of her."

"Ohhhh!" breathed Becca in disgust. "It's a good thing that you *cain't* order a bomb out of the Montgomery Ward catalog, 'cause Jo Howell would have a standing order. I wouldn't trust Jo Howell, even though she is Dean's mama, I wouldn't trust her with enough powder to blow her out of town."

Chapter 15

∞∞∞∞∞∞∞∞∞∞∞∞∞∞∞∞∞∞∞∞∞∞∞∞∞∞∞∞∞∞∞

THE child Mary Shirley was ignoring her father's injunction, and still moving carefully around the edges of the destroyed house, kicking over boards with her shoes, pressing her heel against pieces of broken glass so that they cracked or disappeared into the damp earth.

Her father was in close conversation with the two men from the insurance company, and all three stood in the center of the ruins. Mary could hear what they were saying.

"Corner lot," said the taller of the two insurance men. "The Coppages, them that are left, will make money on it, like they do on ever'thing else. They could sell it for another house, or the city might even buy it, for a supplementary power station."

"I hate to think, though," said the second insurance man, "what it's gone cost for seven coffins and seven graves. They'll have to sell the lot just to pay for the funerals."

"Not much was left," said Officer Shirley sadly, "they could put everything we got out of there in one medium-sized job."

"The family'll never take to that," said the first man, "they'll want it done right. And they've got the money to do it right. What kind of policy did they have, Fred?"

"Theft, life, flood, and fire."

"Don't do 'em no good now," the insurance man said, "we's all could have gone to Atlanta for a week on them premiums."

Mary Shirley was tiptoeing around behind her father, making quite a show to herself of her silence and her care-taking, stepping very high, with her finger to her lips, when she stumbled on a half-brick from a broken foundation. She struggled to keep her balance, and not fall among the cinders, but she came down hard with both feet on a long board, the end of which was about half a foot off the ground. This board was fulcrumed on a small pile of black, wet rubble, and consequently the other end flew up into the air. An object that had been caught, invisible, on the other end was tossed high, and fell directly at Mary's feet.

Mary clapped her hands together in excitement. She had actually found something in the wreckage, something that had not been destroyed by the fire. It was a piece of jewelry, a necklace with a gold and black disc attached to it. The child picked the thing up quickly, examined it, and then called her father.

He turned at the sound of her voice. "Mary," he cried, "I told you to get away from here!"

She did not heed him at all, but skipped through the piles of debris over to his side, and held out the amulet to him. Puzzled, Officer Shirley took it up, and the two insurance men leaned over to examine it.

"Where'd you get this, hon?"

"Right there." She pointed vaguely behind her. It was not clear at all where she had found the thing.

The second, shorter insurance man said, "Was it *in* the house, girl?"

Mary shrugged and pouted. But then she asked, "How come it didn't burn, Daddy?"

James Shirley did not answer. "You take it home, James," said the first insurance man. "It can't be worth accounting for. It can't be worth nothing, anyway."

The second insurance man added, "There ain't much point in burying it with 'em, cause we don't know which of 'em it belonged to, though it was probably Rachel's, and the way they was fried, it's gone be closed coffins all the way. You take it home, girl, and put it aside for your

74

wedding!" The two insurance men laughed, but Mary was taking the whole episode seriously.

"Daddy." Mary whined, "can't I go back and hunt for more stuff?" She looked all round her, and thought of what might lie hidden beneath every board. "Mama says," she added cannily, "that you can't burn a diamond ring."

Chapter 16

A little later that morning, Thelma Shirley sat in her kitchen reading the first edition of the *Montgomery Advertiser*. She was a woman in her mid-thirties, handsome but harsh, of strong will and infinite purpose. She did much good among the poor in the community through her work as president of the Ladies' Auxiliary Union at the First Baptist Church, but she was not an easy woman to get along with.

Gussie Ralph was the Shirleys' maid, a middle-aged black woman, thin and sullen. She had worked for the Shirleys since their marriage a dozen years before, and prior to that time, she had been employed by James' father. It was thought in the black community that Gussie had turned sour after so many years in the employ of Thelma Shirley, and it was universally wondered that she had remained on so long, when it was apparent that the black woman and the white woman had no great liking for one another.

Gussie stood at the sink, breaking up ice cubes with an ice pick. Thelma Shirley insisted on having cracked ice in her tea, midmorning. Without looking up from her paper, Thelma said in a low, bored, unfriendly voice, "You still got to shell them peas for dinner, Gussie. And you don't finish them peas, you not gone have time for the pecans. 'Cause just as soon as you serve dinner, I want you to start on that pie. There's gone be a meeting of the ladies at the church at three o'clock to talk about the Coppages, 'cept I don't know what we're gone say about 'em, 'cept that they're all dead. If there was even one of 'em left alive, why then we could bring him food, or give him a place to sleep, or something, but all their people lived out of town, over there in Brundidge, and wouldn't have nothing to do with us anyway. I said it was a useless meeting, but they want to have it anyway, kind of a pot-luck preparation for the funeral."

Gussie replied sullenly, "Where they gone find a church big enough, Miz Thelma, for all them coffins?"

"Well," her mistress replied, "they talking about the Presbyterian church, which has got removable pews for the first three rows, but I don't know, 'cause they weren't Presbyterian, they were of course Baptist."

"Bad thing, real bad," commented Gussie, but her voice didn't hold much sympathy. It was actually that her animosity was directed toward Thelma, and not at the luckless Coppages.

"And, Gussie, while that pie's in the oven, I want you to run up the street to the church, and make sure that everything's set up right for the women this afternoon. I don't want to show up there and have to go hunting for tablecloths and the like, you hear me?"

"I hear you, Miz Thelma," replied Gussie, and came down so hard with the ice pick, that she chipped a piece of enamel off the bottom of the sink.

"And listen, you'd better check—"

Thelma's next command, whatever it was going to be, was interrupted by the slamming of the screen door. Immediately, little Mary appeared in the doorway, excited, and holding her hands behind her back. A moment afterward James Shirley, still in uniform, entered directly behind his daughter.

Mary's eyes flashed. "Look what I brought you, Mama!" She ran forward.

Thelma looked up at her husband accusingly. "Where you been with this girl, James? Why isn't she in school?"

Mary pulled the amulet from behind her back, and shyly put it into her mother's hand. Thelma glanced at it briefly, puzzled, and then stared hard into her daughter's eyes. "Where'd you get this, girl?"

Mary's lip trembled, and she looked down at the floor, deeply disappointed that her mother seemed displeased with her find.

"Found it at the Coppage place," said James Shirley. "Nothing left there."

"Child," said Gussie, from the sink, "you ought not be picking up things what belongs to dead folks."

Thelma took her daughter by the shoulders, and asked, pointedly, "You didn't see anything, did you, girl?" Mary's eyes widened. She had seen so much, and yet she had seen nothing, for nothing was left at the place. She didn't know what her mother meant. Thelma looked up at her husband. "You didn't let her see anything she shouldn't see, did you, James? Dead folks ought to be seen in their coffins, and not strewed out all over the garden. Children ought not see dead people in the grass."

Mary trembled. She didn't want to see anybody that was dead, and became suddenly fearful that she *might* not have been so lucky. What if she had tripped over one of the bodies, and actually fallen on top of it? Mary thought she was about to cry.

"She didn't see nothing, Thelma. There wasn't nothing to see, by the time we got there. She couldn't have seen nothing at all."

Mary was relieved to hear this; there had been, according to her father, no danger at all of tripping over dead bodies that morning. She became excited again. "Oh, Mama, you should have seen that place! It was all black, and it was wet where they put out the fire, and there wasn't nothing left in the whole place except what I just brought you." Thelma fingered the amulet thoughtfully. "Mama," whispered Mary, "you think it's made of *diamonds*? 'Cause you know, you told me that you can't burn *diamonds* . . ."

Chapter 17

A T least three times a day, Becca Blair and Sarah
Howell complained to one another of the tedium of their
work, the fact that there was no variation in the three
screws they set in, that the rifle that went by at 8:05
looked just like the rifle that went by at 4:55. But the ad-
vantageous corollary to this had always been that you had
plenty of time to think. All the women on the line nodded
solemnly when this point was brought up, but the fact was
that there being such a great space of time to be filled with
thoughts, and the noise of the factory building being of so
high a volume, it was difficult to maintain concentration
on almost any subject. And it was nearly impossible to
think for any length of time about something that was actually pleasant.

Sarah knew this, and Becca knew it too, but the women
wouldn't admit it, even to each other, for then there would
be no consolation for the monotony of their employment.
But in the weeks following Dean's return from Rucca,
Sarah found herself in an even less desirable situation. She
discovered that she could, with astonishing vividness, call
up the scenes of her present life with Dean; tableaux that
were dull, meager, and bleak. The images were like faded
snapshots, carelessly taken and composed to begin with,
found in an album where all the good, happy, or interesting pictures had been removed.

The picture that most frequently came to Sarah's mind

was her coming to Dean in the hospital for the first time, the very night of the accident. He was motionless, seemingly without sense or intelligence or will, wrapped in the bandages that would obliterate his personality for her. At that time, she knew it was possible he would die, and that gave a real substance to her grief, but now when she thought of the body in that ancient army hospital bed, with the rusted iron headboard pushed against a dull green wall, she knew what she hadn't known then—that she would be put through what was perhaps worse than Dean's death: a permanent widowhood in which she must always bear her husband's corpse at her side.

A second picture was Dean's being brought from Rucca to Pine Cone in a military ambulance. It wasn't that he had needed the attention or special care, for Sarah had been told that he could have got along just as well stretched across the back seat of Becca's Pontiac, but until he was installed at home in Pine Cone, and Sarah had signed certain documents, he was still the direct responsibility of the United States Army, and they could not afford to take chances. Dean was carried into the house on a stretcher—Sarah had seen a corpse dragged out of a burning car with a lot more life in it—and deposited on the bed. Sarah stood back, leaning against the window, saying nothing, while Jo, sitting in the plush chair at the foot of the bed, berated the two army medical interns for their clumsiness, which was apparent only to her. Sarah saw the two men to the door, apologized for her mother-in-law, thanked them, and waved sadly as they drove off. She returned slowly to the bedroom, and as soon as she was within the door, Jo was commanding her to do this and do that for Dean's comfort: to loosen the string round his pajamas, to turn his hands so that they rested palm side up, to lower the shades in the room. It was the first time that Jo had seen Dean, and Sarah was very much surprised that she seemed not in the least dismayed by his appearance. For that moment Sarah ignored Jo, and stared at the figure on the bed; it occurred to her forcibly that Dean was now her total responsibility forever and forever. She was a mule, and Dean would be a heavy rider who would never come down from her back—and Jo was a fat, loathsome mongrel, yapping, and biting at her legs, and making her slow, aimless, unceasing progress a torture.

There were other photographs in the mental album: of herself with trays of food, endlessly feeding Dean with a tarnished spoon that sometimes broke off in his mouth; of Jo, in the plush chair, hemming her enormous dresses and talking to her son, of God-knew-what-terrible-things, and leaving off abruptly whenever Sarah came near and tried to hear what she said; of Dean, lying on the bed, lying on the sofa, propped up on pillows, sunk into the back of a chair: silent and unmoving.

The pictures came without her willing them, and stayed though she wished them away. She tried to concentrate on the three screws, but they wavered, and disappeared, and the hateful album fell open before her. Sarah felt that she was as much debilitated by the imaginary photographs as by the actual trouble of maintaining her husband. Becca Blair watched her friend closely through these days and for her sake repeated a little prayer every hour on the hour, and even said two of them, to make up, if she missed her time by so much as a minute.

The afternoon after the Coppage fire, as they were driving home, Becca said without preamble, "What you gone do, hon? What you gone do?"

Sarah knew what Becca was talking about. "I don't know, Becca. Just get used to it, I guess."

"Ohhh!" repeated Becca, with a sigh, "What you gone do?"

In all of this, there was but one thing for which Sarah Howell felt that she could be truly thankful—and that was that she was never there when the doctor changed the bandages around her husband's neck and head.

Chapter 18

THE sun was still shining brightly when Sarah returned from work that afternoon. The air was hot, even this late in the day. She found her husband and her mother-in-law in the backyard.

Dean wore white cotton socks, khaki pants, and a Hawaiian shirt over his bandages. The effect was ludicrous, but horribly so, because his neck and head were completely covered with the tape. He lay in the hammock like a desecrated mummy.

The motionless body of her husband made Sarah uneasy. She had slept on the couch in the living room ever since his return, and she had never gotten over the feeling that she was sharing the house with a corpse, that Dean was somewhere else, still at Fort Rucca perhaps, or already in Vietnam, and that the body of bandages in her bedroom—and here in the hammock—was a practical joke played on her by someone unknown and malevolent.

Jo Howell was spread across the tiny straight-backed chair in a way that only emphasized her obesity. She shooed the flies off her son with a paper fan, and kept the hammock in gentle motion.

"What'd you hear?" said Jo, as soon as Sarah approached.

"About what?" said Sarah.

"About the fire," replied Jo. "Dean wants to hear everything," said his mother, with quiet maliciousness, "Larry Coppage was his good friend for just years on

82

years, and now Larry's done gone and burned up like quail in a brushfire, and Dean wants to hear everything."

Sarah nodded, inwardly wondering how it was possible for Jo to tell whether Dean were listening, or even that he could hear anything at all that they said. She dropped cross-legged onto the grass, and then in a very quiet voice, Sarah told her mother-in-law all that she had heard that day at the plant. She related the gossip, old and new, dredged up from the past, or newly created for the occasion, about Larry Coppage, his wife, and the five children, who had perished the night before in the burning house.

Of course there had been major consternation at the factory over the unfortunate destruction of the Coppage family. Larry was high up in the administration, was kin to the people who owned and controlled the place, and was liked by virtually everyone. Very few who came to the plant on Thursday morning had not already heard about the fire and its melancholy consequences. People felt bad because of it. They pitied the poor family, and were disturbed that not a single member was left on whom they could heap condolences and platters of food. Larry, so far as the administration was concerned, was the only member of the Coppage family that was easy to get along with, and they had depended on him—beyond his capacity in the personnel department—to be an occasional middleman between them and the principal stockholders. He was a severed link now.

Many women on the line knew Rachel through the church or the PTA, and though she was a woman who kept pretty much to herself, she was disliked in no quarter of the town. And if Rachel's children had been rowdy at times, they were indisputably good-natured, and it was a terrible thing that all five had been taken at once. Old Man Coppage, Larry's father, was deprived at one blow of his only son and all his grandchildren. (His only daughter lived alone in New York City, and had declared her intention of never marrying.) Some said he had gone to his bed when he heard the news, and others said he would never leave it again. The Alabama congressional representative had sent a telegram to the Pine Cone

MICHAEL MCDOWELL

Munitions Factory, which was mimeographed and distributed to all the employees.

And all the talk on the morning and afternoon coffee breaks, and across the whole of the lunch hour had been the deaths of the Coppages.

"What they can't figure out though," said Sarah, "is how the thing started. Everything's gone now, so there's no way of finding out. Must have just been something wrong with the wiring."

Jo nodded with a small smile, and then punched her son affectionately with her fist. "You hear that, Dean?" she cackled. "Wiring!" Jo turned back to Sarah. "Wiring's real bad in some houses. Don't know what it'll do sometimes, don't know what!" She laughed again, and Sarah was at a loss to understand Jo's glee over the deaths of the seven Coppages. Jo shrugged contemptuously, and would not explain herself.

"But even supposing it was the wiring, which it must have been," Sarah continued doubtfully, "what they really don't know is why none of them got out. All the children, except the baby, knew how to walk; there wasn't nothing wrong with Rachel or Larry. And the fire wasn't all that quick. So why didn't none of them get out of there?"

"Can't say," said Jo, smiling despite herself, a leering smile that made Sarah uneasy. "Won't never know, will we?" She fairly screamed then at the hammock. "Won't never know, will we, Dean!"

There was no response.

"Now I didn't say nothing at all to anybody," said Sarah, nervously, for she didn't like the way that her mother-in-law was acting, "about your giving that thing to Larry Coppage yesterday when he was over here at the house. And I'm still wondering why you did it. It's gone now, of course, and if you hadn't given it away, we'd still have it. It didn't make a bit of sense for you to give it to him for Rachel, because you couldn't stand Rachel, even when she was alive, which was just yesterday, and Dean couldn't either. And I still want to know what you were thinking of . . ."

Jo had quieted herself a little. Her eyes cast about the yard, avoiding Sarah's glance. In a much more even

84

The Amulet

voice, she said, "I don't know what I was thinking. I don't know why I gave it to them."

"You mean," said Sarah, "it was a story when you said Dean wanted you to do it."

"No, no," said Jo, her hands twisting in her lap, "it wasn't a story . . ."

Sarah realized that she could have continued to question Jo, but the entire subject was distasteful, and even if she could make the woman admit that she had lied, she would have accomplished nothing. It was strange, all of what had happened, and Sarah could not see her way through it. There was one crazy thing, the gift of the amulet; and there was another crazy thing, the deaths of all the Coppages. And because the two events occurred so close upon one another, it looked as if they were related. But that wasn't possible, was it? What could be the connection between that piece of jewelry, and the fire a couple of hours later? Jo could have given them a cake or something and Sarah wouldn't have thought anything about it, except maybe to wonder if they had had it for dessert before they were burned up. It was that piece of jewelry—that she had never seen before, that looked so strange. It was that necklace, and the disc hanging on it, that troubled her, she realized at last; and she knew enough about Jo to be sure that no amount of questioning would get out of her the reason she had given it to Larry. Not yet, at any rate.

Sarah had lied to Jo when she told her that no one else knew about the gift of the amulet; Sarah had not forgotten that she had spoken to Becca of it. But Jo was obviously hiding something, and Sarah thought it best that she hold back a little something herself.

This would bear a little more talking-out with Becca; Sarah wished desperately that her friend had been there when Jo gave the thing to Larry Coppage. Because Sarah had only seen it once, because she had only glimpsed it and not examined it carefully, because it had been destroyed so quickly afterwards, Sarah almost had the feeling that she had perhaps imagined the whole thing. It was almost easier to do that, than to try to find reasons for things happening the way that they did.

85

Chapter 19

$\blacksquare$BECCA knew that on this Thursday, her friend Sarah was feeling even lower than usual. Dean was constantly preying on her mind, and now there were the Coppages. Sarah would probably have taken that pretty hard anyway, but there was the complication that she had been one of the last people—if not the very last—to see the man alive. After their supper that night then, Becca Blair sent her daughter Margaret over to their neighbors' house. "Margaret, you go beat on the door, and ask Sarah if she don't want to come over and play a little Monopoly or Clue or something."

Margaret did just that, and she returned three minutes later with Sarah.

"You came quick," Becca commented.

"I just that minute finished with the dishes . . ."

"You didn't mind leaving Dean?" said Becca.

"Nooo," replied Sarah cautiously, and glanced at Margaret. "It don't seem to matter much if I'm there or if I'm not. It's just about the same. And anyway, Jo is there to keep him company. I think she started to talk to him the minute I left the room. I'm glad she can do it," said Sarah, and shook her head solemnly, " 'cause I sure cain't."

Then she looked up and smiled broadly at Becca and Margaret. "I'm so glad that you asked me to come over though, 'cause there's sometimes that I think I just need to get out of that house. There are some times it seems close and confining to me . . ."

Becca took this as a signal that they were to say no more just then about Sarah's problems; the poor woman spent enough time worrying about them as it was.

"Sarah!" cried Becca suddenly, "it's already past eight o'clock, and if we don't get the board down this very minute, we are gone be here till the world goes black on doomsday!"

Margaret ran out of the kitchen to fetch the Monopoly set, and in the short space she was absent, Sarah reached across the little yellow kitchen table and clasped Becca's hand beneath hers. "I sure do 'preciate it . . ." she said.

Becca blushed, and said with some confusion, " 'preciate what, hon?"

"Ever'thing. Ever'thing you're doing for me . . ."

"I'm not doing nothing," said Becca, with her eyes downcast, and only looked up again when Margaret had come back.

"Ohhhh! Mama," cried Margaret. "Can I be the red piece? The one that looks like the fire hydrant? That's my lucky piece, 'cause I played with the red piece last time I was over at Mary-Louise's, and I won. I beat 'em all! I even beat her daddy, and he's a mean man, and tries to cheat! Isn't that terrible! I mean, him just sitting there at the table trying to cheat, and embarrassing Mary-Louise and me to death, and everybody knows he's doing it . . ."

And so the game began and continued for the next couple of hours. Margaret did most of the talking, telling her mother and Sarah all the gossip from the school, relating stories about her classes and her teachers. Becca thought that this was the best way to keep Sarah's mind off the topics that distressed her.

But it proved impossible to avoid mention of the Coppages' deaths. Margaret recounted all the theories and stories that had circulated that day at the high school in Elba, among the students who were from Pine Cone; but most everybody had seemed to agree that it must have been the wiring, or oily rags in a closet or a can of spray paint that got overheated and exploded or a burner on the stove that Rachel had forgotten to turn off after supper, or any one of the other things that are well known to be home safety hazards. However, no one had any idea why none of the seven members of the family had escaped.

Sarah listened very attentively to all that Margaret had to say on the subject. And, at the end of it, when she and Margaret were playing out the last moves of the game—Becca having been eliminated about ten minutes before—Sarah said, "Becca, you still got that wee-gee board I gave you for Christmas?"

Becca nodded hesitantly.

The first Christmas after they had become good friends, Sarah gave Becca a Ouija board. Sarah had been greatly disappointed with Becca's reaction to the present. She had looked both shocked and displeased when she opened the carefully wrapped package.

"You don't like it?" Sarah said to her friend. "Or you've already got one?"

"No," said Becca. "I don't have one . . ." She spoke this very reluctantly.

Sarah was puzzled. "I knew you were interested in that kind of thing: ghosts and spirits, and talking to the dead, and all that."

"Well," said Becca, "I am. I believe in it. But I like to read about it. And that's all. But a wee-gee board is bad luck, it's real bad luck. It's only the bad spirits that answer the wee-gee board . . ."

"But you think it works?" said Sarah.

"Oh," said Becca. "I know the thing works. I've seen it work a hundred times. But it calls down the bad spirits. They answer your question—perfectly innocent—like who you're going to be dating next year, and then they stay and they kill your dog. Or something worse."

"I'm sorry that I gave it to you then," said Sarah quietly.

"Oh, hon!" cried Becca, "you didn't know. You didn't know about the bad spirits, and I'm real thankful for it. I'm glad to have it, you know, in case of emergency, but I think I'm just gone keep it in the top of the closet, where it won't be no harm to anybody . . ."

"You could give it away," said Sarah. "I wouldn't mind."

"Ohhh, nooo!" exclaimed Becca, "you can't give a wee-gee board away, because then the bad luck goes to somebody else, and it stays with you too. So then there's two people with bad luck. There's only two ways to get rid of a wee-gee board. One it has to be destroyed by accident, or two it has to get stole. And it can't be accidental on purpose either, like putting it in the backyard barbecue, pretending it's charcoal, or anything like that."

But Becca hugged Sarah for the gift anyway, and now Sarah had thought of it again. "What if it could tell us what really happened at the Coppages? What really caused that fire to start?"

Becca looked shocked. "We know what caused the fire! We don't need the wee-gee board for that!"

"What caused it?" Margaret demanded. "How do you know, Mama?"

"I don't know exactly," Becca hedged, "but it was one of them things that people talked about today. Oily rags or something. What else could it have been? There's nobody in Pine Cone that would want to burn up the whole Coppage family. It was a accident, and that's all. That's the important thing: that it was just a accident. We don't need the wee-gee board to tell us what we already know . . ."

It was evident to Sarah that her friend was genuinely afraid to employ the Ouija board, and because she was not sure that she really believed in it herself, she decided that she would not push the matter. But on the way home, across the moonlit patch of grass from Becca's back door to her own, she wondered what the planchette would have spelled out on the board.

Sarah noiselessly entered the house, and closed the door softly behind her, thinking that Dean and Jo were probably asleep by now; but she heard Jo's voice, loud and laughing, from the other end of the house.

She tiptoed softly through the darkened intervening rooms, ashamed of her own curiosity, and approached the open door of the bedroom. She stood in the shadows and tried to hear what Jo was saying, what the woman was telling her unresponsive son.

". . . Wiring!" Sarah heard her fairly scream. "Wiring! D'you hear what Sarah said they thought it was, Dean? They thought it was the wiring!"

Sarah entered the room suddenly, and Jo Howell's laughter ceased abruptly. The woman pouted, and would not greet her daughter-in-law.

Sarah glanced down at the figure on the bed; it was probably nothing more than the misleading shadows of the dim lights, but Sarah thought that the slit in the bandages was open a little wider, as if the faceless mask had been frozen in an inhuman laugh.

Chapter 20

JAMES and Thelma Shirley lived in the house in which the policeman had been born and raised. The couple slept in the room in which James had been conceived, and in which his mother had died fifteen years before. James' father had been killed in a collision with a Greyhound bus three months after that, and most people said it was suicide over the grief of having lost his wife.

That bedroom was not much changed. It contained the same bed and the same dresser, the same carpets on the floor, the same pictures on the wall. It was one of the few things that James Shirley had insisted on in his married life: that he and his wife Thelma should stay in that room and that it should remain as it was when his parents were alive. Though it was old-fashioned, a little faded and a little cramped, it was comfortable and possessed a great deal more character than the rest of the house, which contained new, cheaper furniture that Thelma had thought more stylish.

The night of the day on which Officer Shirley had talked to the insurance agents at the smoldering ruins of the Coppage house, he and his wife were talking as they prepared for bed. The only light in the room was from a small crystal lamp with a fringed shade that sat atop Thelma's dresser; the illumination was soft and flattering. Thelma sat at the dresser, on a wicker bench with a flowered cushion, and was putting up her hair with bobby pins and tissue paper.

The next day was Friday, Shirley's day off, and he planned to get up early, and go off hunting by himself. The quail season had just opened. He sat on the edge of the bed, in his pajamas, lacing up a new pair of boots, purchased for the occasion. He was a large, loose, slow-moving man, with fair hair, light skin, and freckles on his neck.

Thelma spoke to her husband. "Why you want to go hunting when you know it's gone pour is a mystery to me."

James craned his neck, and glanced out the windows. Low gray clouds had already blown up from the south, masking the moon. "Quail don't care what the weather's like," he replied softly.

"Don't you never want to sleep late? Crack of dawn, and you're . . ." She stuck two bobby pins in her mouth, and didn't bother to finish the sentence. She glanced down at the lace runner that covered the shelf of the dresser. On it lay the necklace and amulet that Mary had brought that morning from the Coppage house. She pondered it a moment.

"James," she said.

"Hmmm?" He was still lacing his boots, and did not look up.

"James, you think I ought to keep this thing?"

"What thing, Thelma?"

"*This* thing, James." She didn't touch it. "This necklace Mary picked up this morning. She really find this thing at the Coppage place?"

"That's what she says. I didn't see her pick it up. But I guess I hope she got it there, 'cause I'd hate to think she was picking up things out of people's houses and pockets and purses."

"Mary wouldn't do that. She must have found it at the Coppages. So should I keep it?"

"Well," said the policeman, "won't do the Coppages no good."

"Must have belonged to Rachel, you think?" said Thelma, and moved the chain around with her bobby pin. "She had fat ankles, you remember that, and she was always wearing short dresses, like she was showing 'em off." Thelma had never cared much for Rachel

Coppage, and it was strange now to have something that had belonged to her—the only thing, in fact, that was left of Rachel Coppage. Thelma continued to stare at the amulet. "Didn't have any people of her own, nobody that ought to get this. Larry's people got money to throw down the well, and I'd hate to see them get it. They didn't like Rachel any more than I did. Won't nobody claim it. Probably nobody knows anything about it."

James had set his boots down by the side of the bed, and noted with satisfaction that all the clothing he would need in the morning was set out so that he could dress as quickly as possible. Now he turned himself under the white sheet and chenille bedspread that was almost too much protection in the warm Alabama weather. "You bring me some water, Thelma? I don't want to wake up thirsty in the middle of the night."

"You wait a minute, James. I want to see how this thing looks on me."

Thelma didn't know why she was so hesitant about trying the amulet on; probably it was because it had belonged to a woman who had burned to death only the previous night. When Mary had handed it to her that morning, she had thought at first it might simply be a child's bauble, and during the activities that afternoon at the church, she had forgotten about it entirely. But now that she looked at it again, she saw that it had obviously belonged to Rachel Coppage, and not to one of the little girls. That morning, also, she had not seen a catch in the chain; she wondered if she would be able to pull the thing over her head.

But when she looked down at the amulet now, the chain was separated. She picked it up, and examined the ends of the length of gold; it still appeared that there was no catch at all, simply two unconnected links. This puzzled her, for she could not determine how it had got broken. Obviously a link had snapped and fallen away, leaving the chain in two pieces, but that didn't make real sense either because there still was no clasp or hook, and how were you supposed to get it over your head? Thelma was even a little relieved that now it was broken; she wouldn't have to wear it. With that consolation she didn't feel so badly about the thing, and she lifted it up by the ends of the chain and held them around the back of her neck, spreading her elbows apart so that she could see how it looked on her in the mirror. She couldn't decide. It was a nice enough piece she supposed, and it just might be worth something—though likely as not it had been picked up at Loveman's in Montgomery, which she knew was where Rachel Coppage used to shop a lot—but Thelma wasn't sure that it became her.

Thelma was about to put it back down on the dresser, when she found that the chain had unaccountably attached itself at the back, and when she withdrew her hands, she felt the amulet drop heavily into place on her breast. She felt again for the catch but still found none. That was very strange, she told herself, and had to imagine that by the dim light on the dresser, she had somehow just not seen the catch—after all, it had to have been there. She shrugged, and then turned toward her husband.

"You like that, James?"

He opened his eyes wearily, and glanced at his wife. "Don't go with a nightgown, Thelma."

"Don't you talk to me like that," said Thelma peevishly, annoyed with her husband for being so obtuse, and probably as much annoyed with herself for having accepted this property which was not hers. "I mean," she continued, "how does it look on *me*, James? I'm not gone wear it to *bed* at *night*, James."

James mumbled from the bed, "Real good, Thelma, looks real good on you." Sleepily, he turned over on his side, away from the light. But suddenly, he turned back over and said, with his eyes still closed, "Thelma, will you get me that water? I'm not never gone get to sleep if I keep thinking about waking up thirsty in the middle of the night."

"James," she said, not quite in reply, "you think it'd be real tacky if I was to wear it to the funeral?"

James Shirley did not reply. Thelma looked over at him, and saw that he was impatient to get to sleep. She sighed, and rose. "I'm getting it now," she said, and passed out of the room.

Every night for the past ten years, James Shirley had asked his wife to fetch him a glass of water, so that he

94

wouldn't wake up thirsty in the middle of the night. He never got it himself, and the fact was, that he never even thought of it until he had already got beneath the covers. At first Thelma had taken exception to this, complaining that he ought to get it himself before he had got into bed, but she had given this up because it did no good and she realized that he wasn't doing it on purpose to annoy her. And it had not bothered her again for years, really, before tonight.

Now she hated the man for it, despised him for this silly ritual, which she must suppose would be carried out every night for the rest of their lives. She thought: *If I were to drop dead tonight, he wouldn't last till Monday morning, because there wouldn't be anybody to get his water for him!*

Thelma knew it was a small thing, fetching a glass of water, but she had done it thousands upon thousands of times, and got no more than a mumbled thanks for it, and half the time James was already asleep by the time that she got back from the kitchen with it. That was all she ever got, for all the things she did for him, in fact— mumbled thanks.

Thelma paused as she passed the open door to little Mary's bedroom. The child had been born in pain, and since then, Thelma had had her daughter beside her every day of the child's miserable little life. Every single day for the past eight years, Thelma had had that little girl hanging on to the hem of her dress, whining. And out of little Mary, Thelma hadn't even got mumbled thanks. She had got nothing at all.

Thelma stamped into the room, and turned on the overhead light.

Mary woke suddenly, blinked her eyes open, and stared at her mother. "Oh, Mama, what you want?" she cried. "What's wrong?"

Thelma didn't answer, but stared hard at the child, with undisguised loathing.

With a hard swipe with the side of her hand, Thelma Shirley knocked the light switch off, and said, "Don't let me catch a sound out of you for the rest of the night, you hear me, girl? *Not a sound.*"

Mary was bewildered by the harshness in her mother's

voice, and wondered if perhaps she had been screaming in the course of a nightmare. But she couldn't remember one. She could only repeat helplessly, "Mama, what's wrong?" But her mother was in such a bad mood that little Mary was thinking to herself that she really didn't want to know what the matter was. And she certainly hoped that whatever it was, it had nothing to do with her.

"Go to sleep!" Thelma cried viciously, stepping back out into the hallway, and slamming the door shut. Little Mary cowered beneath the covers for a few moments.

In the darkness, Mary wondered if she were dreaming now. In the moonlight, she had caught the gleam of the necklace that she had found in the burned-down house that morning. Her mother had said that she didn't want to have anything to do with it. Maybe her dream was really about the necklace, and not about her mother at all. Little Mary had fallen back asleep before she could decide whether she had been dreaming all the time or not.

The kitchen was dark, now that the moon had fallen behind the clouds, and Thelma turned on the overhead light. She blinked in its glare, went to the refrigerator, removed the water carafe and poured a glass of water for James. She started to go out again, but with her finger on the switch, about to go through the door, she suddenly paused and retraced her steps. Placing the glass on the counter, she opened the drawer in which all the kitchen utensils were kept and extracted two handfuls of them. She placed a large rubber band round them so that she could carry them in one hand. Then with the glass of water, she started back.

She paused again for a few moments at the door of little Mary's bedroom, beating the kitchen utensils angrily against her thigh, but at last she moved on and returned to her own bedroom.

The glass of water she placed carefully on the table next to her husband. He gave incoherent thanks, and settled himself into his pillow. Already he was asleep.

Thelma sat herself again at the dresser, thoughtfully removed the band from the implements she was carrying, and then slowly laid them out on the shelf of the dresser.

There were two meat forks, a couple of knives, one of them sharp, the ice pick used by Gussie earlier that morning, a long teaspoon, a small eggbeater, a spatula, and a can opener. She stared at them all for a moment or two, and then touched them one by one, testing the tines and the points of the pieces.

"Thelma," her husband grumbled from the bed, "when you gone finish with your hair and turn that light out?"

Thelma rose from the little wicker bench, grasping the ice pick in her right hand. Her knuckles were white from the pressure of her grip round its wooden handle. Unhesitatingly, she moved over to her husband's side, leaned down over him, and let the point of the pick slide into his ear. She twirled it round just the slightest bit, so lightly that James did not even move with the sensation of it. But then Thelma pushed the point toward her husband's brain. She was much surprised how difficult this was, how much resistance there proved in the operation. The pick wouldn't go very far in, and she had to place one palm on top of the other, over the end of the handle, and lean on it with all the pressure that she could bring to bear.

James flailed with the surprise of the assault, and knocked over the glass of water in the process. It smashed to the floor. In the last second of consciousness, he glanced at his wife. There was not even a flicker of knowledge, or remorse, or even intent in her eyes. The expression on her face was the same as when they had breakfast together each morning, across the table from one another. She bore a small, unselfconscious smile.

There was a satisfying crack when the point of the ice pick penetrated James Shirley's skull. Thelma pulled her hands back and crossed them above the amulet.

James was staring at her, but then the pain hit him, a point of screaming pain, that had only begun to expand when he was dead.

Thelma had jammed the pick into her husband's brain, up to its wooden handle. His body buckled at the waist and slid off the bed. A thin stream of blood bubbled out of his ear. Thelma leaned down to try to lift him back onto the sheets, but she slipped in the spilled water. Her legs shot out backward from under her, and she fell flat on her face. The jagged-edged base of the broken water glass caught against her throat, slicing through her jugular vein.

The blood filled her throat so quickly that there was not even time for Thelma to cry out before she too was dead.

Chapter 21

WHEN Gussie arrived on foot the next morning at the
Shirleys' at about seven, she was surprised to see that the
car was still in the driveway. Thelma had told her it was
impossible to pick her up because of one car's being at the
repair shop, and the other being taken out by James on
his hunting trip. *Well,* said Gussie to herself, *she just
wanted me to walk because she knows how much I hate it.
No sidewalks half the way on over here and the gravel
just eating up the soles of my shoes, which don't fit proper
anyhow.*

The back door was locked, which was strange as well,
because usually Thelma got up early just to leave it open
for Gussie on those days when she didn't come to pick
her up. She knocked and there was no answer. The black
woman walked round the house, peering in one window
after the next; all was dark and motionless. When she
came to the room belonging to Mary, she glanced inside,
and saw the child asleep, only a few feet from the window,
but hesitated to knock, fearing to frighten her. Besides,
she liked the child, and had no wish to disturb her sleep.
It would be much more pleasant to wake Miz Thelma,
and make *her* get out of bed to open the door.

Gussie peered in between the curtains of the first bedroom window and could see, to her surprise, that Thelma
was not in bed. That side was empty. She moved to the

next window, and looked in. The sightless eyes of James Shirley stared directly into hers. Gussie jerked out of the way, instinctively avoiding that gaze and only then realized that the man was dead. She drew her breath in quickly, threw her hands up over her face and squinted, between the crossed fingers of both hands, back through the window again. She ducked a little and tried not to look back into James Shirley's eyes. Then it was she noticed the wooden handle sticking out of his ear. *Why!* she thought to herself, *Miz Thelma done that, done gone and left and locked the door behind her and done gone and left that child to find the body!* When she dropped her hands in anger for Thelma's supposed conduct, she suddenly saw the woman's crumpled body, hidden a little behind James', and realized that the murderess was dead too.

But, thought Gussie suddenly, if both of them were dead maybe it was little Mary that had done it. *Gone in there while they was sleepin' and dreamin' and stuck a ice pick in her daddy's ear, and then done somethin' else— I don't know what—to Miz Thelma. Ohhh, that child! Kill her mama and daddy, and then go right back to bed, and sleep the sleep of the righteous!*

Gussie knew that little Mary was not a particularly sweet little girl—but she wasn't a mean one either and Gussie knew anyway, from experience, that it was the sweet ones that were always playing around in somebody else's belly with a butcher knife. Probably then it wasn't little Mary—maybe it was robbers, or an escaped con from the pen come back to settle a score with Officer James Shirley.

The black woman had turned away from the window and leaned against the side of the house. It didn't matter now what had happened or who had done it, but it was very important that she get little Mary out of the house without her seeing the bodies of her parents. The door to the master bedroom was open, and Gussie could see that if she waked the child and told her to come let her in at the back door, Mary would pass that way and see the corpses.

Gussie went back to Mary's bedroom window and tried

it; it was unlocked. Gently she pushed it up, and then called to Mary. The child sat up sleepily in the bed.

"Gussie," she said softly, "why you climbing in my window?"

"Come here, child."

"What?" said Mary, not understanding what Gussie could want with her at the window. "Let me go open the back door, Gussie. You cain't climb in the window. Daddy'll shoot you for a burglar."

Gussie sighed briefly. If little Mary thought that her father was still alive, then it hadn't been she who had committed the double murder.

"Come here, child," said Gussie again.

Mary shrugged, and went over to the window, a little unsteadily.

Gussie thrust her hands beneath the small child's arms, and lifted her out of the window.

"Oh, Gussie!" cried Mary, "Mama is gone kill me if I get my feet on this wet grass. You know how Mama hates the dew!"

"Child," said Gussie, "your mama's not gone never yell at you again!"

Taking the child by the hand, Gussie ran next door, to the Presbyterian manse, and beat on the back door.

Little Mary stared round her and wondered what on earth her mother was going to have to say about these strange, unprecedented proceedings. She had already begun to make up excuses for herself, for she was positive that she would be blamed, and not Gussie.

Chapter 22

SHERIFF Garrett and Deputy Barnes were now the only senior members of the Pine Cone police force, now that James Shirley was dead. They stood in the bedroom of their slain colleague, shortly after the bodies had been removed to the funeral home. They had come immediately after being called, and were sickened by what they had found. It had been obvious to the officers that no one but James and Thelma were involved in the crime, and so they had allowed the corpses to be removed after only a cursory examination.

These were rural southern policemen, used to brutal, sudden murders of passion. Few crimes in Pine Cone went unsolved. A murder was frequently threatened beforehand, and was rarely denied afterward, and there was no great need for sophisticated techniques of clue-gathering. It was obvious what had transpired in this bedroom, or rather it was obvious "who had done the transpiring," but the motives, the causes, would remain forever unknown.

Deputy Barnes shook his head solemnly. "Don't make sense, just don't make no sense."

"Thelma Shirley was a hard woman, sometimes," the sheriff judged, "but I never thought she'd really go and kill James."

"You're sure though that she killed him, and then killed herself."

"It's not a accident, Barnes, to get a ice pick stuck up your brain. So I'd say yes, Thelma Shirley killed her husband."

"He couldn't have done it himself?" asked the deputy.

"Couldn't have got it in that deep 'fore he'd be dead. Would have stopped because of the pain. Couldn't have gone on if he had wanted to, so she must have done it. Bad way to go," the sheriff concluded, and sighed heavily.

"So," said Deputy Barnes, trying to get through this all step by meager step. "Thelma killed James, and then killed herself."

"Nooooo," said the sheriff slowly, and glanced with some distaste at the blood on the floor. So much had been spilled that the center of the stains was still damp. He noticed as well that it had just begun to rain outside. The moisture in the air drew the smell of blood up from the floor. Human blood smelt a lot different from animal blood. It wasn't a buck that had died in the bedroom, the sheriff thought. "I didn't say Thelma killed herself. You don't cut your throat with a piece of broken glass that's been on the floor. I think she must have slipped and fell on it."

"Accident then?"

The sheriff nodded.

"So she killed him on purpose, and then died herself by mistake." The sheriff nodded again, exasperated by Deputy Barnes' unconquerable slowness.

"Well," said the deputy, "how was she gone explain that? If she hadn't of died accidental, I mean? Gussie would have come in here today and she would have found the body, and ever'body in town would have knowed who done it. It's not something she could get away with."

"No," said the sheriff, agreeing almost reluctantly, "it's not." He didn't want to admit what didn't make sense at all: why Thelma Shirley would have killed her husband in so obvious a way.

"Maybe she was planning on getting rid of the body. Burying it. Throwing it in the river. Burning it in the dump."

"Thelma Shirley had a bad back," the sheriff argued, "she couldn't have managed that body by herself, and she would have known that she couldn't."

"Maybe she was gone say robbers did it," suggested Barnes. The sheriff shook his head again.

"Then people would have said, 'Where was you when the robbers come, Thelma? And why didn't they wake up little Mary? And what robbers carry around ice picks for weapons?' "

The men were silent a moment, and then the deputy spoke again. "Sheriff," he said.

"What, Barnes?"

"I don't think it makes sense."

"No," Garrett reluctantly agreed, "it don't make no sense."

At this juncture, Gussie appeared in the doorway of the room. She nodded to the two policemen, and said, "Well, guess I ought to clean up a little in here. Miz Dorothy's on her way down here. She's the only family they had around here, Mr. James's sister, and I don't think she's gone want to see all that blood."

The sheriff looked at Gussie. "Was they getting along, Gussie?"

She shrugged. "Not no worse than ever before."

The two policemen shook their heads, and left the room. Gussie opened the windows of the room, reaching across the bed so that she wouldn't track through the blood. The sound of the soft rain across the lawn was comforting.

On the side of the bed where the bodies had lain, Gussie dragged a throw rug out of her way, and then pulled the bedspread off. Part of the fringe had been stained with blood, and the whole thing would have to be sent to the cleaners. She carried the spread into the kitchen and returned with a large bundle of thick rags and cloths with which to wipe up the blood. She knelt at the edge of the stain, and had just begun to sop up what was nearest her when her eye was caught by something just underneath the edge of the bed. She leaned forward, resting a few fingers on the spilled blood, and retrieved a necklace, a piece of jewelry she had never seen before. It was caked with blood. She took it to the bathroom, put it under running water, and wiped it clean. She examined it carefully as she dried it, and then brought it back into the bedroom. She stared at it a moment, and then dropped it onto the dresser shelf. It wasn't any more strange finding the neck-

lace than it had been to discover the corpses of her two
employers that morning.

As she continued to mop up the blood, she wondered
who was going to pay her for the morning's work.

Chapter 23

GUSSIE had only just finished setting the bedroom to rights, wiping up the blood, mopping and cleaning the floor, dragging a rug from the guest bedroom in to cover the spot, changing the bedspread and sheets, before Dorothy and Malcolm Sims arrived from Montgomery. Dorothy was James' sister, a woman Gussie didn't care any more for than she had for Thelma Shirley. Gussie had worked for the family for years, but she and Dorothy had never gotten along very well, and Dorothy had always translated this dislike into a mistrust of Gussie's honesty. She told anyone in Pine Cone who would listen that Gussie was robbing her brother blind; the town, to its credit, believed not a word of it and for the most part cared no more for Dorothy Sims than Gussie did. It had been a relief when she had married Malcolm Sims and moved to Montgomery. The only thing that people had regretted about that marriage was the contemplation of what would be Malcolm's lot. Everyone was surprised to arrive at the wedding ceremony and find a pleasant, gentle man. There were two questions that were asked about him: how had he been roped into it all? and had anyone had the decency to warn him against what he was getting himself into?

At any rate, Dorothy and Malcolm Sims had disappeared from Pine Cone, making only sporadic return visits. More often, they entertained James and Thelma and little Mary in Montgomery, since of course the capital possessed many more attractions than the small town. But now they were back for a couple of days, and on a very melancholy occasion. What the Shirleys had possessed was left to Mary, and Dorothy and Malcolm had been designated her guardians. James Shirley had been a policeman, and therefore had realized the suddenness and arbitrariness of death; he had thought it wise to provide for the child.

In the afternoon, when the Simses arrived in Pine Cone, it was still raining. They stopped by the funeral home to make sure that everything had been taken care of there. Malcolm looked at the large pile of broken wooden crates in the back of the establishment, wondering at the number of coffins that had recently arrived. Dorothy briefly conferred with the funeral director, and determined peremptorily on closed coffins, though she was assured that the wounds in the two corpses could be effectively disguised. "Well," said the undertaker, "we just make sure that James is lying with his right side to the congregation and that way won't nobody be tempted to look in his ear, and then we just have to find Thelma a high-necked dress."

"Closed coffins for murders," snapped Dorothy Sims, "don't want to have gawkers sticking their fingers in the holes to see how deep they were. And you know as well as I do that that's just what people around here are liable to do."

"Well," said the undertaker softly, seeing that Dorothy was taking this matter-of-fact view, "are you going to have the services together, seeing it was a murder? And do you want them in the same plot—or maybe at opposite ends of the cemetery?"

" 'Course not!" Dorothy cried. "That woman may have killed James, but they were husband and wife right to the very end, and there's no sense separating them in death. Murder's a bad thing, but there's no use being vindictive. I didn't like the woman when she was alive, and that's enough as far as I'm concerned."

Dorothy Sims was motivated perhaps more by considerations of the greater cost of two funerals and two burial places for her brother and sister-in-law, than by any real forgiveness in her heart for what Thelma Shirley had done.

After leaving the funeral parlor, Dorothy and Malcolm went to her brother's home. Dorothy stepped next door to speak to the Presbyterian minister and asked him to keep little Mary for a while longer, while she and Malcolm went over the house. It was necessary to make sure that everything was out of the way; the child ought not to be upset.

Little Mary came out of the den, where she had been watching the Saturday afternoon horror film on television, and spoke briefly to her aunt.

"You all right, Mary?" said Dorothy Sims.

"I sneezed three times, 'cause Gussie dragged me across that wet grass, and she pulled me right out through the window."

Dorothy thought it best not to mention the deaths to her niece, and therefore said only, "You wrap up good then, because it would be a fool thing to catch pneumonia in the middle of summer, you hear me?"

The child nodded, and Dorothy took her leave, perfunctorily thanking the minister for his assistance. He faltered a few words of condolence, but Dorothy shot a quick look at the child, and shook her head for him to say nothing more. It was actually she who didn't want to be bothered with condolences.

When she went into her brother's house she found Malcolm hovering in the doorway of the bedroom, anxious to see the place where the murder had occurred, but reluctant to step inside. "I thought I'd wait for you, before I went in."

"That Gussie's not here, is she?" demanded Dorothy.

"No," said the husband, "I sent her on home. There wasn't anything more she could do, I s'pose. I paid her for the day."

"I don't know why you bothered to do that, Malcolm! Once she found the bodies, I just know she took enough for two months' pay! I'm glad we didn't get here any later than we did, 'cause we might not have found the house here."

Then, without hesitation, Dorothy stepped into the room. She pulled open the closet doors, and looked briefly into them. She pulled out each drawer in the dresser and the chest of drawers, and then set herself at Thelma's dressing table, and began to go through the cases and contents in earnest.

Malcolm was still at the door. "Dorothy," he said, "can't you wait till after the funeral? It was your own brother and he died in this room, right under that rug you're sitting on. I can see the stains, 'cause blood don't come up that easy."

"He was in the bed, Malcolm. That's Thelma's blood. And I'm not going to wait for the funeral. I want to make sure that Gussie didn't take anything."

"How would you know if she did?" her husband asked.

Dorothy did not answer, but was examining each piece of jewelry in the left-hand drawer. After a moment, without looking up, she asked: "Malcolm, you think James's pants'll fit you?"

This time it was Malcolm who did not answer. He was displeased that his wife reacted so casually to what had happened only the night before.

"You look in that closet," she said, choosing not to recognize his reticence and displeasure. "Take out a pair, and try them on. If they fit all right, we'll take 'em all back with us."

Malcolm grimaced and stepped gingerly into the room. He moved swiftly to the closet, pulled out a pair as quickly as he could, and then retreated into the hallway.

Dorothy glanced up, and saw her husband, standing just outside the door of the room, removing his pants.

"Why you doing that out in the hall?" she asked.

"I don't know," he said, "I just don't think it would be respectful to the dead, if I was to take off my pants in there."

Dorothy laughed briefly, and then said, "I know she didn't take any of the silver, 'cause she knows I'd miss it. I know every piece that Mama left to James. But I just bet she went through every piece of jewelry that Thelma had."

From the hallway, Malcolm said. "What about that piece right there on top? She didn't take that." Dorothy looked down at the dresser shelf. There lay the amulet.

"Well, that's 'cause it's not *gaudy* enough! Colored folks like to *sparkle*, Malcolm!"

"That's a terrible thing to say, Dorothy! And you know it's not true. I'm glad nobody heard you say that."

"Well," said Dorothy, "I'm not gone give her the chance to get it now either," and with that, she picked the amulet up, and dropped it into her dress pocket.

Dorothy Sims turned and looked at her husband in the doorway of the room. He was standing uncomfortably in a pair of James Shirley's pants. "They're real tight," he said.

Chapter 24

∞∞∞∞∞∞∞∞∞∞∞∞∞∞∞∞∞∞∞∞∞∞∞∞∞∞∞∞∞∞∞∞∞∞

FROM the Shirley house, Sheriff Garrett had telephoned Malcolm Sims in Montgomery, and told him what had happened. Garrett explained to his deputy, "She was James's sister, and it ought to be broke to her as easy as possible." But the truth was that the sheriff just didn't want to talk to Dorothy at all. She was a difficult woman at the best of times and goodness only knew what she would say to him if he tried to tell her that her brother James had just been ice-picked to death by his wife. Let Sims do it, the sheriff thought, he ought to be used to it by now anyway. It was a bad business all around.

The news lurched through Pine Cone. As soon as the Presbyterian minister's wife had prepared little Mary a tall glass of coffee that was mostly sugar and milk, she ran into her laundry room, closed the door carefully, and plied the pink Princess-phone extension to all her friends. She had climbed on top of the washing machine and was watching out a little ventilation window all the while that Garrett and Barnes were inspecting the scene of the crime. In a short time the details that the minister's wife had got from Gussie, as well as her firsthand report, had taken care of Pine Cone north of Commercial Boulevard.

In the meantime the sheriff and his deputy were having a melancholy breakfast in the diner near the train tracks, and here the two friendly waitresses quizzed the two men

111

on their dour looks. They received the information on the murder-suicide with little endearing screams and great rolling of mascaraed eyes. They distributed the news freely among all the customers who came in afterward, and this provided for the part of Pine Cone below Commercial Boulevard.

When Gussie walked home in the middle of the morning, she was stopped and asked by half a dozen people whether she had finally got fed up with Miz Thelma, or whether Miz Thelma had finally got fed up with her. She replied, "I been fed up since the day that Miz Thelma married Mr. James, and I wasn't fired 'cause there's nobody else in town would work for that woman, and she knew it—but *you are right*. I ain't got no job no more . . ." And she went on to explain why; the news spread on the black side of Burnt Corn Creek as well.

A number of people arrived at the munitions factory not having heard of the deaths, but they were informed quickly enough. Those who had learned of it, at most, fifteen minutes before, invariably cried, "Ohhhhh! You mean you hadn't heard? It's all over town! Nobody's talking about anything else! The seven dead Coppages is old hat!"

Becca and Sarah were a little late for work, and got into their places no more than ten seconds before the conveyer belt started up, and because it was impossible to hear over the noise of it, they discovered nothing until coffee break at ten o'clock. Even before the belt had stopped vibrating the woman on the line next to Becca stood up, leaned over the partition and cried, "Wasn't it *just awful!*"

"What?" cried Becca, for she knew by the tone of the woman's voice that something spectacular had occurred.

"James and Thelma Shirley is *dead!*" the woman cried, and already the assembly line workers were gathering in little groups to talk about it, though there had been no new information available since the time that they had come to work.

"Oh!" cried Sarah. "How'd they die? Car wreck?"

"No," said another woman sternly—an older woman who had lately taken up Christian Science. "She carved out his heart with a paring knife, and then turned it on herself. She buried that paring knife up to the hilt in her very own neck." The others nodded in vigorous agreement.

"Ohhhh!" exclaimed a young girl, just out of high school. "They was just buckets of blood on the floor, *buckets,* enough to fill your bathtub!"

"And little Mary Shirley," stated another, "tripped over the bodies when she got up to go the bathroom, fell down in the blood, and hasn't stopped quivering yet. They got her strapped down at the Presbyterian manse, feeding her chocolate milk through a straw, 'cause she cain't keep anything else down . . ."

And so the talk went, with details of the horror pulled out of God knew where, and much of it contradictory, with nothing really agreed upon but that James and Thelma Shirley both were dead.

Some details were clarified at noontime when people went home to eat or went over to the diner or telephoned their spouses. It became known that the instrument of murder had been an ice pick and nothing else; that it had been found in the policeman's ear; that Thelma had not committed suicide, but had died accidentally, slipping in spilled water and cutting her throat on broken glass. This made the whole thing seem even stranger. Had she thought that she would be able to get away with it?

"Ohhh!" cried Becca to Sarah, "there we were this morning, just sitting on the line, putting in screws like nothing was wrong! And James and Thelma Shirley lying there, wallowing in their own blood the whole time! When we come to work on Wednesday morning they was nine people alive in this town that just don't even exist anymore. D'you think of that, Sarah?"

"I did. That's just what I was thinking," said Sarah sadly. "We were out there in front of the Coppages yesterday morning, talking to James Shirley. And he was talking about Rachel. He brought up her name."

"And I bet," said Becca slyly, "she was at home that very minute, sharpening up the ice pick, just getting it ready for him. You know," she continued, "I thought Jo Howell was mean—don't worry, I'm not gone get on that subject right now—but a woman that would use a ice pick on her husband's brain, that's just terrible. A woman ought to use poison or something like that. James Shirley had lots of guns, I bet, being a policeman. She could of shot him without a bit of trouble in the world—put a gun to his ear and pulled the trigger and he wouldn't feel a thing. Wouldn't ever know it. But a ice pick? What you think she was thinking about when she did something like that?"

Sarah shook her head. "I don't know. I can't even begin to guess."

Chapter 25

WHEN Sarah got home that rainy afternoon, she went directly into the bedroom, intending to find out what Jo had heard about James and Thelma Shirley's deaths. Though Jo Howell didn't have any friends—none, in fact, that Sarah knew of—she seemed to find out things. Small facts, curious circumstances that nobody else knew about. And Sarah, like everyone else in Pine Cone, was curious about the Shirleys.

But there were two voices inside the room, and Sarah's heart beat violently to think that Dean was talking again. Had his speech come back to him so suddenly? Or had he been capable of it all the while, and only refused to speak in her presence? She thought the latter the more likely case, and careered into the bedroom, hoping to catch Dean in mid-sentence. She knew she must actually see him talking, watch that slit move in the bandages, because otherwise she knew that Jo would deny it, would claim that Sarah was only hearing noises.

Dean lay silent and unmoving upon the bed. She looked up, about to protest to Jo that she *had* heard Dean's voice, when she saw that a man, in army uniform, sat uncomfortably on the forward edge of the little straight chair at the foot of the bed. Sarah did not know him.

"You gone crazy, Sarah?" asked Jo, calmly. "You gone

scare the living daylights out of Dean, coming running in here like that."

Sarah caught her breath. "I'm sorry . . ." she faltered. "I thought I heard Dean saying something . . ."

"That was Si talking here, talking to me, talking to me about Dean. Si and Dean was at Rucca together. Si was lying next to Dean in the firing range when the Pine Cone rifle blew up in Dean's face, lying right next to him, and he saw the whole thing."

Si looked extremely embarrassed, but he nodded to Sarah, and said briefly, "Yes, I was. It was a terrible accident."

"Wasn't no accident!" cried Jo. "Somebody made that rifle wrong! Somebody didn't put that rifle together right!"

"It was just terrible," Si repeated helplessly.

"You came to see Dean?" said Sarah.

The man nodded, and said, "I had leave and I'm from Pennsylvania, so I didn't have anyone that I wanted to see in this part of the country. I borrowed the sergeant's car. I parked it down the street, had a hard time finding this place. I thought I would come and see how Dean was getting along." He glanced nervously toward the bed.

"Well," snapped Jo, "he's in pretty bad shape."

Si didn't respond to this.

"That was real good of you," said Sarah, "real good, and I know that Dean appreciates it."

"Si was telling me about Dean being in the army and all," said Jo. "Real interesting. All the stuff they had to do together and so on. I tell you, though," she said to Si, "I hate to think of all you boys going over to Saigon and Asia and all, getting killed like they are over there, but I'd rather have Dean in Saigon than in that bed like he is."

Si looked down at the floor, but said nothing.

"Si," said Sarah, "you were real good to come down here and see Dean. Why don't you let me fix you a cup of coffee?" Sarah could see that the poor man was being made very uncomfortable by Jo, and that he was probably desperate to get out of that room.

Si nodded gratefully, and quickly stood up. He glanced down at Dean's mother, who didn't seem pleased with his defection to the enemy.

"Mrs. Howell, you were very kind to let me see Dean."
She nodded curtly.

"Come in the kitchen with me," said Sarah, and walked
out of the room. Si followed her.

As soon as Sarah had closed the kitchen door behind
them, and motioned Si over to the table to seat himself,
she said, "It *was* good of you to come to see Dean,
'cause he don't get many visitors. I know it means a lot to
him. And you ought not pay any attention to what Jo
Howell says or how she says it . . ."

"I . . ." started Si, but didn't know how to finish his
consolation.

"We're used to it, and we don't pay no attention, so
don't let it bother you . . ."

"I thought she might be upsetting Dean, some of the
things that she said. I think I'd be upset," he said in a
low voice.

"Well, so would I. But Dean's not, or if he is, he don't
show it, and I don't know how to tell. You know," Sarah
shook her head sadly, "I'm not ever sure he knows what's
going on in the room. I don't know if he hears anything
that's said to him . . ."

"It's terrible," said Si hesitantly, "and I'm very sorry
that any of this happened."

"Well," said Sarah curtly, "so am I. So am I." In all of
her troubles, Sarah had never tried to make anyone feel
sorry for her.

Sarah took her time about preparing coffee so that Si
might regain what composure he had lost in the formidable
presence of Jo Howell.

"Mrs. Howell was telling me," he began in a much more
conversational tone, "about all the horrible things that
happened here in Pine Cone, just this week."

Sarah turned to face Si. "What did she say?"

"She talked about the family that got burned up, and
then the policeman whose wife killed him with an ice pick,
just this morning. She said the maid looked through the
window and saw the bodies on the floor and had to lift the
little girl out of the other window so that she wouldn't see
anything. Sounds terrible to me."

"It was real bad," Sarah agreed thoughtfully, "because
what nobody can figure out is why she did it. They weren't

the happiest people in the world, but they weren't talking about divorce either. They had gotten used to each other, they say, and that's why it seemed so strange that Thelma should just up and want to kill James Shirley. Just real strange. I wonder how Jo heard about the maid and the windows and all."

"Mrs. Howell talked about it like she was right there," said Si, with a little wonder. "I mean, she told me all about it. She's got a lot of imagination, because she sure does know how to tell a story. And most of the time, she seemed to be telling it to Dean more than to me."

"Is that right?" asked Sarah curiously. She was desperate to know what happened between Jo and Dean when she was out of the house. "I wonder how she found out about it all?"

"Pine Cone's a small place. I guess news travels fast around here." Si smiled at Sarah.

"I guess it does," she said, and poured out his coffee.

Then Sarah sat at the table beside him and asked him to tell her all the things about Dean that he had already related to Jo—what Dean was like in the army, what his duties had been, and so forth. But she didn't ask him to tell her what had happened on the firing range that afternoon the rifle blew up in Dean's face. Still it was impossible not to speak of the accident, when the bandaged figure lying motionless at the other end of the house was very much on the mind of the man and woman sitting in the kitchen.

"Well," she sighed, "you know I work in the plant that made that rifle."

"Yes," said Si, "I do know. Dean told me that. He sort of thought that the pinecone on the rifle would bring him good luck. I guess it didn't."

Sarah shook her head. "His mama says I made the rifle that blew up in Dean's face . . ."

Si was shocked, and could not reply.

"Oh," said Sarah, "but she doesn't think I did it on purpose or anything like that. But she's got this idea that it's my fault, what happened, and it's the fault of everybody who works at the plant, that it's the fault of the whole town and so forth."

"Well," said Si cautiously, "it *was* an accident. Who knows what made that rifle blow up?"

Sarah shrugged. "I don't know anything about 'em. I just put three screws in. I don't think about 'em. I wouldn't even know how to shoot one of 'em. I certainly wouldn't know how to make one blow up in somebody's face."

"No," said Si quickly, "of course not. Of course you wouldn't."

"I don't know what Dean thinks, whether he blames me or not. He doesn't talk, he doesn't even move, so how can I know what he's thinking about? Whether he's mad at me or anything?"

"You can't. You really can't."

Sarah smiled bleakly. "You were real good to come. I keep saying that," she smiled, shyly this time, "but I really mean it. And I'm just sitting here, depressing all the spirit out of you, talking about my troubles."

"It's all right," said Si kindly, and he meant it.

He left twenty minutes later after saying good-bye to Jo Howell and nodding very uncomfortably at the bandages. After Sarah saw him to the front door she returned to the bedroom, and sat down for a moment at Dean's bedside.

"Dinner's late," said Jo.

"Well, Jo, I couldn't start fixing dinner when Si was here. It was right to keep him company, and wrong to do anything else."

"Dean's hungry."

"I'm about to get up. In a minute," said Sarah. She looked steadily at Jo, and said, "Si said you were telling him all about what happened over at the Shirleys' this morning."

Jo did not reply for a moment, then said huskily, "Thought he might want to know what kind of things go on in a small town."

"He said you knew a good deal about it all, like you had been there yourself, he said."

"That's all anybody is talking about today. There was even a report on the radio at dinnertime. Me and Dean listened to it. Didn't you hear it?"

"No," said Sarah, "I didn't. They give all the details? That where you heard it all?"

"They told ever'thing you'd ever want to know about

how Thelma Shirley killed James with a ice pick, and then died herself accidental on a piece of broke glass."

Sarah rose from the chair with a sigh, and returned to the kitchen. She stood at the kitchen sink for a few moments, and stared out into the wet yard, and wondered if it was ever going to stop raining.

Chapter 26

SARAH Howell thought that there was something horribly unnatural in the way that her husband was acting, or rather, the way in which he did nothing at all. He was supposed to be recuperating, but he didn't move, didn't speak, and didn't react to anything. At least he did nothing when she was with him. If the spoon hadn't come out clean, Sarah would have thought that Dean was dead. Jo always assured her that Dean heard everything, that despite his sightlessness, despite his immobility, he knew everything that was going on in the whole of Pine Cone.

Sarah had begun to wonder desperately what went on in that house when she was away at work. It was true that Dean's legs could be made to shuffle along like those of a rickety pull toy when it was absolutely necessary to get him from this place to that, but it was an enormous chore, and the man, despite great loss of weight, was very heavy. Jo would never help her.

But often, when she came home from work, Sarah would find Dean in different clothing, lying or sitting up motionless, in another part of the house. When Sarah asked Jo how she managed him Jo would only reply, with an annoyed, impatient shrug of her shoulders, "It's not so hard as you make it out to be." But Sarah knew that it was.

The rain continued throughout Saturday. In the afternoon, the sky was dark, and the ground was sodden. Great pools of water had formed in the flat lawns, drowning the grass and beating the first summer blossoms back into the earth. In the bedroom, Sarah had insisted on raising the blinds and pulling back the curtains so that what little daylight there was might come into the room.

"Dean don't like the light," said Jo, again ensconced in the chair at the foot of the bed. Jo was always in the way when Sarah wanted to get anything done.

"Dean's got his eyes covered up," said Sarah shortly, "and it don't matter to him whether there's light or not."

"The light shrinks his bandages. Makes 'em tight," argued Jo, but Sarah thought that she had made this reason up and therefore ignored it.

Sarah pulled the sheets off her husband, and then pulled him to the right side of the bed. Then she went round to the other side, and took the sheets out. Then she had to drag him onto the bare mattress so that she could remove the sheets altogether. It was a great, difficult, infuriating ritual to change Dean's bed, but she hated the way slow healing smelled.

It occurred to Sarah suddenly that she led a hard life —a tiring boring job all week long, every day, and then come home in the evening, and nurse her husband, without comfort, without thanks. The weekend was spent in cleaning the house. It was this train of thought that prompted Sarah to say to her mother-in-law then, "You're here the whole damn day, Jo, why can't you help with Dean? Why can't you do something around the house?"

"You're his wife, it's you that ought to take care of him," Jo replied unhesitatingly.

"What about the house? The house belongs to you. You ought to help with things," Sarah continued.

"I don't charge you nothing to live here, so there's no reason that I ought to help. What you do is for your rent, and from what I see, dust in the corners, and things not picked up like they should be, you're getting the place cheap, Sarah. I think real cheap."

Sarah shook her head, and continued to tuck the sheets in all around the bed. The subject was dropped and when the two women began to talk again, the subject was of course the deaths of the policeman and his wife. Becca

Blair had come over just after breakfast that morning with the latest news, got from Mrs. Nelson by way of Mary-Louise and Margaret.

"First," Becca said, "they had to send out for five children's coffins for them Coppage kids that got burnt up, and that was only Wednesday night. And now the undertaker says if another grownup dies in Pine Cone, and he's full size, he's gone have to put him direct in the ground, 'cause he is running out of caskets."

"And we were talking to James Shirley Thursday morning. And now he's dead."

"Well," Jo said at this point, "looks like you ought to stay inside, Sarah. Anybody you talk to dies that very same day!" She cackled at her little joke, and Becca stared at the fat woman strangely. The series of deaths was hardly a joking matter, she thought.

"Who's gone take care of the funeral?" asked Sarah in an attempt to change the subject.

"James's sister is coming down from Montgomery to head up ever'thing. She used to work at the plant, 'fore you were there, 'fore you married Dean, in fact," said Becca. "But she and her husband moved up to Montgomery about two years ago. He sells insurance but he's still real nice, what I remember of him. Only saw him twice, and one of them times he had his back to me."

But now it was late afternoon, and still raining. "It's real bad, nine people dead in three days," sighed Sarah. "I just hate to think about that ice pick!"

"Well," said Jo, with a smile that was inappropriate to the subject, "a ice pick can't be no worse than a gun blowing up in your face, tearing the teeth right out of your gums, ripping your eyelids off."

Sarah was shocked that Jo would say such things in the hearing of Dean (if Dean could hear); it could only make him feel much worse.

Jo continued, but without the inappropriate smile, "Them people are all dead now, and who gives a damn? Nobody cares any more about them than they cared about Dean! I care about Dean, and I'm the only one! The only reason you're here, Sarah, is that you're married to him and you can't get away. He's your responsibility. He's not mine. I own this house. I could throw him and you out on the sidewalk and not even wait till the rain let up, and nobody could say a word. But I'm not. I want Dean here with me. It was worse when Dean got his head blown off than when his daddy got bit by a infected 'coon down where we had the blackberry bushes. And *he* died! Dean didn't die, but I don't know he's ever gone get out of that bed 'less we pull him out of it!"

Jo could easily see Sarah's discomfort, but she went on with hardly a pause. "He likes to hear it, likes to hear what happened to these people, he wants to know he's not the only one in Pine Cone that suffered. Serves 'em all right. It's their fault that Dean, my boy, is right there in that bed and not off enjoying himself in Southeast Asia. He wanted to get out of this town, get out of the trap he had got hisself into." Here Jo glanced up at Sarah and it was obvious that she considered that Sarah was part of the millstone around the neck of her son. "I'm not sorry, not sorry for a bit of it."

Sarah faltered. "Are you . . . sure that's what he's thinking? Did he tell you that? He didn't say nothing, did he, Jo?" The worst part of all this was the uncertainty.

"He don't need to talk to me, Sarah. I know what he's thinking. He's hearing everything, and he don't need to say nothing, not so long as I'm here with him. It's worked out real good that you're at the plant ever'day, because you wouldn't be no company for him anyway. You don't know what he wants, you don't know what he's thinking —and I do. That's why I let you change the sheets and stuff, 'cause you're his wife, and you ought to be doing *something* for him. I sit here all the day long, when I suppose I could be out doing other things, sit here all day long just keeping Dean company. I don't mind, 'cause Dean is my boy. Even though you think it's hard to look him in the face, I don't."

Sarah trembled. Jo was being vicious, but for the most part it was an accurate representation of their situation.

Chapter 27

THE rain finally let up during supper that Saturday night, and the sky cleared almost immediately. The moon was on the wane.

Jo Howell was in fine spirits and Sarah was at a loss to account for them. Her first thought was that it had something to do with the nine deaths that week—but that was uncharitable—and Sarah then supposed it was just as likely that Jo was pleased with having got so much the better of her during the argument that afternoon.

But now, at any rate, Jo was a little more agreeably disposed toward her daughter-in-law. "Sarah," she said, "why don't we all do something tonight?"

Sarah was very surprised. Was 'we all' meant to include Dean? Or who else? Or what could they possibly do together? "Well," said Sarah cautiously, "like what? What do you want to do?"

"Why don't you go ask Becca if she'll take us out to the drive-in tonight?"

"Well," said Sarah, "all right. But who's gone take care of Dean when we're gone?"

"What do you mean!" cried Jo, "you don't think we'd leave Dean here, do you, when we went out to the picture show! Dean always loved the picture shows, and they was times he went to the drive-in three times a week even when they was showing the same things."

125

"Will he be all right, just sitting up for two, three hours like that in the car?" asked Sarah.

"I'll sit in back with Dean," said Jo. "Why don't you just go ask Becca if she'll take us out there."

Becca was agreeable to this proposition, with one proviso: "I won't go look at no monsters on the screen. I cain't do that. There we are out in the middle of the country, ever'thing black all around us, out in the middle of nowhere, and I'm s'posed to look at monsters jumping out of the bushes . . ."

Sarah reassured her. They were going to see *John Goldfarb Please Come Home* and *Harlow,* on a double bill.

"Well," said Becca, "that's all right. Maybe it'll do Dean a little good, get him out of that house, get him out of that bed."

"You don't mind that Jo's going?" said Sarah doubtfully.

"Honey," said Becca, and hugged Sarah, "if I could, I'd give you the world, and then fence it in. Taking Jo to the drive-in is not as bad as some things I could name."

"Like what?" laughed Sarah.

"Well," said Becca, thoughtfully, "it's probably not gone be as bad as, say, spending the rest of my life with Mike." Mike was Becca's ex-husband, who used to beat her.

Becca and Sarah asked Margaret to go along with them, but the young girl cried, "Ohhh, Mama! You are going to the drive-in tonight! Tonight is Saturday night! Only high school people go on Saturday night! I'm going! I am going with Mary-Louise. We have got a double date —I already told you about it—with the Beasley twins. And I don't want you to park anywhere near us, you hear me!"

Becca laughed, and said that she would not, that she wasn't going to spy on her.

"Well," said Margaret, a little ashamed that she had put her mother off so, "we can meet at a certain time in the refreshment stand if you want to."

Becca laughed again, and said that the reason that they were going, really, was to take Jo and Dean.

Margaret looked darkly at Sarah. "Dean's going to the pictures?"

Sarah nodded. "Jo says he'll enjoy it." Margaret said nothing. "And even if he don't, maybe we will."

It was a strange evening. Becca parked at the very edge of the lot, so that people wouldn't stare in at Dean when they passed by on their way to the refreshment stand. Jo had propped him up in a corner of the backseat, with blankets and pillows arranged all around him, and provided him a running commentary on the two films, crying out, at appropriate moments things like: "Did you see how she did that?" or "I wouldn't put up with something like that! Would you, Dean?" or "Somebody's like to get get hurt they keep on that way!"

Sarah suggested that since the night was very warm and humid, she and Becca might sit outside. Becca took up this notion gladly, and retrieved a beach blanket from the trunk of the automobile, and spread it on the ground so they could lean against the car. Here they sat cross-legged, and watched the previews, the cartoons, and the two films. But sometimes they talked quietly together, about Jo and Dean, about their work at the factory, and about the summer lightning that broke every ten seconds over the western horizon.

The next morning at breakfast, Sarah asked Jo, "Did Dean like the movies?"

Jo nodded. "He liked it a lot. He liked getting out and doing things, just like he used to. He ought to do more things like that."

Sarah said nothing. But she knew that Dean had been stuck like a straw figure in the corner of the backseat, that he had not moved at all, had not even shifted his posture for comfort, had not even tilted and slipped from his own weight. Jo had a peculiar notion of what it was to "get out and do things."

Chapter 28

ＡLL the Coppage family were buried in the cemetery in
Brundidge, where Larry Coppage's wealthy kin had had
a large lot and an option on as many more square feet
of property adjacent. It was an option that was now exer-
cised though the family had never anticipated that the
grave sites would fill so quickly. Though Larry was well
liked throughout Pine Cone, and was thought to be the
best of all his large, moneyed family, most of the town
did not want to mingle and mourn with the owners of the
Pine Cone Munitions Factory. They used the recent rain
as an excuse for not attending.

The funeral service for Thelma and James Shirley was
held on Sunday, in the afternoon, at the Baptist church;
it was respectably attended. Dorothy and Malcolm Sims,
with little Mary between then, had one pew to themselves;
the one directly behind contained more distant relatives
of the husband and wife, whom Thelma and James themselves had never seen except at someone else's funeral;
another was filled with county policemen and their wives.
There were neighbors and friends, those who knew James
Shirley only by sight, and those who were only idly curious to attend the funerals of two who had died so violently. These last were disappointed that Dorothy Sims
had insisted on closed coffins.

James Shirley was known and respected in the black

area of Pine Cone, and therefore the choir loft in the back of the church, reached by narrow winding stairs from the vestibule, was packed with men and women paying their respects to the dead. Gussie was recognized as the chief mourner among them, and given the place with the best view of the pulpit and the two coffins, which stood, end to end, on trestles before it.

Sarah Howell, Becca Blair, and her daughter Margaret sat on a pew by themselves toward the back of the church. The eulogy was short and avoided all reference to the manner of the deaths of the couple; the minister concentrated on the good that James Shirley had done within the community by his valiant efforts on the Pine Cone police force (here the wives of the other officers began to weep), and praised Thelma for her work with the poor and undernourished in the county.

There were but six pallbearers altogether, so that two trips had to be made to and from the hearse before any of the mourners departed. The Simses and little Mary went out first, and climbed into a large black car directly behind that which contained the coffins. Slowly the other mourners filed out of the church, and got into their automobiles, sitting quietly and lighting cigarettes, in preparation for the slow drive to the cemetery, and the brief graveside service there.

When all the white congregation had exited, the black people climbed down from the choir loft. As was correct, Gussie was the first to emerge from the door. As soon as she saw the black woman, little Mary Shirley leaned out the car window and shouted, "You coming to the graveyard, Gussie? Get in! Go with us!"

Gussie approached the car quickly, and said, "Shhhhh, child. I'm gone walk there."

"Well," said Mary, disappointed, then excitedly, "We're gone beat you there, Gussie!"

Dorothy pulled the child back into the automobile, and all up and down the street, at the signal from the undertaker, the car lights went on and the funeral procession took off, in almost complete silence. Irritatingly, a dog set up a hoarse barking, but someone threw a stone at him, and he scampered off. The last three vehicles in the procession were police cars, with their blue lamps revolving at lowest speed.

A much larger crowd was present at the cemetery than had been at the church. You didn't have to dress to attend the graveside ceremony in Pine Cone, but if what you chose to wear was not entirely respectful to the memory of the dead, than you were careful to stand on the fringes of the circle surrounding the holes in the earth and you ducked behind a tree if any of the bereaved family came by. Children could also be brought here, without fear of disturbing the proceedings.

Sarah and Becca stood a little apart, behind a large cedar tree that had rooted itself in an old grave, eventually knocking down the tombstone with its increasing girth. They talked quietly over the distant drone of the minister's voice by the graveside.

"Jo don't get out much," said Becca quietly. "She ought to have come to the service. Do her good."

"She said she wanted to come, but that someone had to be there with Dean. But if she had really wanted to go, Becca, you know she would have had me stay there with him while she went off."

"I guess," agreed Becca. "Jo Howell wouldn't have nothing to do with the police *or* their families. Don't know why that was."

"It's impossible to tell anything about Jo Howell," said Sarah. "I live with her, and I've lived with her for some time, and I still don't know how she's gone react to things, what's gone make her mad at me, for instance. Can't never tell when she's gone be displeased with something you do."

"Odds on though," said Becca, "she's *not* gone like it, no matter what it is."

Sarah's short laugh had little humor in it, but Becca took exception anyway.

"I don't know why you're laughing," said Becca sternly, " 'cause in your place, I wouldn't crack a smile the livelong day. In your place, I wouldn't put up with it at all. You take care of that old biddie, and you take care of Dean, and you practically support the whole house as it is—"

"Things ought to be easier when Dean's benefits come through."

"Well," said Becca, "you just make sure you get those checks. You go down to the bank and you tell them that you are Dean's wife and that you and nobody else has the right to cash or deposit them checks. You tell them not to give a penny to Jo Howell or to Dean's dead bird dog, whichever of 'em comes in with the thing trying to cash it. Don't let Jo Howell get hold of them checks, you hear me?"

Sarah nodded obediently.

" 'Cause," said Becca, "I don't know what she'd do with that money—heaven knows she don't spend it on clothes and the beauty parlor—but I know you'd never see a penny of it and she'd expect you to support her same as usual."

Sarah said nothing. She couldn't in all conscience disagree with Becca because Sarah knew that her friend was right, but she felt that she owed some loyalty and respect to Jo. And besides, Becca always said enough for two.

"Now," said Becca, "Jo Howell lived next door to me for two and a half years 'fore you came to live there, and I tell you something—it wasn't what I'd call paradise. We didn't exactly get along—ever. But she was always calling me up, asking me to do this and that and I'd do it—because she was fat, and my daddy was fat and I know how hard it is for fat people to get around. But soon I found out that Jo wasn't just fat. It wasn't the fat! She was just lazy. She could have taken her stuff to the washateria herself. She could have got Dean—"

Sarah drew Becca's attention to the graveside.

The funeral was over. Mary had stood between her aunt and uncle all the while the preacher had read scripture, craning her neck to catch sight of Gussie, standing a little apart. The black woman and the white girl exchanged several winks, though Gussie did this only to keep the child quiet. Mary seemed not to know what had happened to her or that it was her mother and father that filled the two boxes supported on canvas straps across the open graves. The minister tossed handfuls of earth onto the two coffins, then turned away; the crowd turned with him and began the slow procession back to the parked cars on the edge of the cemetery.

"You know James's sister?" Becca whispered to Sarah.
Sarah shook her head.

"She was down three from me on the 'ssembly line, on
your side, like I told you. I didn't like her then and I
don't like her now. I wouldn't like to be little Mary
Shirley, having to go off with a woman like that."

"They're going to take care of her then?" Sarah asked.

"She's going back with 'em this afternoon, to Montgomery. I spoke to Gussie this morning and she was there
at the house, packing the clothes and trying to keep Mary
out of the room where *it* happened."

Sarah shuddered, and turned her attention to the bereaved family, which was passing near them just then:
Malcolm and Dorothy Sims, and a little behind them
Mary walking along beside Gussie. The child was quiet,
at Gussie's behest.

Just as Dorothy Sims passed, Sarah's attention was
drawn to the woman's dress, a simple black shift, orna-
mented only by the necklace which Jo Howell had
given to Larry Coppage three days before. Sarah was
astounded. How on earth had Dorothy Sims got hold of
it? The thing had been destroyed in the burning house.
Was it possible that somehow Larry Coppage had got the
thing to Dorothy Sims? It was not: Larry was dead two
hours after Jo had given it to him and Dorothy Sims had
been in Montgomery at the time, and anyway why would
he have given it away as soon as he had received it? Sarah
thought Larry hardly knew Dorothy Sims. But how else
could she have got hold of it? Maybe there were two of
them, maybe Dorothy Sims had bought it from the same
place that Jo had. Maybe she had had it for years. By the
time that these thoughts had passed through Sarah's mind,
Dorothy Sims was being helped into the black car by her
husband, and Mary Shirley was getting in behind her.

Sarah hurried forward to the car, but Becca grabbed
her, and held her back. "What are you doing, Sarah?"
she cried. "Ever'body's looking! You can't run at a funeral!"

"Got to talk to Dorothy Sims," Sarah explained breathlessly.

"No, you don't!" said Becca. "You don't even know

her, and it's been a bad day for them. What you got to say to her?"

"She's got on the thing that Jo gave Larry Coppage. I know that's what it is! She's got it round her neck!"

"Can't be the same one. Must be one just like it."

"I never saw another one like it," argued Sarah. "Can't be two of 'em if I never even saw one before."

"Must be. The one Jo had would have burned up at the Coppage house."

"Well," said Sarah, "it didn't, 'cause now Dorothy Sims has got it."

The car had driven off, and Becca relaxed her grip on Sarah.

"Well," said Becca for the sake of argument, "what if she has got it? Jo gave it away, it's not hers anymore. You wouldn't want it anymore anyway, would you?"

"I don't like it," Sarah admitted.

"Then why do you care whether Dorothy Sims has the thing or not?"

"Because I want to know how she got hold of it, that's why. There's something real strange about all of this. That jewelry, all these people buried—seven of 'em yesterday, and two more today."

"People die," said Becca. "They die in fires, and they kill each other. It's just because it happened two days apart, and it happened in a little place like Pine Cone that it seems strange."

"That's not all," said Sarah, "that's not all though. There's something else, and I don't know what it is yet."

Chapter 29

SARAH and Becca were silent on the drive home after the funeral. You are likely to be thoughtful after such a ceremony, even if the man buried had been your enemy, even if you hadn't known the dead woman at all.

It was a crazy thing: Sarah was actually having to decide whether she thought that the amulet had anything to do with the deaths that had occurred in Pine Cone. That *was* crazy. But supposing it was true. Then she had an obligation to warn Dorothy Sims against it. Or even beyond that, since it was Jo Howell that had put it into circulation, it was her responsibility (since Jo wasn't going to do it) to get it back altogether, and hide it or destroy it.

But what could a necklace possibly have to do with so many deaths? Five were obvious accidents, and the other two . . . who would ever know why Thelma Shirley had killed her husband? It couldn't have been a fight over a piece of jewelry. Sarah wasn't even really sure that Thelma had had it in her possession—but then how else could it have got from Larry Coppage's pocket onto Dorothy Sims' neck? The questions were endless, and they circled back on themselves, and not one of them could be answered.

Probably there were two necklaces, and she was imagining everything. One had burned up with the Coppages, and the other one had probably been given to Dorothy Sims at a wedding shower or something. Maybe, Sarah thought, if she had looked more carefully at the amulet that Jo had given to Larry, she would realize that they were nothing at all alike.

But Sarah knew she was only fooling herself; she knew in her heart of hearts that there was only one amulet. Larry Coppage had had it, and now Dorothy Sims had it. Sarah realized in a few moments that she had only been trying to talk herself out of her fears, because the thing she wanted the least in the world right now was to go up to Dorothy Sims and tell her some damn-fool story about a necklace with a curse on it. The woman would stare, and say she didn't know what Sarah was talking about and ask why she was bothering her at a time like this. That was what Sarah didn't want, but that was precisely what she was going to endure. She would have to make a spectacle of herself, and on top of everything she knew that she wouldn't be believed, that the warning, even if it were legitimate, would do no good.

She wished desperately that she had been able just to speak to Dorothy Sims at the funeral. She could have admired the amulet and then asked Dorothy where on earth she had found it—but that wouldn't have worked either, really. It was hard to make small talk at a funeral with the sister of the dead man. Sarah realized, though, that sometime that afternoon she would have to call up Dorothy Sims.

Becca was pulling the car into the driveway, and Sarah said, almost to herself, "I shouldn't have let 'em go."

Becca had been lost in her own thoughts, and didn't hear her friend. "What?" she said. Sarah shook her head, and did not try to repeat herself, but she determined that she would speak to Jo, just as soon as she got into the house. If she could get something out of Jo then maybe it wouldn't be necessary to make that dreaded call to Dorothy Sims.

Sarah nodded good-bye to Becca and Margaret and went inside. Jo was in the living room watching television. The house was dark and airless, for the curtains had not been opened all day. Dean was lying on the sofa, motionless. Sarah didn't like to see him there, on the place that she now considered her bed. His body, and the medicines that were rubbed into his injured skin, left an odor in the upholstery that lasted the night through and were the cause, Sarah was sure, of a series of nightmares that she had been suffering lately.

"Well," said Jo, "how was it? How many people come?"

Sarah replied briefly, "It was all right. Nothing happened. Seventy-five in the church, about fifty more than that in the cemetery."

"Never could abide that woman, or her husband either," said Jo.

"Which ones, the Shirleys or the Simses?"

"Neither one. Sorry lot, all of 'em."

"I didn't know you knew the Simses," said Sarah. She was trying to maneuver the conversation slowly to the amulet.

"Knew 'em when they lived in Pine Cone. We weren't friends then and we're not friends now that they moved away either."

"Well," said Sarah, "this is a bad time for them."

"If I was to go up to them—or go up to Dorothy Sims I mean, 'cause I never met her husband—and say I was sorry that James and Thelma Shirley was dead, why she wouldn't believe me! She'd say I was a hypocrite—and I would be!"

"I don't think anyone in this town has ever said that you were a hypocrite. It's not one of your faults," commented Sarah, trying hard to keep the sarcasm out of her voice.

"I went to her daddy's funeral, right after he run his truck into that Greyhound, and you know what?" said Jo, "Dorothy was wearing navy blue! Like she didn't have a black dress to her name!"

"Well," said Sarah, "she had on black today. And you know what else she had on?"

"What?" asked Jo.

"She had on that amulet that you gave to Larry Coppage the night his house burned down. Wednesday night."

Sarah waited to see what effect this had on Jo. The old woman said nothing for a moment, but stared hard at Sarah. Sarah couldn't tell if she were angry or surprised or puzzled, but it was evident that Jo Howell was repressing some emotion.

"How do you suppose she got hold of it?" said Sarah. "I'd have thought that the thing would have burned up in the Coppage place."

Still Jo did not answer.

At last, when Sarah continued to stare, Jo faltered, "It's . . . none of my business. None of yours neither. Dean and me gave the thing to Larry Coppage, and it was up to him to do with it what he wanted."

"But Larry Coppage didn't hardly have time to get the thing home, much less to give it away."

"Well," said Jo, a little more easily, "if Dorothy Sims has it now—and I'm not saying that she does, you could be mistaken—then how else could she have got it if Larry Coppage hadn't give it away to her?"

"She was in Montgomery, so he would have had to give it to James and Thelma Shirley. That's the only place that Dorothy could have got it."

"Look," said Jo peevishly, "I don't know why you're going through all this with me. I don't care what happened to it. It's not ours no more. I don't know why you keep harping on the thing. It wasn't worth much—I ordered it out of the Montgomery Ward catalog. You didn't like it, so you can't want it for yourself. What does it matter who's got the thing now?"

With this anger, Jo felt that she had regained her poise, and Sarah knew that she had lost the argument, at least at this point.

"It don't matter to me," said Sarah, "I'm just curious, that's all. It seemed peculiar—to see Dorothy with it on, I mean."

"If that woman would wear navy blue to her daddy's funeral, then I don't think I'd be surprised at anything she did! And, Sarah," concluded Jo, "there's dishes in the sink that's left over from dinner, and if you don't wash them, then they're just gone sit in there and rot to pieces!"

Chapter 30

"WELL," said Dorothy Sims to her husband, as soon as they were back inside the Shirleys' house, "if there is one thing that's worse than a wedding—and you know how I hate and despise weddings—it's a funeral."

"Shhh!" her husband cautioned her, and inclined his head toward little Mary, who had entered the house directly behind them.

Dorothy turned on the little girl and said, "Mary," in a commanding tone.

"Ma'am?" said little Mary. She knew that she had behaved herself, and feared no reproach.

"Mary, do you know what all that meant, what happened at the church and the cemetery today?"

"Dot, don't," pleaded her husband.

"Yes'm," cried little Mary. "They was burying Mama and Daddy. Only I didn't see no headstones. Where was the headstones? 'Cause when the paperboy got run down in the road last year—I almost got to see it—they buried him and he got a headstone. They's a lot of headstones in the cemetery, and what I cain't understand is why Mama and Daddy didn't get one. Is it because Mama killed Daddy? You cain't get a headstone if you kill somebody? Is that it?" Mary lowered her voice toward the end.

Dorothy nodded in satisfaction. Little Mary was a levelheaded if somewhat superstitious little girl, and

Dorothy approved of that. The child had not wept at the service in the church, and she had not been in shock at the graveyard afterward. Dorothy had seen what the death of even a single parent had done to some children, and it wasn't a pretty sight. Dorothy was very glad that Mary was taking it all so well, and she said so to her husband.

"The child don't realize yet what's happened to her," said Malcolm in an anguished whisper.

"I do too!" cried Mary, whose hearing had not been impaired by her grief. "Yesterday morning—no it wasn't yesterday, it was Friday morning right after Gussie lifted me out of the window and took me over next door to Mr. Berry's house—I heard Miz Berry talking on the phone and she was telling ever'body in town that Mama killed Daddy. She said she did it with a *ice pick*. I told Gussie that, and Gussie told me not to believe a word of it, but I know it was true. I *know*."

"How do you know, Mary?" asked her aunt, curiously.

"I *know*," repeated little Mary adamantly. "That night I had a nightmare about Mama, and she came in my bedroom, and she was waving a ice pick around in front of me, and I said, 'Mama, what you want in here with that ice pick?' And she said, 'Mary, you be quiet and go to sleep.' And I did, 'cause I knew if I didn't, that Mama was going to stick me with it. And when I woke up, there was Gussie wanting to haul me out of the window . . ."

"You were real confused," said Malcolm kindly. He hoped that Mary had only made up the story about being threatened with the ice pick.

"Mama scared my pants off," said Mary.

"I don't think we ought to talk about it anymore," said Malcolm. "We don't want you to have bad dreams, and your mama and daddy would want you to remember that they loved you very much, Mary. You meant more to them than anything else in the world."

"Mama sure could get mad though," said Mary, and whistled a little tag of emphasis to the remark.

This conversation was making Malcolm Sims more and more nervous. The deaths of James and Thelma Shirley had sorely tried him, and he was even more upset that his wife showed so little apparent concern. He was very sorry for the little girl, and he knew that his own life with

Dorothy would be changed immeasurably now that Mary was coming to live with them in Montgomery. Dorothy had refused to bear him children. She had declared from the beginning that she didn't want to be "saddled with a baby," and had also refused to consider adoption. Malcolm was fond of little Mary, but he also knew that perhaps she would not be the child he would choose if he had his pick of all the little boys and girls in Alabama. She was a little too much like her aunt: very shrewd in a fashion that was somehow completely wrongheaded. But he had no intention of shirking his duty or of being anything but the most affectionate and caring of foster-parents to Mary.

"Dorothy," this good man said to his wife, "why don't we get ready to go? There's not much more that we can do here today. I'd just as soon get home as soon after dark as possible. I'd like to have supper at home." He desperately wanted for this day to be over; he hated being in this house, surrounded by all the things that had belonged to the dead couple. He could not understand how his wife could have brought herself to wear Thelma's necklace to the woman's very own funeral. And now she was fingering it as if it had belonged to her forever and ever.

"You think I'm gone fix supper for you when I been through what I been through today?" his wife protested. "We're gone pick up some fried chicken or some barbecue on the way. I'm not fixing supper after a funeral."

"No," said Malcolm, "that's not what I meant. There's plenty of food in the kitchen, and we ought to take it back with us, so it won't spoil. There's no need for you to fix anything. I just want to get back to Montgomery. That's all I meant, Dot."

Dorothy Sims looked about her. "I sure hate to leave all this stuff here. You just know that Gussie got herself a skeleton key made, and right now she is probably right outside the door hiding in the bushes and waiting for us to leave! Then she's gone back some broken-down pickup truck to the door, and not a stick is gone be left by tomorrow morning."

"Dot," sighed Malcolm, and glanced toward Mary's bedroom where the child had gone to begin packing, "you ought not talk that way about Gussie, 'cause you know how fond of her that child is. We'll lock the house up, and I've already told the sheriff to keep an eye on it till I get back next week. You can come back with me and decide what you want to keep. Everything'll be all right till then."

Dorothy allowed herself to be persuaded and consoled herself with taking only the two flat chests of silver and the cut-glass punch bowl, which she declared were "absolutely unreplaceable." While she was packing these items carefully in bedspreads and other linens (she might as well take what she could, she thought), Malcolm went in to help little Mary.

The girl pranced about self-importantly, for she had come to realize that considerable interest had been attached to her person because of her nearness to the heinous crime of Thursday night. She was also the only full-fledged orphan in her class at school. In the midst of folding up some of her dresses, little Mary turned to Malcolm and said, "What is my teacher gone think when I don't show up at school tomorrow morning? Is she gone think I got kidnapped?"

Malcolm laughed briefly. "No, Mary, I talked to your principal before the funeral and I told him that Dot and I were taking you back to Montgomery with us. Dot's going to take you to school tomorrow. Do you think you'll still be too upset to go? 'Cause I guess you could stay at home with Dot for a couple of days or so, and wouldn't nobody know—and even if they did, they probably would say it was all right. You've gone through a lot, girl," he concluded with a lugubrious sigh. "We all have."

"I sure *will* be upset!" cried Mary. "I don't know a single person in that school. You think they're gone make me write real writing there? They let me print here. I'm not any good at real writing, and I think I'd just die if I had to go up to the blackboard and do real writing on the board." Mary paused, and trembled at the thought.

Her uncle reassured her. "It's all gone be fine, Mary. You're gone make lots of new friends, and everybody's gone love you like Dot and I do . . ."

Mary ran over and hugged her uncle around the waist. She burst into tears. Malcolm clasped her tightly to him, and did not think it so terrible a thing that she was crying.

Chapter 31

I‍T was a full two hours after the funeral that Sunday afternoon before Sarah Howell had decided that she *must* telephone Dorothy Sims, and ask her about the amulet. It would be going too far to warn her that her life might be endangered by the necklace that Sarah had seen her wearing at the service. At the beginning Sarah planned only to ask Dorothy Sims where she had got it. But what could she say to the woman when she answered the phone? They had never even been introduced. Maybe she could ask if there was any way she could help little Mary prepare for the sudden move to Montgomery. But Sarah knew that no matter what she decided to say, it would come out sounding foolish. But that didn't matter, and it certainly shouldn't stop her from calling.

Yet it did. Sarah dialed the number, but hung up the receiver before the ringing began. Then she washed the dishes that had been left in the sink. Again she dialed, let it ring twice and then hung up. She was doubly ashamed of this—for her cowardice and for the discomfort that would doubtless be occasioned in the mourning household by the nuisance of the phone ringing without any caller. Sarah waited fifteen more minutes—an excrutiating quarter hour in which she told herself over and over again that she had to go through with it. She dialed the number once more. Ten rings, and no one answered at all. She dialed again. Twenty rings and no one answered. They had already left, and Sarah was sure that Dorothy Sims had taken the amulet with her.

Sarah was displeased—with herself and with the situation—but there was nothing that she could do. She remembered then that she had heard that Malcolm Sims was going to return the following week and it might well be easier to talk to him anyway; he seemed a good-natured, well-meaning man and certainly more approachable than his wife. Sarah resolved, with some small easing of her conscience, that she must simply wait until the following Saturday. But how would she feel if something terrible happened to Dorothy Sims during the week? Sarah shook her head and shuddered. Was she going crazy to have such thoughts? They didn't make sense; nobody else—not even Becca—would believe them. Jo might well know more than she was telling, but who could say what Jo really thought about anything at all?

Margaret Blair knocked softly on the back door. When Sarah approached, the girl whispered conspiratorially, "Mama said to ask you if you want to drive around town —get out of the house for a while."

"I'll be there in a minute." Sarah smiled. It would do her good, she knew. Margaret's secretiveness only meant that Becca didn't want to have Jo come along; the trip to the drive-in the night before had taxed her tolerance excessively.

Sarah went into the bedroom and told Jo where she would be for the next hour or so and Jo began to complain immediately that Sarah was never there to take care of Dean. "Away at the plant all week long, and you come home for fifteen minutes on the weekend, just long enough to change your clothes before you're off gallivanting again with Becca Blair, and that little hellion of hers. Won't nothing good come of that one, and—"

"Jo," said Sarah. "I'm gone." And with that, she left the room.

Becca drove directly to the Nelsons' to drop off Margaret, and for a few minutes Becca and Sarah stared at the devastated lot on which the Coppage house had stood only a few days before. They shook their heads in wonder and sorrow. Next they drove to the Shirleys' house, for neither of the women had seen the place since they had first heard about the two deaths. The house looked deserted and the driveway was empty.

"What you supposed happened to their cars?" said Becca.

"Well," said Sarah. "James had the cruiser, and I imagine the sheriff just had it taken away since it belonged to Pine Cone anyway. I don't know what happened to Thelma's car."

"I wouldn't be surprised if Dot Sims made a deal on it with the preacher this afternoon at the cemetery!"

Sarah laughed despite herself—and despite her fears for Dorothy Sims—and Becca drove on. They rode all over the town, down nearly every street, waving to people on their front porches, and even stopping for a moment to speak to men and women working in their gardens by the side of the road.

When they were going through the black section of Pine Cone, Sarah suddenly asked Becca to pull up by two black women in conversation on the sidewalk. One of the women was Gussie, and she and her companion stopped their conversation, waiting politely to hear what the two white women had to say.

Sarah leaned out the window and said, "You worked for the Shirleys, didn't you? Didn't we see you at the funeral today?"

Gussie nodded.

Sarah proceeded hesitantly, for she didn't like doing this. "I . . . just called up the house . . . wanted to talk to Miz Sims for a few minutes. But there's nobody there."

"They's already gone," said Gussie. "They was in that house and out again. Didn't want to hang around that place, and I don't blame 'em. They must be halfway back to Montgomery by this time."

Sarah sighed and ignored Becca who was tugging at the sleeve of her blouse, wanting to know what all this was about. Sarah pushed her hand away and said, "What's you name?"

"Gussie."

"I'm Sarah Howell. I work at the plant."

"How you, Miz Howell," said Gussie cautiously. She couldn't yet figure out what all this was about.

"And Mr. Sims is coming back through Pine Cone next week?"

"That's what they tell me," said Gussie, after a moment's hesitation.

"Well, thank you, Gussie. I'll see you soon," said Sarah, nodding both to Gussie and to her companion. She drew her head back inside the car and Becca drove off with alacrity.

Sarah had turned round to wave good-bye again, and Becca demanded, "What'd you call up the Simses for, Sarah? Right after the funeral? Making the telephone ring in a dead man's house? Don't you know that's bad luck?" Becca was upset.

"No," said Sarah wonderingly, "I never heard that."

"Well," said Becca adamantly, "it sure is. You ought to go see people, not call 'em up. Telephone's for business and making dates, not for telling somebody you're sorry his mother got run down by a Mack diesel. I wish I would have known you were going to try something like that . . ."

"Would you have tried to stop me?" asked Sarah.

"Maybe," shrugged Becca. "But that wouldn't have done no good. I'd have driven you over there." She shuddered again at the thought of the telephone ringing in the house of mourning. "Those people don't need any more bad luck. What were you gone call Dorothy Sims about anyway?"

"The amulet. That necklace. I wanted to find out about it."

Becca threw up her hands and nearly lost control of the car. "Oh, honey!" she cried, "leave it alone. There's nothing to it! I mean if you thought I had it or something, you could ask me about it. If somebody at the factory had it, you could ask them. But you don't even know Dorothy Sims to spit at, and she's just been presiding at a double funeral. Leave her alone. Or talk to her husband when he comes back to town next week, but I hope you've forgot about it before then."

"I hope so too," said Sarah, and she meant it.

They returned home shortly after this, and spoke no more of the amulet.

In what was left of the afternoon, hot and golden, with the leaves on the trees sodden with humidity, Sarah brought out a folding chair into the backyard, and set it up in the shade of the pines on the back part of the property. Jo had wanted her to give Dean a sponge bath, " 'cause he's sweating under them bandages, and he won't say nothing 'cause he don't want to bother you, which is all the more reason for you to take care of him." For once, Sarah did not give in.

"This funeral has upset me, Jo," she said, "Dean is just going to have to wait." She turned her back on the house, and on the mother and son who were still in it, with hate boiling in their mouths like the foam of a rabid dog. Becca had loaned her a stack of *Life* magazines, and these Sarah leafed through until there was insufficient light to read any longer.

Chapter 32

LATE on Sunday afternoon, with the dusk gathering in the hollows and creeks of the rolling countryside of central Alabama, Dorothy and Malcolm Sims were finally on their way back to Montgomery. The scenery was familiar to them and they paid little attention to it. The road was not much traveled at this time, so that the drive was easy for Malcolm. The vegetation was lush and cooling; the car ran quick and smooth and quickly lulled little Mary to sleep in the backseat.

Dorothy had changed her dress, for the black had been too hot, but she had kept the amulet on; it was possible, she considered, that she might wear it all the time. It was a simple stylish piece that was sure to attract attention and admiration. Dorothy glanced into the backseat and looked at her niece a moment, turning uneasily on the vinyl upholstery. She whispered, "I don't know what we're going to do about that child, Malcolm."

Malcolm spoke low as well. "Terrible thing to have happen, Dot, Mary's a good little girl."

"Well," said Dorothy, "she eats as much as you do, Malcolm, and I don't know where the money's coming from that's gone keep her in clothes. And there's books to buy when we put her in school, and I don't know what all. Next thing you know I'm gone be talking to Mary Edwards down at the welfare office."

Malcolm sighed. "We can manage with Mary, Dot. Terrible thing, what happened. James left money for the girl. There's insurance. There's no need to set on the child because of money. We won't go without."

Dorothy touched the amulet round her neck, and rubbed it between her fingers. All this had been a great nuisance, one of the greatest nuisances of her life. It wasn't just that James had gone and got himself killed and left her to tend to the coffins, the services, the plots, the headstones, the selling of the house, and all the rest; he had also left her his little girl. Dorothy truly had never wanted children, and though she had no particular dislike for them—at least when they were quiet she didn't mind them much—she simply didn't want to be bothered. But now there was little Mary, and little Mary was going to be around for at least ten more years—demanding attention. And if she went to college there would be tuition, and if she got married there would be the wedding to pay for, and so on, probably for the rest of her life. That was the greatest nuisance: the child dropping so suddenly into her lap. And it was very bad about James too. He hadn't deserved to die with an ice pick. He hadn't deserved to spend his life with a woman like Thelma, and he certainly ought not have been murdered by one. It would have been much better if James had died in the line of duty. Then Thelma would have been around to take care of little Mary and Dorothy wouldn't have had to bother with either one of them. If that had been the case, she and Malcolm would be driving back to Montgomery now and they would never ever have had to give another thought to Pine Cone.

It was all Thelma's fault, then. Her fault that James was dead, her fault that Dorothy had had to worry with the funeral, her fault that little Mary was going to cost them umpteen thousand dollars over the next dozen years. Dorothy had never liked Thelma, and now she was furious with her. *It's a good thing she's in her grave,* Dorothy considered, *because it's the only place where she's safe from me.*

Malcolm had always stood up for Thelma; had stopped a number of quarrels between the two woman at various holiday get-togethers and now Dorothy turned and stared at her husband beside her and thought how none of this need have happened if Malcolm had only minded his own business. He had stood up for Thelma more than once, even when directly opposed to Dorothy's interests; there had been no call for that, no call at all. Maybe, Dorothy considered suddenly, Malcolm had talked Thelma into killing James, so that they could run off together. Thelma was to kill James and then call up Malcolm. Then Malcolm would have killed *her* and he and Thelma would have run off together. That was probably it. But something slipped up and Thelma died by accident, and since she was dead there wasn't any need for Malcolm to go through with his part of it. Dorothy shuddered to think how very narrowly she had escaped death that previous Friday.

She looked at her husband with violent loathing, and wondered how on earth he had thought he was going to get away with so foolish a plan as that. She and James would have been dead and Malcolm and Thelma would have gone to jail and God only knows what would have happened to little Mary. *He wanted to kill me, he wanted to kill me,* Dorothy repeated to herself, but strangely she was less angry with him for that than for the fact that the plans had been upset in such a way that she was now saddled with the little girl in the backseat. She hated him for it, and could barely keep herself from drawing her fingernails down the great expanse of smooth cheek below his melancholy eyes. She continued to twist the amulet between her fingers.

The automobile went suddenly up over the crest of a hill and down into the shadowed darkness on the other side. Below, a swift shallow creek was crossed by a flimsy bridge with aluminum railings. Thick forest of oak and pine crowded in on both sides of the road, with borders of red clover in violent bloom. The sky was unmarred dark blue.

The sudden increase in acceleration as the car moved downhill woke Mary in the backseat and she sat up, puffy-eyed, to see where they were.

Just as the car reached the bottom of the hill, Mary was very surprised to see her aunt reach over, very calmly, and wrench the steering wheel sharply to the left.

Malcolm was so surprised by her action that he allowed the wheel to leave his grasp. When he tried to regain it, Dorothy pushed even harder to the left.

The automobile slammed into the side of the bridge, shuddered a moment before breaking through the aluminum cordon, and then plunged into the waters of the creek. In a few seconds, water had broken up through the floor and was pouring in underneath the dashboard. Malcolm had opened his door before the car fell off the bridge, and now he struggled out into the shallow water. In the backseat Mary tried to open her door, but the force of the water kept it closed; she began to scream. The car had settled into the hard bed of the creek at a place where the water ran not more than three feet deep.

"Let down the window! Let down the window!" Malcolm called out to Mary, and still screaming, the child turned the handle to let the window down. In the meantime, Dorothy Sims was squeezing across the seat underneath the steering wheel, to climb out of the car.

"Dorothy," said her husband, with great anger, "why in the hell did you want—" He interrupted himself to reach in and pull Mary out of the backseat. She squirmed a little, and drew back from him.

"They's snakes in that water!" she gasped.

"No snakes," said her uncle. "Come on, Mary, you gone drown in that car, you don't let me pull you out of there." It was an empty threat, for the water outside the car was barely breast-high on the child.

Mary moved back toward her uncle, still whimpering to herself, "Snakes. I know there's snakes in that water."

But before Malcolm could pull Mary through the car window, Dorothy pushed him down into the water. He looked up at the woman in considerable surprise. "Dorothy—" he began, but she kicked at him. He struggled out of her way on his hands and knees, scraping himself badly on the sharp rocks on the bed of the creek. All his clothing was wet through, and impeded his movement severely.

Mary stared at her aunt apprehensively. Dorothy Sims pulled out of the water a newly fallen branch of oak that was tumbling downstream. She lifted it high over her head and advanced slowly on her husband. He continued to crawl away, repeating her name softly. "Dorothy. Dorothy. Dorothy . . ."

Mary reached over into the front seat and got Dorothy's pocketbook; the child leaned out the window and threw it at her aunt, but it fell several feet short, and dropped into the water.

Dorothy came nearer her husband, and before he could get out of the way, she brought the branch down against the side of his head. The rough surface of the branch tore open the side of his face, tearing away skin and nearly severing his ear. He paused quivering on all fours, dazed and already bleeding heavily, while the water of the creek flowed swiftly beneath him. The pebbles under his hands began to give way under the pressure of his weight, and he was about to slip over when Dorothy lifted the branch high above her head and brought it down squarely upon Malcolm's upturned face. He screamed, flailed briefly, and then collapsed into the water. The branch had smashed his nose, plunged splinters through his lids deep into the eyesockets, and split open his cheek from the side of his mouth to the dangling ear. He tumbled sideways into the water, unconscious and staining the water with his blood.

Dorothy dropped the branch into the water. It submerged a moment, paused, and then was spun away over a fall of tiny rapids. Mary stared at the branch out the rear window until it was out of sight and imagined somehow that it was more responsible for what had been done to her uncle than was her aunt.

Dorothy Sims knelt over her husband, took both his arms and dragged him back to the side of the car. Mary crouched on the other side, as far away from her aunt as she could get. Dorothy pushed Malcolm's unconscious form under the car between the wheels. She held tight onto him by his ankles so that he would not be borne away by the rushing water. For a few moments there was a slight struggle and one of Malcolm's feet escaped her, but she caught it quickly enough again and held ever more tightly. In a couple of minutes Dorothy let the body go, assured that her husband had drowned.

Mary, still inside the car with the water a few inches over the level of the back seat, was rigid with fear. She had rolled down the window and was about to crawl out of it into the water despite her fear of the snakes, when Dorothy released her husband's ankles. The corpse of Malcolm Sims knocked about under the car for a moment, and then emerged on the downstream side. His purple face appeared just beneath the surface of the water, a halo of blood surrounding it. Mary screamed, dropped down onto the seat, and began to cry. Her uncle was dead, her aunt was doubtless going to kill her next, she was like to drown in the backseat of a car, and the creek was filled with snakes.

Dorothy Sims, however, ignored her niece and waded to the shore. Bedraggled, she struggled up onto a sandbar, stepped across a narrow muddy streamlet, and then climbed up a clayey embankment about three feet high. She sat for a moment in a nest of pine needles to catch her breath, then made her way along the creek bank to the bridge; she made slow progress because of the denseness of the vegetation. It looked as if she were going to flag down the next vehicle that came along in the dusk.

She was nearly to the road when a farmer's pickup truck appeared at the top of the hill. Though the dusk was deepening into night in this small valley, the truck did not yet have its headlamps on.

Dorothy Sims struggled against the briars, which tore her dress and slip, and leaped out into the road, trying to catch the attention of the driver of the truck. But she tripped on the uneven edge of the pavement, and stumbled headlong into the highway.

Her clothes were dark, so that the driver of the truck did not see her before he was almost upon her, and by then it was too late to stop. He swerved to the right, but Dorothy had not the sense to dart backward, and so was caught by the right fender. She was knocked clear across the road and against the concrete piling at one end of the bridge. Her spine was snapped instantly.

Mary heard the screeching of the truck's brakes and she stared out the window but could see nothing of what was happening. Making sure that her uncle's corpse was farther downstream, Mary struggled out the right-hand window of the backseat and fell into the water; she came up sputtering and screaming, "Snakes! Snakes!"

Chapter 33

❦❦❦❦❦❦❦❦❦❦❦❦❦❦❦❦❦❦❦❦❦❦❦❦❦❦❦❦

JACK Weaver backed his truck off the bridge, and onto the narrow shoulder of the highway. Shaking, he climbed down out of the cab and ran quickly over to the body of Dorothy Sims. It was apparent from the abnormal way in which her torso was bent that her back had been broken. He took Dorothy's hand; there was no pulse. He breathed an automatic but thoroughly sincere prayer, and closed the woman's eyes.

His wife Merle was also out of the truck now and had approached timorously. "Jack," said the woman, "is she dead? Did we kill her?"

"She's dead," he replied. The middle-aged couple then looked up, and saw for the first time that the bridge had been broken through, and that there was a car in the water. Mary had just come up out of the water and begun to scream for fear of the snakes.

"Oh, Jack, they must have been a accident, and we run the poor woman down when she was trying to get help!" cried Merle.

"You go get the child, Merle. Poor thing's in hysterics. Get her out of the water."

"What about this lady?"

"I'll put her on the back of the truck. I don't want the little girl to have to see her, and then we'll drive into

Brundidge. Looks like that was where they was headed."

"Maybe the girl will know," said Merle.

Merle and Jack Weaver were good, conscientious people and this accident was an enormous burden on their minds, not because of the possible consequences of it to themselves, but simply because of the death of the unfortunate woman whom they had killed and because of the child. They owned a small farm on hard acreage and had worked all their lives tearing a living from the stubborn earth. They were pious, well-meaning people, whose only child had been electrocuted during a rainstorm.

Merle climbed down to the creek bed, and waded out into the water toward Mary, soothing her with her words. "They's no snakes, child. No snakes! I'll carry you, come here, child!"

Mary stopped blubbering and began walking toward Merle through the water. Merle snatched her up out of the creek and brought her to the shore. There she waited a few minutes in order to give her husband time to place Dorothy's body out of sight on the back of the truck.

"You tell me what happened, child," said Merle, piteously.

"Well," said Mary, with a conspiratorial air, "we was going to Montgomery—"

"You and your mother," interrupted Merle.

"My mama's *dead,*" whispered Mary.

"You saw it then!" cried Merle, thinking that the child had been witness to the accident.

"My mama's dead, because we buried her today. This afternoon. My daddy's sister was in the car, and she just now run up here into the trees."

Merle was shocked and dismayed to think that the child had lost her mother and now her aunt in so short a time.

"We was going to Montgomery," Mary continued, with her eyes almost shut tight, "and we come to this bridge and Aunt Dot turned the wheel of the car, and we went in the water with all them snakes in it. And then Malcolm —that was Dot's husband—tried to get me out of the backseat, where there was all this water, you know, and Aunt Dot beat him over the head with a big stick and killed him and he is floating off down to the Gulf of Mexico right now! I thought she was gone kill me next, she could have put a snake in the backseat! You better watch out," Mary warned her rescuer, " 'cause she might try to kill you too!"

"Jack! Jack!" Merle screamed, and pulled the child after her back toward the highway. Jack was just covering the body with a piece of canvas. He turned at his wife's voice.

"Jack! There's another body, floating down the creek—this woman's husband. The girl says she killed him and then ran up on the road."

Jack Weaver's eyes widened. He ran to the cab of the truck and brought out a heavy-duty flashlight. He stood on the downstream side of the bridge and flashed the light over the surface of the creek. He caught sight of another corpse about twenty yards away, caught in the exposed roots of a cypress that stood at the edge of the water. Jack sickened at the ghastly sight.

"Merle," he turned to his wife, "you get in the car with the girl, and don't you let her see a thing. Don't you let her look out the window, whatever you do."

Merle climbed into the cab, and coaxed Mary in after her. While they waited for Jack to retrieve the body of Malcolm Sims and place it on the truck beside that of his wife, Merle pieced together the events of the past few days from Mary's rambling narrative and was appalled by all that the child had suffered. When finally, grimly, Jack got into the cab Merle repeated to him what the child had said, being constantly interrupted by Mary with new and inconsequential details, and it was decided that they ought to return to Pine Cone right then.

Chapter 34

IT was the early part of the evening, but the streets of Pine Cone were already deserted. The Weavers' pickup truck was parked directly in front of the courthouse, with the headlamps still on. The harsh light from a mercury lamp shone down into the cab, directly onto Mary Shirley and Merle Weaver. The little girl was still wet and bedraggled, and lay with her head in Merle's lap, very weary and confused by all that had happened since that morning. Merle Weaver stroked the little girl's hair, and thought of the two corpses in the rear of the truck.

Presently, Jack Weaver came down the front steps of the courthouse. Sheriff Garrett and Deputy Barnes were directly behind him, talking in low voices. Jack went down and was about to uncover the corpses for their inspection, but the two men first glanced into the front of the truck and saw that it was Mary Shirley inside.

"Hey, Mary, how you doing?" said Deputy Barnes automatically, but very infelicitously. The sheriff punched him and they moved away before Mary had the opportunity to reply that she was very very wet.

From Jack's description of what had happened on the road and of the story related to him by the little girl who had survived the strange happenings on the highway and in Burnt Corn Creek, the sheriff and his deputy had concluded that the bodies must have been those of Malcolm and Dorothy Sims.

Garrett and Barnes glanced at one another and shook their heads. Then they moved round beside Jack, one on either side, and glanced as he pulled back the canvas, uncovering the upper portions of the two corpses. The faces were ghastly in the mercury light, and still wet with thin blood and creek water.

"The girl," Jack repeated, "say *she,*" and he indicated Dorothy Sims, "beat *him,*" and he nodded at Malcolm. "Beat him over the head with a pine branch until he was dead, and then she ran up on the bridge."

Sheriff Garrett pulled the canvas entirely off. "If she'd have been wearing something light colored, maybe you'd have seen her," he said, trying to console the farmer, who was obviously greatly distraught.

The deputy said then, "She was at her own brother's funeral today—he was a deputy just like me—and so she wouldn't have been wearing white in no case."

"And this wasn't *their* little girl, then?" said Jack.

"No," said the sheriff. "Like I said. Mary was James Shirley's little girl. James Shirley was this woman's brother. James Shirley's wife pushed a ice pick into his brain and then cut her throat. That was on Thursday night."

Jack shook his head and whistled. "What's gone come of her now?"

Sheriff Garrett shrugged.

"We gone get in trouble, Sheriff?" the farmer asked. "You know," he said piteously, "I didn't mean to run the woman down."

"Well," Garrett replied, "wasn't your fault, like you said. She wasn't wearing white, and she ought not be running up on bridges when the sun's gone down. And she ought not be killing her husband with pine branches either."

"Ought not do that in any case," added the deputy. "No, sir," he added a moment later, for emphasis, when no one thought to second his opinion.

"It's real peculiar," mused the sheriff.

"What is?" said Jack.

"Ever'body dying like they are . . ." said the sheriff. "You mean these two, and then the policeman and his

157

wife?" asked Jack. "Not much family left there, is there?"

"Wasn't just them," said Deputy Barnes, " 'cause last Wednesday night, seven people burned up on the other side of town."

"Well," said the farmer, "burning up's a lot different from stabbing and shooting and getting run down on bridges and being hit on the head with pine branches in the middle of the creek."

"Maybe," said the sheriff, "but I tell you, sir, I just can't say I was surprised when you folks pulled up and said you had two bodies in the back of your truck, what with all these people dying. And if I had thought about it for twenty seconds I think I could have guessed that it would be Malcolm and Dorothy Sims."

"And you know what's funny too?" said the deputy.

"What?" asked the sheriff, pulling the canvas back over the corpses; there wasn't any point in examining them further now.

"For the last nine dyings," said the deputy, "we ain't had one open coffin, and from the looks of these two, we're not gone get it now."

"We not gone get them anyway. They was from Montgomery, just down for the funeral."

"You'd think she'd have waited till they got back to Montgomery," said the deputy.

"I sure do wish she had," said Jack Weaver, shaking his head slowly.

At this point, little Mary Shirley leaned her head out the cab of the truck, and said loudly, "And you know what, Sheriff? She did it on purpose! She pushed the car off the road! I saw her turn the wheel! She did it 'cause I saw her do it!"

"Mary," said the sheriff, "you be quiet, till we know what's gone come of you."

"They's all dead," said the little girl with more gravity. "I don't know what you gone do 'bout me. They's Gussie, I could go live with Gussie, 'cept I just know she's gone make me eat collard greens, and I *hate* collard greens."

Merle Weaver drew the little girl back into the truck and held her tight against her breast for warmth and comfort.

Chapter 35

∞∞

THE parking lot of the Pine Cone Munitions Factory was two acres of packed red dirt that was bright blood-colored dust in dry weather and thick, sucking mud after any amount of rain. A small corner of paved ground was reserved for those high up in the company. A great array of automobiles crowded this lot every working day: cars that were twenty and even thirty years old, cars that had been purchased only the week before and still retained the dealer's stickers on the side windows, all manner of trucks and vans, a couple of motorcycles, and even a school bus.

At lunch time every day, many workers came out into this dusty, dry, barren area, not because it was inviting certainly, but because it was a change from the interior of the factory. Here they stood about and talked in little groups, sitting on the hoods of cars, crouching in the shade of the larger vehicles, even catching little naps in the backseats if the sun had not made the vinyl upholstery unbearably hot. They drank soft drinks out of cans with straws, or smoked cigarettes lifted out of large purses with loud catches, or even passed around a thermos filled with rum and Coca-Cola.

On Monday afternoon Becca Blair made a date for the following Saturday night with the man who daily checked the electrical wiring of the plant; she then joined Sarah Howell, who was leaning against the side of Becca's

Pontiac, flipping through a copy of *Reader's Digest* looking for the jokes.

They had hardly had time to exchange a few words, when the woman down four from Becca on the line approached them hurriedly. "Let me tell you what I just heard!" she cried breathlessly, and the three women automatically made a little circle between the two cars.

"First," said Becca, "you tell us who told you, 'cause I want to know if I'm gone believe it after I hear it."

"I heard it from my own Anna-Lee," said the woman, who had a girl the same age as Becca's daughter Margaret, "and Anna-Lee is a good girl, wouldn't tell no lies—not to her own mother—and she got it straight from one of the colored ladies in the lunch line at school not fifteen minutes ago. I had to pick her up at the school and drive her over to the dentist, so that's how I found out so quick. Anyway, this lady on the lunch line is the sister of Gussie who used to work for the Shirleys, course that was 'fore she killed him. I mean, before Thelma Shirley killed James. So far as I know, Gussie didn't have a thing to do with it."

"All right," said Becca, laughing shrilly, "we'll believe it. Anna-Lee's word is good by me!"

"What'd you hear?" said Sarah.

The woman spoke with great significance. "Little Mary Shirley is *back in school!*"

Becca and Sarah could make nothing of this.

The woman continued, "Little Mary Shirley was in school this morning."

"That supposed to mean something?" asked Becca.

The woman nodded mysteriously.

Sarah said uneasily, "But she was off to Montgomery with her aunt and uncle yesterday. They were supposed to leave directly after the funeral. They did leave,"she said after another moment, "because I called the house, and Gussie said that they were on their way."

"Didn't never make it to Montgomery," said the woman gravely.

"What do you mean?" demanded Sarah.

"Well," said the woman, and then she related in a quick, low voice, "Car jumped the road, flew in the creek, smashed up on a sandbar, burst into flames in twenty-five seconds, and then that woman, the policeman's sister—who was already acting very peculiar at the funeral if you ask me what *I* thought about it—hit her husband over the head with the right front fender till his eyes bugged out . . ."

Sarah and Becca gasped in surprise.

"Choked to death on his own blood, and floated down the river till he got picked up by a colored man fishing for rainbow trout since early that morning. It was his only catch of the day. That corpse would have made it to Elba in two more hours . . ."

"What happened to Dot Sims?" demanded Becca. "Why'd she do it?"

"Well, that's the thing," the woman replied. "Don't nobody know why she did it, don't make no sense, 'cause little Mary saw it all, trapped in the backseat with the car on fire and ever'thing. And if the woman was planning to get rid of him, you wouldn't think she'd have done it in front of a child—that wasn't even her own. She must have known that the child would say *something* about it later, you know what I mean? Unless she was planning for the child to be cremated right then and there, in the middle of the creek!"

Sarah and Becca nodded. "So what happened to her?" Sarah asked. "Where is she now?"

"She run up on the road, trying to flag down the Montgomery bus, which was due just about then, and got run down by this fourteen-year-old boy in a Oldsmobile, who didn't have a learner's permit yet, and the police found two quarts of moonshine whiskey in the backseat. The boy said they belonged to his father, but the police made him walk down the line in the center of the highway and he couldn't do it. And that child, poor boy, is gone get sent down the river for running down a woman that had just gotten through killing her husband."

"Little Mary Shirley," said Becca, "what become of her?"

"She was drowning in the back seat of the car, or burning up, I don't know which, 'cause Anna-Lee didn't get *all* the details, and she saw everything, like I said. She's all right, 'cause she's in school, 'cept I don't know how she got rescued, unless it was the bus driver that did it."

Becca shook her head sadly, "That poor child is gone
have bad dreams for the rest of her life. First her mama
and daddy, and then her aunt and uncle. All in the same
week. The women in that family are just no good; I
wouldn't let no man I had around marry into that pack.
Just wouldn't be safe."

Sarah objected. "Dot Sims and Thelma Shirley wasn't
related by blood, they was just sister-in-laws. There must
have been something else . . ."

"Something else what?" asked the woman.

"Poor little girl," Becca said, thinking of little Mary.

The whistle sounded, and the three women hurried back
into the factory.

Chapter 36

BECCA and Sarah's friend was not the first person working at the Pine Cone Munitions Factory to hear of the deaths of Malcolm and Dorothy Sims. The wife of one of the policemen on the Pine Cone force was the switchboard operator in the main administration building of the factory, and when her husband called for his midmorning check-in (she lived in constant fear of his untimely demise) he told her of the two corpses in the back of the truck. She managed to relate the story to a number of her friends and co-workers in the next hour, but these women had not known Dorothy intimately—the dead woman had been on the assembly line, but that was several years before—and so the tale did not spread as far as it might have.

In the middle of the morning, one of the two black utility drivers was sent to the Piggly Wiggly supermarket to buy coffee for the administrators' lounge. Since the driver did not enjoy such an amenity at the factory, he felt he was at least entitled to a cup of coffee and a piece of pie and stopped at the diner by the railroad tracks, where, in slack hours, black men were served so long as they did not seat themselves. There he overheard the two friendly waitresses tell breathlessly of what had occurred the previous evening on the road north out of Pine Cone. When this man returned to the factory the information traveled

quickly enough among the black employees, not because
they had known the unfortunate couple but because it was
another example, and a fine one, of white immorality and
imbecility.

The assembly line knew very little. Only Becca, Sarah,
and Anna-Lee's mother had heard anything at all, and
Anna-Lee had not got everything exactly right. The news
traveled no further than these women in the next two
hours, for they were pinned to their places on the line, and
deafened by the noise of the machinery. During the afternoon coffee break, however, the word was passed down
the line.

After lunch in the administration buildings, the more
recent murder and death, so strangely paralleling those of
the policeman and his wife, were noised about. Bosses
perched on the corners of their secretary's desk, telling
the story, and invented grotesque details to make them
squirm and certain other secretaries and female file clerks
related the incident to their employers as a subtle object
lesson in what may happen to a man if a woman is
driven too far.

Strangely enough, much of this was done in great fun.
The employees at the factory had not yet heard enough
circumstantial detail to be properly shocked and they
waited for the end of the day when they could return
home to the newspaper and radio reports which would no
doubt tell them what had really happened. Until that
"official" announcement by the media, people in the factory enjoyed themselves with the unexpected, strangely ef-
fected deaths.

The rest of Pine Cone was not so isolated as the Pine
Cone Munitions Factory. In stores and in homes and on
the streets of the town, the deaths of Malcolm and Dorothy Sims were known and discussed with considerably
greater accuracy.

Certain persons in Pine Cone could be counted on to
know more about those incidents in the town than anyone
else, and they were applied to by all who were curious. To
begin with, the two friendly waitresses in the diner by the
railroad tracks were inexhaustible funds of information
and editorial comment on any act of violence in Pine
Cone, for it usually happened that they were intimately

acquainted with either the perpetrator or the victim. They would shriek discreetly and cover their eyes dramatically against the terrible things they related, but their sources were impeccable and their details reliable.

Another source was the three bag boys at the Piggly Wiggly supermarket, who managed among them to speak to three quarters of Pine Cone's female population over the course of any given weekday. With equal enthusiasm they received and offered the news of the moment, and acted as white-aproned clearinghouses for all the more malicious gossip of Pine Cone. These three boys were not particularly well thought of outside their two capacities as movers of packages and broadcasters of domestic information, but within those fields, they were trusted absolutely.

Those who were finicky and wanted the most accurate information available usually called the radio station and talked to the manager. He might not know as much as the sheriff, but he was more willing to talk. And because the radio station in Pine Cone had been set up more as a service for the rural portions of the county than simply for the town's convenience and the sheriff's jurisdiction ended at the town limits, there were often things that were known to the manager of the station that were wholly unfamiliar to Sheriff Garrett.

Today the sheriff wasn't answering any questions at all. Garrett had been very upset by the murder of his colleague the past week, and now the death of James Shirley's brother-in-law depressed him further. There was something about the murders of the two men and the subsequent accidental deaths of their wives that confused the sheriff beyond his even beginning to understand it all. Why had the women done it? For the same reasons, perhaps? What were those reasons? Or had Dorothy Sims acted in imitation of her sister-in-law? But Sheriff Garrett knew that the two women had not got along together and Dorothy Sims was unlikely to follow the example of Thelma Shirley in anything at all. On the other hand, how could the two murders—being so close together, so similar, among members of the same family—be unrelated? And the women dying afterwards, *immediately* afterward—had they only looked like accidents? Had

Thelma Shirley sliced open her neck on purpose? Had Dorothy Sims deliberately jumped out in front of Jack Weaver's truck?

Sheriff Garrett knew one thing though: It was senseless to prosecute Jack Weaver—a *good* man—for something that was obviously not his fault. The only one who ought to have gone on trial was Dorothy Sims, and she was on the embalming table that very minute. Even if the case were brought before a jury, not a single man or woman in Pine Cone—much less twelve of them together—would think anything but that Jack Weaver had acted as an administrator of divine retribution. He would be let go with only a caution by the judge to turn his truck headlights on earlier in the evening. Dorothy Sims and Thelma Shirley, in getting themselves killed, had saved the county a lot of money in trial expenses and the state wouldn't have to pay for their upkeep in prison, and their punishments had been commensurate with their crimes. But still, Sheriff Garrett considered, it was just real strange.

Until he could figure all of this out satisfactorily for himself, Garrett refused to say anything, except to the manager of the radio station and to the editor of the newspaper, whom he informed at length of the circumstances of the new set of deaths. He didn't want to be distracted by his friends—and the wives of his friends, and total strangers—calling up to get a firsthand account of this new horror. He left the gossiping to Deputy Barnes who enjoyed the sense of self-importance he received from the wholesale dissemination of this official information.

By six-thirty that Monday evening, the news had spread all over town, and many of the pertinant facts had been got straight. Then, working from the same basis of information, the same questions that had plagued Sheriff Garrett now fell upon the general population of Pine Cone. Everyone was at pains to determine why on earth the two sisters-in-law had murdered their husbands, who both had been very good men. It was a great, great mishap, and on top of everything, what would come of little Mary Shirley? The poor girl now had no one in the world, except those people who had showed up for James and Thelma's funeral, and who were they? Relatives who never show up except at a funeral may be looking for money, but they certainly aren't wanting a little girl to take back with them.

Some people said it was a suicide-murder pact between the two women. But nobody could guess when they had made up their quarrel. Even those who set forth this idea admitted that it didn't make much sense, but what other explanation was there? Other opinions, such as that it had really been Malcolm Sims who had murdered both James and Thelma Shirley—and that Dorothy was avenging their deaths—were even more farfetched. In fact, the town was stumped and could make no sense out of it at all. In the course of that Monday evening, the only theory that was *not* put forth was that the deaths of the two married couples had anything to do with the seven-times-fatal fire at the Coppage house.

Chapter 37

▄▄

SARAH Howell grew more upset with the hours that afternoon. Two more people were dead and they had died
as mysteriously, as unaccountably as the others—and
Sarah had seen Dorothy Sims only a few hours before
she murdered her husband, had seen that she was wearing the amulet. The details that the woman in the parking
lot had given her had been confused, but it seemed fairly
certain that Malcolm Sims and his wife were dead.

The afternoon break came and the news spread among
the women on the assembly line, but no one had any new
information. Sarah had hoped against hope that someone
would be able to tell her of a simple reason for the deaths
of Malcolm and Dorothy Sims, but instead, the women
pressed *her* for details of what she had heard from Anna-
Lee's mother. In the last hours of the working day, the
assembly line rattled on, lurching and grinding, and
Sarah's thoughts were fixed on the amulet. Where was it
now? Who had it? Were there to be more deaths? More
unhappiness? What seemed most likely, she had to admit,
was that little Mary Shirley now had the amulet. It was
necessary, if so, to get the thing away from the child before anything happened to her. Sarah didn't like the idea
of going over to the Shirley place trying to find the little
girl and take the amulet from her. Mary might not want
to give it up, Sarah might look as if she were trying to

steal it; she would look crazy. But no matter how unpleasant a task it might be, her duty was to get hold of
the thing, and destroy it, or put it in a safety deposit box,
or *something*.

Therefore just after work, Sarah asked Becca to drive
her over to the Shirley house. Sarah didn't want to tell
Becca why she wanted to go, because she didn't want to
be talked out of her feeble resolution. She had barely
persuaded herself to take on this foolish project and she
knew that just a couple of well-directed sarcastic remarks
from Becca would be enough to send her scurrying home,
leaving that poor child with the amulet in her possession.
Therefore she refused to tell Becca anything beforehand,
but promised that she would inform her in detail afterward, whether or not she was successful with her un-
named project. Becca was suspicious of all this—more
suspicious than curious, in fact—and she said she was
perfectly willing to wait in the car while Sarah went into
the house. Sarah gratefully accepted this offer. She felt
much better about going into the Shirley house knowing
that Becca was out in the car waiting for her.

"You sure do put up with me," said Sarah to Becca
affectionately.

"I sure do!" her friend cried. "I don't know why I do it.
And I'm blasted to hell and back if I know why you want
to come to this place. James and Thelma Shirley are
dead! You wanted to come over and speak to Dorothy
and Malcolm Sims yesterday, but they're dead too!
There's nobody left!"

"There's little Mary Shirley," replied Sarah cautiously.

Becca's brow darkened. "Why you want to see that
little girl? That little girl's had a peck of trouble since
last week, and you ought not go in there upsetting her.
You ought—" Becca suddenly broke off in the middle of
her low-voiced cautions, and cried loudly, "I don't know
why I'm talking to you like this! This is absolutely crazy,
Sarah Howell. You following up these dead people like
you are. It's worse than chasing fires! What do you think
you're doing? You didn't hardly know these people when
they were alive, so why are you hanging around 'em after
they're dead?" She shook her head slowly and Sarah

made no immediate reply, but allowed Becca's accusations to stand, for the moment.

Then, slowly, she said, "Becca, listen, you've just got to put up with me on this. I don't like it, you know I don't. I don't want to go in there and talk to little Mary Shirley, I didn't want to call up Dorothy Sims on the phone yesterday, but I did it. You don't think I would be doing *any* of this, do you, if I didn't absolutely have to do it? I don't like going around asking questions about dead people."

Becca said nothing for she knew that Sarah was in great earnest. "Why do you do it then?" she asked grudgingly.

"I was scared to death yesterday afternoon to call up Dorothy Sims and when I finally did get the gumption to call, she and Malcolm had already gone. If I had got to them first, if I hadn't been such a fraidycat, Dorothy and Malcolm Sims would be alive today. Or even if they had died anyway, I wouldn't be feeling now like I was responsible for it."

"You're not!" cried Becca. "What were you going to say to them? Tell Malcolm his wife was going to bash his head in later on in the afternoon in the middle of Burnt Corn Creek? Or what were you gone say to her? If she wanted to kill the man, *you* or anything you said to her wasn't going to stop the woman."

"It was the amulet, I think, that did it. Or it might have been. It don't matter right now if it did or didn't, just so long as I find the thing."

"The *amulet!* You still harping on that thing? How can a hunk of jewelry cause Dorothy Sims to beat her husband over the head with a automobile fender?"

Sarah shrugged. "I don't know. I don't know how it could. But I do know how to count, and I count eleven people dead in this town since last Wednesday evening when Jo Howell gave that thing to Larry Coppage. I saw him with it, and I saw Dorothy Sims with it. They're both dead. Maybe it's just bad luck, but that's still enough reason to try to get hold of it again. People ought to be warned against bad luck." Here Sarah looked sharply at her friend, knowing how superstitious she was.

Becca had to agree. "Maybe you're right. I'm willing to

believe that it's bad luck. They're some people that have bad luck, and there's certain pieces of furniture that's bad luck, and there's probably pieces of jewelry that's bad luck."

"And I was thinking," said Sarah, "that maybe it was little Mary Shirley that's got it now." She paused and allowed Becca to think of this for a moment; Becca nodded slowly. "And little Mary Shirley," said Sarah, "is a very little girl, and she ought not have to put up with bad luck. It didn't do Dorothy Sims a bit of good, and I sure don't want anything to happen to little Mary."

"I guess you're right," said Becca. "You go on in there and talk to the girl. I guess you might as well find out what she knows. If we can get the thing back, we might as well try, 'cause this town has had bad luck this past week, and it don't need no more."

"You want to come in with me?"

Becca shook her head. "I don't want *none* of what happened in that house to rub off on me."

Sarah started to open the car door; they had been parked for some few minutes in front of the Shirley house. Becca said, "But you know, Sarah, I don't believe a word of it. Not a word."

Sarah laughed silently, a mournful little laugh, and got out of the car.

"You get that thing," whispered Becca, "and you bring it back out here with a pair of ice tongs, 'cause I don't want you to touch it, you hear me?"

Sarah nodded and moved up the sidewalk. Gussie answered Sarah's knock, and with a slightly puzzled expression, invited Sarah into the living room. Little Mary sat on a couch in the living room eating a sandwich and watching cartoons on television.

"Who's she staying with now?" Sarah asked Gussie.

"I'm staying here with her right now," said Gussie. "And the sheriff, he's trying to get hold of some relatives Miz Thelma had in Ohio. She didn't like 'em and they didn't like her, so far as I know, so I don't know what's gone 'come of this child. People are bringing by food, but Mary's just in the second grade." By this, Gussie meant that Mary was being helped by the community right now, directly after her multiple bereavements, but that she had many many years of dependency left.

"Well," said Sarah, "she seems to be all right for now, and that's a blessing."

"Tore up," said Gussie shortly, "she's just tore up!"

Little Mary Shirley looked up during the commercial, and stared inquisitively at Sarah Howell.

"Mary . . ." said Sarah.

"Ma'am?" said the little girl.

"Mary, can I talk with you a few minutes?"

"You come sit by me. You gone talk about Mama and Daddy, or you gone talk about Aunt Dot and Malcolm?" The child was wary, and had had enough of consolation for the time being.

Sarah moved into the room followed by Gussie, who turned off the television set.

"I want to ask you a few questions, Mary."

"What do I get if I get the answers right? I sure could use a new box of colors. My green broke to pieces, and my black's all used up."

"Yes," said Sarah, "I'll give Gussie the money, and she can buy you some new colors."

"How many questions do I have to answer?" the child demanded.

"Just a few," said Sarah. "Now Mary, I don't want to upset you, but I want to know what your Aunt Dot was wearing when you had that accident on the way to Montgomery."

"Wearing a dress. Mama always said Aunt Dot's hips was too big to wear pants decent."

"No," said Sarah, "did she have on a necklace, that's what I want to know."

Mary shrugged.

"You don't remember?"

Mary shook her head. "Do I still get the colors?"

Sarah nodded. "You don't have a necklace, do you Mary, that's a gold chain with a thing on the end of it that's round and black and gold?"

Again Mary shook her head. The child shrugged dramatically, and looked very sad indeed, afraid that she would not get the crayons, being unable to answer Sarah's questions satisfactorily.

But Gussie spoke then. "That's Miz Thelma's necklace you talking about."

Sarah looked up in surprise.

"I found that thing right under the bed on Saturday morning, when I was cleaning up. I didn't never see it before. You know where it come from?"

Sarah did not reply to that question, but only asked, "You haven't seen it since then, have you?"

Gussie shook her head.

Sarah then told a little lie. "That thing belonged to my husband's mama, and she had lent it to Thelma. So if you do come across it, you be sure and call me, will you, Gussie? It's real important, you understand me?"

Gussie nodded, and after leaving a dollar with which Gussie was to buy Mary's box of crayons, Sarah left the Shirley house.

Becca quizzed Sarah immediately on what she had found out. "So," said Becca, at the end of Sarah's relation, "it's not there. It got broken off or something when Dorothy got run down in the road. Or it's still on her, and is gone get buried with her." She was trying to reassure Sarah.

But Sarah was not so easily consoled. "All we know is that little Mary doesn't have it, and that's something, I suppose."

"Why do you look so unhappy, then?" said Becca.

"Because," said Sarah, "of what Gussie said. She said that she found the amulet under Thelma Shirley's bed when she was *cleaning up . . .*" Sarah and Becca both shuddered at the thought of the two corpses and the great pools of blood. "That means that Thelma Shirley had it in the house. And that means I was right. Larry Coppage didn't give it to Dorothy Sims direct. He gave it to Thelma and then Thelma killed her husband and died herself. Then Dorothy Sims found it, put it on—we saw her with it on—and then went and killed her husband and got killed herself."

Becca whistled.

"You know what that means?" asked Sarah.

"What does it mean?" demanded Becca. "I think I know what it means," she added sourly.

"It means," said Sarah, "that we know of three people

who got hold of that amulet, they're all three of 'em dead, and their families with 'em. 'Cept for little Mary Shirley, and who knows what's gone come of her now?"

"That's the worst luck I ever heard of," Becca judged.

"That's worse than bad luck," said Sarah. "Bad luck is just sort of coincidence. I don't think that this was coincidence. I really do think that amulet's got something to do with it."

"That's crazy, Sarah, and you know it! What could it have to do with it, except being bad luck and all?"

"I don't know, but I do know I got to find it and get rid of it before anybody else gets hold of it. I mean, what if somebody else was to die? How would you feel, knowing what I just told you, knowing that we didn't do everything in our power to get hold of it and get rid of it?"

"I just cain't believe it . . ." Becca maintained. "It's too crazy." Then she thought for a moment. "But if there was something wrong with that necklace, I mean something *really* wrong with it, then that means that Jo Howell probably gave it to Larry Coppage on purpose, knowing what it would do. That's what it means, don't it?"

Sarah didn't answer.

"That means that Jo Howell is responsible for all them people dying, don't it?"

Again Sarah said nothing. This was the part of it that she disliked thinking about most of all.

"I believe *that!*" cried Becca. "I wouldn't put it past her. She found out where to get them things and she was the first in line for it. She probably ordered two of 'em! That woman peeves me, that woman hasn't done nothing but peeve me since the day I laid eyes on her broad behind! I wouldn't be surprised if she set out to get back at Larry Coppage for not giving Dean a job. You said she was mad at him for it."

Sarah nodded.

"She tried to get back at him with a *amulet*."

Becca paused, breathing heavily, and looked at her friend. They had just pulled into the driveway, and Becca turned off the ignition. "Isn't that what you think, Sarah? Isn't it?"

"I don't know, Becca, I don't know what to think. I didn't want to think about that. I'd hate to think that Jo

Howell was capable of such a thing. Just right now I'm pretending that she didn't know anything about it, about what it would do, and it was all just a accident."

"Jo Howell don't have accidents. She's mean on purpose, she's mean 'cause she wants to be mean, and no other reason in the world. She wasn't born that way, I bet. She practiced. Went out in the field by herself for just hours on end when she was a little girl, practicing being mean. She wanted Larry Coppage burnt up to a crisp. She didn't like Rachel neither, and she threw in them five kids for good measure. You know she did, Sarah!"

"No!" cried Sarah, "I don't know it! She couldn't want to kill all these people! There's eleven of 'em, Becca, eleven people dead in Pine Cone. And you think I could go back in that house right now if I thought it was Jo Howell that did it? I cain't think things like that!"

Sarah jumped out of the car, and ran toward her back door.

Becca leaned out of the passenger window, and exclaimed softly, "It's crazy, Sarah, just too crazy, and I don't believe a word of it. Not any of it . . ."

Chapter 38

᭗᭗᭗᭗᭗᭗᭗᭗᭗᭗᭗᭗᭗᭗᭗᭗᭗᭗᭗᭗᭗᭗᭗᭗᭗᭗᭗᭗᭗᭗᭗᭗

Later that night, after Sara Howell had washed up the supper dishes and turned off the lights in the kitchen, she peered through the door into the living room. The only light there was from the television set, and it flickered ghastly illumination on the bandages around her husband's neck and head. Dean lay on the couch with his head thrown back, sinking down between the tattered sofa arm and the tattered cushion, his feet lying heavily in his mother's lap. Jo Howell, who sat at the other end of the couch, was slowly massaging her son's ankles.

Sarah had refrained from mentioning to her mother-in-law her visit with Mary Shirley and Gussie. She was not yet sure that it was best to let Jo know what she was up to. Jo Howell was a secretive woman and Sarah felt that until she got some straight answers about the amulet, it was probably best to say as little as possible about her own suspicions. It would not do to put Jo Howell on her guard.

Sarah sat in a chair apart from her husband and Jo and tried to interest herself in the television program, but could not for thinking of the amulet. She cast sideways glances at her mother-in-law and began to think she had gone absolutely insane to imagine that such a great fat woman, who wouldn't move out of her chair if the vice-president of the United States were choking on a fishbone

at the other end of the room, would be able to engineer
the horror that Sarah was tempted to credit her with.
She was fat and she was mean and it was very unpleasant
to spend an evening with her, but was she any more than
that, an obese country woman who hadn't taken to farming, who hadn't taken to marriage, who had never even
really taken to mothering until her son came home from
the army a scarred vegetable?

"What you staring at?" Jo demanded, at the onset of a
long commercial break.

"Nothing," replied Sarah quickly. She was used to Jo's
quick interrogatories and was rarely caught up by them
anymore. "I was just looking at Dean, trying to see if he
was reacting to anything, trying to see if he had improved,
or anything."

"Oh, yeah," said Jo. "I think he's a lot better today.
A lot better."

"How can you tell?" said Sarah.

"You can tell, that's all. He's taking more interest in
things, you know what I mean?"

"No," said Sarah, "I don't know what you mean at
all."

"Well," said Jo, "I mean that like this afternoon, I
was telling him everything about the Simses getting killed
up on Burnt Corn Creek. You know, I used to live up
that way. I know right where that car went in the creek.
I used to have to go pick blackberries near there every
summer. I hate picking blackberries. Cut your fingers to
pieces on them thorns."

"It was real bad, what happened up there. I don't
know why she did it," said Sarah, but there was an edge
in her voice.

"Well, she was a mean woman, and that's about all
there was to it. I used to live up that way, and that's
where Dean's great-aunt got drowned, right down near
there."

"How do you know that's where it happened?" asked
Sarah.

"That's the only bridge on Burnt Corn up that way.
Can't be nowhere else. Real pretty spot, too. I was the
one that found the body. There wasn't much traffic on that
road, way back then. People didn't go to Montgomery

like they do today, they didn't just pick up and go off to buy a quart of milk in Montgomery like they do now. So I found Dean's great-aunt down there in Burnt Corn Creek, right in the same place where Dorothy Sims beat her husband over the head with a pine branch, and I had to drag the body out. You know, Sarah, how hard it is for a girl—and I wasn't much more than fifteen then—how hard it is to drag somebody out of a creek when they got their lungs full of water? But there wasn't nobody else to do it and if I hadn't done it right then and there, then she would've been washed down to the Gulf, and there wouldn't have been nothing left to stick in the grave. And you know what?" Jo smiled maliciously.

"What?" said Sarah.

"I bet it was harder to pull ol' Malcolm Sims out than it was for me to drag Dean's great-aunt out of that water. Ol' Malcolm Sims was a big man. And Dean's great-aunt was a little bitty thing."

Sarah didn't reply to this observation. Jo didn't often talk at such length, and almost never spoke of her past, so Sarah was inclined to let her go on without interruption in the hope that she would give something away. But though Jo seemed to speak with narrative abandon, there was very little that Sarah could deduce from what was said.

Jo cackled then, "They ought to put up a sign down by that bridge, telling people how dangerous it is, that people get drowned and beat over the head there, and that they ought to watch out. Somebody ought to put three little white crosses by the side of the road, just 'fore you come to the bridge, to tell about the three people that died right there. Dorothy Sims and Malcolm Sims and Dean's great-aunt."

"What was her name?" asked Sarah.

"Bama," said Jo. "Her name was Bama. That was short for Alabama. She was named after the state."

"That's real peculiar," said Sarah. "I thought Alabama was a man's name."

"It is," said Jo argumentatively, "but her name was Alabama, and she got herself drowned in Burnt Corn Creek, and I found her 'fore she had time to get washed away. Don't nobody know why she was down there. Didn't like her much, but she taught me a lot of things."

"What sort of things?" questioned Sarah.

"Shhhhh!" cried Jo, "the show's back on now, and Dean don't want to miss a word of it."

Sarah sighed heavily. She had the distinct feeling that Jo was toying with her, that the old woman knew that Sarah was trying to find something out. Jo was deliberately feeding her information that sounded good but was actually worthless. Sarah knew that it would do no good to talk to Jo longer that evening so she rose, saying, "I'm going to speak to Becca for a few minutes." Jo replied nothing at all, but only motioned for Sarah to move out of her line of vision.

Sarah let the kitchen door swing noiselessly shut behind her and then stepped quietly out the back door, into the moonlit yard. She knocked on Becca's back door and Margaret appeared presently, cradling and stroking a small white cat in her arms.

"Mama's just about to put her hair up. Come on in, Sarah," said the young girl.

"No," said Sarah, "ask you mother if she won't bring her pins out here, and sit with me a while in the back-yard."

Margaret nodded and disappeaed into the house. In a few moments, Becca Blair appeared with a scarf around her wet hair and a small tin box filled with bobby pins.

"Ohhhh," she cried, "what a good idea you got, Sarah! Let's go right out in that yard and you talk to me while I put up my hair by the light of the moon. I got a little mirror with a hook that goes right on my neck and I can see everything I'm doing. I just love to do these little things outside. You just got to promise me one thing, and that's that you won't mention word one about that *thing*, that necklace. 'Cause you got me upset this afternoon and I don't want to hear a word about it, you hear me?"

Sarah nodded, and smiled. "No, I promise, I won't say a word."

And so the two women settled themselves into the iron chairs in Becca's backyard. Sarah arranged hers so that she could watch her own back door and see if the light went on in her kitchen, sign that Jo was looking for her.

Becca set the mirror around her neck and the box of bobby pins in her lap.

"You gone have to talk to me, Sarah," she said, laughing, " 'cause you know I can't put my hair up 'less I got half a dozen of these things in my mouth! You know how it is, just a habit that don't make no sense . . ."

The moon was bright, and the shrubbery in the yard so thick that it blocked from view the harsh mercury lamps and the sharp illumination from kitchen and living room windows throughout the neighborhood. A cat in heat screamed in the next block and frogs in a drainage ditch croaked loudly from a nearer distance.

"I don't know, Becca," Sarah began sadly, "I don't know what to do about—"

" 'Bout what, Sarah?" said Becca peremptorily, and stuck four pins in her mouth. She widened her eyes, to show that she would not be able to speak again for some minutes to come.

"To do—don't know what to do in general. Dean's coming home has upset me, coming home like he did. There's this *thing* in there on the couch that I'm supposed to take care of, but it don't seem like it's Dean inside there. I think of Dean, and it's not that thing in there on the couch that I'm thinking of. You know what I mean?"

Becca nodded her head somberly, her fingers still twirling spirals in her wet hair.

"I don't know why I'm here. Jo and Dean, they belong together, they seem to get along together. But Dean, he don't move, he don't say a word, if the spoon didn't come out clean, I wouldn't even know he was alive inside there. And I'm his wife, Becca! They get along fine, and they need me to clean up after 'em, and that's all. Am I supposed to spend the rest of my life doing that? Going to the plant every day, sitting at the 'ssembly line, getting a little money and a lot of hemorrhoids? And then coming home in the afternoon to cook supper and clean the house and run errands for 'em? Spending all the money I get on prescription drugs?"

Becca whistled sympathetically through the bobby pins in her mouth.

"I'm stuck in this, and I don't like it a bit. I'm stuck in it, and I don't know what to do to get out of it. It don't seem like there's anything that I can do to get out of it. I don't know where to start. There's not *time* to start. There's not time to do anything but the things I do do, go to work, clean house, cook, go to the drugstore for Dean's medicine. You know, I tell myself things will be better when Dean gets better, when he gets out of the bandages, when he can get a job or disability insurance or something. But I feel it in my heart that he's not never going to get any better, that he's gone spend the rest of his life wrapped up in white, lying in the hammock, lying in bed, lying on the sofa, and doing nothing but listening to Jo Howell talk to him."

Sarah paused a moment, and then concluded, softly, with despair, "Becca, I tell you something else. I don't like this, I don't like this a bit in the world."

Chapter 39

JACK and Merle Weaver had been considerably upset by the accident that occurred on the Montgomery road, and slept restlessly that Sunday night, both dreaming of the woman that they had knocked into the bridge piling, dreaming of the face of the man caught in the roots of the cypress. Over and again in their sleep they heard the frightened cries of the small child in the half-submerged car, screaming out for fear of the snakes.

On Monday the couple drove back into Pine Cone and gave their deposition to the sheriff and his deputy. Again, they were assured that they would not be held culpable for the accident. Though technically Jack Weaver could be charged with manslaughter, the accident was clearly not his fault, and certainly any guilt on his part was more than balanced by the crime that was committed by his unintentioned victim. No jury in the Wiregrass region of Alabama would convict him and therefore, in the sheriff's practical eyes, there was no point in bringing the incident to trial.

The Weavers then visited the Baptist preacher in town, having heard that the couple were of that denomination; and again they were assured of their moral innocence in the matter; and that the only real problem was what was to become of the little girl, who now was wholly alone in the world. The Weavers shook their heads, and drove away. Late in the afternoon, they purchased a dozen bags of feed grain from the Farmers' Exchange in Pine Cone, with the vague idea that by doing business in the town where the people had been driving from, they would be making some sort of reparation, even if it was only after the most indirect and purely financial fashion.

Monday night as well proved sleepless for the unfortunate couple, and they rose, as usual, at dawn, however ill-prepared for a thoroughgoing day of strenuous farm activity.

Directly after Merle Weaver had prepared breakfast for her husband and herself, she sat down at the table across from him, with a cup of coffee held just below her lips, and said: "You know Jack, I thought all night long."

"About that woman," said her husband.

Merle nodded. "But about the little girl too. It's our fault really that she's alone in the world, that poor little girl, with nobody left—all of 'em dead that would have taken care of her, and it's our fault. It was a accident, but it's our fault."

"My fault," said Jack. "I ran the woman down."

"Not your fault," said Merle. "*Our* fault. Though I don't know if it would have done any good *not* to run the woman down, 'cause she would have been sent up the river anyway, for murdering her husband, and it's probably just as well then that the little girl didn't have to testify in the trial. They say testifying in trials is real hard on little girls."

Jack nodded. His wife had put a better light on it than any that he had been able to strike, but he still judged against himself. "I still wish I hadn't done it though."

Merle nodded. "I wish we hadn't either. And that's what I was thinking about. I was thinking that maybe we ought to see what we can do about the little girl. I mean we don't have any money to give her, and for all we know, there may be insurance, but I wouldn't count on it, but I was thinking that maybe we could bring her out here to live."

"You mean live with us?" said Jack.

Merle nodded. "We could adopt her or something."

"Would they let us do it? I mean, we run down her only surviving relative in the middle of the road, and are they gone let us adopt the little girl then?"

"She was a sweet little girl."

"Oh, she sure was," agreed Jack. "I'd sure like to do something for her, like you said. Maybe we *could* adopt her. I mean, it's all right with me if we do. I'd like to have a little girl, and seeing she needs somebody real desperate to take care of her, it might as well be us."

Merle nodded.

"If they let us," said Jack, "and if she wants to. She may not want to live out on a farm, but you're right, and I think we ought to offer, because I think it's the least we can do, offer to adopt her."

"You think she'd keep her own last name?" asked Merle, and so the conversation continued throughout breakfast, and both Jack and Merle were immeasurably heartened by the exchange. They were perfectly serious about this project, and had every intention of offering a permanent home to little Mary Shirley. They had a fair idea of the trouble involved in raising a child—and the expense—but what did that matter, when the child was in need, and they were to some extent responsible for her predicament?

"I feel so foolish," said Merle, "I don't know why we didn't think of this before."

Jack nodded. "People in Pine Cone must think you and I are the meanest people in the world, abandoning that little girl the way we did."

Jack and Merle Weaver walked out through a long path of dewy red clover—glaring, brilliant red in the early morning light—to their barn. Here it was necessary to unload the bags of grain that they had purchased in Pine Cone the day before, from off the back of the truck. The single farmhand that they employed, who normally would have assisted Jack in this work, was off on the far side of the property, mending a section of broken fence.

Working together, Jack and Merle pulled the bags off the back of the truck and together carried them into the barn, where they stacked them near the rear door. After their third trip, on their way back to the truck, Merle's eyes caught the glimmer of metal in the sand near one of the rear tires of the truck. She stooped and picked up a necklace, of simple, forthright design. She had never seen it before. She shook the sand off it, and held it close to her eyes.

"What you got, Merle?" said her husband.

She handed him the piece of jewelry.

"This yours?" he asked.

"No," said Merle, "don't know where it come from, Jack."

"Where'd it come from though?" Jack asked.

"Right there in the dirt," said Merle. "You saw me pick it up, right then, didn't you?"

Jack shook his head. "It didn't drop out of your pocket?" he asked.

"What'd I be doing with something like this? You know I don't have nothing like this."

"Maybe it fell off the truck," said Merle's husband. "Maybe that woman we ran down in the road was wearing it yesterday, and it came off her neck getting jostled around in the back when we was on the way back to Pine Cone."

"Maybe," said Merle, "maybe you're right."

There was a pause. Jack handed the amulet back to his wife. "You think it's worth anything?" he asked.

"I can't tell," his wife replied.

"Is it gold, you think?" he asked.

"Gold's gold, not black," Merle pointed out.

Jack stepped forward and pointed to the gold band in between the wider bands of jet. "There's gold right round in there, between the black part. Maybe it's all gold, and just part of it's painted black . . ."

"Maybe you're right, Jack."

"Maybe it's worth money."

"If it's gold, then it's bound to be worth something," said Merle.

Jack looked cannily at his wife. "Hold it up to your wedding ring, and compare 'em," he said. This seemed a brilliant idea to him, a way to ascertain whether the necklace was really of gold or not.

Merle held up the amulet next to her wedding band, and examined them both in the light of the sun.

"Can't tell, still can't tell," she judged, after a moment.

This was a thing not in their experience, the finding of an object that might be valuable, and something that very certainly did not belong to them. In any of its multitudinous forms, luck had rarely made an appearance on the Weaver farmstead.

"What you think we ought to do about it?" asked Jack quietly.

"You think we ought to tell the sheriff?" his wife replied.

"Can't keep it, not ours," Jack stated, simply.

Merle shook her head. "We ought to take it into Pine Cone, when we go over and see about that little girl." Her husband nodded. "You think they'll think we took it?" The idea occurred to Merle suddenly, and just thinking that she might be considered a thief appalled and frightened her.

"Nobody's asked us where it was, or if we had seen it."

"Maybe they don't know about it. Maybe they don't know it's missing yet. Maybe we ought to take it in right now." Merle was upset to hold on to something that so definitely belonged to someone else.

"We'll go in this afternoon. That'll be soon enough," said Jack. He knew that his wife was nervous, and so tried to console her. "We're not sure now, Merle, that the thing did belong to the woman that was killed on the bridge, and it might just not have, for all we know. But we'll take it into the sheriff and leave it with him, and if somebody's missing the thing, then he'll step forward and claim it. And we'll go back by the Baptist preacher's, and see about that little girl. That poor little girl!"

Merle stared a few moments at the amulet in her hand, absently feeling for the catch, wondering whether she ought not to put it around her neck. It was a heavy piece, and would feel good. She had had a heavy necklace once, when she was a little girl, but not since then.

But she shuddered; there was something about this necklace that she didn't like at all. Besides, it didn't belong to her. She glanced at her husband, stiffened her shoulders, and dropped the amulet into the waist pocket of her dress.

Chapter 40

∞∞∞∞∞∞∞∞∞∞∞∞∞∞∞∞∞∞∞∞∞∞∞∞∞∞∞∞∞∞∞∞∞∞∞∞∞

MERLE Weaver smiled to herself as she began work that morning, exulting that she had discovered a way to expiate her and Jack's guilt over running down that poor woman, at the same time that she provided herself with a permanent cure against loneliness. That little girl—they couldn't even remember her name, they had been so upset at the time—would come out to live with them, and they would raise her as if she were their own child. They had had a boy themselves, about ten years back, but he had died in a rainstorm on the last day of August, hit in the head with a bolt of lightning when he was dragging in a croker sack of pecans out of the downpour. That little girl had grown up in town all her life, Merle thought, but she didn't have anybody else, the sheriff said, and probably she would be wanting to stay in Pine Cone, with all her friends at school. Where did they send children who didn't have anyplace to go? Merle supposed there were orphanages, but she didn't know where any were located, and she couldn't imagine that it could be a very happy existence there, with no one to love you especially. She had high hopes that the little girl would come to live with them, and Merle even decided that the little girl could keep her own name if she wanted to, whatever that name might happen to be.

"Oh," said Merle to Jack, when the last of the sacks had been transferred from the back of the truck, "I'm just looking forward so much to having that child out here with us."

"Well," cautioned Jack, "we haven't got her yet, and we may not get her, you know. I don't know much about how these things work."

"But she don't have nowhere else to go. Used to be, somebody's mama and daddy died, somebody in the church would take 'em on, but I don't think that happens much anymore. They say there's not enough money, and the other children don't take to it or something."

"Well, Merle, if she wants to come, and they'll let us take her, then she'll be here. And there's nothing more to be said about it till we get into town. I don't want you thinking about it, 'cause what if we don't get her? Then you'll be disappointed, and I don't want that. I don't want to see you unhappy . . ."

Merle nodded, and went to feed the pigs. She resolved to say nothing else, but the excitement would not go away. Merle stepped merrily up onto the lowest rail of the fences that encircled the pigpen, located next to a blank wall of the barn. She leaned forward against the upper rails to maintain her balance while she tossed ears of corn, from the crib by her side, into the pen. She delighted in hearing her sows and hogs squealing, and loved to watch them plow through the earth and mud after their morning's food. Merle was sorry that this chore came so early in the morning, because it was her favorite task of the day. She knew every pig from every other, and to most of them she had given names; she had come to know them for intelligent, if not affectionate, creatures. And, it happened, they were the only thing on the farm that produced profit year after year after year.

Two ears of corn slipped over the edge of the crib, and fell just inside the pen. One of the larger sows rushed over to get at them, and in so doing, brushed against Merle's foot. She stumbled on the rail, and barely managed not to fall; but in the process, the amulet slipped out of her pocket and disappeared into the mud on the inside of the pen. Merle was very annoyed by her own clumsiness, and set her lips in malediction against herself.

She turned to see where her husband was. In a moment

he emerged from the barn, scratching his head, and approached her.

"I've done gone and dropped it in the pen, Jack."

"What'd you drop? That thing we found?"

Merle nodded. "Dropped right out of my pocket, I don't know how."

"Where'd it go?" Jack moved over to the fence, and stared over into the mud. The animals were still squealing in pursuit of their breakfast.

Merle pointed directly downward over the rail. "Right down there," she said. "It was right there, Jack. Because when I knew it had fallen I looked over and saw it sliding under the mud, and then Louise must have stepped on it, because I can't see it no more." Louise was the great sow that had knocked against Merle's foot.

"You want me to go after it?" said Jack, and without waiting for a reply, he began to scale the fence. "You show me where it went, and I'll find it."

But his wife held him back, grabbing the straps of his overalls. "No," she said, "it was my fault, so I'll look for it. Got to do what's right."

"You gone ruin that dress," her husband said, with kind concern, "and I really don't mind doing it."

"It's my fault," his wife repeated. "If I hadn't found the thing, we wouldn't be having this trouble now. Now you just stand here and help me down over into the pen."

Merle climbed over the fence, and her husband held her hand so that she would not fall headlong into the mud. The wet earth was ankle deep, and Merle bent over gingerly, toeing the mud with her shoe trying to locate the amulet. All the while, she and Jack talked reassuringly to the pigs, who were a little alarmed to find a human in their pen. But Merle was unsuccessful, and could not turn up the amulet.

"Fell right here," she murmured again, with annoyance. "Jack, you go get me a broom or something, something with a long handle, maybe that'll help."

Jack stepped down backward off the rail and went into the barn. There he looked around a bit, but saw nothing that would be of use. The broom that usually stood on the inside of the front door was missing. He thought a moment, and then went through the barn and out to the truck. From the back he pulled a pitchfork, and then plunged it idly into the ground, thinking that this, with its long prongs, would be just right for retrieving a necklace out of the mud of a pigsty.

Jack Weaver had started back toward the barn, when he heard a terrified scream from the direction of the pig-pen. The voice was so strained, so filled with horror that he could not even recognize it as his wife's, though he knew it must be hers. A tall picket fence separated him from the pen, and he was forced to run back through the barn again. He stumbled in the relative darkness of the structure, tripping on a length of hose, and fell against the packed-earth floor. He picked himself quickly up, and ran, leaving the pitchfork behind. The scream had not been repeated, and he called out his wife's name. "Merle! Merle! Merle!"

As soon as Jack had disappeared into the barn after something to help her locate the amulet, the sow Louise had knocked against Merle, and the farm woman tumbled into the mud. She fell forward and sprawled helpless there a moment, upset by the combined misfortune. Her feet slid in the mud, and it was difficult, in her distress of mind, to raise herself out of the mire. She had made a half turn on her hands and knees, intending to take hold of the rails and lift herself out by that expedient; she had even reached out to grasp one, when suddenly Louise scurried forward, right up to Merle, and bared her teeth menacingly in Merle's face.

Merle was alarmed. She had never seen her own pigs attack before, though she had heard stories, and she wanted to know no more about it then she did. She sup-posed she had fallen onto one of Louise's piglets, or that Louise was just angry at the intrusion, but in any case, Merle made a great effort to scramble away. Other pigs gathered round her, curiously, and began to nudge her. Louise advanced slowly on the crawling woman. Merle backed away from Louise, looking like a crab in a flow-ered dress, until she came up against another great hog, the largest in the pen, who impeded her path. The bristles in its coat scratched the flesh from her arms. It was at this point that Merle screamed in terror.

Merle tried to raise herself against the back of this

great animal, but she kept slipping in the mud. All the pigs in the pen began to scream together, and the sound made Merle very, very cold. "Jack! Jack! You come here!" she cried, wanting to shout, but her voice was only a whisper.

Merle was opening her mouth, prepared to scream again, scream in terror, when Louise suddenly lunged forward, and in one swift motion tore out the poor woman's throat.

Jack emerged from the barn only in time to see his wife's body falling back, stiffened with horror, into the mud.

"Merle! Merle!" he screamed and ran back through the barn, and out to the truck. He pulled open the cab door, and took down the rifle that was set on a rack in the back window. He scrambled for shells in the glove compartment, and then loaded the piece as he ran back through the barn.

When he had reached the pen again, he was weeping, moaning his wife's name. He shuddered to see her body again, floating on top of the mud, with a number of piglets burrowing in the earth at her side, as if she were a nursing sow, and all squealing that they could find no teats to suck.

Louise had blood all around her snout, and was tearing viciously at Merle Weaver's feet. It was a horrible, vindictive action that was wholly out of keeping with what Jack Weaver—if he had had the presence of mind to think about such things—knew about the habits of pigs, and especially of Louise, who had been something of a pet to his dead wife. Jack Weaver stared at the bloody tendons of his wife's foot as it was scraped between Louise's jaws. The sow began to drag the resisting corpse through the mud.

Jack took aim and shot the sow through the spine; the animal collapsed suddenly. Wailing piteously, Jack Weaver climbed into the corncrib, and began to hurl ears of corn at all the pigs, hitting them as hard as he could with the cobs. The pigs squealed, and ran about, and trampled the body of the dead woman beneath their hooves.

Chapter 41

❦❦❦❦❦❦❦❦❦❦❦❦❦❦❦❦❦❦❦❦❦❦❦❦❦❦❦❦❦❦

WHEN the house was quiet and dark, and Sarah Howell lay turning, sleeplessly, on the couch in the living room, she thought about Jo and Dean and the amulet. She would contrive all manner of stories that explained where Jo had got hold of such a thing, would think of ways in which it would cause somebody to die, would imagine herself snatching it out of someone's grasp to grind it beneath the heel of her shoe. In those long, hot minutes Jo and Dean became powerfully evil in her imagination, and in the blackness she could not tell when her directed thoughts left off and when her nightmares began.

In the morning, when she first awoke, things seemed better. There was light in the room, for when she went to bed, Sarah pulled the drapes and opened the windows for air. She dismissed all her thoughts about the amulet, about murder and revenge and intended evil, as she would disregard any discomforting dream. For a while she would be overcome with pity for Dean, lying in the next room, in exactly the position in which she had last viewed him six hours before. Jo woke, and from her bed began telling Sarah to do this and bring her that for the woman was simply lazy and cantakerous, and Sarah was relieved to imagine that she was no more than that. And the amulet was a hunk of cheap jewelry brought to the house through the mail, from Sears or Montgomery

Ward. And Dorothy Sims had had one just like the one that got burned up in the Coppage house.

Sarah rose at five-thirty and left for work at a quarter of eight and in that two hours, she got enough of her husband and her mother-in-law to last the whole day. She had to prepare breakfast for them, after she had attended to Dean's sanitary needs in the bedroom—or what was worse—had to clean up after him. Some days Sarah put a load of laundry in the washing machine first thing, so that she could hang it out before she went off to the plant, and on other days Jo liked to see her take a broom and dustcloth to the rooms, "just so she could earn her keep."

And invariably, just before Sarah was about to go out the door, with Becca honking the horn in the driveway, Jo would think of one more thing that absolutely had to be accomplished before Sarah went off. This was usually to move Dean somewhere else; to guide him to the sofa, help him struggle into the backyard, to set him down on the living room floor in front of the television set that he could not see. Dean's legs shuffled along—almost comically—and Sarah wondered that if he could do this much, if he actually remembered how to walk, even in this limited, depressing fashion, why could he not respond to anything else? Why did he never move again once he had been put into his bed? Why didn't he even try to talk; why wouldn't he chew his food?

It was horrible for Dean; Sarah knew that. If he could think at all, then he must be thinking about nothing but the difference between what he had been and what he was now. But there was such great disparity between what the doctors said his progress should be and what she had to put up with every day; even such disparity between his complete motionlessness and insensitivity for just hours on end, and this staggering gait which got him from the bed to wherever his mother wanted him—that Sarah occasionally entertained the thought that Dean was deceiving her, that he was better than he let on, that he was only pretending that he had no speech, no mind, no control over his limbs and digestive tract. But these thoughts only came to her late at night, when she did not have before her the utterly debilitating spectacle of the man himself, head and neck swathed in reeking bandages. That sight demanded that she do for him what was asked of her by Jo, by the doctors, by her own conscience.

Every morning Sarah would leave the house distrustful of Jo and Dean. One day after another, she would find an excuse to run back inside, in hope and dread that she would catch Dean and Jo in some unexpected commerce. But no matter how quitely Sarah would reenter whatever room she had left them in—and sometimes she simply stood outside the closed doorway and listened intently—there was no sound, and Dean was in the same position, atom for atom, in which Sarah had left him.

Jo always laughed at Sarah for these contrived entrances, as if she knew what was behind them, as if she were gloating: Dean and I'll never be caught at it, never be caught!

These little traps, that invariably failed and that Sarah still couldn't refrain from executing each morning, left her unhappy and frustrated. If she could only see some little change in Dean, something that indicated that he wasn't as bad off as he seemed, she wouldn't even mind that he was trying to trick her.

The drive away from the house was welcome, even though it meant that there were eight long hours ahead of her at the assembly line. Sarah smiled and joked with Becca, and did not speak at all of her husband and mother-in-law except to reply with a brief "all right" to Becca's unvarying interrogatory: "How you this morning? How's Dean and his mama?"

Becca Blair and Sarah Howell arrived at work just a few minutes earlier than usual. The two friends arranged themselves leisurely in their little cubicles, procured cups of coffee, and then talked idly to one another over their partition, nodding greetings to the other women who passed by them every minute or so. The belt was still, and the Pine Cone rifles lay in every stage of assembly, like a textbook diagram of the fashion in which such a piece of goods is constructed.

"You know," said Becca, "I think that this is the sweetest five minutes of the day."

Sarah nodded her agreement to this proposition.

"But then it goes on until five," sighed Becca.

"We get dinnertime," said Sarah.

"Dinnertime's not hardly enough time to get home and back though," said Becca. "You practically got to stay around here." Becca paused in these reflections on the workday, and said suddenly, as if she had just remembered something. "You know the Weavers, Sarah?"

Sarah shook her head.

"You know who I mean though," said Becca. "They was the ones that run down that woman in the highway, and then brung poor little Mary Shirley back into town. Two corpses in the back of the truck, and a orphan in the front. And driving that way at night! Can't be no fun driving corpses around the back roads at night! But that was the Weavers—so you *do* know who I mean . . ."

Sarah was suddenly very interested in Becca's story. "What about them?" she demanded. "They aren't dead, are they?"

"*She* is," replied Becca, wonderingly. "How'd you know, Sarah?"

Sarah did not reply; she avoided Becca's glance. Her lips were set in anger and alarm, and involuntarily she thought of Jo and Dean, as she had left them at the house that morning: Jo spread across one of the living room chairs watching the *Today Show,* and describing to Dean what everyone was wearing, and her husband lying on a quilt spread lengthwise on the floor at the foot of the couch. He looked like a mummy that had been tipped out of its sarcophagus onto the floor of the tomb.

But much worse than this involuntary vision, which she had hoped to avoid through the course of the day, was the knowledge that her nightmares had not gone away with the morning light. Becca had very often told her never to tell a dream before breakfast, because it was sure to come true; Sarah always took that precaution, just to be on the safe side, but it hadn't done her a bit of good.

"How'd she die?" asked Sarah after a moment.

With a little hesitance, Becca said, "Rooted to death by her own pigs." Sarah grimaced; that was worse than she could have guessed. Becca continued, "While her husband was *watching,* and they say he's just not the same. She fell in the trough, and they just tore her throat out, right by the roots!" Sarah's glance still wandered over the large room, focusing idly on this woman and that, but her mind raced. Becca waited for her friend to say something, but when she did not, Becca went on. "Terrible way to go, and I bet you wouldn't be the same now, if you had seen it, like Jack Weaver did."

"Becca?" said Sarah.

"What?" Becca still wanted to know how her friend had found out that Merle Weaver was dead.

"Becca," said Sarah cautiously, "what you think's causing all these people dying?"

"What do you mean?" Becca asked.

A whistle sounded, and the two women broke off their conversation; in a moment, they knew, it would be impossible to continue it.

"Get ready, Sarah," said Becca, "here we go."

Sarah was thinking hard. "Becca," she said, "did you know these people with the pigs?"

"Daddy knew 'em," replied Becca.

"Let's you and me go out there," said Sarah.

Becca was surprised. "What for?" she asked.

"I want to see the place," said Sarah softly. The assembly line began to vibrate, and Sarah picked up her screwdriver. Becca stared a moment longer at her friend, over the partition. She started to say something else, but the noise of the machinery grinding up to begin the day covered her speech and her thoughts on the subject.

Chapter 42

▬▬▬▬▬▬▬▬▬▬▬▬▬▬▬▬▬▬▬▬▬▬▬▬▬

At five o'clock, when they left the factory building and got into the purple Pontiac, Sarah again asked Becca Blair to drive her out to the Weaver farm.

"You crazy," said Becca shortly. "You crazy to want to go out to that place."

"Maybe," said Sarah, quietly. "But will you take me out there?"

"No," said Becca adamantly. "I'm not gone do it. I know what you're thinking about, and I think it's crazy for you to think that way, and I'm not gone be no part of it."

"Well," said Sarah seriously, "would you let Margaret take me out there?"

"I wouldn't let Margaret have this car to do a damn-fool thing like that for you, Sarah Howell!" But Becca wasn't refusing her friend so much as pleading with her to give up these nonsensical ideas. Becca was a superstitious woman, but the things that Sarah was hinting at were ideas too unpleasant and too dangerous to entertain.

"Well, that means I got to get on the phone and see if I can find somebody who *will* take me out there."

"Why you want to go?" Becca demanded.

Sarah replied slowly and quietly, "Because when she died, that poor Weaver woman must have been wearing the amulet. Somehow she got hold of it from Dorothy

Sims when they ran her down in the road. Now this poor woman's dead, and she died horrible, and I intend on getting the thing back. I intend on getting rid of it."

Becca threw up her hands. "You know I'm gone take you! You know I'm gone do it for you. And you know I think you're out of your mind! You decided to go out there, and nothing's gone stop you, and I'm not gone let anybody else find out how crazy you are. You think I'd want it all over Pine Cone that my best friend was ready to be carted off to Tuscaloosa?" Becca shook her head in despair; she had given in entirely.

Sarah took Becca's hand and squeezed it; Becca pulled sharply out of the parking lot. "We going by the house first so you can tell Dean and his mama where we're going?"

Sarah shook her head. "I don't want 'em to know. We'll be back 'fore long. I don't want 'em to know where we went. I'll tell 'em something later—I don't know what."

Becca grinned, for she liked the idea of deceiving Josephine Howell. "Well," she said, much more brightly, "it's only 'cause the clover's in bloom, and that it's the prettiest road in the world this time of year, that I'm 'llowing you to drag me out to look at the place where that poor woman got her throat tore out by the roots . . ."

But Sarah was very serious, and would not allow her friend to sidestep the issue. She turned in her seat, and placed her legs beneath her. Becca kept her eyes on the road, and listened without comment, and very sadly, to all that Sarah had to say.

"Now, you listen to me, Becca. You don't think I like this, do you? You don't think I want to go out there, and throw myself on poor Mr. Weaver, who I don't know from Adam's first cousin, when his wife is dead just this morning. It's *intruding*. But honey, I thought about this all the afternoon long, all day since you told me what happened. That necklace just gets around, it gets around, and whoever gets hold of it dies. Ever'body in Pine Cone that got hold of that necklace this past week is dead. What if Mr. Weaver has it? What if he's got hold of it? Is he gone run out and kill somebody? Is he gone get killed himself? And when he's dead, who finds it, who picks it up? And they gone die too? I can't just sit back. It was Jo Howell

198

that started all this. She won't stop it, and I'll just have to. It's not my fault, but I got to do what I can."

"You really believe this, hon?" asked Becca desperately.

"No!" cried Sarah, to her friend's surprise. "I *don't* believe it! You're the one who believes in all them things, not me. I don't believe in 'em. But I know what I know. I never saw that thing till Jo Howell gave it to Larry Coppage for no good reason in the world, and I know all them Coppages burned to their frying ashes not two hours later. Gussie told me that Thelma Shirley had it, and Thelma Shirley went and stuck a ice pick in her husband's ear. And Thelma herself is dead. I saw it on Dorothy Sims, and Dorothy Sims is dead. And so's her husband. Now we hear that the woman who run her down in the highway is dead too, and what else can I believe? I don't believe it's possible for a piece of jewelry to do that, 'cause how could it? But I tell you something, if I got hold of that thing, I wouldn't think twice about smashing it with a tire iron. I wouldn't think twice. Don't you see, Becca? I don't believe it, but I just got to be sure! All I could think about today was that I was just chicken to call up Dorothy Sims after the funeral. Now she's dead, and her husband's dead, and this poor woman out in the middle of the country's got trampled to death by her own pigs!"

Sarah and Becca were silent for a few moments, while Sarah's labored breath gradually subsided.

"Lots of people dead, Sarah," said Becca cautiously.

Sarah nodded grimly.

"And you think if they get hold of that necklace, then they die, whoever gets hold of it dies?" Becca demanded.

Sarah nodded again.

Becca silently pointed out the Weaver farm, coming up on the right. They turned down a side dirt road, and headed away from the farmhouse, toward the barn. Becca pulled the car up next to a pickup truck parked in a space of packed red clay, and turned off the ignition. Then Becca placed her hand atop Sarah's on the seat, turned to her friend, and whispered huskily, "What you think it's made out of?"

Chapter 43

❦❦❦❦❦❦❦❦❦❦❦❦❦❦❦❦❦❦❦❦❦❦❦❦❦❦❦❦❦❦

THAT afternoon, there was considerable activity in that corner of the barnyard where Merle Weaver had died so wretchedly the morning before. Morris Emmons' large yellow truck was backed up to the pigpen, and a ramp let down into the mire. Two teenaged boys, one lean and pimply, the other fat and redheaded, were nervously loading all the hogs up onto the truck. Normally, these two boys would have gone right down among the animals, pushed and urged and driven them up the ramp, but to-day they coaxed and prodded with long poles from the good side of the fence. They very much feared that one of the sows would go on the rampage, and neither of the boys wanted to end up like poor Miz Weaver. The piglets rushed up onto the truck after their mothers, but the two boys reached in, scooped them up with their hands, and tossed them squealing back into the mud.

Morris Emmons ran the country store on the road be-tween the Weaver farm and Pine Cone, where the inven-tory was so varied it put the Sears catalogue to shame. A slaughterhouse was attached to the place in back and it was in his capacity as butcher that Morris Emmons had been called out to the Weaver farm. All these animals had been sold to him the afternoon before, and he had got them cheaply with the promise that he would slaugh-ter them—every one, and as soon as possible. Emmons

stood to one side, watching his two nephews at their work.
Emmons was corpulent, red-faced, and had a belly that
was large from biscuits and beer. He scratched his throat
thoughtfully.

Two recalcitrant hogs were all that remained in the pen
when Becca Blair and Sarah Howell pulled up into the
packed red dirt area in front of the Weavers' barn. The
two women got out and looked about them. Timorously
they approached Morris Emmons. Both women at first
mistook him for Jack Weaver, and they were hesitant to
approach him in his grief. Sarah was doubly nervous, for
she was not sure just what questions she ought to ask in
regard to the circumstances of Mrs. Weaver's death. She
liked being out here even less than Becca did, but it was
necessary that she find out about the amulet. It was a
mercy, she considered, that Jack Weaver himself wasn't
dead, and she hoped that he would be able to tell her if
his wife had been wearing the necklace, or if she had not.

Becca and Sarah came close to the man, who leaned
against the fence that bordered the pigpen. He regarded
the two women with a cool, disfavoring eye.

"You're not Mr. Weaver, are you?" asked Sarah. He
had not at all appeared a man prostrate with grief over
the death of his wife.

"You a friend of his?" said Emmons, paying no attention to the illogicality of the question: if Sarah were a
friend of Weaver's, then she should certainly know what
the man looked like.

"I used to know him when I was little," said Becca.

"You hear what happened?" said Morris.

The two women nodded.

"Come to pay your respects, or just curious?" he demanded.

"Both," said Sarah hesitantly.

"He's not in much mood for talking," said Emmons,
"and they's not much to see, either."

Sarah didn't know what to do then. This man, whoever he was, wasn't being of any help at all. She wondered
if she shouldn't go over to the house and try to talk to
Mr. Weaver. Perhaps she would even have to pretend
that she had known his dead wife. But it was also possible
that this man knew something that would be of use to her.

"These the animals?" Sarah asked.

Morris Emmons nodded, and broke a little grin. "Them boys is scared," he said. He pointed to the teenagers, and laughed shortly. The two boys turned and stared at their uncle with no great goodwill. They were having difficulty in coaxing the last two pigs up onto the truck.

"Scared that the pigs'll turn on 'em."

"Pigs don't usually turn, do they?" said Becca.

"Well," drawled Morris Emmons, and leaned back against the fence, "my granddaddy used to say he knew of five pigs what teamed up and used to kill Yankee salesmen and preachers when they come down the road on the way to Mobile. But other than that, I never heard of it. And truth to tell you, I don't rightly know as I would take much stock in my granddaddy. He was a liar, even after he started teaching a Sunday school class. Used to make up Bible stories hisself. So, to answer your question —no. I don't know of no other pigs what turned."

After a pause, Becca asked, "Mr. Weaver all right? You know?"

"Well," said Morris, with an unpleasant laugh, "how'd *you* feel?"

Becca's eyes widened, but she said nothing. She hoped, though, that this man wasn't any close friend of Mr. Weaver's, for it would be a chilly brand of comfort that he would administer.

With as little emphasis as she could, Sarah said, after another little pause, "D'you find anything here?"

Morris stared at Sarah incuriously. "Like what?" he said.

"Anything," she said vaguely. "Like a necklace. Miz Weaver was wearing a necklace when she was killed."

Becca made a little nervous jump. Morris Emmons saw this but lazily chose not to interpret it.

"How'd you know that?" said Morris. "You see the body?"

Sarah didn't answer.

"Come to think of it," said Emmons, "she didn't have no throat to put a necklace on, when she was pulled out of here." He waited for Sarah to explain herself. Becca stared at her friend.

"I just know that she had one on, that's all," said Sarah bravely, "and I want to know what became of it."

Emmons shrugged, accepting her flimsy explanation. "Nothing here but mud—mud mixed with a little blood. Jack Weaver said he didn't never want to ever see these animals again. I'm taking 'em off his hands. They get slaughtered tonight. Jack wanted me to come take 'em away yesterday, but I had the boys working on the carburetor yesterday, and they didn't get it fixed till this afternoon."

Sarah said to Emmons then, "My name's Sarah Howell. Dean Howell's my husband." There was no real reason for her to expect that this man had ever heard of her, or Dean.

"Heard 'bout the accident," Emmons said—for he had listened to the talk in the county. "Real shame. And a Pine Cone rifle that done it, too, wasn't it?"

Sarah nodded briefly, and said, "If you find anything you call me, you hear? I work at the plant."

"Well," said Morris Emmons, "if I find anything, Miz Howell, I reckon it'll belong to Jack Weaver, won't it?"

"No," she said, "that necklace, what I'm looking for, belongs to Dean's mama. It's hers, and I just want to know if it gets found."

It was a peculiar story, and one that didn't make a whole lot of sense to Morris Emmons. He looked the woman up and down, and still could not decide if she was telling the truth.

"Well, Miz Howell," he said at last, "if I do find something—and there ain't nothing in that pen but mud and blood—I'll give you a call."

"Thank you, Mr.—"

"Emmons. Morris Emmons."

"Mr. Emmons," said Sarah, "you be sure and call me."

He nodded, and then Sarah said, "Well I guess, Becca, you and I had best get on up to the house and talk to Mr. Weaver a minute."

"He's not there," said Emmons quickly. "He's seeing about the funeral. He went into Pine Cone this morning, but they was a shortage on coffins, and he had to drive over to Brundidge to get one. Won't do that wood no good, getting bounced around in the back of a pickup truck. Nothing worse than a funeral where the coffin got all sorts of dents in it, like it's been used before—"

"Much obliged," said Becca, cutting the man short. She and Sarah hurried back to the car, and got in. Becca quickly turned the engine over, and drove swiftly away from the Weaver barnyard.

Chapter 44

IT had taken some time for Becca and Sarah to get out to the Weaver place, the conversation with Morris Emmons was halting and slow (it is impossible to rush certain country people, especially if they tend to distrust you), and the return trip was made with the lowering sun shining bright gold and still hot against the side of Sarah's face.

"Well," said Becca, "you satisfied? That man said that there wasn't no necklace round Miz Weaver's neck when they pulled her out of the pen . . ."

"He also said she didn't have no neck—"

"Oh!" cried Becca, "when you gone give up?! It's not there, and she probably didn't never even lay eyes on it. And if Dorothy Sims had it on her when she got run down, then it's probably gone be buried with her in the coffin. You don't need to think any more about it."

"I bet it was out there in that mud, come off her neck when the pig attacked her, and fell in the mud . . ." Sarah said thoughtfully.

"So let it stay there! Not nobody is gone go out to Mr. Weaver's place, and go trampling around in the pigpen looking for a piece of jewelry they don't even know is there. It's just as safe in that pigpen as it would be in Dorothy Sims's coffin. So why don't you just let it alone, Sarah?"

"I would have thought it got burned up in the Coppage house. That's 'xactly what I did think—and that's what Jo Howell wanted us to think. But it didn't. If it can get out of a burning house by itself, then it can get out of a pigpen. Or a coffin."

"What? Does it just fly out when we're not looking? We turn our backs on the pigpen, and this necklace jumps up out of the mud? That's just the craziest thing I ever heard of in my life!"

"I don't know," replied Sarah. "I don't know what it does. But I'm going to get it, and then I'm gone smash it to bitty pieces. But until I do, I don't think that there's a single person in this county that's pure-and-teed safe!"

"So what are you going to do now?" Becca asked.

"I haven't decided. I got to talk to Mr. Weaver. I'll call him up, give him time to get back from Brundidge."

"Don't you think you ought to at least wait till after the funeral?"

"I waited till after the funeral for Dorothy Sims, and Dorothy Sims has now got a funeral of her own. I'll call him when I get home. I guess he's probably got a phone."

Becca paused, and then she said, "You gone let me know what you find out, aren't you, Sarah?"

Sarah turned to her friend. "You're starting to believe in it, too, aren't you?"

Becca shook her head. "No, I'm not. I don't want to. I won't believe it till I have to. But you do, and as long as you do, then I'll do what I can. I mean I'll drive you around and all that."

"You gone be sorry you said that," laughed Sarah. "I was just about to ask you if you would get up real early tomorrow morning with me, and let's go back out to the Weaver place. I'm gone talk to the man tonight, and if he says he don't mind, then I'm gone take a leaf rake out there, and go through that pigpen . . ."

"You mean you are gone set foot in all that mud!" cried Becca.

Sarah nodded. "But you don't have to. I wouldn't ask you to do that. I just want you to drive me out there before work. But I still got to talk to Mr. Weaver first, see what he says. If he says that Merle never had hold of

that thing, then I'm not gone bother. Not much point then,
I guess. But if he says his wife did have something like
that, then somebody's in trouble . . ."

Sarah thanked Becca several times for having driven
her out on the fruitless errand, and the two women paused
at their respective back doors for an instant, waving to
one another sadly across the top of the purple Pontiac,
in the driveway.

Sarah walked into the dusky kitchen slowly, hoping
against hope that Jo would have begun preparations for
supper that evening so that she wouldn't have so much
to do now, but when she turned on the light she saw that
nothing at all had been done. Dishes from the afternoon
meal had been stacked unwashed in the sink.

Sarah didn't even want to tell Jo and Dean that she
was home. She wanted to have nothing to do with them.
It was the death of Merle Weaver that upset her so, the
strange and horrible destruction of this woman, who by all
accounts was good and simple and completely unac-
quainted with Jo Howell or Dean Howell, who had nothing at all to do with the Pine Cone Munitions Factory. But
it was necessary that she inform Jo that she was there, so
that she wouldn't start calling Sheriff Garrett or anything
like that. She stepped quickly through the living room,
leaned briefly into the bedroom, and said, "I'm back!"
with some small amount of entirely fabricated cheer.

"Where you been?" Jo demanded. "You're late!"

Sarah shook her head. "I'll tell you later. I got to get
supper started . . ." She moved away, and knew that Jo
Howell would be too lazy to follow her into the kitchen,
where she might end up having to do something.

Sarah turned on the water and washed the dishes,
sadly thinking out the rest of the evening and the rest
of her life, wondering what she should say to Jo; wondering how she was going to survive an infinitude of days
that were as wretched and horrible as this one.

A thought occurred to Sarah that turned around all her
ideas about the amulet. If it was Jo that had set all this
evil into violent motion, then by destroying the amulet,
the cause of it all, she would have her revenge on the old
woman. Now suddenly Sarah was doubly anxious to

find it, now she was willing to go to all lengths—to badger perfect strangers, go crawling about in pigpens, chase ambulances and police cars—so that she could put an end to Josephine Howell's despicable plan.

Sarah quickly finished the dishes and left them to dry in the rack. She cracked the door to the living room, to make sure that Jo was not there, and then went to the telephone by the refrigerator. The information operator gave her Jack Weaver's telephone number, and she called the bereaved farmer.

She apologized for disturbing him at such a bad time, told who she was, and why she had called.

Jack Weaver was much too burdened with his own grief to find anything really strange in Sarah's questions. And Merle was so much on his mind that he didn't mind that Sarah wanted to talk about her.

"Yes, ma'am," he said limply, "I know what you're talking about. That necklace thing we found out by the truck. We was right then in thinking that it came off the body of that poor woman we ran down."

"What happened to it, Mr. Weaver?" asked Sarah in a voice that she tried to control.

"It was that necklace that caused Merle to die," the farmer stated in a flat, tired voice.

Sarah was so shocked that she could not for a moment reply. "I'm so sorry," she faltered at last.

"She found it on the ground, and put it in her pocket. We were gone bring it back into town, thinking it might be buried with that woman. It was in Merle's pocket when she was feeding the pigs, and it slipped out into the mud. She went in after it, and then Louise got her. Her pocket didn't have no button on it," the farmer explained piteously. "If she had had a button on her pocket, then she'd have been alive today."

"Where's the necklace now?" asked Sarah.

"Didn't never find it, I guess. Is it yours?" the farmer asked.

"Sort of," Sarah replied. "Would you mind," she asked, "if I came out and looked for it?"

"It's not mine," said the farmer, "it wasn't Merle's. It caused her death, and I don't want no part of it. Do what you like, Miz Howell. Do whatever you want . . ."

"Thank you, Mr. Weaver," sighed Sarah. "I'm really sorry to have bothered you at a time like this."

"Don't much matter," said the farmer, and Sarah heard the receiver click softly.

Chapter 45

THE phone call to the bereaved farmer had confirmed Sarah Howell's worst suspicions: the amulet had been at the scene of this last, most recent death, and beyond that, the man even went so far as to blame it for his wife's death. Sarah breathed heavily, at that moment hating her mother-in-law, hating her own husband as being somehow involved in these evil transactions.

Sarah had turned out the lights in the kitchen, and made that terrible phone call in the darkness. Now she sat a few moments at the kitchen table, the light from the last quarter moon casting cold through the small window above the sink; she was mustering her strength and her thoughts.

She sat, and even as she sat and thought she felt a change coming over her, inexorable and harsh—yet relieving. She was convinced now that not only was Josephine Howell, her mother-in-law, somehow mixed up in all the evil that had befallen these dozen people—an even dozen lives violently ended—but so was her husband. Sarah tried to tell herself that Dean could have had nothing to do with it, that his inert body with neither will, nor pleasure, nor defiance was incapable of contributing to the engineering of this bizarre tangle of accident and murder. But she couldn't accept that reasonable conclusion; she was certain that her husband was involved, and she knew it for gospel at the same time she was convinced that he could not move to the other side of the bed if he wanted to. She was not even sure he was capable of forming the desire. Dean Howell was so helpless he couldn't hit the floor with his hat, but with his mother's abetting assistance, he had somehow managed to slaughter twelve people in the past week, to avenge himself against the town of Pine Cone.

Sarah dropped her head in her hands. She was crazy to think those things, crazy to sit in the darkness and accuse her invalid vegetable husband of mass murder; out of her mind to see calculated, spiraling mayhem when there was only accident and not uncommon domestic homicide. She was crazy to think it, but there was no way any longer to believe anything else.

She no longer loved Dean. With what she knew about him, how could she? Besides, it wasn't Dean that had come back to her, but a breathing corpse, a sweating sack of warm lard surrounding a tube that ran from the top to the bottom, from the mouth to the rear end—and that was all. Josephine Howell, she was the crazy one, for sitting there all day talking to such a thing.

Sarah at last admitted to herself that she no longer had a husband. That Pine Cone rifle had done worse than even what Jo credited it with. It had blown away not only Dean's face, but it had torn off everything that was good in the man, leaving a rotting carcass of single-minded wickedness. Sarah was not even allowed the comfort of mourning the loss of her husband, for legally the man was still there: he had a Social Security number, and he occupied a certain space, and dozens of government forms had to be filled out with his name on them. And worst of all, he had the right to demand attention of her. The thing that lay in there on that bed, however, was no more Dean than if Sarah had stuffed a dozen dead cats in a pair of pajamas and arranged them on the bed to look like the figure of a man underneath the covers—and stuck a white gourd on the pillow for the head.

Much of Sarah's discomfort in the past week had come from the knowledge that she was fighting against Jo and Dean. She could reconcile herself to her war against Jo, for Sarah knew how wicked the woman could be, but it

was very difficult to explain to her conscience her frenzied
battle against the inert figure on the bed. How could she
attack something that could not defend itself? If she were
to leave off sticking mashed carrots into the black hole,
then the rest of that loathsome body would shrivel and
die, turn black and rot. She could roll it off the bed onto
the hard tile floor, and it would be unable to climb up
again. She could plunge Jo's sewing scissors into its belly,
and it would not be able to pull them out again. And she
had tried to convince herself for weeks that this was the
man she had married, this the man she loved when he
went away to Fort Rucca, this the man for whose sake she
had listened intently to all the news of the progress of the
war in Asia. It didn't work anymore.

But what discomfort need she feel now? For whose
sake should she hold back? For Jo's and Dean's? She
believed them culpable, and if they were, then they deserved anything that might come to them for it. More
importantly, she had an obligation to all the people in
Pine Cone who might be put in danger if she did not retrieve and destroy the amulet.

But what if Jo and Dean were entirely innocent? What
if she really were just out of her mind—temporarily, understandably, from all the strain, from overwork, from
just having shared a house with Josephine Howell for the
past two years? Then she could get herself into trouble.
She might get Jo and Dean into trouble. At the very least
she would be making a fool of herself, and probably of
them too.

Sarah considered these two sides of the question, but
she knew that her decision was already made. She couldn't
take the chance; if she gave it all over, took the easy,
blind way of ignoring all that she had seen and heard,
then more people would die—and she would be more
responsible. It was terrible that she had been so cowardly
in not going up to Dorothy Sims right away—but at that
time, she hadn't been sure about the thing. It was all just
a guess, a cloudy guess in her mind, and she had been
working on intuition. Now it was still cloudy—exactly
how the amulet worked, for instance, and where Jo had
got it—but it was no longer a guess that the thing did

work. And it would be inexcusable now for her not to work on that premise.

But Sarah, once this great decision was behind her, asked herself a depressing, despairing question: what would come of her? She was sure to lose no matter what happened. She saw that it was possible that she would alienate the town, that at best would think that she was "touched" and wouldn't be so careful of her feelings as was Becca Blair. If she were wrong in all of this, she was sure to anger Jo even more, and make the woman so distrustful of her that there would never be hope of stable truce between them. And even if under the best possible circumstances, nothing were changed at all—if the fears about the amulet subsided, if the people stopped dying, and if Jo never discovered what it was that Sarah was doing behind her back—she was still trudging through life with Dean strapped to her back, like two seventy-five pound bags of seed corn. Sarah considered ruefully that her twenty-first birthday wasn't even for another month.

Suddenly, Sarah had an image of herself in the Coppage house, upstairs, in one of the bedrooms (though she had never been there before). The house was on fire, and everywhere she turned the flames were neck-high, and they had the substance and smell of soft-boiling candy on the top of the stove: thick and syrupy. She turned and turned and tried to decide which of the four walls of flame she ought to try to jump through to safety, but failing to decide, she grew despairful as the fire crept closer to her all around.

She shook her head forcibly; she had not been asleep, but nevertheless she had been dreaming. She sat still a few minutes longer, making sure that she was entirely awake. She hated having to think things out the way that she had, but in truth it was the only real way of making the hard decisions. She shrugged. It was then to be war against the amulet, and if necessary, against Jo and Dean. In this, there could be no more thought or pity for herself, and for her situation. The only important thing was to make absolutely sure that no one else died.

In a few minutes she rose, moved quickly through the living room, and softly opened the door to Dean's bedroom. The light of a mercury lamp shone through the

213

venetian blinds of one window, across the body of her husband lying crossways on the bed. His head hung over the edge slightly. He looked like a corpse found on the desert, with bleached skin and a black, desiccated mouth. Jo was seated in her accustomed chair at the foot of the bed.

"Dinner ready yet?" the woman said surlily.

Sarah moved quietly into the darkened room.

"Why you so late tonight?" her mother-in-law continued. "Dean's hungry. I'm hungry. Where were you?"

Sarah did not answer. She turned on a small lamp on the dresser; it was of low wattage and covered by a shade of thick red material, but she and Jo both blinked several times, unaccustomed to the light.

At first Sarah and Jo spoke in low voices, almost in whispers, out of consideration for Dean, who might well be asleep; but quickly they fell into normal voices, forgetting his comfort and his presence.

"Where were you?" Jo repeated.

"Somebody else got hold of that amulet," said Sarah quietly.

Jo spoke quickly. "Who?" Her lips clamped shut after that, and Sarah could tell that she was thinking hard. Sarah did not immediately reply, and Jo refused to repeat the question. At last Sarah said, "The woman that run down Dorothy Sims on the Montgomery highway."

Jo chose her words carefully. "I thought it was a man that was driving the truck."

"It was," said Sarah, "it was her husband that was driving the truck. Merle Weaver was in the cab with him."

"Didn't know 'em," said Jo, recovered now from her momentary surprise.

Sarah stood at the dresser, and stared at her mother-in-law. After another pause, Jo asked, "Now, what you mean she got hold of what amulet?" Her voice sounded curious, but Sarah thought she detected a note of urgency in it as well.

"Merle Weaver's dead," said Sarah slowly. Jo Howell never answered a question directly, never gave the answer that was strictly called for, and Sarah considered that she could play that game as well.

"I told you," said Jo, commandingly, "that that thing burned up in the Coppage place."

"Hogs got her," said Sarah quietly.

Jo squinted. "Hogs?"

"Out on their farm," said Sarah grimly. "She's dead, and I don't think her husband's right anymore."

Jo shifted uneasily in her chair, as if she wanted to remove herself from her daughter-in-law's directed gaze. "Well," she said, "what do you want me to do about it?"

Sarah was calm. Her fingers played with the switch on the small lamp. She said quietly, "You plan these things, don't you—you and Dean?" She glanced down at her husband, motionless, a bizarre figure of immobility and helplessness.

"You not talking sense, Sarah," said Jo, with a grim smile that turned into a prolonged sneer.

Sarah decided that she must continue the attack. "You sit there all day and plan."

"We sit in this house all day," echoed Jo, "and we watch television, and we look out the window, except Dean, he can't see, and he can't talk. I watch television, and I look out the window, and I keep Dean company while you're away at work, and *that's* what we do all day." Jo's words protested her innocence, but the tone of her voice was insolent, as if she were daring Sarah to prove her guilty. It was the ironic denial of the murderer who knows he can never be convicted.

"Becca and I went out to the Weaver place," said Sarah.

Jo looked displeased, and a little startled: "What'd you want to do that for?" she asked uncomfortably.

"I wanted to talk to Mr. Weaver, and I wanted to find that thing—that amulet," said Sarah. All this while, she watched her mother-in-law very closely, trying to find out all that she could from the way that Jo responded to anything that she said.

"D'you find it?" Jo demanded, but in a way that suggested that she did not expect an affirmative answer.

Sarah shook her head.

"Well, what makes you think that it was out there?" Jo said, once again on the offensive.

"Merle Weaver's dead, that's why. Died peculiar, just

215

like the others. A whole line of 'em, and I didn't want anybody else to die. The others had the amulet and they're dead. Merle Weaver's dead, and so she must have had the amulet too. I went out to find it."

"That don't necessarily follow, Sarah, you know that," said Jo, with another derisive smile. "Just because she's dead, don't mean she had the thing on her. It got burned up, like I told you."

Sarah stared at Jo a few moments, and then said, "I talked to Mr. Weaver too. He said that his wife had the amulet. They found it yesterday morning, the day before. It came off of Dorothy Sims's body, when they were driving her back to Pine Cone."

"It still don't prove nothing," said Jo. "How could a piece of jewelry cause all them deaths? You're still talking crazy, Sarah."

Sarah realized then that no matter how convincing her evidence was, no matter how closely she could get to the sequence of events, and reproduce them in front of her mother-in-law, the old fat woman would fall back on the same argument: "You're talking crazy, Sarah." And she was, because it was a crazy thing to begin with. There wasn't any sense to make out of it. It was magic—black magic, and black magic didn't make sense, it didn't even exist. Suddenly Sarah was very angry. Without thinking about it, Sarah turned off the lamp, a little involuntary movement of her fingers. In a second, she flicked it back on, and said to her mother-in-law, in a vicious voice. "Why don't you just shoot 'em in the head, be a lot better than these terrible things that are happening to everybody. There's twelve of 'em, Jo, twelve people dead, so far!"

Jo was petulant. "They got Dean in the head, didn't kill him."

"You blame me too," cried Sarah, " 'cause I'm on the 'ssembly line, don't you? And you blame Becca Blair too! 'Cause we had our hands on that rifle that blew up in Dean's face. It was a accident. He could've got his legs cut off in a jeep. You wouldn't have blamed the people in the factory up in Ohio that made the jeep."

Jo made no reply.

"Do you two plan who's going to get it next?" Sarah looked with loathing at her mother-in-law, and then transferred the gaze to her husband, who had not moved at all in the course of the conversation. In a slightly calmer voice, she said, "These people didn't have nothing in this world to do with what happened to Dean. Miz Weaver, the Simses, the Shirleys, they didn't none of 'em have nothing to do with the Pine Cone rifle that blew up in Dean's face. The Weavers was good people, James Shirley was a good policeman, they was five of the Coppage kids and they probably never even set foot one in the Pine Cone Munitions Factory. You want to get back at somebody, you ought to burn the factory down, you ought to stop the war."

Sarah turned away in disgust.

"Well," said Jo, after a few moments in which the only sound was Sarah's labored breathing, "well, who's got it now?"

Quietly, Sarah replied, "I don't know. I couldn't find it. It's still in the mud out at the Weaver place."

"You'd better find it then, you better crawl through that mud and get it before someone else finds it, and dies too, 'long with their husband, and their children, and the animals in the barn." Jo was sarcastic, and it sounded really as if she didn't believe that the amulet had anything to do with the deaths.

Sarah did not reply to all of this. "One day . . ." she said quietly.

"One day what?" snapped Jo.

"One day," repeated Sarah, "we are gone take those bandages off Dean."

She switched off the light and walked swiftly out of the room, leaving the mother and son alone in the stuffy darkness.

Chapter 46

EARLY the next morning Sarah and Becca rode back out to the Weaver farmstead. Along the way they said very little, for it was very early in the morning and neither of the women had much liking for the errand.

"Well," said Becca, "you came in late yesterday afternoon, you're leaving early this morning. What'd you tell the old biddie?"

"I told her that I had been out to the Weavers—she didn't like that—"

"Good!" interjected Becca.

"—and then I told her I was coming back out here this morning, and she didn't like that either. She told me I ought not be going around causing people anguish."

"If Jo Howell didn't like it, then I'm glad we're doing it. If she did something wrong, I mean something real *bad*, then we've got to get her on the run." Then Becca laughed at the image called up of that great, fat, greasy woman trying to propel herself on her two short thick legs.

Sarah had wondered if she shouldn't go up to the house first and speak to Mr. Weaver, introduce herself and explain to him again why she wanted to go through the mud in his pigpen with a leaf rake. Farm people got up with the sun and there was no danger of awakening him,

218

but still she hesitated to intrude upon his grieving solitude.

But from the main road, Sarah could see a figure moving about the barnyard, and she had Becca drive directly there. Jack Weaver stood in the open barn door and waited patiently, and without any expression of curiosity or interest, for the two women to get out of the Pontiac and approach him.

Sarah introduced herself and Becca to him, reminding him that she had called the night before, and asked if he would allow them to search the pigpen for the amulet.

"Worth something?" the farmer said automatically, but his eyes moved vaguely over the barnyard.

Sarah nodded. "It's been in the family a long time, and we just didn't want it to get lost." This was a lie made up on the spot, and Sarah realized even as she spoke, that it made no sense, for how would a Howell family heirloom come into the hands of Dorothy Sims? But Jack Weaver was in no emotional shape to cross-examine Sarah on her motives, and in fact he did not even notice the logical discrepancy. Sarah wanted to tell the farmer nothing about her fears concerning the amulet, for she saw he felt bad enough already, and was better off believing that his wife had died simply by horrible accident.

"It's bad mud in there. You gone get yourself filthy," said Jack kindly. "Why don't you let me go in there and try? Give me that rake, and I'll look for the thing for you. It wasn't ours, and we was on our way practically to go back into Pine Cone and give the thing to the sheriff, when Merle,"—he broke off and looked away, then picked up again—"Merle said she thought it might be worth something, and I guess she was right. I sure do wisht she hadn't never found it though . . ."

Sarah refused the farmer's offer; she didn't want to put him to any trouble, but also she knew that she would not be satisfied unless she examined the pen herself. Without ceremony then, Sarah simply climbed over the fence into the pen and, starting in the far corner, began to rake through the mud. This was a difficult enterprise, for since the pigs had been removed the ground had not been disturbed and had begun to firm. For a few minutes, Jack

Weaver and Becca watched the young woman at her strange task.

Becca had told the farmer who she was, and reminded him that she used to come out here with her mother and father fifteen, twenty years before. Jack smiled mournfully and started immediately to talk to Becca of his dead wife. He spoke quietly and with great feeling for some minutes, and Becca wouldn't look into his face for fear that she would see him crying and embarrass him. The two leaned forward on the fence and watched as Sarah raked carefully through the congealed mud.

Suddenly, Jack Weaver shook his head and exclaimed loudly to Sarah, "I'm just standing here, talking my head off, when you are in there breaking your back! You got to let me help you!" He ran back into the barn for another rake, and returned presently.

Now Sarah allowed him to assist her, for the work was hard and she knew that, though this was not a common task, the farmer would probably be better at it than she was. In another twenty minutes the two had gone over every square foot of the pen and turned up nothing.

"I don't know where it could have gone," said the farmer, "but I sure don't think it's here." He moved over to the spot just where Becca was leaning on the fence. He faltered, "Merle . . . Merle was standing right there . . . when the thing fell out of her pocket. She couldn't find it either, but it must have fell just about here—" He raked through the stiffening mire for another few minutes, but still came up with nothing.

He turned to Sarah apologetically. "I'm real sorry. I'm real sorry that we couldn't find it. I know how much that thing means to you, to come out here and look for it like this. If I come across it, I'll call you right up."

Sarah nodded nervously. She was worried about the amulet, but she was even more concerned for this unfortunate, good man and his grief just now. Obviously he had nothing on his mind but his wife, and yet he had been willing to spend a good hour raking up the mud in a pig-pen as a favor for two women he didn't even know, searching for a piece of jewelry that she credited with the death of his wife.

Sarah thanked him profusely and motioned for Becca to

get ready to go. "We don't want to take up any more of your time, Mr. Weaver. We really do 'preciate your help, 'preciate you letting us come out here like this."

"I'm just sorry we didn't find it," repeated the farmer.

"So am I," agreed Sarah sincerely.

"Sarah," said Becca, "we got to get going, if we're gone get to work on time. We got to go by the house and let you change them pants."

Sarah nodded. The two women got into the car and drove off, Sarah and Becca both waving out the window to the farmer standing forlornly in his barnyard.

"What does it mean?" asked Becca: "What does it mean that you couldn't find it?"

"It means it's not there anymore," said Sarah simply. "It means it got somewhere else."

"How?"

"I don't know. Mr. Weaver would have said if there had been anybody else out here going through the pen. That man Mr. Emmons may not have cared much for us yesterday afternoon, but I think he would have told us if he had got hold of it."

"I bet if he found it, he'd keep it," said Becca. "He looks like the type."

"You think we ought to stop at his store and ask?" Emmons' store would be coming up on the left in just another mile or so.

Becca looked at her watch. "We can stop and get a drink or something. Feels like its noontime to me, I been up so long this morning, and it's just seven-thirty. But we got to hurry."

They did stop, and Mr. Emmons behind the counter provided them with bottles of soda and the information that he had not found anything in the mud that afternoon before. "I didn't step foot in there, and them boys didn't either. Didn't want to get all that mud and blood on my boots and cuffs. Don't like to go trampling on the scenes of murder anyway. Bad luck."

Becca nodded her sympathy with this opinion.

Back in the car, headed for Pine Cone, Becca and Sarah agreed that they believed him. He might have picked up a double-barreled shotgun if he had found it on the ground out at the Weavers', but what would he do with a piece of jewelry? Becca had noted that the man was not wearing a wedding ring, and he didn't even have a wife to give the thing to.

"So where is it?" said Becca. At last, she was convinced herself that there was something terribly strange about the amulet. Concrete information had been received, not through Sarah, but directly. Becca had heard Jack Weaver say that his wife had the amulet, that it fell into the mud, that no one had taken it out of the mud. But it wasn't there, and that was inexplicable. And Becca did not like to have the inexplicable so close at hand.

"I don't know who's got it," said Sarah. "It's got beyond me, I think. I can't figure it out. And I don't know where to go from here."

"I know what," said Becca, "let's you and me think about it on the line this morning, and see if we can't come up with something by dinnertime. Maybe by then we'll have thought of something."

Sarah laughed, and Becca asked her why.

"Because," said Sarah, "you said yesterday afternoon that you didn't believe in any of this."

"Still don't," said Becca curtly, "but I'll do anything that looks like it'll make Jo Howell mad."

"That's not all though, is it?" said Sarah seriously.

Becca shook her head. "No, it's not," said Becca. "I listened to that poor man talk this morning, talking about Merle Weaver. Now I don't remember her too well, but she was always sweet to me, I do remember that. What happened ought not to have happened, and I'm just sick about it. That man went through what I hope I never have to go through in my life, and I don't want to hear of it happening again."

Sarah said nothing, but she knew that now, in whatever she proposed, Becca Blair was sure to assist her.

Chapter 47

ALL that morning, Sarah hardly saw the three screws before her. Her thoughts were confused and undirected. To begin with, she was upset because she had not been able to find the amulet. That meant either it was still in the mud, or else that it had already moved on to its next victim. There was no doubt that Merle Weaver had got hold of the amulet. Jack Weaver had described it roughly, but well enough for Sarah to equate it with the piece that she had passed from Jo Howell's hands into those of Larry Coppage. If only she could see the thing again! It was infuriating that she was always a step or two behind it. She dreaded finding out who had it now, dreaded stumbling over another corpse in Pine Cone.

But she was also relieved by having Becca with her, backing her up. It made it much easier to deal with the whole situation now that there was someone who sympathized with her. Neither of them, when it came down to it, could credit the amulet with the twelve Pine Cone deaths. There had to be some explanation behind it, some reason or sequence of events that they simply hadn't the imagination or brains to reason out for themselves. Maybe when they got hold of the thing themselves they would be able to make everything clear. But until that time, it was an enormous reassurance that Becca, at least, would not make fun of her, would take her part against Jo and Dean, and if necessary, against the rest of Pine Cone.

The two women smiled at one another many times over the partition, and were very anxious to talk with one another, though when the noon break came, both had to confess that they had no new ideas.

"I thought about it till my eyes rolled," said Becca, "and I can't make heads or tails of it. What I did start to think about, though, was Jo Howell. I mean, you saw her give the thing to Larry Coppage, and we think that the thing had something to do with everybody dying. But what we don't know is how much Jo Howell knew. It's possible she didn't know anything about it; it's possible that she was just giving him a present like she said she was, and she just gave him a necklace that was unlucky, *real* unlucky. Or it could be she just wanted to get back at Larry Coppage, and wanted him to have a car wreck and get his arm broke or something, and wasn't even thinking about Rachel and the kids and all them other people. She may not have wanted all them people to die, but once she gave the thing away she couldn't control it anymore." Becca sighed in perplexity; she did not like to defend Josephine Howell, even by hypothesis.

Sarah considered this, and realized that Becca was right. It was possible that Jo Howell was not so culpable as she thought. But no matter the extent of the woman's guilt, it was still imperative that they get the amulet back and destroy it. " 'Cause when she found out it was killing all these other people, she was surprised, I think. I would tell her about it, and it was like she didn't expect to hear it. And that means she can't control it. And that still means we got to get it back."

"Maybe if we knew how it worked. Maybe if she told you how it worked, Sarah, we could find out how to find it and stop it. Maybe you can talk Jo into telling you about it."

"I'll try," said Sarah. "I'll try anything, but I don't think she will. She won't admit anything about it, and keeps saying it was burned up in the Coppage house. She won't admit it, 'cause if she did, then she would be responsible."

"And where'd she *tell* you she got it?" asked Becca.

The Amulet

"Montgomery Ward catalogue," replied Sarah, "but I just bet she made that up."

"Well," said Becca, "when you and I get home this evening, we ought to go through them catalogues—I never throw anything out like that—and see if we can find a picture of it. I don't know what good it'll do us even if we do find it, except to tell us how much she put out for it, 'cause it's doubtful if the catalogue is gone say something like: 'Comes in black and gold only. Good for getting rid of people you don't like.' "

Sarah laughed; both women laughed, and then spent the remainder of their lunch hour together carefully talking of things that weren't so unsettling.

Chapter 48

∞∞∞∞∞∞∞∞∞∞∞∞∞∞∞∞∞∞∞∞∞∞∞∞∞∞∞∞∞∞

THE back room of Morris Emmons' country store on the Pine Cone road was large, squarish, and low-ceilinged. The walls were roughhewn wood, one with shelves attached at every height, another with hooks for the hanging of carcasses. More hooks were set in the crossbeams of the ceiling. Now the room—chill but perhaps not so cold as it ought to be for the preserving of meat—was burdened with the slaughtered carcasses of Jack Weaver's hogs and sows. They hung from the back set of hooks in two rows against the back wall, stalagtites of livid pink flesh. The heads of the animals were stuck in a square pattern, four down and five across on hooks in a side wall; they were to be picked up soon by a black butcher whose clientele were much taken with head cheese and certain soups that were best made with the head of a pig.

Late in the morning, Morris Emmons entered this back room in the company of two farmers—hard, thin men, poor and dirty, with evil smiles, and great curiosity to see the animals that had killed Merle Weaver. The two farmers, Jim Coltrane and Mal Homans, had married sisters and their farms were adjoining. They got drunk together, they played practical jokes together, and they banded together in general to protect themselves against the onslaught of their wives. Mal Homans was the senior of the two farmers, and though it is difficult to judge such things, was probably the sneakier of the two—though Jim

Coltrane, from inclination and long practice, was acquiescent in anything that the other suggested or opined.

"Which one of 'em was it got Miz Weaver, Morris?" said Mal, with a wicked smile. Peculiar delight flashed in his eyes. His brother-in-law laughed conspiratorially.

Morris pointed vaguely toward the heads on the wall; they looked like the trophies of a cowardly hunter. "That one right there," he said, "the mean-looking one."

"They all look alike to me," said Jim, "which one you talking about? All hogs look mean to me. You know what I mean, Mal?"

Morris walked over to the wall and pointed to the head in the lower left corner. "It was this one," he said, and nodded significantly.

Mal had moved over behind him, and he placed his hand over the snout of another glassy-eyed pig. "You sure it wasn't this one, Morris?" Mal and Jim laughed boisterously at this, which they considered to be a fine joke. "Sure looks meaner to me . . ." added Mal, and the two farmers erupted into more unpleasant laughter.

"Naaaah," said Jim, "I think it was *this one!*" And he stuck his finger right into the eye of yet another pig's head. The eye burst and fluid poured down the snout and over Jim's hand. He wiped his fingers off on his trousers, but did not stop laughing.

"Yep," said Mal, "I think Jim's right, this one looks the meanest to me, it must have been this one that done away with poor Miz Weaver."

Morris Emmons was patient through this teasing, and when the two brothers-in-law had quit their snickering, he said, "That's not the one. This is the one, and I tell you how I know. 'Cause Jack Weaver shot the sow that got his wife, and this is the only one that was already dead when we got out there." Again he pointed to the sow's head in the lower left-hand corner.

The two farmers shook their heads seriously, and disputed.

With a little anger, Morris Emmons then said, "Look here, you two, you can still see the woman's blood on the snout here!" He pointed to the two little streams of dried blood that could be discerned through the bristles round the snout of the animal.

"That's hog blood, Morris, you can't fool us!" cried Mal.

"Hog blood! Hog blood!" Jim echoed, with choking laughter.

"No, it ain't!" shouted Morris Emmons, in indignant reply. These two men were getting on his nerves. They would talk this kind of nonsense throughout the day; they could maintain a falsehood through months of ribbing, just for the hell of it—and Morris Emmons didn't like to be made a fool of. "Damn it!" he cried, "you just put your hand up there, and look at it, you touch it, that's real human blood."

"Women's blood," snickered Jim.

Morris Emmons reached out and touched the snout of Louise, the hog that had killed Merle Weaver.

"You don't believe me," he said, "so I'm gone open her snout, and I bet you she's still got part of Merle Weaver's throat in there. And I'm gone give it to you, and you can take it to the funeral, and lay it in the coffin with the rest of her body! You can take her throat away with you, you hear me, Mal Homans!" Mal and Jim laughed again, uproariously, at Morris Emmons' excitement and anger.

Morris Emmons pried open the mouth of the decapitated sow; ligaments in the jaw were torn apart, and the mouth fell suddenly open. A piece of jewelry on a chain fell out into Morris Emmons' hands.

The two farmers drew back in surprise, and both cried, "Heeeey!"

"Morris, you son-of-a-bitch!" cried Mal Homans, very much rattled by the effect, at once bizarre, surprising, and uncanny, of the amulet dropping out of the pig's mouth. "Morris, you put that thing in there!"

Morris was as amazed as the two farmers. He turned the amulet over in his hand. "No, I didn't," he protested. "I didn't know it was in there!"

The three men stared a few moments at the piece of jewelry.

"Miz Weaver must have had that thing 'round her neck, and the hog just tore it off," said Jim.

Mal Homans shivered a little to let off superstitious steam, and then jocularly remarked, "Hog must've liked jewelry."

228

Jim and Morris Emmons laughed a little nervously, but were obviously glad that the incident was going to be taken lightly.

"Well," said Mal, pleased with the tack he had taken, "not never gone wear my wedding ring in the hog pen no more, I tell you!"

"Get your finger bit off!" shouted Jim. "You wear a wedding ring in the hog pen! Finger bit right off at the knuckle!"

The three men then indulged in a spate of laughter that relieved them somewhat; it had been a fright to see the amulet pop out of the hog's mouth, almost as if it had been cast up in derision.

Mal choked off a final laugh, whistled, and commented in a breathless whisper, "Sure must have been a mean one to do what it did."

Morris Emmons looked thoughtful a moment, and then said to the farmers, "You know who Dean Howell is?"

It was Mal Homans who commonly made the joke about Josephine Howell having poisoned her own husband by biting him in the ankle. And he had heard of Dean's accident, as had, in fact, the entire county. Jim Coltrane was reminded of the accident by his brother-in-law. "You 'member—got his face blowed away at Rucca." Jim nodded, and grinned, but then said, "But what's that got to do with Miz Weaver or that thing? He's laid up now. They say he's got the brain of a winter turnip."

"His wife was out to the Weaver farm," said Emmons, "looking for this thing. She described it 'xactly."

"It was hers?" asked Jim. "It was Miz Howell's?"

"But Miz Weaver was wearing it," protested Mal.

"She must've been wearing it, if it just then fell out of the pig's mouth," agreed Jim.

"But how'd Miz Howell know about it then?" asked Morris.

The two farmers shrugged.

"She told me to call her if I found this thing."

"Maybe it's worth something," said Mal, "maybe she knew it was worth something, and when she heard Miz Weaver was dead, she thought she might just as well try to get hold of it for herself. Take it to Montgomery to sell it in a pawnshop or something like that."

"Maybe it's made of gold," suggested Jim.

"Let me see it," said Mal, and Morris handed it over to him. Mal turned it in his hands and held it up to his eyes. Jim watched his brother-in-law jealously, and as soon as he could, reached for the piece and took it away, examining it in exactly the same fashion.

Morris turned his back on the two farmers for a moment in order to peek through the door into the store to see if there were customers or if he were wanted there.

Mal glanced at Jim mischievously, and took the amulet away from him. In the transfer, the chain came apart, and the two farmers glanced with wondering grins at one another, for they had not seen the catch in its length.

Then Mal snuck up on Morris, Jim following only a step or two behind. The first farmer draped the amulet round Morris' neck, and—just as surprisingly as before— the two ends of the chain came together and locked shut. Mal laughed loudly and backed away, knocking into his brother-in-law.

Morris protested in a gruff voice, "Hey, what you doing? You're both good-for-nothing bastards!"

Mal and Jim convulsed themselves in laughter at the sight of Morris Emmons wearing a necklace. "Goddamn trouble-making hippie!" Mal cried, and Jim echoed, "Goddamn hippie! Goddamn hippie!"

Then Morris laughed too, and pushed Mal and Jim out of the cold storage room into the front of the store. He flicked off the light, and pulled the door closed behind him.

Chapter 49

WHEN Morris Emmons, Mal Homans, and Jim Coltrane emerged from the storage room in the back of the store, there were only two customers to be seen in the long wooden aisles. A little boy was standing in front of the counter near the cash register, picking through the cookies in a large display jar. An old countrywoman in a poke bonnet, who was the little boy's grandmother, was peering at cans of vegetables and soups on the shelves, trying to find the cheapest among a lot of containers that were all marked with the same price. She glared at Morris Emmons when he came out of the back.

"Can't hardly hear myself think out here, trying to decide about little Fred's dinner, come to visit me, with all that racket there in the back of the store," she murmured, and then commanded in a large voice, "Fred, don't you put none of them cookies in your mouth!"

The child paid no attention to his grandmother, but broke one of the large flat cookies in half, and then pushed both pieces into his mouth at once.

Morris Emmons rolled his eyes in consternation that it was old Miz Baines, who would be a trial to the devil himself, come to do her afternoon shopping. "You two get on, I got Miz Baines to wait on out here."

"Don't you let the hog head bite you, Morris!" cried

Mal, and his brother-in-law echoed, with variation, "Don't you let it get its teeth sank in your arm, Morris!"

"You better open up all them mouths, on all them animals, Morris, and make sure you ain't got wedding rings and bracelets and belts and things all hidden inside there! Might be a treasure trove in them pigs' mouths!"

The two men laughed again, and Morris shooed them out from behind the counter. Their stupid jokes and taunts infuriated him. He had put up with these two brutes for close on to ten years, and they had even annoyed him when they were boys. But they were good customers now, and he had had to put up with it. Well, he considered, and cursed himself that he had never thought of it before: they needed him more than he needed them. He kept them supplied with their machinery, with the parts for those machines when they broke down, with the best seed, with the right fertilizer for their impoverished soil, with the only decent advice on how to run their dilapidated farms that they were likely to find in the whole of the Wiregrass. No matter what he did to them, they would continue to come back, because they had to. If they went into Pine Cone for their supplies, they'd soon enough fall over into bankruptcy—and then Morris Emmons would have a fine laugh himself.

Those two sorry men: they spoke evil, they smelled evil, and they were always willing to do a bad turn for someone, always ready to kick a staggering man. Their farms were falling to racking ruin, their wives—the ugliest two women ever to come out of the same womb—would fall down in the dirt not to have to speak to you when you passed 'em on the road; and them bird dogs that the two men claimed they "raised" couldn't tell a quail from a polled Hereford.

Morris Emmons glanced angrily down the center aisle of the store, through the screen door, at Jim Coltrane's truck, parked just outside. In the cab, one of those stupid bird dogs was barking furiously at having been left for so long a time in the stifling enclosed space.

"Can't you keep that dog shut up?" Morris demanded.

"He's a watchdog," said Jim, "and watchdogs s'posed to bark."

The constant hoarse barking of the bird dog was irritating. Morris Emmons twisted the amulet between his fingers; it was still around his neck.

"What you got to be watched, Jim Coltrane? You got nothing," snapped old Miz Baines.

"Don't you pick on him," said Mal, in an amused teasing voice. He actually relished the idea of a little verbal altercation between the old woman and his brother-in-law.

"Your no-good dog bit my little girl's little girl last blackberry season. I hope your no-good dog barks his throat out!" said old Miz Baines.

Jim Coltrane had moved over to the screen door; he was a little afraid of the old woman's tongue, and had just as soon depart Morris Emmons' store. But Mal lingered behind, leaning against a wall of canned goods and paper products. He leered at old Miz Baines, and said, "Your little girl's little girl was pulling down my scuppernong vines, and I catch her over at my place again, Miz Baines, *I'm* gone bite her!"

During this short exchange Morris Emmons squatted down behind the counter, and from the small rack just below the cash register, took the shotgun that he kept loaded, just in case of robbers. Laying this across his lap, he carefully filled his shirt and pants pockets with ammunition. Slowly he stood, pointed the gun directly down the aisle, and fired it at Jim Coltrane. Coltrane saw what was happening, but did not have the time to protest or move at all, before he was struck in the chest. He fell backward through the screen door into the red dust of the bare ground outside. He writhed a moment, twisted over on his stomach, and was dead. Mal was so surprised he fell back against the shelves, knocking over a whole row of tinned peaches and pears, but he was much too frightened to say anything.

"You gone crazy, Morris Emmons?" shouted old Miz Baines, shaking in her poke bonnet. "What you want to do that for?"

Morris stepped from behind the counter, pushing little Fred out of the way, whose mouth, full of cookies, had gone suddenly very dry. Emmons walked slowly down the center aisle of the store toward the screen door. Mal Homans crawled down along the lowest shelf, upsetting whole rows of canned goods as he proceeded. He imagined that if Morris had killed Jim for no reason at all, then it was probable that the man would turn on him next. Morris reached the door, and stepped through and over the corpse of Jim Coltrane.

Old Miz Baines turned to her grandchild and commanded him, "Fred, don't you go looking at the dead man now, you get out of here before Morris Emmons comes back for *you!*"

The child grabbed a handful of cookies and scampered out the side door of the store. The old woman looked at Mal Homans and sneered, "That's what you get for raising scuppernongs, Mal Homans!" and then she followed her grandchild out of that place of sudden death.

Mal crawled to the front window of the store and peered through; he saw Morris advancing slowly on the truck. Mal stared a moment at the corpse of his brother-in-law, watching the blood form a thick pool underneath the body, and then he began to shake. He faltered backward and staggered out the side door, running after old Miz Baines and little Fred. They were stepping gingerly over some electrified fence into the safety of a neighboring cow pasture.

Morris Emmons walked slowly and deliberately to the truck that had belonged to the man he had just killed. The bird dog inside, sensing that something was terribly wrong, had stopped its barking and set up an even more fearsome howl. Morris peered through the window by the driver's side of the cab, and the dog leapt viciously against the glass. Morris Emmons stepped back a couple of feet, raised the rifle and fired directly at the panes. The side windows on both sides of the cab were blown out in an instant. The dog had dropped below the level of the glass and was uninjured; it jumped through the window and smashed against Morris' chest. The animal careened to the ground, and set up another round of barking, snapping at Emmons' ankles and pulling at his pants legs. In a moment the dog went and sniffed at the corpse on the ground, while Emmons tried to kick it. The dog turned and bit Emmons' leg, and then ran off, barking.

Emmons fired at the dog, but missed, and only blew up a great cloud of red dust. When that had cleared, Emmons could see that the dog had crawled between the rails of the border fence, and was running away across a pecan orchard, heading for the peanut and cotton fields a few hundred yards away.

Grimly, Emmons gave chase. He was awkward in running, in climbing over the fence, in trying to load his rifle again as he ran across the uneven earth of the pecan orchard. He had to stop several times to retrieve shells that bounced out of his shirt pocket. The dog kept always a few dozen yards ahead of him, and when Emmons paused, the dog turned back and began to howl.

But despite Emmons' hurry and his flailing limbs, and his sweating back, the man's face was set and expressionless—as blank as the gold-and-jet surface of the amulet bouncing on its chain around his neck.

Made curious by the gunshots, a number of black field hands had gathered in twos and threes at various fence posts within sight of Emmons and the dog, and among themselves discussed that the dog might be rabid, or wondered what it had done to make Emmons so angry. As they watched, however, Emmons' jerky movements and his feverish chase of the dog made them nervous, and they realized that they had much more to fear from the man with the rifle than from the dog. The field hands—men, women, and children—who had been weeding the rows of cotton and peanuts, moved swiftly along the fence, well out of Emmons' way, and then circled back toward the barn and outbuildings of the farm where they were employed. Emmons and the dog were headed that way, but there was much more protection in buildings than in open fields and orchards.

Emmons would raise his gun to fire; the dog would stop a moment, then suddenly leap to one side, or behind a tree, and the shot would miss him. The game had become stylized, and the crazed hunter and his canine prey progressed slowly and lurchingly toward the barn, crossing the several acres of low cotton and peanut plants.

All the black workers that had been gathered around the barnyard had scattered, retreating around the back of the building, or into a neighboring field of corn where they dropped to the ground below the level of the yard-high plants. A brave few climbed into the upper platforms of the barn, where hay was stored, and stared down through cracks between the planks, watching to see if Morris Emmons was going to be successful in killing the dog. They all abandoned the baling machine into which they had been feeding the last cuttings of the winter ground cover; the machine, set just inside the great front door of the barn, hummed softly, its gears turning against nothing, the wire inside poised to wrap securely the shredded dry grass.

The barking dog stopped just at the entrance of the barn, snarled fiercely at the approaching Emmons, and then turned inside into the darkness. Without hesitation, Morris Emmons stepped into the barn, but unable to adjust immediately to the dim light inside, he peered about a couple of times, not able to see much of anything. The dog had stopped barking, and Morris was confused by the sounds of cats that made their home in a near corner and by the shuffling of the very nervous men on the platforms above him. Emmons lifted the rifle to his shoulder, and turned around slowly, with the intention of shooting the dog as soon as it came within his vision.

The dog snarled behind him, and Morris whirled suddenly, sliding on the damp straw beneath him. Before he could regain his balance, the dog had leaped against his chest, propelling him backward and into the maw of the baling machine. In a moment, full of screams, Emmons was drawn by studded treads into the interior of the machine. The rifle fired once.

Two farmhands from above climbed swiftly down a ladder, and stared with real horror at the man's legs disappearing into the contraption. The machinery ground harshly, with muffled difficulty for a few moments, and then suddenly, with loud whistling and even louder grating, it began to spew out silver-dollar-size bits of bloody flesh, torn clothing, and mangled metal. The baling machine ground to a broken halt while one booted foot still protruded from the hopper.

One of the farmhands rushed out of the barn, calling for help. The dog rushed out after him, still barking. The other farmhand, a strapping black man in his mid-forties, stood still, glanced around to see that there was no one around him. Then he stopped and retrieved the piece of jewelry that had been flung out of the machine and at his feet. He glanced at it briefly, wiped the blood from it with the tail of his shirt, and then placed it in his pants pocket.

The Amulet

The female farmhands timidly entered the barn to determine what had happened to Morris Emmons. When they saw the single foot in the baling machine, they screamed, and ran back out into the sunlight, declaring how that foot was a great deal worse to look at than a whole churchful of open coffins.

Chapter 50

MORRIS Emmons had paid Jack Weaver half the sum for the pigs in cash when the distraught farmer had come to him the day of Merle Weaver's death, and had promised that the remainder would be available at his store sometime Thursday afternoon. Jack was to go by and get it then and also confirm that, according to the bargain, all the murderous animals had been slaughtered.

Jack Weaver, then, thinking of other things, pulled his pickup onto the red-dirt area in front of Morris Emmons gas pumps. He got out of his truck, scratching down on the back of an envelope a list of items he needed for the remainder of the week. The farmer was beneath the awning that protected the pumps and shaded the front of the store before he saw Jim Coltrane's corpse spread before the screen door. A pool of blood had flowed out beneath the body, and the tire tracks of a vehicle had spread and splattered the liquid farther.

The farmer put his hands over his face and leaned against the ethyl pump for support. He had not one coherent thought. He could not think who might have done it, could not think what he ought to do next, could not even decide whether he himself might be in danger. He shook his head without understanding, and turned only with the approach of an automobile. It was a highway patrol car, with two officers in the front, and another man

The Amulet

in the back. This last proved to be Mal Homans who jumped out and ran over to the corpse crying, "See, he's dead! Morris Emmons went and killed him! No good reason! No reason at all! Pulled out a shotgun and blew him to hell!" Mal Homans shook his head dismally, and stared at Jack Weaver and the two officers. The two policemen stood over the corpse, carefully avoiding stepping in the blood, and appeared to be at as much of a loss as the two farmers.

A second car soon came up and two women, so similar in appearance, that they were distinguished only by their dresses, stepped out and approached the body. They were both determined and solemn, and so alike in demeanor that Jack Weaver could not tell which was the widow, and which only the sister-in-law.

"Ya'll watch out!" cried Mal Homans suddenly, "he's probably still in there!"

The two women retreated to their car, got in and drove off without having spoken a word, either to each other or to anyone else. Jack Weaver and Mal Homans hurried to the pickup truck, and stood on the side away from the store. They peered through the window of the cab, and watched as the two officers carefully made their way around to the back of the store, surreptitiously peering in the windows.

"They gone get their heads blowed off, I know it!" cried Mal Homans, in great agitation.

"What happened?" stammered Jack Weaver.

Homans ignored him. "You hear a shot, we gone get in this truck and ride straight out of here, and we not gone look back, 'cause that man is out of his mind."

"What happened?" the farmer repeated, and then before the other could reply, Weaver suggested, "Let's get out of here now. Let's leave this place."

Homans shook his head. "I want to see if them men get killed. They are crazy to stick their heads in front of the window like that. If I was Morris Emmons inside there, and I had already killed one man, I wouldn't stop for no highway patrol."

"Morris Emmons killed Jim?"

Homans nodded distractedly, then said, "No reason. Didn't have no reason for doing it. I don't know why he did it. We was in there in the back, looking at them pi

239

that went and killed——" Homans broke off, realizing who
it was that he was talking to. Weaver looked down at the
ground, troubled, but then raised his eyes bravely.
Homans continued: "We was in the back, and then we
come out, and was about to go. Emmons told Jim to make
the dog shut up, and then he shot him dead. Didn't even
give him a chance to make the dog get quiet. Then he
tried to kill the dog too! Dog got out and Morris began
to chase that dog like there was no tomorrow! I don't
know if he got him. I ran out the side door, and snuck
'round the edge out here"——he pointed at a fence around
the property behind which was a thick hedge of crepe
myrtle——"and I saw Morris was gone. I run out here, and
made sure that Jim was dead—and he was—so then I
jumped in the truck and got the hell out. Got goddamn
glass in my ass, and near 'bout run poor Jim over. Went
straight home, and called the patrol. Them crazy men—
you wouldn't catch me doing anything like that . . ."

The two highway patrolmen had just entered the building when Sheriff Garrett and Deputy Barnes drove up
from the direction of Pine Cone. They hopped out of the
car, the deputy with his gun drawn and waving unsteadily
in the general direction of the two farmers.

"They're in there!" cried Mal Homans. "Don't know if
Morris is in there with 'em or not."

The sheriff and the deputy advanced cautiously on the
building, but the two patrolmen sauntered out, shaking
their heads and shrugging. All the law officers then gathered round Mal Homans and listened to his story told
again, and every few seconds they glanced uneasily toward
the corpse.

At the end of the tale, Mal Homans pleaded, "Hey,
cain't we move him, ya'll? He's starting to draw the flies.
Is the ambulance coming out here?"

Sheriff Garrett nodded. "On their way now. Ought to
have been here already."

"Where you suppose he could be? Morris, I mean. You
didn't see nothing, did you, Mr. Weaver?" asked the sheriff.

Jack Weaver shook his head. "That's his truck I see
'round back. He didn't take it. He must be around."

"He went after the dog," said Mal lamely.

All six men looked around themselves uneasily, and moved into the shade of the tin awning, where they weren't such targets. "Maybe we ought just to go on inside and wait for the ambulance." This suggestion was taken up, but just as the sheriff stepped through the door, he heard the radio in his patrol car. He sent Deputy Barnes to receive the information.

Barnes moved warily out to the car, and actually lay down across the front seat before he took the receiver. A few moments later he hurried back across the lot to the store, motioning the men out.

"Come on!" he shouted. "Morris Emmons is dead too!" He pointed out across the field. "Mr. Crane called in. Morris Emmons chased that dog through the peanuts, ran in the barn, and then jumped in the baler. Tore the damn thing up. Mr. Crane's gone have to buy a new one. He's real mad about it too."

The men winced. The two highway patrolmen got into their car, neglecting Mal Homans, and drove off in the direction of the neighboring farm.

The sheriff turned to Homans and Weaver. "You two want to come? You might not want to see."

Mal Homans replied immediately, "Yeah, I wouldn't miss it for the world. He killed ol' Jim, and Jim was practically my brother and he deserves whatever he got. He deserved it, and I want to see him in it."

Jack Weaver touched Homans on the shoulder, and said, "You go on. I don't want to see nothing. I'll wait here for the ambulance."

Homans glanced guiltily at the corpse of his brother-in-law; he had forgotten. "Yeah, I'd be mighty grateful, Jack, if you would. I just cain't bear looking at poor Jim."

Jack said nothing, and stood stiff armed against his truck while the sheriff, the deputy, and Mal Homans drove off.

A car drove up a few moments later, wanting gasoline, but Jack kept them back from the pumps and explained that there had been a terrible accident and that they would have to go on to the Shell station three miles up ahead. The two women inside demanded to know what sort of accident, but Weaver only shook his head.

The farmer then went inside the store and came out

MICHAEL McDOWELL

with a large piece of canvas with which he covered the
body of the slain man. He stood for a moment in the doorway, waiting for the ambulance, but when it failed to
come he moved briefly to the back of the store, opened the
door of the cooling room in the back, and stared at the
wall laden with the heads of his own slaughtered swine.
He recognized Louise, and made note that her jaw had
been ripped open. That seemed fitting.

He came out front when he heard the ambulance siren,
and while the undertaker and the coroner made themselves busy with the corpse of Jim Coltrane, Jack Weaver
told them what he knew of the motiveless murder. "And
you better put him over to one side, 'cause you got another stop to make over at Mr. Crane's." The coroner
and the undertaker looked up curiously. "And you better
take a couple of croker sacks, too, cause a stretcher is not
gone do you no good at all . . ." The farmer was not trying to be humorous.

Chapter 51

❊❊

On the short ride from Morris Emmons' store to Mr. Crane's farm, Sheriff Garrett questioned Mal Homans again on the possible motive for the unexpected murder. Homans again went over what had happened, and in the third telling, he mentioned the necklace that had fallen out of the sow's mouth. He also recalled that it was Dean Howell's wife who had been looking for it.

"That's just real peculiar," said the sheriff thoughtfully.

"Sure is," chimed in the deputy. "I never heard of nothing worth having coming out of pig's mouth before. They say sometimes you cut open a fish and find a ring that somebody throwed off a ship or something, but hardly nobody—and for sure nobody around here—throws jewelry in the pigpen."

"So, anyway," said Mal. "Jim and I put it 'round his neck, just making fun you know, calling him a goddamn hippie and like that, and he laughed, and then five minutes later he went and blew Jim to kingdom come, and I don't know why. I don't know why he took out after that dog like he did either—but better the dog than me."

Sheriff Garrett was puzzled by the motiveless crime and the subsequent death of Morris Emmons in the baling machine. He simply dismissed the part about the amulet as having nothing really of importance to do with the actual

243

fact of the murder. Morris Emmons, the sheriff considered, knew what a baling machine was; he knew how the damn thing worked, and he knew that you weren't, above all, supposed to jump inside it. The sheriff was as uncomfortable now as he had been last week, with the deaths of the Shirleys and the Simses.

Why had Emmons killed Jim Coltrane? Why had he killed himself? Why had he *not* killed Mal Homans? And Mal Homans, thought the sheriff, glancing in the rear-view mirror, had *not* been the more likable of the two.

Sheriff Garrett and Deputy Barnes did not enter Mr. Crane's barn happily. They had lost count of the number of maimed and disfigured corpses they had come across in the past week. It wasn't something that they had yet grown used to, and they hoped that they never would.

Garrett prodded the protruding foot with the handle of a shovel, and thought that investigation enough. He came back out into the sunlight, sweating not entirely from the heat, and prepared to wait for the coroner and the undertaker. "I think I'm just gone let them take care of this one," the sheriff said in an undertone to the two highway patrolmen. "I mean, I don't mind when they just get shot up, 'cause they're in one piece, and you can pick 'em up and throw 'em in the backseat if you have to, but I don't want to have to go around and start picking 'em up over all creation. You know what I mean?"

The two patrolmen nodded, and indicated that since there was nothing else really to be done, they might just go on off and share a couple of beers. It was early in the day for it, but staring at corpses made a man thirsty. And they might need it, just to get through the remainder of the afternoon.

The sheriff nodded and waved them off. While the deputy questioned Mal Homans again on everything that he had already said three times over, and attempted to give the farmer the impression that he was under suspicion for both deaths, the sheriff went over and talked to a number of the farm hands who had been witnesses to the dreadful accident.

The sheriff was best acquainted with Johnny Washington. This man had spent a couple of weeks in the diminutive Pine Cone jail, under indictment for second-degree murder, and the sheriff knew him for a trustworthy man. Johnny had seen the accident from above, and was able to tell the sheriff that Morris Emmons' death was entirely an accident, that the bird dog had pushed him off balance, and that, quite by accident, Morris had tipped over backward into the baling machine.

"I'm pleased to hear it," said the sheriff. " 'Cause that makes a lot more sense than him coming over the fields over here in order to do away with himself in somebody else's baling machine. Can't be a clean way to go, can't be easy to take, I don't imagine . . ."

"No, sir, Sheriff," said Johnny Washington, "I don't 'spect so."

The coroner and the undertaker arrived, and began cursing that this was going to be the most unpleasant job in a hectic week. While they went about their business, the sheriff tried to calm down Mr. Crane, who had come out complaining to the deputy and to Mal Homans about people committing suicide on his property without his permission, interrupting the business of the farm, destroying the machinery, giving the place a bad name and maybe even an evil spirit and so forth. He admitted without much prompting however that he had never cared for Morris Emmons much anyway.

When Morris Emmons had been gathered up in two great green-plastic trash bags, and set heavily inside the ambulance next to the body of the man that he had killed, the sheriff and the deputy drove Mal Homans back to his home.

"They find that necklace he was wearing?" asked Mal, when he could think of nothing else to say.

"They didn't say nothing about it," said the deputy. "And I didn't see nothing like it."

That was satisfactory to Mal, who didn't care anyway, but the sheriff considered, "I should have asked Johnny Washington about that. But I don't guess it really matters much. If Emmons had it on, then it probably got chewed up in that machine, and wouldn't be no good to nobody anymore. And if he didn't have it on, then it must have come off him, and somebody'll find it some time. But I just wonder how something belonging to Sarah Howell come to be in the mouth of the pig that killed Merle

Weaver. That don't hardly make more sense than why Morris Emmons went and killed Jim, does it?"

"Morris Emmons," said Mal Homans darkly, "couldn't take a joke."

Chapter 52

ოოოოოოოოოოოოოოოოოოოოოოოოოოოოოოოოოოო

THAT afternoon, at the very moment that the coroner
and the undertaker were wondering how on earth they
were going to arrange the remains of Morris Emmons in a
coffin, Sarah Howell was telling Becca Blair of her intention of badgering Jo Howell until she got at the truth
about the amulet.

"Good luck," said Becca significantly as they parted in
the driveway. "You call me if you need any help, and I'll
come a'running. You and me—we'll bolt her to the 'frig-
erator!"

Sarah smiled briefly, and then entered the house, determined to speak to Josephine Howell immediately about
the amulet, and about the dozen deaths it had precipi-
tated.

There was an unfamiliar noise in the house, a low-
pitched, muffled hum. Sarah walked directly through,
wondering what on earth it could be, and opened the
closed door of Dean's bedroom. She was met with a blast
of frigid air, and saw immediately that an enormous air
conditioner had been set in the back window. The machine operated at its maximum, very loudly blowing a gale
of icy air into the interior of the room. Jo sat placidly in
the plush chair at the foot of the bed; Dean lay beneath
the covers, only his bandaged head and neck stuck out

from under the blankets. It was an Alabama February in that room.

"Where'd that come from?" Sarah asked immediately, forgetting the amulet and her resolve in the surprise.

"I ordered it from Sears," said Jo. "They brought it today, and the man put it in for us."

"Well, that's just real nice. It's freezing in here, Jo. Who's going to pay for it?" Sarah was tight-lipped, sarcastic, and very angry.

"It got put on Dean's account," smiled Jo smugly.

"Who's going to pay for it?" demanded Sarah. "Dean can't pay no monthly payments. Dean couldn't stick a nickel in a parking meter if you gave him the nickel and tore the damn thing out of the curb and brought it in here to him!" Sarah was beside herself. There was no way in the world that they could afford an air conditioner. "Why'd you do it?" she demanded.

" 'Cause Dean was suffering in here. Burning up all the time. Suffering. Uncomfortable. He might have died in this heat with them bandages making him suffer like they do."

Sarah jerked back the covers on the bed. Dean's naked arms and chest were covered with goose bumps. "Jo," she cried, "he's freezing to death in this room."

"Well, cover him up. You shouldn't ought to let him get cold like that. He wouldn't be so cold if you hadn't pulled the covers down off him."

Sarah rolled her eyes, put the covers back up around Dean's neck. She went to the closet and pulled down from the top shelf a large pink comforter which she tossed over her husband's body.

"Jo," she said, "why don't you let me turn down this thing just a little bit?" She moved over toward the machine, which already had made her shiver, though she had only a minute before come in out of ninety-five-degree heat.

"No!" cried Jo. "You leave them controls alone! Dean's got to keep himself cool!"

"Dean's gone have ice in his veins you don't let me turn this thing down a little."

"Don't you do it, Sarah," her mother-in-law warned.

Sarah turned, and then said flatly, "You're right. I don't care if you both freeze to death in here. It's not gone be in here that long, 'cause they're gone come back and take it away, 'cause I'm not gone make the payments on it." She stared at Jo, and was glad to see that this had some effect on the woman.

"You *got* to pay for it," said Jo, with not so much strength as before, "it got bought in your name."

"The account's in Dean's name," said Sarah. "Dean's gone have to pay for it. I'm not. I don't have the money. If I had the money, I'd buy it for him. I'd buy him anything that he needed, or that I thought he wanted—but I don't have the money, and I'm not gone pay for it."

"Well," said Jo, "what about when the money comes from the army? Then you can pay for it. Dean's got to have it, Sarah."

"Dean hasn't got to have it, Jo. They didn't have the hospital at Rucca air-conditioned. He got along without it all these years, and he don't have to have it now. And when the money comes from the army, then it goes to pay the doctors and for the medicine and for the therapy, whenever we can get him started on that. If there's anything left over, then we can see about the air conditioner. We're gone have to see about getting a car too, 'cause there's gone be trips to the VA hospital in Pensacola. You can't go through the Sears catalogue, picking out your heart's desire, Jo, 'cause we just don't have the money."

Jo was silent, and Sarah knew that this once she had got the better of her mother-in-law, and she knew that she had won because she hadn't given in when Jo pricked at her about "not taking care of Dean like he should be." Sarah knew that she was doing all that she possibly could for Dean, that in fact, she was running herself into the ground for him. She would never allow Jo to goad her in that way again.

Sarah also realized that now was the best time to pursue her attack on the amulet. Without a pause, without even a heavy breath to betray her excitement, Sarah said, "Becca and I went out to the Weaver place this morning, went all through the pigpen looking for that amulet. Didn't find it."

"Why'd you think you would?" said Jo maliciously.

"Because," said Sarah, "that's where Miz Weaver dropped it. It fell out of her pocket. Mr. Weaver says that's why she got killed, went in the pen after it and the hogs attacked her. That's why he blames it on the amulet. He saw it happen."

"Looks to me like he ought to blame them hogs. They're the ones that did it. Killed her."

"Killed her and eleven other people, you mean."

"That's not what I mean," said Jo. "That's not what I said at all . . ."

"Now, listen to me, Jo Howell. There's twelve people dead in this town since yesterday was a week ago. That thing was there in every one of the cases—every single one. I know that for a fact."

"You cain't know," protested Jo.

"I *do* know. I saw you give it to Larry Coppage. Gussie found it under the bed the morning after Thelma killed James Shirley. I saw it round Dorothy Sims's neck 'fore she went and killed her husband. Jack Weaver saw his wife pick it up off the ground ten minutes 'fore she got done to death by them hogs. Twelve people's dead, and I just want to make sure that there's not any more. You understand? I don't want you and Dean to be responsible for no more bodies in Pine Cone."

"Why you think we're responsible for houses burning down, and wives killing their husbands and all, and pigs going on the rampage?"

"Because you gave Larry Coppage that thing, and that started it all off. And I got to know how it works. I got to know how it works, so I can stop it from doing any more damage."

"A amulet don't *work*, Sarah, it just sits there. It's got no moving parts, it's not like a watch. What can it do? You saw the thing. It was just a piece of metal with a chain on it. Got it from Montgomery Ward."

"I thought you said your cousin Bama gave it to you, back when you were little."

Jo hesitated, then replied, "I was thinking of something else. I got it out of the Montgomery Ward Christmas catalogue."

"Show me the catalogue, Jo. Show me where you ordered it, and I'll believe you."

"It was years ago. I don't keep catalogues."

"Well," said Sarah, "Becca does. I'm going over there

tonight and look through the Montgomery Ward catalogues and find where you bought it."

Jo stared hard at her daughter-in-law.

"I'm not gone find it, am I? It's not gone be in that catalogue, is it?"

"Well," said Jo, "I ordered it out of a Montgomery Ward catalogue—I *think* it was a Montgomery Ward catalogue—or it might have been one of them jewelry catalogues that we get from Mobile, maybe it was one of them. It was so long ago, I don't hardly remember which." She looked about the room uneasily.

"When did you order it?"

"I don't know," she said vaguely, "sometime 'fore you married Dean. I don't know exactly when."

"How much did you pay for it?"

"Four ninety-eight."

"That all?"

"I couldn't afford no more."

"Why'd you want it?"

Jo twisted uncomfortably in her chair. "I don't see why I'm supposed to answer all these fool questions. I didn't have nothing to do with them people dying. I gave Larry Coppage this piece of jewelry that I didn't have no use for no more." She paused, then added suddenly, "I gave it to him, 'cause one time Rachel Coppage was over here, and I was wearing it, and she said she liked it. So when Larry Coppage come over here, I thought I'd give it to him, 'cause I didn't wear it no more, and Rachel had said she wanted one like it. What she did with it after I give it to her is no business of mine. If she wanted to run right out and give it to Thelma Shirley that's all right with me. I give it to her, and she could do with it whatever she wanted to."

Sarah knew that Jo had made this story up on the spur of the moment, and she knew too that if she continued to question the woman about it, Jo would only make the lie more elaborate. She wanted to cut through all that.

"I don't care about that. I still got to know how it works, what makes people die that get hold of it. Why didn't you die, for instance?"

Jo shrugged. "I think all this is crazy. I don't know why you so worried about that thing. It's got no moving parts.

251

It just hangs there. Even if you got it back, you couldn't get your money back for it. Those places in Mobile don't give refunds, you know."

Sarah shook her head in frustration and walked out of the room. She hadn't found out what she wanted to know, but she had made progress. Jo was on the defensive, and she had admitted that it was the same amulet that had appeared in all the deaths and no longer maintained that there was more than one. Sarah only hoped she found out the rest before someone else died. She dared not trust that the thing was buried forever in the mud of Jack Weaver's pigpen.

Chapter 53

❧❧❧❧❧❧❧❧❧❧❧❧❧❧❧❧❧❧❧❧❧❧❧❧❧❧❧❧❧❧❧❧❧❧

Iᴛ was almost six o'clock on Thursday afternoon. The undertaker and the coroner were drunk, and still had not decided what to do about Morris Emmons' fragmented body. Sarah Howell had begun to fix Dean's supper. She was still angry about the air conditioner and hadn't decided yet whether to make anything for Jo or not. On the other side of Commercial Boulevard, a fifteen-year-old black girl sat in the kitchen of the house belonging to Mildred and Graham Taylor, watching after the two Taylor children, little Graham, about three, and his brother Ralph, who had just passed his first year. Audrey Washington was a skinny, slightly haughty girl, but extremely good with children. She came over to the Taylor house each afternoon after school, and kept the boys so that Mildred could go out and run the day's errands. This afternoon Audrey was anxious, for Miz Taylor had promised her that she would be able to leave by five-forty-five, but the woman had not yet returned from shopping.

Nervously glancing at the clock above the stove, Audrey crooned to the infant in her arms, who dozed peacefully. Little Graham was playing quietly beneath the table with a set of square wooden blocks.

Audrey was surprised by a knock at the back door. She rose slowly, trying not to disturb the baby, and stepped onto the latticed back porch. Out here, a radio played

253

MICHAEL MCDOWELL

country music softly and the washing machine had just begun its second washing cycle. Audrey rocked the child in her arms, and continued to sing as she kicked the back door open. She was very much surprised to see that it was her father on the back steps. She glanced at him with annoyance, and peered down the driveway to make sure that Mrs. Taylor was not in sight.

"Daddy," Audrey said, "what you doing here? You know Miz Taylor don't like to find you here . . ."

Audrey's father, Johnny Washington, was a good man, but he had been involved in a fight two years back in which another man had been killed—the victim was Johnny's brother-in-law. Johnny stood trial and was acquitted, but Mrs. Taylor still didn't like to have the man around her house, even though it had been her husband Graham who had defended him.

"Audrey," her father said, "they was a accident out at the farm, Mr. Crane's place . . ."

"What happened?" cried Audrey, "was you hurt?" Then she glanced at her father sternly. "D'you hurt anybody?" Her father, even though let off, had been guilty of the crime two years before. Audrey continued to rock the baby slowly in her arms.

Johnny Washington shook his head meaningfully. "No, sir, I sure didn't. But you should have seen it, Audrey! Mr. Emmons what owns the store where we buys drinks at dinnertime, Mr. Emmons done went right out of his head, start chasing round this bird dog right through the peanuts waving a gun all 'round him, and then jumped right in the baler! Come right in the barn and jumped in the baler, and is got parts of his head and his shirt spread out over all creation out there! You never saw nothing like it in your life! I was up top in the barn, scared for the life of me he was gone take me for that bird dog and shoot my legs off!"

"Ohhhh!" cried Audrey, "but he didn't get you, did he? He didn't aim at you or nothing did he?"

"Nope!" her father exclaimed. "Didn't see me, didn't *let* him see me! Nearly got hit with flying teeth and things though—nearly got hit . . ." he repeated.

Audrey sighed dramatically, in relief for her father's safety, but then she quickly cautioned him, "Daddy, Miz

254

The Amulet

Taylor's right now on her way back here, and you know she don't want to find you here."

Johnny's wife had died five years before and Audrey had been their only child. Audrey, though young, had stood valiantly by her father during the time of his incarceration and trial, and he knew that Graham Taylor would never have defended him at all—much less for a fee of only fifty dollars—if Audrey hadn't begged the man (her employer then too) to help her father. In that difficult time Audrey had cared for her father, and gained some ascendancy over him. They both had come to believe that it was only because of Audrey's constant watchfulness that Johnny was kept out of trouble. Johnny was very thankful for what Audrey did for him, seeing that he got employment in the fields, seeing that he didn't spend all of his paycheck on whiskey, seeing that income tax and welfare forms got filled out and filed properly, seeing that the house was kept in good order. Every night Johnny asked his daughter if she was planning on leaving home, because maybe she found him just too much trouble to bother with, and every night Audrey replied, "When you get to be too much trouble for me, Daddy, you'll know it, 'cause I won't be here no more." And that satisfied the man until the next evening.

"I brought you this," Johnny Washington said, and fished the amulet out of his pants pocket. He dangled it before her a moment; Audrey stared at it, and then reached out and took it from him.

"What is it?" she demanded.

"You s'posed to put it on your neck, I s'pose," he replied.

Audrey swung it before little Ralph's face. The baby reached for the piece. Thoughtfully the black girl said, "That's real sweet, Daddy, but where'd you get hold of this? I was in Woolworth's yesterday, and I didn't see nothing like it. And I *know* that jewelry counter!"

Her father did not answer her.

"All right if people see me wearing it, Daddy?" she inquired suspiciously. "I don't want to get in no trouble 'cause of a little necklace, and I got no kind of sales slip for it . . ."

"It's all right, Audrey, it's all right, I think."

255

Audrey pulled the amulet out of the reach of little Ralph.

"Put it under your dress for the next couple of weeks or so, that's all," her father cautioned, as an afterthought.

Audrey smiled knowingly. "Thanks a lot, Daddy," she said. "Now, you better go on home, and I'll be there 'fore long. Miz Taylor don't want to find you here, and I want her to be back here any minute now."

Audrey's father nodded, and turned to go. Audrey let the door slam shut behind him, and latched it. Then she moved down to the end of the latticed porch to the washing machine. She opened the top and made sure that the clothes were being agitated properly and that the water level was correct. Miz Taylor had had trouble with the appliance in the last month and had asked Audrey to keep a sharp eye on it. Audrey sang a little formless tune with incomprehensible words to the infant in her arms, and stared at sheets and pillowcases being sloshed around at a furious rate.

Audrey set the baby carefully down in a pile of folded laundry in a great wicker basket set beside the washing machine, and then examined the amulet for a moment. In the dim light of the back porch she could not see the catch, but she figured she must have pressed it, for the chain came apart in her hands. She held it around her neck and pressed the ends of the chain together and they caught—though she still could feel nothing but the two unbroken links at either end. She stared down at the amulet, wishing she had a mirror handy; well, she could go look in the mirror that was in the dining room.

She reached down to pick up the baby, and found to her acute dismay that little Ralph had wet not only himself but also the freshly washed blouse of Miz Taylor's directly beneath him. This infuriated Audrey, for she knew that Miz Taylor would jump down her throat for it. That stupid baby couldn't hold himself for twenty seconds, that stupid baby wasn't any better than his fool brother had been. She'd like to take that baby home for a month, and then she'd whack it into some kind of shape. White people didn't know what to do with a baby. They thought you ought to stop it from crying, no matter what you had to do for it, but Audrey figured that the best thing was to make it remember for a long, long time when it had done something bad. Well, this baby had just done something terrible. Audrey reached down and snatched the blouse out from underneath the baby, who tumbled over in the basket, gasping in surprise. She plunged the article into the washing machine, even though it was the wrong cycle for such clothing—and told herself she didn't care if the thing was torn to shreds. Little Ralph had banged his head against the side of the basket, and set up a dismal howl. That noise drove through Audrey's skull, and she cried, "Damn you, baby! Damn you to hell for that!" She picked the infant up and shook it, so that its head rattled on top of its pudgy shoulders.

And when she returned to the kitchen a few moments later, Audrey no longer bore the slight burden of the year-old Ralph Taylor.

Chapter 54

Mrs. Taylor pulled up into the driveway of her home, a little flurried; she had promised Audrey that she could leave by five-forty-five, and it was well past that time now. Audrey was a good girl, and Mrs. Taylor trusted her with the children, so she liked to treat Audrey as well as possible. It wasn't the girl's fault, after all, that her father was a killer (even though Graham had got him off for lack of evidence), and so long as the man didn't come around along with his daughter, everything was all right.

There were four great bags of groceries in the backseat of the car; she ought not to have gone to the store right at five-thirty, for that was when all the women from the munitions plant went as well, and there were great lines at the check-out counters. Mrs. Taylor got out of the car, and called toward the kitchen window, "Audrey! You come on out here! I need some help!"

Mrs. Taylor opened the back door of the car, and lifted one of the heavier bags into her arms, and turned toward the house. Audrey had not come out, so Mrs. Taylor called again. "Audrey!" she cried, and walked to the back door. She supposed that the girl was in the far part of the house, perhaps with the baby in his room. She tried to pull open the latticed door, but found to her surprise that it was latched on the inside.

"Audrey!" she called again. "Come unhook the door!

This bag is heavy, girl!" She shifted the weight in her arms and waited a moment; it was then that she heard clearly, for the first time, the terrible racket that the washing machine was making, rocking from side to side as if with a greatly unbalanced load of heavy clothing, or rugs, even.

Mrs. Taylor stamped her foot with impatience. What had become of that girl? She had hooked the back door, she was letting the washing machine get away from her—and Mrs. Taylor had specifically warned her about the machine—and for all she knew, Audrey might even have left the dishes from dinner! She feared for a moment that Audrey might have gone off just at five-forty-five, locking the two children inside, but reassured herself that Audrey, young though she was, was much more responsible than that, and would never leave the two children alone for a minute.

Again Mrs. Taylor shifted her weight, and listened with some little alarm to the violent rumblings from the washing machine on the porch inside. She glanced down toward the kitchen window, to see if she could catch sight of Audrey inside; but what she saw frightened her severely. She screamed loudly, and threw down the bag of groceries, so that cartons of milk and eggs broke open, and spilled out onto the back steps. The washing machine had overflowed and water was pouring underneath the latticework and onto the plants that bordered the house; but the suds from the machine were red—red like blood.

Mrs. Taylor flew down the steps, slipping in the spilled liquid and kicking cans out of her way, and ran over to the side of the house. She cupped her hands beneath the liquid. It *was* blood, blood mixed with soap. Again she screamed, and frantically attempted to wipe it away on her dress.

Inside the house, Audrey was humming soft and low in the kitchen. Mrs. Taylor's calls were plainly to be heard, and the child Graham looked up at Audrey inquisitively, wondering why she did not respond.

Audrey took up a large butcher knife from the rack of drying dishes by the sink, and walked with it out onto the back porch. There the washing machine was rocking violently from side to side, almost shaking off its concrete-

MICHAEL McDOWELL

block foundation; the crimson suds flowed in lugubrious
pulses from underneath the lid. There was a great slippery
pool of dyed water in the middle of the porch, through
which Audrey had to go to get to the back door.

But the thin film of soap on top of the pool caused the
young black girl to slip as she was reaching for the latch
on the back door, and she fell backward against a shelf
on the wall. The radio dropped to the floor and smashed
open.

Audrey lay full-length in the pool of blood and soapy
water. Her slick shoe heels would not catch against the
painted floor, and she could not immediately get up. She
rolled over on her stomach and was raising herself on all
fours, when she inadvertently placed her hand swiftly
down on the blade of the butcher knife. Her wrist was
sliced open, and the blood began to flow prodigiously
from the wound. Audrey scurried to raise herself, and
unthinkingly grabbed hold of the electrical cord of the
radio to pull herself up with, but this had been pulled
from the appliance, and was live with electricity. She was
stunned into unconsciousness, and in only a couple of
minutes had bled herself beyond the hope of recovery.

Mrs. Taylor went again to the back steps and began to
pound on the door. Now more blood—thicker, darker,
less diluted with water—began to flow out over the edges
of the porch. Again Mrs. Taylor set up a round of screams,
and ran around the other side of the house. She was on
her way to the front door, but stopped at the kitchen
window and peered inside. There, she could see her three-
year-old son little Graham playing with a great bloody
butcher knife, trying to carve up one of his wooden blocks.

Hysterically, his mother screamed at him, "Graham,
you put that thing *down* 'fore you cut yourself! You hear
me! You put it down!!"

Chapter 55

❦❦❦❦❦❦❦❦❦❦❦❦❦❦❦❦❦❦❦❦❦❦❦❦❦❦❦

SARAH did fix Jo her dinner that night, but the two women, sitting across from one another at the tiny breakfast table in the kitchen, spoke hardly a word. And those few words that did pass between them had nothing to do with the amulet or the air conditioner. Sarah cleared the table, and said, "I'm going over to Becca's now. We're gone look through some old catalogues, I think."

Jo sat very still and said nothing, but she glowered a monstrous frown, and her eyes disappeared into their sockets.

Sarah shrugged and walked out the door without another word. Why mollify a woman who had, in effect, murdered a dozen people?

Sarah and Becca went through seven years' of Montgomery Ward's and Sears' catalogues, but found no item that resembled the amulet. Becca was not on the mailing list of the wholesale jewelry houses in Mobile, and had none of those books.

Sarah sighed when she closed the cover of the last and oldest catalogue, "I didn't think we'd find it anyway. The first time Jo talked about it, she said her cousin gave it to her just years and years ago, and I think she made it all up about the Montgomery Ward catalogue, trying to confuse me."

"Well," said Sarah, "what do we do now?"

MICHAEL MCDOWELL

Becca shrugged and looked away. Sarah could tell that her friend was thinking of something, but she did not prod.

"I tell you what," said Becca after a few moments, in a low, cautious voice, "I think we're gone try the wee-gee board." Sarah started to protest; she knew how much Becca feared the thing. But Becca held up her hand, and shook her head. "It's not gone be as bad as all that. Besides, this whole town has had bad luck, and we ought to do what we can to stop it. We're just gone be real careful, that's all . . ."

"How do we do that?" asked Sarah curiously.

Becca didn't know, and therefore didn't answer; but she went to the closet and brought down the set. They placed the board between them on the kitchen table, and Becca took the suddenly inspired precaution of sprinkling the planchette with holy water taken from a bottle in the pantry placed next to the vanilla extract.

"Shouldn't we turn down the lights? Or maybe we should do it in the living room or something," suggested Sarah, who thought that Becca's brightly lighted—even garish—kitchen provided insufficient atmosphere.

Becca shook her head. "Don't need it, don't want it. Spirits come crowding down thick enough as it is. Don't want to *draw* 'em in here with setting the place up spooky and all. And I wouldn't do this if Margaret was here, but she isn't. She's too young to fool around with this kind of thing. I wouldn't want nothing to happen to Margaret 'cause of a wee-gee board."

"How do we do it?" asked Sarah, a little impatiently. She didn't believe it would work, but then, she didn't believe in the amulet either.

Becca instructed Sarah to place two fingers of one hand on the planchette, while she did the same. "Now we ask it a question, just a little everyday something, something we don't care about. Then we just sit, and this thing starts moving around, pointing at letters and numbers and so on, and that's the answer to the question. Sort of. Sometimes. You write down what the thing points to, to keep a record, 'cause spirits don't spell remarkable. You got to ask things you don't care about first, so that it's got time to know what you're like, and to gather the spirits 'round the board, I guess. 'Cause they're out there, just waiting for a chance to say something to us. Sometimes they don't answer the questions that you're asking, and they just start talking to you, and that's when you got to stop it, right then and there, 'cause if you don't, you gone find out things you don't want to know."

Sarah nodded, and Becca continued, for in dealing with so dangerous a device as the Ouija board, too much instruction was barely enough to protect against the evil spirits that were able to speak through the little pointed wooden tongue that moved about on the brightly painted board. "You not supposed to laugh, but I don't hardly need to say that, 'cause after the first five minutes, don't nobody laugh no more. Sometimes it works, sometimes it don't. When it don't, you cain't make it work. And you don't need to try to push the thing, 'cause it just goes by itself. When I was first doing it, I used to try to push it— just a little—to send it where I wanted it to go, and I couldn't do it. I'd send it off to the *H* and it would head right for the *M,* and it spelled out *M-I-K-E,* even though I didn't want it to. And then I went and married the man, and that was the worst luck that I ever did have in the whole of my life! So you don't have to push it."

Sarah shuddered. She had never done this before, and she couldn't conceive that the strange little board before her, with the two crescents of alphabetic letters, the row of numbers, the *Yes* and the *No,* and the small wooden triangle were anything but a gift for a child born on Halloween. It certainly wasn't as dangerous- or evil-looking as the Pine Cone rifles that passed before her on the assembly line every day.

"I'm ready then," said Sarah. "What do we ask it first?"

"Well," replied Becca, "like I said, something that don't matter. Like, 'What day of the week will my next date be on?' "

Sarah laughed, but Becca held up a warning finger. "Don't giggle now. This is serious, or we not gone find out anything, and we gone get the bad luck to boot. Now you look here, this board's special, 'cause it's got the days of the week on it, up there at the top, and most of 'em don't. I still wish you hadn't given me this thing. Now, Sarah, we got to be serious."

Becca dropped her hands into her lap, and closed her eyes briefly; when she opened them again, her face was blank and solemn. She looked like a snapshot of herself taken at a bad moment. This made Sarah even more jittery but she closed her eyes and in a few moments, when she had calmed a little, she opened them again.

Becca stared vacantly at the buttons on the front of Sarah's blouse, and she said, "When will I have my next date?"

The two women raised their hands out of their laps, and placed two fingers each on the planchette. It stood still a moment, and then moved irresolutely among the letters of the alphabet. In a few seconds, it had rested on the circle which denoted *Yes*.

Sarah thought that this made no sense, for the planchette ought to have headed for one of the days of the week. Becca was unperturbed. "What night of the week will I have my next date?"

Their fingers, which had been lifted from the planchette when it came to rest, they dropped down again, and the wooden piece struggled, this time stopping above the number *4* .

"That's next Saturday," said Becca when she lifted her fingers. "Saturday's the fourth."

"Have you got a date then?"

"Don't know yet for sure. Jimmy Mack Jones was talking to me yesterday about something next Saturday night, but he didn't made no commitment, really, so I don't really know yet for sure. Wrestling in Opp or something like that. I'll see him tomorrow, and then I'll find out."

Sarah was impressed, but she did not comment for fear of breaking the spell. Three more questions were asked, of an equally innocuous nature, and the Ouija board answered in either an ambiguous or senseless manner. Becca wasn't sure that they were getting through.

"We gone try one more time, and if it don't work, this thing goes back up in the closet for a good long while. All right then, here's the question: 'What's Margaret doing right now?' "

The two women placed their fingers on the planchette, and slowly it moved from one corner of the board directly toward the letters on the far side. It stopped dead on the letter *M* and then moved suddenly again to the letter *L* next to it.

Sarah was very much surprised, for before the planchette had seemed to waver all the while, to be unsure of itself, but now there was no question but that *M* and *L* were the letters intended. It was as if they had only been playing around before, but now that the board had been threatened with its removal, the planchette moved in earnest.

"*M-L*," said Becca, after a moment. "That's Mary-Louise, and that's where Margaret is tonight."

The planchette moved suddenly to the other end of the board, pulling their fingers across so suddenly the muscles knotted in Sarah's upper arm with the strain of maintaining so light a touch on the wood. *N*, then across to *E*, then to *L*—and Sarah suddenly removed her fingers.

Becca glanced at her reproachfully. "It was gone write out Nelson."

"I know," whispered Sarah, and trembled. She had not wanted to see the board spell it out with such hideous ease. She knew that none of the movement in the planchette was of her volition, and she was frightened.

"Do you know about the amulet?" Becca asked sharply, and in so matter-of-fact a tone of voice that Sarah thought the question was intended for her. Their fingers were on the planchette, which trembled slightly and then moved first to the figure *1* and then to *6*, and then stopped. Sarah pushed, but it would not move.

"Sixteen," said Becca. "I think it means twelve, twelve people killed so far. Is that what you mean?" said Becca, again in the matter-of-fact voice. Once again the planchette moved; Sarah tried to push it toward the letters, away from the *Yes*, but it moved only one figure over, to the *7*, paused, then *2*, danced a little circle and returned to the *2*, then over to *1*, and then—though Sarah was desperate to remove her fingers altogether—the planchette dived straight again to the *2*, moved away, and then returned resolutely to the same figure. Sarah trembled as she recorded the figures on the back of an envelope: 7 2 2 1 2 2.

"They add up to sixteen," said Becca, and Sarah nodded reluctantly.

"The seven is the Coppages," said Sarah.

Becca nodded thoughtfully. "And the first two is the Shirleys and then the Simses and then poor ol' Miz Weaver. But they was two more two's, and there's not nobody else dead."

Sarah shivered violently. "Nobody we know of. Becca, you think this means there's four people dead we don't even know about yet?"

Becca shook her head. "We would have heard, don't you think? Pine Cone's not that big, you cain't just go and cover up for people being dead, even when they been dying like they have this week. As it is, there's bodies just right in the streets, seems like."

"Can we ask it anything else?"

"Sure. That's why we're here. If there's gone be bad luck, we already brought it down, so we might as well find out what we can."

"Ask 'em if that was right. There're really sixteen people dead because of the amulet."

Becca did so, and immediately the planchette began the sequence again, but in reverse: *2 2 1 2 2 7.* Sarah lifted her fingers so quickly that the planchette skidded across the board.

"That answers the question," said Becca with a little irritation. "You ought not be so jumpy, Sarah. Don't want 'em to start lying to us."

"They lie?" She was almost hopeful.

Becca shrugged. "Who knows what they do? I don't like this, but we're doing it, and we might as well do it right."

Sarah was surprised and troubled by Becca's hardness in all of this.

"Ask 'em," said Sarah, and paused, "ask 'em where it came from."

The planchette didn't wait for Becca to put the question: it moved quickly, but with a certain lurch it had not had before, and spelled out *D E N I J O Z A F A N A N A N A N,* and looked to be stuck between the *A* and the *N* just below it, until the two women, puzzled and troubled, raised their fingers.

"I tell you what it looks like," said Becca. "It looks like Dean and Josephine and somebody getting strangled."

Sarah sighed heavily, not that there wasn't more specific information, but that all that she had feared was being confirmed. And now she had begun to fear this board as well.

"What else?" demanded Becca of her friend.

Sarah's mouth was grim. "Who's next?"

Both expected that the planchette would move, but there was not even a quiver. Sarah pushed a little, but the wooden triangle did not budge.

"Who's next?" repeated Becca sternly.

Now the planchette moved, unsteadily and slowly, spelling out: *A N R A B U A N N R B R Y.*

Sarah was nervous, and all the concentration on the board, after a good hour and a half poring over the catalogues, had enervated her. "That don't make no sense."

Becca shrugged. "See if you can make something out of it. Looks sort of like Robert and maybe Andrew. The thing about the wee-gee board, Sarah, is that it don't spell real good, and sometimes you got to use your imagination. I mean the spirits aren't moving the thing around themselves, they're on the inside of our brains, telling our fingers what to do, without our fingers knowing what's going on, and they probably don't have complete control, you know what I mean. I mean, it's like they got a stutter or something . . ."

Sarah nodded. She was nervous, and didn't know whether she wanted to go on with this at all. It was a painted piece of wood, and how could it tell the future? How could it know about Dean and Jo? How could it tell who was going to die next? But their questions were being answered. She wanted to stop, she—"How many more are there going to be?" she gasped, and wondered where the question had come from. It hadn't been in her mind.

The planchette wavered, swung around the numbers without pausing, and then returned to the alphabet where it spelled out *B A K A B L E R K A B L A R.*

"Well," sighed Becca and sat back, "I think that's about it. It's just doing nonsense. I don't think we're gone get anything more out of it tonight."

Sarah stood up hastily. "Honey, thank you so much. It was exciting, real exciting." Becca looked at her friend strangely; it wasn't like Sarah to depart precipitously. And she was acting as if the whole thing had been a game, and Becca knew her friend well enough to know that she had been very much troubled. "It's late," Sarah faltered, "I got to get back and make sure Dean's all right. I'll see you in the morning."

"We could wait a few minutes and try again," suggested Becca, but Sarah shook her head emphatically.

"No, no, no. I probably just don't have the knack for it. It's probably never gone work for me, and right now, I'm dead on my feet." She hurried out the door. Becca stood on the back steps, and stared after her friend. Then she returned inside to put up the Ouija board and the planchette, and only then did she notice that Sarah had taken the envelope on which they had transcribed the messages that had been indicated on the board. Becca shrugged, and with only the tiniest shiver, put the board back into the closet.

Sarah Howell went directly into her husband's bedroom and turned on the dresser lamp. She was alone in the room with Dean, but after glancing at him briefly, she ignored him. She smoothed out the crumpled envelope, which she had secreted in her closed fist, and stared at the last set of letters, *B A K A B L E R K A B L A R*, that had appeared as the nonsensical answer to the question of how many more deaths. She drew three slashes to divide the letters, thus, BAKA/BLER/KA/BLAR, and could see nothing but her friend's name—Becca Blair— written out twice.

Chapter 56

PINE Cone, Alabama, was not a large town, but it was sizable enough for two mortuaries, one catering to the white population and the other to the black. This was still only a few years after the great Civil Rights legislation and there were many institutions, many customs in the Deep South which remained segregated at this time. Congress had not even stated at the time that undertakers must accept the dead of any race, and so, as had been the custom in the past, corpses of different skin colors were kept separate.

The black and white morticians were not in direct competition since their perspective customers were already slated to take the service of one or the other, and so it was not with any great envy that Washington Garver counted the number of white people who had died in Pine Cone in the last couple of weeks. The white undertaker had even had to come to him and purchase a casket in which to bury one victim but he had taken the merchandise away in the middle of the night—so that no one would know that the farmer was to be buried in a "Negro" coffin.

The black community in Pine Cone did not number above a thousand persons, and that included babies who had not even yet been given a name. Washington Garver was therefore almost sure to know any corpse that he laid

out and embalmed; that made even sadder a profession
that was not known for its cheer.

The Silver Pine Funerary Home was not so grandiose
as its name, but was merely a one-story house of eight
rooms that Washington Garver had set up business in.
One room he had saved for himself, and another for his
son Roosevelt, who assisted him in the business, but all
the other areas of the house were given over to the preparation of the corpses, and the holding of services.

A large addition to the back of the house, adjacent to
a screened driveway, was where the corpses were brought
by the ambulance, by the police, by the family; and it was
here that the bodies were drained of their blood, and in-
jected with fluid that would preserve them through a
funeral in July. This room was cluttered with tables and
shelves holding chemicals, with surgical instruments that
never wanted sterilization, with racks of clothing, and
boxes of makeup and perfumes. It was nearly always
decorated with flowers—chrysanthemums and carnations
mostly—smelling of florists' coolers.

Washington Garver was a large man with shining black
skin and a wheezing voice; he stood at the foot of one of
these embalming tables now. He was having some difficulty in pulling the shoes off the corpse of Audrey. The
pool of blood and water in which she had lain had swollen
her flesh and shrunk the leather.

A bright white lamp directly over the girl's body was
the only illumination in the room; every crack in her skin,
every speck of dried blood upon her damp dress was
clearly visible, but all the edges and corners of the room
and the things that were stored there were invisible in the
surrounding darkness.

A young black man, not much more than eighteen, and
looking much too young to be doing this sort of thing, was
cutting through Audrey's wet dress with a pair of scissors.
Her body was already stiff, and since the dress was ruined
anyway, there didn't seem much point in trying to salvage
it.

Washington Garver finally succeeded in getting the
shoes off Audrey, and quickly he pulled off her socks as
well; these he tossed into a large box that rested by the
side of the door. They would be given to the black Baptist

church ladies' group, who would discreetly mend and clean the items, and then distribute them through the community, never letting on that they had belonged to the homicidal baby-sitter.

Washington Garver spoke to his son, who was very carefully peeling the dress from the corpse. "Real bad what this girl done, Roosevelt, and I feel bad for her daddy, real bad. He was in trouble, you 'member, 'bout killing somebody, and he got out of trouble. Audrey would've been in trouble too, if she'd have lived, but now Audrey's out of trouble forever. Ain't gone be no jury for her, Roosevelt."

"Why you think she'd do it, do something like that?" Roosevelt Garver stared a moment into the face of the corpse, as if he thought he might read an answer to the question there.

"Just a accident, I reckon, Roosevelt, just a accident, but I still think it was real bad."

"Well, Pa," said Roosevelt, "it can't have been no accident, not putting a white baby in the washing machine, and then killing herself with a butcher knife *and* a electrical plug."

"Had to be a accident," Washington reiterated. "Black people don't kill white chil'ren. Black folks don't kill theirselves either. Black folks only kill their family and their friends. It's the white people that kill just anybody. Only the white people do that." Washington Garver shook his head sadly over this melancholy reflection.

The doorbell rang, and Roosevelt looked up. "You better get it. I probably smell of her, and if it's her father there, he'll smell her on me, and that'll make him feel bad."

Washington nodded, and walked out of the room. While his father went to get the door, Roosevelt cut Audrey's slip in half, from the bottom to the top, and pulled it open. When he did so, a necklace slid off her breast and onto the floor at his feet. He glanced down at the floor but could not see it. He stooped to retrieve it, feeling all around beneath the table, and in a few seconds brought it up to the light.

It looked expensive, not the sort of thing that a fifteen year-old black girl would have when she was just about to commit murder. The chain was still hooked—and that was strange. If Audrey had been wearing it around her neck, then it would have had to come unhooked to fall off the way it did. And if she hadn't been wearing it around her neck, why was she keeping it in her dress like that? It was just possible that she had stolen it, Roosevelt thought.

After all, he considered, a girl who was capable of throwing a baby into a washing machine was certainly not above taking a piece of jewelry off a white woman's dresser. He stared at the necklace a moment longer, lifted his head at the sound of his father's footsteps, and then thrust the amulet into his pants pockets.

Washington Garver entered the embalming room. "It was Audrey's daddy," he said. "I told him to sit out on the front porch till we're done. There wasn't no sense in letting him see her like this."

Roosevelt nodded his head in agreement.

Chapter 57

JOHNNY Washington sat on the front porch of the Silver Pine Funerary Home, rocking disconsolately in a caneback chair. It was the middle of the evening, not much past nine o'clock, and Johnny had just brought over the choir robe in which his daughter was to be buried. He had seen Audrey's body when the ambulance brought it to the funeral home, and Johnny was disturbed that his daughter had appeared so ill-content in death. The dead ought to lie peaceably and calm. But even motionless as she was, Audrey appeared sullen and nervous. Johnny had asked that the coffin be closed during the service. But the undertaker replied, "Not no need, Johnny. No marks on her 'cept the butcher knife cut on her wrist. We gone cross her hands, palm down, and not nobody gone see it, 'less they lift up her hand—and who's gone do that?"

The evening was warm, and bullfrogs in a ditch nearby croaked loudly, trying to drown out the crickets. Johnny Washington sat and rocked, and tried to think of nothing at all. An old black man came down the sidewalk presently, saw Audrey's father there, and called out to him in a friendly voice.

"Hey, Johnny, what you doing here?"

Dolefully, Johnny replied, "They got Audrey inside."

"Oh, I'm sorry," said the old man, "I'm just *sorry* for you, Johnny Washington."

273

Shortly thereafter, Johnny Washington got up from his chair and descended the steps of the mortuary. On the sidewalk he met a young girl, not much older than Audrey had been. He would have passed on by, but she stopped him.

"It's Ruby, Mr. Washington," she said. "I heard about Audrey, and I just want to tell you how bad I feel about it, how *bad*."

"Thank you, Ruby," said Johnny.

"We wasn't close, you know, Audrey and me, but that's no reason why I shouldn't feel bad for you, and that's no reason why I shouldn't go in that house right now and do her hair up right for the service." Ruby was a beautician, and a capable one. She had been Roosevelt Garver's girlfriend for two years and so it was she who got all the business of fixing the hair of female corpses. It was not a task that she was particularly fond of, but Roosevelt always stayed by her and she was never alone with the body, so that it wasn't too bad. And she was well paid for her services.

Ruby was subdued when she spoke to Johnny Washington, but normally she was energetic and voluble. She stood at the top of the steps to the Silver Pine Funerary Home and watched the bereaved father disappear around the corner. Then she knocked on the door, and presently Roosevelt appeared. Instead of letting her into the house, he came out onto the porch, and led her to the swing at one end of it. He wanted to spend a little time with Ruby in the dark before they started in again on Audrey, readying her for the service the next day. He was about to tell Ruby just how tired he was, but she didn't give him the chance.

"I heard *ever'thing*," she gasped, "right thirty minutes after she done it, and I knew they'd be bringing her right here. Didn't wait for you to call me over. Lying in that blood and them soapsuds, gone be a real mess, and I know it's gone take me a hour and three-quarter to get her hair done. Audrey," she whispered, "wouldn't come to me to get her hair done, she'd go 'cross the tracks to Marjorie, 'cause she's cheap. Her daddy's a cheap man, wouldn't give her no money, wouldn't hardly let her keep what she earned for herself over at the Taylors—and I bet the Taylors are sorry now they ever gave that girl a dime, after what she did to that baby. Her daddy's a cheap man, and I bet she's only gone get a pine coffin out of him."

"Cedar," Roosevelt sighed.

"Well," said Ruby, unabashed, "I tell you, right now I am *glad* she didn't come to my place, 'cause I don't want to do the hair of people what's gone go out and put white babies in washing machines."

"If white people gone spend their money on washing machines," said Roosevelt sententiously, "then that's what they got to expect . . ."

Ruby laughed shrilly, then stopped short, and whispered: "But I am *glad* that I'm gone get to do Audrey's hair, 'cause it will serve her right! Serve her right for going 'cross the tracks when I was right there 'cross the street from where she lived and if she would have walked ten steps out of her way she could have looked at me through my own picture window. She thought I wasn't good enough to do her hair, but now she don't have no choice. She gone look real good in the church tomorrow."

"Service gone be held here," said Roosevelt.

"Why? 'Cause she murdered that baby? Her daddy's not never gone be able to look a washing machine in the face again!"

Ruby's nonstop conversation wearied Roosevelt as much as working on a corpse, so he asked, "You ready to go in, Ruby?"

"Your daddy through with her yet?"

"I think so," said Roosevelt.

"Don't you help him no more?" asked Ruby, with a little friendly sarcasm. "Lazybones!"

"I'd rather sit out here with you."

"Um-hmh," said Ruby with a doubting smile, but she was evidently pleased with the compliment.

"I got something for you, Ruby," said Roosevelt slyly.

"Ohhh?" she cried, "what you got for me, Roosevelt?"

Roosevelt pulled the amulet from his pocket and dangled it before Ruby's eyes. It glinted softly in the distant light of a streetlamp.

"Where'd that come from?" said Ruby.

Roosevelt did not answer her.

"Lot of colored people got to be dead in this town, 'fore you can afford something like that for me, Roosevelt Garver."

"Didn't cost me nothing," said Roosevelt.

After a pause, Ruby leaned over and whispered harshly in her boyfriend's ear, "You got that thing off Audrey!"

Roosevelt nodded slowly.

Ruby drew back, and whistled loudly. "And you are giving it to me?" she squealed.

Roosevelt knew Ruby. He smiled and nodded.

"I don't want it," said Ruby hastily.

"Audrey got no use for it," said Roosevelt.

"Something like that," said Ruby, "somebody's gone miss."

"But they not gone know I got it," replied Roosevelt. "Audrey's mama's dead. Buried her two years ago. It was after her funeral that Johnny Washington got in trouble, killing that man. Dying and killing runs in that family, looks like."

"What 'bout Johnny Washington? He's gone know something is missing off his little girl's body, and he's gone know what it is, and he's gone know who took it!"

"He's not gone notice. He's tore up 'bout Audrey. I don't even think that the thing belonged to Audrey"—He swung it around by the chain—"I think she *took it!*"

Ruby whistled again.

"He may not even know about it. I don't think he does," continued Roosevelt. "And even if he does, how's he gone know I got it? Or had it? 'Cause I'm gone give it to you."

"I can't wear it," whispered Ruby, " 'cause people'll see it, and then they'll ask me where I got it, and what am I gone say then, Roosevelt Garver?"

"Put it down your front. Nobody'll see it!"

Ruby grinned, and laughed, and then took the amulet from her boyfriend.

Roosevelt stood, pleased that Ruby had taken the amulet. "Now you come on in with me, 'cause you got to do Audrey's hair."

Ruby remained seated. She shivered dramatically. "You not gone leave me alone, are you? You know I can't stand them dead bodies, just can't stand the way they feel. Shampoo don't never take right on a corpse . . ."

Chapter 58

∞∞

T HE news of poor Audrey Washington and her diminutive white victim spread all through the black section of
Pine Cone that Thursday night. On those evenings when
the lights of the back room of the Silver Pine Funerary
Home were burning, the neighbors did not rest until they
had discovered who was dead, and of what cause. Sometimes, when there was no other way to obtain the information, one of Washington Garver's domino cronies
would knock softly on the front door and ask of the undertaker, or his son, who it was that they were working
on in the back.

Audrey's body lay in its coffin in the front parlor of the
Garver establishment, and three of her good friends from
high school, and the black Baptist preacher's wife for
chaperone, sat up all night with the corpse. They ate
popcorn to keep awake. At his own home, Johnny Washington did not lack for company either. Many of his good
friends came over and helped him to demolish that afternoon's paycheck in red wine and liquor. Johnny even
bought Scotch whiskey, " 'cause it's the best, and Audrey
was the best too." Women from all over that section of
town came over, and in an effusion of sympathy, cooked
enough ham to send hog futures soaring, and wept enough
to raise the water table.

Not a word was mentioned to Johnny of Audrey's

crime. The most charitable whispered among themselves that Audrey had, entirely by mistake, dropped the Taylor baby into the washing machine, and then killed herself in remorse. But they didn't really believe it. Others said that it was no wonder she did what she did, what with all the white murders and suicides in town that week. She was just imitating them. The shame however was that she had chosen to murder one of the Taylors, seeing that Mr. Taylor had kept Johnny Washington out of the pen for a murder he had unquestionably committed. It looked like ingratitude. But most people could see no reason at all for Audrey's action. The girl had been a little stiff, sometimes, and sharp of tongue, but she was completely trustworthy—they had thought—and had been universally admired for the way that she kept Johnny Washington in check. Lord knew what would become of the man now that he didn't have Audrey, who told him when to stop drinking and when to start working; who bought his clothes and made sure he didn't get in trouble with the police and the welfare department. It was a terrible thing, and just real bad, *real bad,* in that it came so soon after all the trouble in Selma. Selma wasn't much more than eighty miles away, and there were some people—white people—who hadn't known Audrey, who might say that she had killed the little Taylor baby just because it was white and she wasn't. This was such a terrible thought that the black people did not even dare speak it outside their own families.

Of course, there was great consternation in the white section of Pine Cone as well, especially among the families who had black maids and gardeners. Would they turn too? Nothing like this had ever happened before. It was the first time anyone could remember that a black person had killed someone white; and it was the first time anyone could remember that a baby had been murdered. No one knew how to look at it. At first people were inclined to speak ill of Audrey, who was, they said, nursing a grudge against Mrs. Taylor, or was trying to start a racial war, or something else equally improbable; but Mrs. Taylor and her husband told anyone who asked their complete bewilderment over the murder of their year-old child. "Audrey was a good girl. She was always here on time. She didn't mind working on Saturday. She'd do the floors. She was good to the two boys," said Mrs. Taylor, and whimpered at the last.

"I don't know what possessed her to open the lid of that machine. I don't know why she would do such a thing," said her husband, and at this point in their tale of woe Mrs. Taylor always began to cry in earnest.

The whole thing was even more difficult to understand than why Morris Emmons had shot Jim Coltrane. This latter story had been brought back to Pine Cone that afternoon by Sheriff Garrett and Deputy Barnes, and had just begun to circulate through the town when it was overtaken and surpassed by the horror of Ralph Taylor sloshed to death in the washing machine. Emmons and Coltrane were grown men, after all, neither of them particularly likable. And grown men were prone to fire guns at one another for insufficient reasons. The disturbing part of the Emmons thing was the cotton baler; even if he hadn't jumped into it, even if his death had been an accident, why was he chasing a dog through the peanuts? Why hadn't he just tried to get away after killing Coltrane? Why had he committed murder so casually, in front of witnesses?

"Both of 'em," the sheriff said, and shook his head, "they committed murder, and there wasn't no way for 'em to get away with it. Emmons shot Coltrane right in front of Homans and ol' Miz Baines. If he was planning on doing it, he should have got the man alone, by himself. And Audrey Washington, and I'm *surprised* at what that girl did, if she wanted to kill that baby, she should have given it poison or something. She could have dropped it headfirst on the floor. She would have lost her job, letting the baby get killed, but wouldn't nobody know she did it on purpose. That's what don't make no sense—why witnesses? why the washing machine?"

"Well," said Deputy Barnes, "they both got theirs back. We don't have to put 'em on trial. They didn't get the chance to get off. And they died painful. Cotton baler's worse than gunshot. I don't know which one would be worse though—'lectrocution or the washing machine. Not much choice there, so far as I'm concerned, though I 'spect that 'lectrocution's got more dignity.'"

The sheriff and his deputy then noted the similarity between these four deaths, and the other four that had occurred the week before when Thelma Shirley and Dorothy Sims had murdered their husbands. Both had seemed not to care that they would be caught, and both then died themselves, apparently by accident.

"Yeah," said the sheriff, "it's a pattern, and I don't like it a bit. I mean, it's probably just as well that the people who do the murdering die, but I just wish it'd stop altogether."

Other people in town also drew the parallels, but no one could make anything of them. It was like a fever or the measles or something, only much worse, because people died from it. Eight people dead, and that wasn't even counting the other eight who had perished in Pine Cone in the last week as well, from accident: the seven Coppages and poor old Miz Weaver. People weren't even surprised on Friday morning to see a little article on the town in the *Montgomery Advertiser* which told about the four murders of particular violence and unknown motive, and the strange and providential deaths of these murderers immediately thereafter.

Chapter 59

It was in Friday morning's paper that Sarah first learned
of the four deaths in Pine Cone the previous day, four
deaths that had occurred before nine o'clock, when Becca
and Sarah had manipulated the Ouija board.

Becca handed the *Advertiser* to Sarah, when they met
at the purple Pontiac. "I just now saw it," gasped Becca.
"I'd have called you up, but I just this minute looked at
it."

Sarah read the article hurriedly, but by the time she
had finished, she was sweating. "That's four more. That
makes sixteen. And the wee-gee board was right. All
four of these took place before we started on the wee-gee
board last night." Sarah was grim, and she closed her eyes.

Becca backed the car out of the driveway. "Sarah, we
don't know for sure. We don't know anything for sure. I
mean, it sort of makes sense that it was Morris Emmons,
'cause we saw Morris Emmons and he was hanging around
the pigpen and maybe he did find it after all. But this
little colored girl, I mean how did she get it from Morris
Emmons? That don't make sense. Morris Emmons was
way out in the country, and this girl wasn't hardly old
enough for a learner's permit. How'd the amulet get back
in town? How'd it get from Morris Emmons to a little
colored girl who was taking care of Miz Taylor's kids?
That's what don't make sense."

Sarah shook her head. "Why are you trying to argue with it, Becca? There was twelve people dead that we knew about. The wee-gee board said it was sixteen, and now we hear there's four more people dead in Pine Cone, and don't it make more sense to believe that them four all died because of the amulet too?"

Becca shook her head. "Maybe the wee-gee board was lying. Maybe it was lying to us. You know, when we asked it about who was gone be next, and how many, and it just talked nonsense . . ."

Sarah moved uneasily in her seat. "Maybe it just cain't tell the future. Maybe it can only talk about things that's already happened," she suggested faintly.

Becca shook her head, but would not continue the argument. "I don't know what to think. What are you gone do now? What are we gone do now?"

Sarah didn't know. "Let's you and me try to think this thing out. We couldn't do anything till dinnertime anyway, and probably we won't be able to do anything then. But let's just think about it this morning."

On their coffee break Becca and Sarah talked with other women on the line, and got what additional information they could about the four deaths in Pine Cone the day before. Much of the gossip was patently false, and made up to fit the strangeness of the events, but what was apparent in all the stories that Becca and Sarah heard, was that the crimes were essentially motiveless, that the deaths of the murderers were unintentional and terrible.

Sarah went out of her way to speak to one of the black women on the cleaning crew that morning, and from her Sarah learned a little about Audrey, and about Johnny Washington. She also learned that Audrey could be "visited" at the Silver Pine Funerary Home over on Swiss Street. "But, I tell you," the women cautioned Sarah, "not gone be many white folk over there, 'cause white folk been talking about how Audrey was thinking about voting rights and sitting at the back of the bus when she stuck that poor little baby in the washing machine." Sarah protested that she didn't think anything of the sort, and that she was sure that Audrey had just gone crazy for a few minutes, and simply hadn't known what she was doing.

Sarah debated whether to go to the funeral home at

noontime with Becca, but decided against this. She had never heard of any white person visiting the Silver Pine Funerary Home to view a corpse. They frequently attended funerals in the black churches, and would go by the houses, but following etiquette that was alike unknown in origin and unbroken, they avoided Mr. Garver's establishment.

But Sarah did get Becca to drive her over to Johnny Washington's house. Sarah approached the place cautiously, and was stared at by eight or nine glum-faced men and women on the front porch. Sarah asked timidly if she could speak to Johnny Washington, but she was informed that the man was sleeping off a drunk, and couldn't be waked for no reason a-tall, unless she had come to offer him a job. Sarah shook her head, and apologized sincerely for intruding. She thanked the people and turned to go, but one old man, seeing that Sarah had meant no harm, called out, "Hey, ma'am, you can talk to him tomorrow at the funeral. He'll be up by then. He loved Audrey. He wouldn't miss Audrey's funeral. She was all that he had."

Sarah nodded and walked back to the car. Becca had heard the exchange, and she turned to Sarah, about to ask her again, "What now?" when she saw that her friend had begun to weep.

Rather than provide consolation in that exposed place, Becca drove away immediately, and in another two minutes they were outside the town limits, on a dirt road that skirted Burnt Corn Creek. Becca pulled up into a little paved area with three rotting picnic tables in an artificial clearing at a picturesque bend in the stream. No one else was about.

"Let's go sit out there, just a few minutes," said Becca soothingly to Sarah, who still was crying. "We got time —just a few minutes—and you'll feel a lot better."

They got out of the car, and moved down to the table nearest the water. Here they sat next to one another on the weathered green bench. Sarah broke down entirely, sobbing and gasping, for perhaps a minute, while Becca grasped her round the shoulders tightly, and whispered incomprehensible consolations in her ear.

Sarah at last placed her hand over her mouth, until she

had stopped crying. She rubbed the tears from her eyes, and said, "What am I gone do, Becca?"

Becca shook her head.

Sarah continued, "I cain't put up with this! People dying, and it's Jo Howell's fault. It's Dean's fault. It's my fault 'cause I cain't stop that thing. Today I should have gone up to that funeral home, and walked right in it, and tore that poor girl's dress off her corpse, just to see if she was wearing that thing. That's what I should have done, but I didn't. 'Cause I'm chicken. I was chicken to go up to Dorothy Sims, and now sixteen people are dead. And I'm still chicken."

"No, you're not. You're doing everything that you can."

Sarah shrugged. "I don't know what to do. You think we're wrong? You think maybe we're wrong about all of this, that it's maybe just people killing people, and that's all there is to it? That makes more sense, don't it, than talking about this piece of jewelry?"

"It don't none of it make no sense at all," said Becca. "It don't really matter what we believe. It don't make no sense. If it made sense, they wouldn't write about it in the *Montgomery Advertiser*, would they? If there was a explanation, we wouldn't have read about it in the paper this morning."

"This afternoon," said Sarah, dry-eyed, "after work, you gone take me to see the sheriff. And we gone talk to him, just talk, and I'm gone ask him about the amulet. I'm not gone tell him what we think, I'm just gone ask him if he's seen it. And if he sees it again, then I'm gone tell him to get it, and give it to me."

"You think he's gone believe you?"

"I don't care. But we got to do something. We'll see what he says, and if we have to, we'll go to that poor little colored girl's funeral tomorrow."

For another few minutes the two women watched the muddy swirling waters of Burnt Corn Creek as it ate away at the clay banks, and then they returned to the assembly line of the Pine Cone Munitions Factory.

Chapter 60

"I was meaning to talk to you anyway," said Sheriff Garrett to Sarah Howell and Becca Blair late that Friday afternoon.

On the way home from work the two women had been trying to screw their courage up to see the sheriff, when they had seen his cruiser parked in front of his house. Garrett himself had been standing in the bushes in front of his picture window, turning on the sprinkler. Becca pulled the Pontiac up behind the cruiser, and the two women hesitantly got out of the car. The sheriff waved to them, and moved cautiously around the circular fountain of water.

"What'd you want to talk to us about?" said Becca, trying to put off the evil hour of speaking to the sheriff about the amulet.

"This necklace you were looking for . . ."

Both women trembled. "How'd you know about that?" Sarah faltered.

"Mal Homans told me."

The women stared at the sheriff blankly. The name meant nothing to them.

"Mal Homans was Jim Coltrane's brother-in-law, the man that Morris Emmons killed. Homans told me you was out looking for a necklace . . ."

Sarah nodded hesitantly. "That's right. Morris Emmons

286

must have told him, 'cause I told Morris Emmons about it."

The sheriff cocked his head curiously, evidently wanting to ask Sarah why she had gone to Morris Emmons about a missing piece of jewelry, but instead, he continued with his story. "Well, this necklace—and it seems real peculiar to me—was in the pig's mouth that went and killed Merle Weaver—"

Sarah and Becca both gasped, but the sheriff went on. "Fell out of the pig's mouth. Mal Homans and Jim Coltrane took that necklace—after Emmons told 'em that you was looking for it, Sarah—and went and put it round Emmons's head. Then Emmons come out front in the store, and blew Jim Coltrane to kingdom come."

Becca and Sarah nodded dismally; they had heard this part of the story.

"I mean," said the sheriff, eyeing the women closely, but not with any hostility, "don't all of that seem peculiar? You don't shoot somebody because of a practical joke, and putting a necklace round somebody's neck don't seem much of a joke anyway, does it?"

Becca and Sarah shook their heads.

"I was just wondering if you knew anything about all this? I mean," said the sheriff with a furrowed brow, "you was looking for a necklace, Sarah, said it belonged to you, so how did it come to be in the mouth of a marauding pig?"

"Where is it now?" asked Sarah. "Did you find it?" She realized that this was a senseless question, since it had obviously already passed on to poor Audrey Washington, and heaven only knew where it was by this time.

The sheriff shook his head. "It probably got mashed up in the baling machine with the rest of Morris Emmons."

Sarah shook her head. "No, it didn't."

The sheriff looked at her quizzically, and then Sarah recounted to him the history of the amulet, how it had got from the Coppages all the way through to Morris Emmons. She did not say anything about Jo and Dean, except that it was Jo that had given the piece to Larry Coppage in the first place. Sarah told it carefully for she had gone over it many times in her mind, and was able to prove, sufficiently for the sheriff, that indeed the amulet had been present at each of the deaths in question.

"But," she concluded, "I don't know how it got from Morris Emmons to Audrey Washington. Audrey fits right in the pattern"—the sheriff nodded reluctantly—"but I just cain't figure out how she come by it."

"Johnny Washington gave it to her," said the sheriff quietly. "He saw Morris Emmons die. He was out there at Mr. Crane's place, and he must have picked it up off the ground, and carried it to Audrey."

Sarah winced. There was now no doubt that Audrey Washington and Ralph Taylor were the latest links in the ever-lengthening chain.

"You believe us then," said Becca simply.

"I don't think so," said Garrett after a moment. "I mean I believe you about following this thing around. You wouldn't lie to me about something like that. You saw it, or you talked to people who saw it. I can go and ask 'em myself. And I will. There's something real peculiar about all of this, and if it's that thing that you're talking about that's causing it all, then maybe if we can find it, we can stop it."

Sarah explained that she had gone by Johnny Washington's that afternoon, but had not been able to talk to him. She had also not gone to the funeral home, and apologized for her cowardice.

"It's all right," said Garrett kindly. "You let me do that. It's easier for me. They're not gone object to me talking to Johnny Washington about that piece of jewelry. I'll find it, if it's there."

Sarah started to weep with relief. It meant much—it meant everything in the world—to have some of this burden lifted from her. Now there was someone else fighting. For the second time that day, Becca placed a comforting arm around her friend's shoulders.

The sheriff talked on, in a low, respectful voice. "It's sort of a relief to hear it. All these people dying in the past two weeks got on my nerves, I tell you. It was bad to have to go out yesterday and look at Jim Coltrane and Morris Emmons, and then I come back into town, sitting down to supper, and I get this call that says that Audrey Washington done gone and stuck Graham Taylor's little boy in the washing machine, and then has killed herself with a radio plug." He shook his head. "I don't believe all this that you're telling me, but at least it's something that I can go on, it's something I can do."

Sarah nodded gratefully.

"I'm gone go by and speak to Johnny Washington tonight, and I'll talk to Washington Garver too, see if that girl had the thing on when they brought her in. We can find it," he added reassuringly. "You call me up tomorrow morning, and I'll probably be able to tell you that I've located the thing . . ."

"Sheriff," cried Sarah, "you find it, and you *kill* it."

"Just tell me one thing," said Garrett. "Where'd Jo Howell get hold of a thing like that?"

"It weren't Montgomery Ward," snapped Becca.

Chapter 61

about It on the phone. There was something about it in the paper.

... wonderful what ever were ...

W<small>HEN</small> Sarah returned home after the small but infinitely reassuring talk with the sheriff, she was in a mood which, in comparison with what she had felt for the past ten days, might be considered exultant. She had wondered whether she should tell Jo the progress of the search for the amulet, but decided against this and the short term pleasure of what Becca had called "sticking it to the old witch." There would be more to gain in keeping Jo in suspense. In any case, Jo wasn't going to reveal anything, and Sarah didn't want the woman to make any attempt to upset the sheriff's investigations. In parting, Sarah had assured Garrett that there would be no use at all in talking to Jo, that she apparently knew nothing about the amulet, and that she had given it to Larry Coppage because Rachel had once admired it. This was not the truth, but Sarah was afraid that if the sheriff talked to Jo, the old woman would convince him that the whole business about the amulet was nonsense—and the sheriff's belief, Sarah thought, was what had saved her life.

"D'you hear about that little baby? D'you hear about the cotton baler?" cried Jo, as soon as Sarah stepped foot into Dean's bedroom. Sarah was surprised by Jo's nervousness. The other deaths had not affected her in this way.

"I heard," said Sarah cautiously. "They were talking

about it at the plant. There was something about it in the paper this morning."

"D'you bring me a copy of that paper?"

Sarah smiled briefly with wondering what was now pushing Jo. "No, I didn't. I didn't know you wanted to see it. It didn't tell much though."

"Well," demanded Jo, "what'd you hear at the plant?"

Briefly, Sarah told her what had happened at Mr. Crane's farm and on Graham Taylor's back porch the previous day. But she gave no indication that the amulet was present at both places, and did not even mention it as a possibility. She was careful to speak of the deaths as accidents unrelated except in their barrenness of motive. Sarah watched Dean as she talked, and tried to detect motion in the figure on the bed, but could not.

"What you think of all that?" said Jo hesitantly, and with averted eyes.

"I don't think anything about it," said Sarah quietly. "I think it's real bad what happened. Don't like to hear of people killing, getting killed. Who does, Jo?"

Jo leaned back in her chair, and said nothing else. Sarah noted with satisfaction that the woman seemed distraught, and puzzled. Sarah waited several moments for the woman to say something else, to give herself away further. But she said nothing. Sarah then wondered if she shouldn't continue herself, perhaps just mention the amulet in passing, but decided against that too. It would be best to wait for what the sheriff had to say in the morning. There would be time then to confront Jo, and maybe by then there would be hard evidence. Maybe if the amulet were destroyed—and what happy news that would be—there would not be any need for a confrontation at all.

Sarah slept soundly that night, and though there were nightmares that woke her soon after dawn, she could not remember them. She worked about the house, got Jo and Dean their breakfasts, and was just wondering how early she might telephone the sheriff, when Garrett himself called. Sarah took the call in the kitchen, well away from Jo and Dean on the far side of the house.

"Went over to see Johnny Washington last night. He's in bad shape, wasn't that bad off when he knifed his brother-in-law. And I talked to him, and he said he *did* find that thing, and he brought it to Audrey not thirty minutes 'fore she went and stuck that poor little baby in the washing machine."

"Did she have it on her?"

"Well, then I went over to see Washington Garver, and he said she didn't have no kind of jewelry on her, except two cheap dime-store rings, and them he gave back to Johnny to keep 'em as souvenirs."

"So we still don't know where it is?"

"No," said Garrett, "we don't. You let me think about this awhile. You know, the girl had it when she killed that baby. And Morris Emmons had it when he shot Jim Coltrane. And that's enough. That's too much. We'll find it, just in case. I don't want to have to go find any more bodies."

"No . . ." agreed Sarah.

"But listen," said the sheriff sternly, "I don't want you doing nothing else. You been chasing 'round this town, and you let me work on it for a little while. This thing could be dangerous, and you ought to let me handle it. You stay home, take it easy, keep company with Dean. He'll appreciate it, and I'll call you soon as I know anything."

Sarah thanked the sheriff and hung up. She was much disappointed that the amulet had not been found, but she was also very glad that she had been commanded to give over the search. She didn't want to have to think of it any longer. She did not allow herself to imagine that there would be another death. Right now she had to rest, had to ease her mind of this great burden. Maybe if she just took this weekend and thought it all through again she could come up with an answer. Maybe Josephine Howell, overwhelmed with guilt, would give in to her and tell how to stop the devastation. Maybe, Sarah thought, Burnt Corn Creek would rise, and just wash them all away.

Chapter 62

It was eleven o'clock in the morning on a hot, dusty, still day in Pine Cone. The wind whipped clouds of red dust up from the parking lots and threw it in the faces of countrywomen who had just arrived in town for an afternoon of gossip and shopping. The hours were relaxed and lazy and passed with a frightening slowness. No matter how much food you had for breakfast, all you could think of was, how long is it before dinner? The drawing was three hours away, but already the town was packed.

Shopkeepers were in an emotional quandary. No time is so sweet for fishing as Saturday morning, but they were behind their counters with ties and white shirts that were damp-stained across the shoulder blades. It would be an easy thing to be nasty to the customers for keeping them inside on such a hot day, when you just knew exactly where the fish would be, swimming slowly among the roots in a grove of cypress. But this was a day when all the county came to town, men and women whose dollar bills had been counted again and again, for whom a pair of socks was a major purchase, and a new dress was to be thought of only on Easter and birthdays. It was not possible to resent these good, hard men and women, with their dusty, barefooted children, whose lives were so difficult. And so the shopkeepers sweated and smiled, and sighed at the end of the day, wondering if the receipts (which often totaled as much as the other five days put together) were worth having to watch the sun make its slow progress across the sky, and miss the best fishing of the week.

School had let out on Friday, and students would return on Monday for only a few hours, to turn in their books, and pick up their report cards. This was the sweetest weekend of the year for them. Hot weather had started long before, of course, but this was the beginning of *summer*, and these two days, Saturday and Sunday, tasted most of freedom.

Despite the heat and the dust, there was still a lush sweetness in the air, all that can really be called spring in the Deep South; that sweetness was loved the more for the knowledge that it would be soon burned away in the scorching days of June.

The black part of town was very quiet at this time. All the children had run down to the creek, and were swimming in the shallow water or playing complicated games in the cool forest. Women were in their kitchens, preparing the midday meals, and the men were either away working as gardeners (as supplement to a weekly paycheck at the factory), or were sitting on their front porches, silently rocking. Audrey's funeral would be held late that afternoon.

Ruby's House of Beauty was actually a single room— low, narrow and long—that had been built onto the back of her parents' house. It was dimly lit, in an attempt to keep a little of the heat out, and two great ceiling fans whirred quickly overhead. The room was crowded with chairs and sinks (Ruby sometimes had an assistant who specialized in permanent waves), and shelves built floor to ceiling at one end contained all of Ruby's supplies.

There was a single customer in Ruby's House of Beauty, a young black woman about nineteen. Her name was Martha-Ann and she had been a friend of Ruby's for many, many years. Ruby didn't like to take customers on Saturday morning, but this was a favor, since Martha-Ann was going out on a date, just as soon as she could get changed after the funeral.

". . . and Roosevelt," Ruby was saying, as she shampooed Martha-Ann's hair, "he say he gone take me down to Apalachicola just as soon as he gives that hearse another coat of gloss black, and we are gone go to the Dew Drop Inn, and just injure that floor with our feet . . ."

Ruby and Martha-Ann played out a little rivalry with one another about their respective boyfriends, as to which girl was promised more, which was given more, which was treated with greater deference.

"Well," said Martha-Ann, "George, he say he gone take me 'cross the *line* tonight!" Ruby paused momentarily; she had been topped. Martha-Ann was talking about the Florida state line, above seventy miles to the south. There were dance halls just over the border where liquor was served to anyone who could pay for it and those dance halls, at least to the people who had never been in them, were wild, mythic places, where people gathered who were very wicked, and got their money in ways it wouldn't do to tell.

Martha-Ann could see that she had gotten the better of her rival, and continued: "And George, he say he not gone promise *nothing* to me, girl, so I want you be sure to get *all* them kinks out of my *unruly* hair, you hear me?"

"I hear you, but I tell you something, girl . . ." began Ruby. She had moved away, and climbed the little stepladder. From behind two bottles of liquid concentrate shampoo, where she had carefully hidden it, Ruby fished out the amulet. She knew it wouldn't do to show the thing to Martha-Ann, who would be sure to ask questions and spread the tidings, and there just might be talk of a missing necklace at Audrey's funeral. No, Martha-Ann couldn't see it for at least a month, by which time everyone would have forgotten about Audrey and the washing machine, but it would make Ruby feel a lot better just to have it around her neck, out of sight under her dress. Martha-Ann's boyfriend had given her a rhinestone clip six months ago, but that was Christmas and birthday combined, and Ruby knew that Martha-Ann hadn't got a thing out of him since then. But this thing that Roosevelt had given her looked like it was worth something, and not the least attractive part was that it had belonged to a murderess.

Ruby grimaced when she saw that the chain had broken in half, and she couldn't imagine how it had happened. It was a shame, because now she couldn't wear it, and because it hadn't really been Roosevelt's to give her, she couldn't take it to the jewelry story in town to get it mended either. *Damn,* she thought to herself, and with some exasperation she held the two ends of the chain around her neck, and let the amulet fall over her breast. *It would have looked good,* she nodded to herself ruefully. But then she found, to her surprise, that the chain had somehow hooked itself back together. It had not broken at all. Maybe it was one of those invisible catches that was advertised on television commercials.

Ruby nodded with satisfaction, dropped the amulet beneath her blouse, and descended the ladder, bringing a couple of bottles with her.

"What's that, Ruby?" said Martha-Ann, who had been buried in a movie magazine, "what you got to say to me?"

"I *say*," said Ruby, "you want to get rid of them kinks for good, Martha-Ann, then you gone have to get me to shave your head . . ."

"Ohhh!" cried Martha-Ann, "don't you say nothing like that to me, Ruby, 'cause I am *paying* you."

Martha-Ann made a little pretend pout, which Ruby took great exception to. She couldn't understand why her friend was always so nasty, why she was always making snide remarks about Roosevelt's profession, and what was it gone be like when he and Ruby got married. "I tell you," Martha-Ann would say at least once a week, "I don't think I'd want a man to put his hands on me, right after he's had 'em all over a corpse. I don't know how you put up with it, smelling them dead people on the tips of his fingers . . ." Well, Martha-Ann's boyfriend was no good, couldn't hold down his job at the munitions factory cause he was always damaging the vehicles there, running 'em into telephone poles and fence posts, and Martha-Ann had no business saying the things she did about Roosevelt, just because of what he did for a living. It didn't make *no* difference to Martha-Ann that Roosevelt was doing it because his daddy did it, didn't make no difference to her that there was a good living to be made in a funeral parlor, didn't make no difference to her that Roosevelt looked more like a football player than a mortician.

Ruby stared at her friend in the swiveling chair, and wondered why, if Martha-Ann was going to insult her all the time, she had allowed herself to be roped into doing the girl's hair at all, much less on a Saturday morning. Ruby had much rather have been downtown in all the crowds. Everybody else was downtown, and would stay there till after the drawing. Then everybody was coming home to get ready to go to Audrey's funeral. Ruby had tickets in that drum, and this new necklace around her neck made her feel lucky. It was just possible that she'd win today—if she was there. But if Martha-Ann didn't hurry up and stop her chattering and get her nose out of that magazine, Ruby would never get there in time. They'd call out her name and she wouldn't be there and all that money would go to somebody else, somebody who didn't need it the way Ruby did.

Martha-Ann was doing it on purpose, Ruby decided, because she was really jealous of Ruby for having snagged Roosevelt Garver, because in ten years Roosevelt Garver, if his father died like he should, was going to be the richest black man in Pine Cone, and he would be married to Ruby.

Martha-Ann, without looking up from her book, said, "Ruby, you didn't do your best on me last time, and I was walking around with a tin bucket on my head, 'cause I didn't want people to see what I let you do to my hair. I want you to be real careful today, you hear me?"

"Oh," said Ruby, "I'm gone take real good care of you today, Martha-Ann. I'm gone massage your scalp."

"Oh," cried Martha-Ann, "that sounds real good. Good for the roots, good for ever'thing."

Ruby laughed softly, and reached down below one of the sinks, and brought out a bottle of thick green liquid. She poured a little out into the palm of her rubber-gloved hand, and then began to rub it into Martha-Ann's scalp.

"That feels just real good," said Martha-Ann with satisfaction. "I ought to get you to . . ." Martha-Ann stopped suddenly, realizing that something was wrong with the way

that the scalp treatment felt. "Ruby—" she protested, but
Ruby did not answer, and continued to rub her fingers
into Martha-Ann's hair. Martha-Ann squirmed; it felt as
if her hair were being pulled out of her head entirely.

"Ruby!" she cried, and tried to twist around to get a
look in the mirror at what was happening. "What's that
stuff you putting on me? What you putting in my hair
now?"

"Gone take the kinks right out," said Ruby softly.

"Feels like you gone take my whole head off, Ruby,
that's what it feels like!"

Martha-Ann got one foot on the floor, and with hysteri-
cal strength pushed the chair around. She stared in the
mirror and screamed. Her hair was almost gone, and
Ruby continued to pull handfuls of it out. The scalp itself
was bloody. Martha-Ann threw her hands over her face
and tried to stand up out of the chair, but Ruby pushed
her down and continued to massage. Martha-Ann moaned
and writhed, but she felt herself growing weaker; she
could not even stop to think why there was so little pain.
She opened her eyes and stared into the mirror, just as
Ruby carefully peeled away her scalp.

Martha-Ann screamed faintly, and rushed out of the
chair, eyes closed with the horror of the sight. She ran in
the direction of the back door, but tripped over the corner of the carpet and fell against the window. Martha-
Ann broke through the glass, and fell down into the flower
bed below, moaning and screaming. But in only a few
moments, her scream was cut by a rattle in her throat and
she was dead.

Amid the screams of her friend, Ruby took the bloody
scalp and carefully arranged it atop the white Styrofoam
head of a wig dummy, and then went over to the stepladder again, and mounted it, reaching upward to replace
the two bottles on the top shelf. But one spilled on her
and she pulled back instinctively to avoid the liquid. She
lost her balance and caught at the shelving to keep from
falling. But the shelving was not support enough, and it
pulled away from the wall. Ruby fell backward in the
air, directly against the rapidly spinning blades of the
ceiling fan. In a moment, cleanly, her neck was severed.

Body and head fell to the floor separately, blood gushing from both.

The falling shelves had caught momentarily on the edge of a chair, but now they broke in two, and dropped heavily onto Ruby's separated corpse.

Chapter 63

DIRECTLY after the noon meal on Saturday afternoon,
Becca Blair and Sarah Howell had driven a mile or two
out into the country to visit a farm-produce stand that was
reputed to have the best berries and fruits in the county.
Jo Howell had been complaining that Dean was finding
his food dull, and that he surely could do with some
mashed strawberries, that he was, in fact, aching for fresh
mashed strawberries. Sarah suspected that it was Jo that
hankered after the strawberries, but when she told this to
Becca, Becca had said, "Well, honey, I don't mind going
out there, won't take twenty minutes, and I might get some
for Margaret's picnic on Monday, she's going on a picnic
to celebrate school's being out, you know. Going with
those people, the Nelsons, that lived next to the Coppages
and watched 'em burn up with us, gone take little Mary
Shirley long too, 'cause that child can't be having much
fun anymore, not with so many people dropping around
her like flies, and not nobody left to take care of her.
Who'd take her on picnics if it wasn't for Margaret?"

This trip into the country was a real luxury, for on it
Sarah did not allow herself to think of the amulet, to wonder around whose doomed neck it now hung. The sheriff
had assured her that he was going to take care of the entire business, and the sheriff, even more importantly, had
told her to leave it all alone. And that—at least for the
weekend—was exactly what Sarah Howell intended to do.

The Amulet

Becca was very pleased with the alteration in Sarah's attitude. She seemed freer, less worried than at any time since the news had reached her, through Jo, that Dean had been wounded on the Fort Rucca firing range. All the way out and back, Becca made jokes about Jo Howell, and Sarah giggled uncontrollably.

And now Sarah and Becca were driving back into Pine Cone, with a cardboard box on the backseat filled with sacks of sweet fruits, and even sweeter berries. Their way lead them through the blocks of the town where all the blacks lived, and they were surprised to be forced to slow up for a great crowd that had formed in front of one of the houses. Cars were parked along both sides of the street, and a great number of black people were standing around in the yard.

"Ohhhh!" cried Becca, "Sarah, let's stop and see what's happened!" Her tone was still gay and abandoned. "Knifing, I bet," she said, with an amused conspiratorial voice. "Playing poker on a Saturday afternoon, and somebody up and knifes somebody else. Ohhhh!" she exclaimed then, in a lower-pitched voice, "Sarah, look! It's the hearse. It's not the ambulance—there's somebody dead . . ."

As soon as Sarah had seen the crowd of seventy-five or so, with none of the noise usually attendant upon such a gathering, all the day's good spirits flooded out of her. Very suddenly she became weary and despairing.

"It's the amulet," she whispered to Becca, but did not look at her friend.

Becca pulled up to the curb half a block away from the crowd. She spoke hurriedly as they got out of the car, trying desperately to reassure her friend. "Maybe it was a heart attack. There's the fat woman who works at the plant, I cain't remember her name but she lives right around here. She's real fat, and they say when you get like that, it's good chance that you're gone have a heart attack. It can come like that—" and she snapped her fingers desperately.

Sarah shook her head. "It's the amulet, Becca, and you know it. Audrey Washington had it in this part of town. It wasn't on her in the coffin, and her daddy didn't have it. Somebody got hold of it, and now somebody else is dead."

301

Sarah and Becca, the only two white bystanders in the crowd, moved up toward the front. Sarah had turned to a woman beside her, and was about to ask what had happened, when all at once, there was a gasp from all the crowd, and as sudden a return to the solemn silence. Silence, except for a pitiable uncontrolled whimpering—a frightening whimper, because it was a man that was crying.

Around from the back of the house appeared two men carrying a stretcher between them. The first was Deputy Barnes, very pale, and the second was Roosevelt Garver, weeping copiously, and moaning with an open mouth, so violently he could barely keep the stretcher steady. A bloody, flowered sheet covered the body being borne toward the hearse. The crowd drew well away, but they all stared intently at the strange lump, the size of a small pumpkin, sitting on the chest of the corpse beneath the sheet.

Sarah and Becca stared and were silent also; instinctively they grasped one another's hands.

Sheriff Garrett and another black man appeared presently, carrying another body on another stretcher, and all the crowd shook their heads in wonder and in pity.

The two corpses were placed in the back of the hearse, and Roosevelt Garver staggered around to the front and threw himself behind the wheel. His wailing voice was the only sound apparent among the men gathered there. In another moment the hearse careened away with the screech and stink of burned rubber.

The sheriff and the deputy turned and mounted the steps of the little frame house and spoke in low voices to a weeping couple standing there who Sarah and Becca took to be grieving relations of one or both of the corpses.

"Let's go, Sarah," pleaded Becca. The scene was painful, and she did not want Sarah to get worked up.

"No," replied Sarah peremptorily. "I want to find out what happened." She turned to a woman who stood beside her. "You know what's going on?"

"Ohhhh!" the old black woman wailed softly. She faced Sarah and Becca, but her eyes were turned toward the couple on the porch of the house. "I don't know what happened. They was best friends, they was borned weeks apart, weeks! And I don't know what happened! Ruby done took Martha-Ann's scalp off! Took it off with chemicals and rubber gloves! They was the bone and they was the blood, and why she do it? I don't know. I don't know what happened. And Ruby! Ruby got paid back for it! Ruby got her head taken off by a ceiling fan! Blades are still going!"

Sarah and Becca were wide-eyed, and could hardly credit the story they had been told. They questioned the woman again on all these points, and received corroboration from another woman who was standing by. This second woman pointed to the couple on the front steps. "It would have been better for them if the finance company hadn't have give them the loan to build Ruby her House of Beauty, better for them if the electric company had shut off their power 'fore that ceiling fan took off their little girl's head! They got nobody now but Jesus and the Dove of Peace to help 'em through their lives!"

Becca shuddered, and motioned to Sarah that they should return to the car now. "The sheriff knows what to ask 'em," whispered Becca. "He knows to look for the thing. We don't have to have nothing to do with it, the sheriff told you to leave it alone."

Quietly, resolutely, Sarah replied, "We got to talk to the sheriff. We got to find out what happened."

"You *heard* what happened today," argued Becca, a little panicky, "and you don't want to see where it happened. Sarah, let's get out of here."

Sarah shook her head, and moved along the edges of the crowd, around toward the back of the house. For a moment Becca stood behind, faltering, but she caught up with Sarah in a few steps. "Let's don't go in, Sarah, please let's don't go in there!"

The people in the crowd looked at them wonderingly, but said nothing, and made no move to stop the two white women as they mounted the steps in back, and opened the screen door that led into the House of Beauty.

Chapter 64

FOR having been in the last hour the scene of a violent and heinous crime, Ruby's House of Beauty was a lively, almost cheerful place. The sheriff and his deputy stood at one end, talking to one another volubly, and several brave, middle-aged black men hovered about the doorway, staring into the room—though they dared not cross the threshold. Four tiny children were squeezed into two chairs in the room all chattering and arguing with bright garrulousness; it is certain that they did not understand the enormity of what had transpired.

When Becca and Sarah entered the room through the back screen door, the policemen turned around.

"Miz Howell? Becca?" said Sheriff Garrett, surprised.

"Hey, Sheriff," said Becca in a low voice. She looked all around her, at the window whose frame had been broken through, and at the ceiling fans, whirling softly above.

"You two taking to chasing murders?" asked Deputy Barnes.

Sarah did not answer. She suspected that the sheriff had not told his deputy about the amulet. She didn't blame him, and she was relieved in fact to think that the story had gone no further than Garrett himself. In support of this theory, Garrett nodded knowingly to Sarah, glanced at the deputy, and held up his hand for Sarah to say nothing more at the moment.

"You hadn't ought to be here, Becca," said Deputy Barnes. "You neither, Miz Howell."

"Sarah made me come in," said Becca, a little peevishly. She had not noticed the exchange of signals between Sarah and the sheriff.

The deputy laughed uneasily. "Why?"

Sarah coughed lightly, trying to indicate to Becca that she should say nothing more; but Becca did not heed her, and said: "She wants to know if one of these two girls was wearing a necklace."

The deputy glanced uncomprehendingly at the sheriff, who refused to acknowledge his glance. "Why you want to know something like that?"

Sarah did not answer, and neither did Becca.

The deputy cocked his head, and said severely, "This the same one that you was asking Morris Emmons about? Why you think just dead people in town gone have that thing?"

Barnes again looked to the sheriff, hoping that he would be backed up in this attack on Sarah Howell, but the sheriff said nothing. The deputy saw that he had best not continue. He shrugged. "No, didn't neither one of 'em have nothing 'round their necks. And one of 'em didn't even have a neck no more . . ."

He laughed at his little gruesome joke, but stopped abruptly when the four children in the two chairs laughed uproariously, jabbing one another in the ribs, and repeating in little screams, "No neck! No neck no more!"

"You kids hush!" commanded the sheriff. "You ought not be in here nohow!"

During this little exchange, Becca had caught the smell of blood in the room, underneath all the cosmetics and shampoos, and had turned her back on the others, momentarily, to take a piece of tissue out of her purse, and hold it to her nose. She stood still a moment, trying to catch a calming breath; the amulet, which had been caught on one of the blades of the ceiling fan, slipped off, and fell neatly into her handbag, which sat open on a small table next to one of the chairs. She did not notice it, but two of the children in the room did see the thing happen. They exchanged surprised glances and began to giggle, pointing at the purse. Becca glared at the children, thinking that they were making fun of her, and she snapped the handbag shut.

"You two girls go on home now," said the sheriff. "I know what I'm looking for here. I haven't found it yet, but I'll know it when I do. I'll give you a call if anything comes up, and I'll probably give you a call if it doesn't." The deputy stared at his superior during this speech, which made no sense at all to him.

"We didn't mean to bother you," apologized Sarah, "but we saw the crowd, and we knew that something else had happened." She smiled bravely. "I guess we're just gone have to leave it up to you."

The sheriff nodded.

"But you see what happened—" said Sarah, with furrowed brow, —"what's gone continue to happen . . ."

"What's she talking about?" demanded the deputy of Becca Blair.

Becca shrugged and turned to go.

" 'Bye, ya'll," said the sheriff, and Sarah and Becca hurried out of the building.

As soon as they were gone, the deputy turned to the sheriff, about to demand an explanation, but both men were distracted by sudden loud laughter among the four children in the room. One little boy had taken Martha-Ann's scalp off the wig stand, placed it over his head, and was parading about the room in it. "Miss America!" he cried. "Look out for Miss America!"

Chapter 65

SARAH said nothing at all on the drive home. Becca thought that her friend was only distraught—though understandably so—by the new set of double deaths in Ruby's House of Beauty. It was just as well to leave her in her thoughts. But when Becca had pulled the purple Pontiac into the driveway between their houses, and had herself got out, she was surprised that Sarah remained in the car. The reflection of the bright afternoon sun on the windshield prevented Becca from determining Sarah's expression. She went around and leaned in the window. "Sarah," she said, "what's wrong? Come on out of there. You gone burn up in that car."

There was no response from Sarah, who sat motionless —still as Dean himself, thought Becca involuntarily.

"Sarah?" said Becca questioningly. "Sarah, is something the matter?"

The troubled woman didn't move, and Becca, with much concern, pulled the door open. She placed a hand on Sarah's shoulder, and shook her. Sarah's head waggled a little, but there was no other response.

Becca drew in her breath sharply, much concerned that something was very wrong.

Slowly, Sarah turned her head towards her friend, and Becca was at first relieved, crying, "Well, thank heaven, Sarah, I thought—" But Sarah's glance was uncomprehending, blank, corpselike. Becca shuddered, and without stopping to think about it, she reached in, and dragged Sarah out of the car.

Sarah stumbled out, and would have fallen to the ground if Becca had not, with extraordinary strength, heaved her up onto her feet.

Margaret appeared at the kitchen window and seeing that something was wrong, hurried outside and helped prop Sarah up.

"Mama, what's wrong with Sarah? Mama, we gone take her inside her house?"

"No," said Becca; "bring her in here."

Mother and daughter half pulled, half dragged Sarah to their back steps. Becca hissed, as much to convince Margaret as reassure herself, "She's all right. She just got upset. She got too hot sitting in the car." Becca pushed Sarah up her back steps, and added: "She smelled too much blood this afternoon."

Margaret looked up sharply. "Somebody else dead?"

Her mother nodded.

They put Sarah down on the couch, laid her out, removed her shoes, and loosened her clothing. Margaret brought a dish towel wrapped round half a tray of ice cubes and placed it carefully on Sarah's brow.

Becca knelt at the side of the couch, and held Sarah's hand tightly between hers. She was considerably relieved when Sarah moved her head a little, focused her eyes, and said, in a weak small voice, "Becca, I cain't walk."

"Yes, you can," said Becca softly. "You walked in here. You just got excited. You gone just lie here till you feel like getting up."

"Jo," whispered Sarah. "What about Jo and Dean?"

"I'm gone sit here with you for a few minutes, till you feel better, then Margaret's gone come in here and sit. I'm gone go over there and tell Jo that you aren't feeling too well, and that tonight, for a change, she is gone have to take care of Dean by herself. She's gone have to fix him dinner by herself, and if she wants anything to eat herself, why she's just gone have to go over to the refrigerator and open the door. And I hope it kills her to do it!"

Sarah smiled wanly, and then turned her head toward

the back of the couch. Becca remained beside her friend until she was sure that she was asleep. Then she called Margaret in, and instructed her to sit in the room—and not to leave it for anything—until she got back from next door.

Becca Blair was furious with Jo Howell, for she blamed her entirely for what had happened to Sarah. Sarah was a fine girl, and everybody in Pine Cone knew it, and Jo Howell had run her into the ground. It was bad enough that she had made Sarah unhappy—now she had made her sick.

Becca wasn't even thinking about the amulet—that was neither here nor there so far as she was concerned right now. Jo Howell had a lot to answer for in any case. Becca stormed across to the other house, saying to herself over and over, "She's not worth the trouble to pull a double-barreled trigger on . . ."

Becca found Sarah's husband and mother-in-law on the couch in the living room. All the curtains had been closed, so that the room was dark; the new air conditioner in Dean's bedroom was on extra-cool, and the two rooms were frigid. Dean was propped up in the corner of the sofa with pillows. Jo Howell, gross and fat, was sitting up close to him—it looked to keep her son from sliding off onto the floor—and sponged the bandages on his brow with a damp cloth.

She had not seen that it was Becca Blair who entered, and assumed it was Sarah. "Ohhhh!" she said reproachfully, with her back to Becca, "Dean is burning up, Sarah! We gone have to get a machine for this room too! In them bandages, Dean's not gone be able to take this summer, he's not gone be able to take it, I tell you! I think I'm gone put another order in—"

She turned at this, and seeing that it was Becca in the room, said coldly, "Where's Sarah?"

"Sarah's sick," said Becca quietly. She tried to avoid looking at Dean, for she didn't want her anger mixed with either the pity or the revulsion that the sight of him raised in her.

"Where is she?" Jo demanded.

"She's at my house. She's asleep."

"She's all right then," said Jo, and turned back to Dean.

309

"You tell her," said Jo, "that's she got to get back here by four-thirty so that Dean'll have his supper on time."

"You listen to me, Jo Howell, I'm not letting Sarah step foot out of my house, till I'm convinced that she's well enough to, and until I'm convinced that she *wants* to leave it."

"What do you mean?" demanded Jo, and her eyes disappeared behind rolls of enraged fat.

"I mean," said Becca, "that Sarah is very sick, and you were the one that made her sick, and right now, she's not in no condition to fix you and Dean a plate of white bread. Now, I'm gone go back over next door, to my house, and I'm gone tell Sarah that you said you could get along just fine without her, and that you told her to rest up—"

"I'm not gone tell you any such thing—" protested Jo.

"—or else," continued Becca, running over Jo's objection, "I'm gone take her, and put her in the back of the Pontiac, and drive her over to the hospital in Enterprise. That's what I ought to do anyway, probably . . ."

"You bring Sarah back over here where she belongs. I don't know how you expect her to get well—if she's really sick—when she's not in her own house."

"She's *sick*," cried Becca, " 'cause of what you're doing to her, making her wait on you like you didn't have two legs and two arms and all your fingers, Jo Howell, that's why she's *sick*, and for no other reason in the world! That poor girl works hard as I do every day at the plant, and that's *damn* hard, and she comes back to this house that's stuffy and dark, and she does and does and does for you and Dean till she cain't do no more!"

"Sarah is Dean's wife," said Jo petulantly, "and Dean cain't do for himself, so she's got to do it for him."

"But she's not *your* wife, Jo!" cried Becca. "And she don't have to do for you like she does."

"She's been complaining, hasn't she?"

" 'Course not," said Becca, "Sarah don't complain," which wasn't true, but the situation demanded that Becca stand against Jo Howell on every point. "Sarah's just tired, and she's gone tire herself into the grave, you keep running her like you do."

"She'll get used to it," said Jo, "she's got to. Dean's gone take a long time to heal."

"She'd be all right if you'd get off her back, Jo! And she'd be all right if she didn't worry like she does about this amulet thing . . ."

Jo's neck twisted strangely, and by mistake she pushed the wet cloth with which she had been mopping Dean's brow into the black slit of his mouth. "What you talking about? What you mean Sarah's worried about what amulet?"

"You know what amulet. The amulet you gave Larry Coppage. That necklace that went and killed the Coppages, and the Shirleys, and the Simses, and all the rest of 'em, and now it's done and gone got two more colored girls right this very afternoon. We saw where it happened. And the sheriff still can't find the damn thing!"

Jo was livid with rage. She sputtered, "Sheriff? What's the sheriff looking for it for?"

"We're all looking for it! Sarah keeps trying to find it, 'cause it just keeps killing people, and that's what's making her sick like she is this afternoon. That poor girl is in there lying down on my couch, and she's got no more will in her to move than Dean has . . ."

Jo spoke slowly. "Sarah told you about the amulet, and then she went and told the sheriff?"

Becca nodded, and then was unable to hold back a sneer of disgust. "Jo Howell, you always was mean, but I never thought that you would go around killing perfectly innocent colored girls with a piece of jewelry. I never heard the like of it in—"

"Get out! You get out, and you go get Sarah, and you send her right back over here!"

"No!!" shouted Becca. "I'm not gone do it. You gone sit there, or you gone get up and fix supper for Dean and yourself, or you're not gone get any—"

"You just shut up, and go get Sarah."

"You shut up! I've had just about enough, Jo Howell. Now you listen"—and Becca's voice dropped to a hoarse whisper—"I'm not kidding when I tell you that you have just about drove Sarah into the ground. I send her back tonight, and maybe she's gone get you supper, but then she's gone fall apart. She's gone fall apart tonight or to-

311

morrow morning, and then she's not gone get supper for you ever again. She's not gone be going to work either, and then what's gone happen to you and Dean? Now, I don't care. I don't give a damn what happens to you, Jo Howell, and I had just as soon that you had gone over to the Coppages and burnt up in the house with 'em, but you didn't. Sarah wouldn't mind taking care of you and Dean if you was just nice to her for five minutes a day, but you're not. I'm gone try to get Sarah on her feet, so she can come back over here and take care of you. That's what she wants—though I sure don't know why she wants it. But not tonight. She's not gone come back to this house tonight. She's gone sleep in my house."

Jo said nothing. Becca's tone had convinced her that it might indeed be necessary for Sarah to have that single night's rest.

"You understand what I'm saying?" said Becca.

"All right," said Jo grudgingly after a moment. "But let me tell you something, Becca Blair. You look around this room, and you look good, because when you walk out that door in ten seconds, you never gone see the inside of this house again, you understand me?"

"Jo," said Becca, "if an escaped con from the Florida pen came up to me, and put a shotgun to the back of my head, he couldn't get me to come within twenty feet of you. If I never see you again after this very minute, I will count this the luckiest day of my life. I would buy a new set of tires for the piggyback diesel that ran you down in the middle of the road." And with that she walked out of the room, and returned to her friend next door.

Chapter 66

SARAH was indeed ill. The deaths of the two young women on the other side of Burnt Corn Creek had smashed through the careful support in her mind that had kept her going all this while, from Dean's coming home, through her early suspicions about the amulet, to her absolute certainty that this piece of jewelry had been responsible for the deaths of sixteen men, women, and children in Pine Cone. Sarah relaxed a little after she found herself supported by Becca and Sheriff Garrett, and she had not been prepared for the stink of freshly spilled blood in Ruby's House of Beauty.

She knew that Becca was lying when she said that Jo had made no objections to her staying over the night, but Sarah did not contradict her friend. She slept the rest of Saturday afternoon, and sat up to eat the supper that Becca set out on a TV tray for her. Sarah even smiled a little through Becca's nervous volubility that entire evening: ". . . almost glad it happened, 'cause it gives you the chance to get out of that house for just a little while, let Jo take care of Dean for a bit, 'cause she is perfectly capable of mashing up them strawberries we brought back for him, and if I thought she couldn't take care of Dean, why I'd be over there myself . . ."

Sarah nodded, and said in a low hoarse voice, "Jo can take care of Dean . . ."

313

MICHAEL McDOWELL

Becca nodded vigorously, glad that Sarah seemed to be coming out of it. Her immobility had frightened Becca, and she still wondered if Sarah would be able to go to work on Monday morning.

Becca telephoned the head of the Pine Cone telephone office, and broke the date she had made with him the previous day.

"When he asked me, I told him yes, even though I didn't want to go—don't like him—but I thought if I went out on a date, I would prove that the wee-gee board was wrong, when it said I wouldn't have a date till next Saturday."

Sarah didn't laugh. "Looks like the wee-gee board's gone turn out to be right. Just like when it said that Dean and Jo were responsible for all them deaths . . ."

"Shhhh . . . !" cautioned Becca, "let's don't talk about it no more tonight."

"It also said that—" Sarah began, broke off, and spoke no more of the Ouija board, the amulet, or the eighteen dead citizens of Pine Cone.

The two women watched television, though Sarah fell asleep shortly after ten o'clock. She was well enough the following morning to sit up at the breakfast table.

Becca feared that Sarah would now start making motions to return to Jo and Dean next door, weak as she still was; and she began thinking of ways to talk her out of it. But Sarah said nothing about going back, and seemed content to sit and read through the Sunday papers, while Becca and Margaret got ready to go off to Andalusia for late morning mass, a trip Becca enjoyed despite not being a Catholic.

"You gone be here when we get back, aren't you?" she said, a little doubtfully.

Sarah nodded and smiled. "I'll go back over there in time to fix Dean's supper. Not before then."

Reassured, Becca soon left with Margaret. Not an entire minute later, the telephone rang. Sarah was sure that it was Jo, who probably had been waiting for the purple Pontiac to pull out, and she did not answer it. She sat at the kitchen table, with a second cup of coffee, and a little plate of toast that Margaret had fixed for her just before they left.

314

In another few minutes, she heard Jo's voice calling out from the kitchen window just across the way. "Sarah! Sarah! You come back over here! Dean needs you, Sarah!"

Sarah did not get up from the table, did not even lift her eyes from the comics.

Late that afternoon, when Sarah was just about to return to Jo and Dean, Becca said, "You're all right now, aren't you?" Sarah had rapidly improved during the time that Becca and Margaret were in Andalusia, regaining her spirit entirely, and by five o'clock had apparently recovered her strength as well.

Sarah nodded in response to the question. "I'm fine, Becca, just fine."

Becca looked askance and reluctantly said, "What you think was wrong with you, Sarah?"

"I was a little tired, that's all. Probably I don't need anything more than a little nap every afternoon, that's all." She said this with a smile, but Becca didn't believe her.

"You not still thinking about that amulet, are you?"

Sarah smiled again, and Becca thought this very strange, for her friend had never spoken of the amulet but with the greatest seriousness. "No," said Sarah, "I cain't do anything about it. I'm just gone leave it all up to the sheriff . . ."

Becca didn't believe this either.

Chapter 67

Margaret Blair, on this particular Monday, was very happy, for at noon she was to become a senior in high school, a position which conferred many social and psychological benefits to a young girl. She in fact was going to celebrate, with a few of her friends, with a picnic on a special sandbar in Burnt Corn Creek, a favored location that was known and frequented by a certain set of boys —soon also to be seniors themselves. They were charitably taking along all their younger brothers and sisters, so there promised to be quite a little crowd on the strip of pebbly sand and coarse grass.

Margaret stood over the stove in the early morning, fishing apples out of a great pot of boiling sugar syrup. She was preparing two dozen of these, and that was to be her contribution. She and her friends would be going down to the creek just as soon as they could get out of school, and those minutes just before noon were perhaps the most precious of all the year to them.

Margaret's mother entered the room then, dressed for work, her handbag over her arm, and sat at the breakfast table.

"That gone be enough, Margaret?" asked Becca.

Margaret nodded absently, and then said, "Mama, you better get ready, 'cause I see Sarah out in her back yard putting up clothes on the line, and she don't have many.

She's gone be through in twenty seconds, and she's gone be ready to go."

"I'm ready," said Becca, "soon's I do my lips."

Becca rummaged in her purse for her lipstick. But pulling her hand out, she came up with the lipstick and with the amulet as well. Becca looked at it and shuddered. "M-Margaret . . ." she faltered.

Margaret let an apple slide off the spoon back into the pot. It disappeared beneath the surging sugar-water. "What, Mama?" She turned down the burner just a little, for the syrup had raised itself to the ideal temperature, according to the candy thermometer attached to the side of the pot.

"Margaret," Becca said, "did you put this thing in my purse?" She held up the amulet by its chain.

"What is it, Mama? What is that?"

"It's a necklace, with a thing on the end of it, just like the one that Sarah's always talking about. What I'm asking is, d'you put it in here?"

"Mama," replied Margaret, "I never saw that thing before in my life."

Becca stared a moment at the amulet, and then looked up again at her daughter. "Margaret," she said, "you call Sarah and you tell her to come on over here right now."

Margaret called out the window, "Sarah, can you come here half a second?"

Becca could hear her friend's voice from outside, calling in reply, "Soon as I get these sheets up!"

Margaret moved over to her mother's side. "Mama, I've never seen that thing before, but it's real pretty. If you don't like it, why don't you let me—"

Margaret reached out for the amulet, and Becca, fearful that her daughter might take it and put it on, suddenly pulled back, clapping the amulet to her breast. The sudden movement knocked her chair against the wall; and Becca grabbed the edges of the chair as she scurried to keep from falling over.

"You be careful, Mama!" cried Margaret, "if you don't—" She stopped abruptly. "How'd that happen?" she asked, surprised.

"What?" said Becca.

"That chain's 'round your neck. You had it in your hand not two seconds ago, and now it's hooked 'round your neck."

"No, it's not," said Becca.

"Yes, it is, Mama!" exclaimed Margaret, who couldn't understand why her mother was contradicting a self-evident fact. She laughed in her perplexity and returned to the apples. Becca tugged at the amulet, and with an expression of intense disgust, followed her daughter's movements at the stove. Margaret peered out the window, and said, "Mama, Sarah'll be right here."

Margaret carefully brought another apple up to the surface of the pot. She heard her mother rise from the breakfast table behind her. "Mama," she said, "you think I ought to make eggs too? I mean, they's gone be nearly fifteen of us, and that's not counting little Mary Shirley, and you know what that little girl told me? She told me that now that her mama and daddy is dead, she's not ever gone eat a egg again when the sun is up! She said to me that eggs was for the nighttime!"

Suddenly Margaret felt herself grabbed from behind. Her mother had her hand on her daughter's throat, tight and stifling. Margaret was so surprised that she did not even think to struggle; but in a moment, when that hand began to push her face down toward the violently boiling syrup in the pot, Margaret tried to squirm out of her mother's grasp. She opened her mouth to scream, but the liquid flooded up into her throat, and searing pain that seemed to melt her consciousness was all that was left to the unfortunate girl.

Sugar syrup boiled out all over the stove and the counter and floor. Steam hissed up from the contact with the electrical coils beneath the pot. The apples rolled off the counter and smashed solidly against the linoleum. Margaret's body went limp under Becca's hands, and fell to the floor under its own weight. The pot of seething sugar toppled as well and poured out all over the girl's corpse, cooking her flesh until it was the color and consistency of deep-fried chicken skin. Becca had had to spring well out of the way so that she would not be burned also.

Margaret's face was a featureless, bubbling lump of pink candy. With a broom handle Becca overturned the

The Amulet

corpse, so that it lay face down, and then she gingerly reached over to turn off the stove. She heard Sarah's voice, calling softly from just underneath the kitchen window. Becca stepped to the sink and looked out at her friend.

"What'd Margaret want, Becca?"

"She just wanted to know if you're ready to go to the plant," Becca replied with a smile.

"I'm ready," said Sarah, "don't even have to go back inside."

Becca nodded, and backed away from the window, at the same time carefully slipping the amulet beneath her blouse. She retrieved her purse from the breakfast table, and went out the back door without even glancing at her daughter's corpse on the kitchen floor, lying in a pool of still-bubbling sugar syrup, with the brilliantly red candied apples scattered all round her.

Becca pulled out of the driveway a few moments later, and the two women drove down the street in front of Sarah's house. Instinctively, Sarah stared out the car window at the front of her house. Suddenly, the curtains in the living room were jerked open. Sarah could see Dean, bandaged and motionless, propped up in a chair in the little alcove there. Jo was in the chair beside him, staring directly out at Sarah. She jumped, and averted her eyes: who had pulled the curtains open?

319

Chapter 68

∞∞∞∞∞∞∞∞∞∞∞∞∞∞∞∞∞∞∞∞∞∞∞∞∞∞∞∞∞∞∞∞∞∞

WELL," said Becca, "did you two have it out? What'd Jo say when you came in yesterday?" These were Becca's first questions to Sarah, even before they had got into the car.

Sarah looked well, and appeared stronger than before the attack had occurred on Saturday.

"No," said Sarah, "we didn't have it out. I went in yesterday afternoon and I fixed supper and I took it to them. And Jo didn't say a word about my being gone."

"I cain't hardly believe it," said Becca, but asked no more questions on the drive to work.

But Sarah was thinking, and thinking hard: herself wondering why Jo had said nothing to her. She had been prepared for an onslaught of abuse and recrimination, but none had been forthcoming. Jo had been sullen and even more watchful than usual, but there was no blatant hostility.

The fat woman sat by while Sarah fed Dean, and Sarah began to think that she had got away with it. But she also wondered about Jo's strange and unexpected behavior in this. Sarah had come back from Becca's with new resolve to take control of her life again, to fight Jo—and fight Dean—to the last drop of her blood, and if necessary, theirs. Now she felt as if she were lying in wait

for them, preparing herself for a long siege against the mother and son.

That would take time, however, and while she played her games with Jo, other people in Pine Cone might die. But Sarah knew that haste and hysteria and strident accusations against Jo would do no good, and that the only way to get at Jo was by the same methods she used herself: silence, deviousness, and treachery. All Sarah's strength was gathered up from her heart, from the whole of her body, and set right against the backs of her eyes. Nothing would escape her, and she would feel no remorse for anything that happened, for anything that would have to be done.

At last, after Dean had finished his supper, Sarah's patience was rewarded. Jo said, "Becca told me about them two colored girls that died in the beauty parlor."

Sarah looked up but said nothing. She doubted if Jo was telling the truth.

"She said you went in there, and saw where it happened, and all."

Briefly, Sarah told what she knew of the circumstances of the deaths of Martha-Ann and Ruby.

"Becca said that you told the sheriff about the amulet."

Sarah nodded. "I told him I was looking for it, and I described it to him."

"What else did you tell him about it?"

"Nothing else. I just told him I had lost it, and was looking for it, that's all. If I had told him . . . anything else, he wouldn't have believed me."

Sarah saw that this lie pleased Jo, and relieved her of some anxiety.

"But you told Becca . . ." said Jo.

"Becca believes in all sorts of things. Becca would believe anything you said to her. You know, we were watching *The Song of Bernadette* on TV the other night, and Becca made Margaret sleep in the same room with her, 'cause she was afraid that the Virgin Mary was gone make an appearance in the bedroom closet . . ."

The two women were in a standoff now, and neither said anything for a few minutes. Jo continued with her sewing, and Sarah read through two short articles in *Redbook*.

"What you gone do now?" said Jo.

Sarah folded the book in her lap, but kept her place. "I'm gone see what happens tomorrow . . ." Then she smiled, and opened the magazine again.

That had been an act to scare Josephine Howell; Sarah really wasn't sure what she would do next—but it was above all necessary to keep Jo on her guard. That morning, as she prepared herself for the beginning of the week at work, Sarah had noticed with satisfaction that Jo was nervous, and so distracted that she forgot to be irritable.

Sarah dreaded the beginning of this week, another forty hours on the assembly line in which she would have nothing to do except think of Jo, and Dean, and the amulet. But she had drawn her strength up, and was, in fact, reassured to know that she was willing and prepared to fight, that she was ready to risk everything. She had got beyond despair.

Chapter 69

THE Monday morning on which all the young people were to be let out of school was bright and warm. And though it was the first day of the week, the great crowd of workers that entered the Pine Cone Munitions Factory did so cheerfully. Playfully they shoved one another up the small narrow flights of wooden steps into the factory and managerial offices of the place.

After Sarah and Becca had parked the car in the parking lot and had got out, they became separated, moving along with different groups of acquaintances into the building. It was a happy morning, for the end of the school year, even for those who hadn't been inside a classroom in thirty years, still meant the beginning of summer in Pine Cone. And summer in south Alabama despite the worsening heat meant trips to the Florida coast, going fishing in the late afternoon after work, picnics, and barbecues.

A couple of minutes before the whistle was to blow, Becca and Sarah seated themselves at the assembly line, arranging for two hours of work before the coffee break.

Becca checked over her religious artifacts on the boards beside her, and then pulled the amulet out from underneath her blouse, setting it to best effect. Sarah stood up and leaned over the partition that separated them, in-

323

tending a final few moments of conversation before the belt started up.

"Margaret told me yesterday she was going picnicking today," she said. "She told me—"

Becca had turned to face her friend, and Sarah stopped short when she caught sight of the amulet around Becca's neck.

"Becca!" Sarah cried.

"What?" said Becca, with surprise.

"Becca, where'd you get that thing?" said Sarah, in great alarm. Sarah was very frightened, and completely at a loss to know how Becca had come by the amulet. She could not even stop to think of possibilities.

Becca stared at her friend blankly and grasped the amulet protectively to her breast.

Sarah reached for the amulet, and actually had her fingers around it, but Becca pushed her hands away violently.

The machinery ground up suddenly, and the assembly belt quivered and moved forward. Sarah again spoke to her friend, but her question could not be heard over the sound of the machinery. Again she lunged for the amulet, but Becca jerked away. The partition behind her was upset and fell against another female worker. Two figurines smashed to the floor.

Becca stared around her, as if in panic, and Sarah made a move to come around the partition to get at her. The women in the immediate vicinity, those who could see what had happened, stopped to stare. What had come over these two women, who were best friends in all the world?

Becca fled from Sarah down the aisle. Workers stopped and looked, and tried to shout their curiosity and wonder to one another over the sound of the machinery. Sarah ran after her, determined now to get the amulet, no matter the cost, no matter the embarrassment.

Becca turned a corner into an aisle bordered with much larger pieces of machinery. These were die presses and the like, all operated by men. She whirled around to see where to go next, and then fled down the aisle, heading toward the door that opened onto the parking lot. All the men turned and stared, but none tried to stop her. Sarah

was almost as quickly around that corner as well and gave
chase. Becca was an older woman and not as quick, so
that Sarah soon caught up with her. Sarah reached forward and grabbed at the amulet. Becca lunged to the side
to get away from her friend, stumbled and careened; she
fell beneath the dies of a metal-punch machine.

The operator of the machine, even as he saw Becca
stumbling, moved to turn off the machine's switches. He
was too late. Two of the large circular dies, like pistons in
an automobile engine, cut through Becca's body. The
sickening sound of crushing bones could be heard above
everything else. Sarah screamed Becca's name.

The dies came up again, dragging Becca's body a couple of feet into the air before letting it drop again. The
machinery halted. Blood gushed from the obscenely
large wound in Becca's body. The operator had run away,
and Sarah continued to stare at her friend's corpse. Becca's eyes remained open. Sarah could no longer see the
amulet about her neck.

She screamed at the corpse, though she could hardly
hear herself over the machinery. "Where is it, Becca,
where is it?"

Sarah spun around in panic. Becca was dead, Becca
had died in front of her eyes, Becca had died because
Sarah had chased her through the plant. Sarah had wanted
to protect her friend against the prediction of the Ouija
board, and had succeeded only in fulfilling it. Becca had
had the amulet around her neck when she fell into the
machine, and now it was no longer there.

With revulsion matched only by her determination,
Sarah knelt beside the corpse, ignoring the crowd of men
that in the past few seconds had begun to gather. She tore
open the top of Becca's blouse. Blood dyed Sarah's hands
to the wrists. The amulet wasn't there; it must have come
loose in the fall, and dropped somewhere near. Maybe it
had been smashed in the machine. Sarah dropped to her
hands and knees and scurried around on the bloody hard-
wood floor searching for it, and violently resisting the efforts of the men around to raise her.

Because of the great size of the factory, and more especially because of the tremendous volume of noise in the
place, only a few people realized that something terrible

had happened. Because the machine in which she was killed was set back a little from the others, only a couple of people had actually seen Becca Blair die. The women who worked on the assembly line had only seen the two women running off, and with the rifles still coming through they had not the leisure to follow after them. The two women on either side of Becca's and Sarah's places had to work double-time while those two were absent and perform their tasks for them on each rifle that was to go through. They cursed Sarah and Becca both.

Sarah stared round her. She had no idea what she ought to do now. The man who operated the die press had gone off to get help, but had not yet returned. Several more men, also mechanics, stood staring aghast at Becca's corpse. Two workers had pulled it out into the aisle and hidden it, as best they could, beneath a canvas cover. They stared at Sarah in great apprehension, for in their eyes it was she who had caused the horrible death of Becca Blair. Sarah staggered away. She came around another corner and was once again within sight of the conveyer belt and the long line of her friends and acquaintances.

Sarah looked about her distractedly and attempted, without knowing what she was doing, to wipe onto her dress the blood that stained her hands. Suddenly she gasped. The amulet, gleaming gold and black, was caught around the barrel of one of the weapons on the conveyer belt.

A woman with a drill faltered when she saw the amulet appear before her, and in her surprise she drove the drill through the palm of her hand. She screamed shrilly in pain, and all the workers near her pulled back in alarm. The injured woman overturned her chair, and lurched across the floor. In another moment her friends rose and gathered around her.

Sarah tried to get at the amulet, but could not reach the assembly belt through the knot of people blocking her path. She screamed for them to get out of her way, but they only stared at her uncomprehendingly, and then turned back to the woman whose hand was being bandaged.

Sarah knew now that she had to get hold of the amulet before anything else happened, so she picked up a rifle that lay atop an unclosed box along the outside wall. She waved it round menacingly, and though the women all knew that it was unloaded, instinctively they drew back. By this action, and by the blood on her dress and her hands that they noticed for the first time, all the women were sure that Sarah had gone entirely out of her mind.

A woman, who had never liked Sarah, ran up and attempted to wrest the rifle from her. Sarah pushed her down onto the floor with the butt of the weapon, but had to work to disentangle her foot from the woman's crossed arms.

On the other side of the building there was now a large amount of shouting and a general commotion over the discovery of Becca Blair's mangled body. Nothing was intelligible because of the noise of the machinery.

The men gaping around Becca's corpse had no idea of what was happening on the other side. Most of the women from the assembly line had abandoned their positions, and were now crouching behind their partitions, or the shelving, and stared in wonder at Sarah Howell, who scrambled among the partitions, knocking the incomplete rifles onto the floor.

A very few workers had remained in their places as long as possible, but they had now given up in frustration, when the rifles shuddered past them having been neglected in the previous stages of assembly.

Never before had the Pine Cone Munitions Factory fallen into chaos. Machinery had broken down before, even the conveyer belt, and people had sat on their hands until it was repaired. But now everything moved on, and none of the machinery was still—but nothing worked properly. The male workers attempted to shut off their machines, but the switches were ineffectual in cutting the power. Even the die machine under which Becca Blair had perished so miserably suddenly reactivated itself, and punched at a terrible speed, as if greedy for another victim. The men cautiously backed away from their machines with the growing, terrifying realization that they no longer had control over them.

The chief electrician ran to the main power boxes at

the end of the great room, and though he changed the position of all the levers, no alteration was apparent. None of the machines was shut off.

Beneath all this, the conveyer belt had continued to move, and even to accelerate beyond its accustomed pace. The rifles shook and danced around on the belt; some were shaken off onto the floor. The wail of the machinery increased in volume and in pitch, until it was a piercing, unavoidable scream. All the shouting stopped, and every worker—even the woman who had pushed the drill through her hand—stood still, with their hands over their ears, and looked open-mouthed at the assembly belt. When they turned around again, Sarah was nowhere to be seen. The belt went faster and faster, and all the rifles were shaken apart into their components. Those scraps of metal bounded, and flew about, and were thrown off the belt. Several women who had sought to retrieve their purses and other personal belongings from the partitions, were brutally injured by the flying bits of metal, which seemed to seek out their eyes, mouths, and throats.

Two rifles at the very end of the line unaccountably exploded, with bright sparks and terrific reports. A woman standing nearby threw her hands above her face, and collapsed onto her knees, swaying widely in intense pain.

On the other aisle, several of the largest pieces of machinery, which were operating at twice and three times their normal speed, began to smoke. White gasps of clouds shot out from their tops at first, but soon the double row of machines was billowing forth black smoke along its entire length. In another few moments, these dark clouds were shot through with shooting sparks and small, licking flames.

One worker, who took hold of the handle which controlled the velocity of his machine, had his arm wrenched out of its socket when the handle suddenly reversed the direction of its circular motion.

Every worker in the building at once directed his gaze upward. The incandescent lights in the rafters above had suddenly increased in brightness. Then the workers, who were standing together in the aisles, as far from the machinery as possible, stared down at the floor, so as not to be blinded. The lights went searing white and then burst, showering hot glass everywhere and on everyone, inflicting small painful cuts on every inch of exposed skin.

Throughout the building, windows shot up so suddenly and so forcefully that the glass in the panes shattered, and the frames of the windows splintered. The factory workers turned and gaped, astounded by the sight of the factory falling apart around them. They had not yet the sense to leave the place, so surprised were they by the extraordinary events themselves. Because of the noise, no communication was possible. Each worker was alone in his fear.

The clothing of two workmen was ignited by stray sparks and the men ran down the aisle followed by a third, spraying a foaming fire extinguisher at them. The sight of these two men, fleeing in their flames, scared the workers more than anything else, and as one man they started to run for the door. It was as if they had realized, each at the same moment, that they were doomed if they remained inside a moment longer.

Shelves and cases filled with tools and spare parts toppled over in quick succession, as during an earthquake. Three women were caught beneath the largest and heaviest of these.

A man was jostled by his own wife in their attempt to escape and he fell against a machine used to fashion and attach serial-number plates to the rifles. Two small bolts drove through his arm, riveting him to the machine. He tore away from it, leaving behind two bloody mounds of flesh, muscle, and splintered bone, but fainted from the shock before he could reach the exit.

In the managerial offices in a different building, all work had stopped for a moment while everyone discussed the news that had just been phoned over: that one of the assembly line workers had died on the job. They wondered who it might have been, how she might have died, and whether the accident would entail an investigation. The machinery in the plant was a distant, constant hum under these whispered conversations, only a little louder than a refrigerator motor.

Conversation stopped altogether when that hum greatly increased in volume, peaking in a piercing whine. All the office workers—executives and secretaries and stock-room

clerks—ran to the windows that faced the factory buildings to see what had happened. They all gasped to see the
first few workers spilling out of the plant. They cried aloud
when a young woman fell down the stairs and was trampled in the rush.

"Let's go see what's wrong!" someone shouted and there
was a general movement to the front door of the offices.
But before even one man had gone through those double
doors, every telephone in the building rang at once, setting
up an intolerable jangling. The workers looked at one another in perplexity. A secretary lifted one of the phones;
there was no one on the other end, but as soon as she
replaced the receiver, it began to ring again.

Two frosted-glass partitions between executive offices
shattered noisily and the glass poured onto the floor, again
with small but painful injury to those standing nearby.

All the water fountains in the corridors suddenly arched
their jets of icy water far into the air, and could not be
stopped. The floors became spotted with slippery pools of
cold water. In hurrying from one room to another, people
skidded and fell in their haste.

Bracketed walls of shelves gave way in every office,
sending hundreds of pounds of books and supplies onto
the heads of those who turned helplessly about in the
rooms, unable to conceive of what was happening to them.
Filing drawers shot out of their casings with force great
enough to crack the ribs of those unlucky enough to be
standing near them. All the toilets overflowed at once so
that even more water poured out into the corridors.

One by one, piles of stationery on typists' desks toppled, and the sheets flew out in all directions, as with will,
and literally shredded the skin of the women who hud-
dled around their desks, whimpering. Untouched, the type-
writers in the room set up an intolerable clacking, joined
by the adding machines, the duplicators, and the posting
machines, until the machines erupted with an oily smoke.

In every office, the lights in the ceiling glared brightly,
more brightly still, and then exploded. Immediately after,
the ceilings started to give way, and great clouds of plas-
ter filled the rooms. Pipes burst in all the walls, which
bellied ominously, and water poured out of every crack
and seam.

Workers trying to leave were hampered by the water that was now inches deep in some places, by doors that suddenly swung open or locked shut, by drawers that shot out of desks and cabinets, by piles of anything at all that without cause toppled heavily over. But they stumbled forward, screamed and struggled, and a few even aided one another. Some even managed, whimpering and scared, to get out of the building.

Those who tried to escape by the windows regretted the attempt, for when they were halfway out, the window would smash down heavily enough to shatter the glass, splinter the frame, and break the back of the secretary or administrative assistant caught beneath. One of these unfortunates could be seen in half a dozen windows all around the building, dazed, or unconscious, or already dead.

Smoke gathered in the rooms, and fire traveled from office to office, apparently unhampered by the quantity of water on the floors.

Nearly all of the workers were now out of the main plant building, in which Becca Blair had died. Two women were still trapped beneath shelves that had fallen, but they were likely to remain there, since no one had seen them disappear. Those workers who had been near the exits now stood about the parking lot, staring at the factory, still unable to comprehend what was happening. Smoke billowed from the center of the building where a portion of the roof had collapsed. Everyone was watching for flames. The last workers were struggling out, many with torn and bloody clothing, some limping. A female worker held the hands of a man while he lowered himself out one of the side windows. He ran off immediately, and she jumped down to the ground after him.

An explosion, loud but still somehow indistinct, blew out part of the side wall of the plant, and directly afterward large sheets of flame appeared in that part of the building. When it seemed likely that there might be more explosions, the people panicked and ran to their cars.

Many had left their keys inside the building, and banged futilely on the car doors; others who had left the automobiles unlocked cowered in the backseats. Those who could drive away immediately locked bumpers in their rush, or dented fenders so that tires would not turn. A limping woman was run down, and the guilty driver, though he knew he had been seen, kept going. Two pickup trucks parked on the edge of the lot drove off, each carrying twenty people in the back.

In the line of cars parked nearest the building, one automobile suddenly began to roll backward, and ran down a man with a broken leg who had taken shelter just behind it. In halting succession, the other vehicles in that row also began to move backward, or turn in wide slow arcs, until they had smashed into something else. This set up a chain reaction that spread all over the lot, but in a haphazard fashion, so that it was impossible for those fleeing through and among the automobiles to avoid being hit by the rolling, unoccupied cars.

These collisions were not violent, but they prevented any more cars from leaving the lot. Those fortunate enough to have remembered their ignition keys were now forced to abandon their vehicles. The injured and the simply frightened fell over into babbling hysteria and uncontrolled weeping when they realized that they had to dodge through nearly an acre of these marauding vehicles before they reached the safety of the street—and who knew if they would be completely free of these inexplicable dangers even then?

Residents of the houses directly across from the lot came out and stood on the curb, staring with wonder at the destruction of the factory, and the lumbering mayhem of the automobiles. The braver and kinder of these ventured across the street and helped to the relative safety of their front yards the workers who at last had made it to the edge of the factory property. But there was nothing to do for those who struggled and stumbled and screamed, trying to avoid the cars that rolled about the lot at random, nothing to be done for those with broken limbs and severe burns who had taken shelter in the automobiles, and were now rigid with fear at being trapped in cars that were driverless but mobile.

After the second explosion in the building there was sudden quiet. The automobiles in the parking lot halted, as if hundreds of emergency brakes had been drawn on at once.

Under the smaller, random screams of the injured and the merely frightened, it was possible to hear the soft sounds of the fire, peeling along the wooden floor of the buildings. Someone pointed to the administration building; it too was on fire, though it appeared impossible that the flames would have spread from one building to the other across a barren strip of asphalt forty yards wide.

Those who remained to observe the destruction turned at the sound of sirens behind them. At last the fire department had been alerted, and was on its way, though the executives of the place whispered that it would do no good. These men began to speak of sabotage and the two hippies who had passed through town the week before. It was probably they who had planted a bomb in the factory, set to go off a week later, when they would be long gone.

What other explanation was there?

Chapter 70

█ARAH Howell was out of sight of the factory, running down the sidewalk on a shaded street a few blocks away from the Pine Cone Munitions Factory. She turned to glance behind her and saw a great cloud of black smoke churning up from behind a clump of oaks. Sirens wailed before and behind her.

A car coming down the street pulled up to the curb near Sarah. An old woman leaned out of the passenger window, and asked, "What's happened, dear?"

Sarah shook her head and hurried on.

The old woman and her husband exchanged curious, concerned glances, then turned to watch Sarah running away.

The town's second fire engine wheeled around the corner just then, and Sarah leaned against a light pole for a moment, to allow the vehicle to pass and to catch her breath.

In ten minutes more she was home. She struggled up the sidewalk, disheveled and panting. There were oil stains on her forearms, and one of the straps of her shoe was broken. Jo rocked peaceably in a chair on the front porch, and with an idle hand she was pushing the glider back and forth. Dean was scrunched into the corner, unmoving. The sun shone hotly against his bandages.

Jo stared at the column of black smoke in the distance

and smiled. Wearily, Sarah threw herself onto the bottom wooden step. Her breath for a time was hot and irregular. She sat very still until it was under control. The sun dried the sweat on her brow. She moved her head slowly about, and stared at the smoke in the distance. Jo stared as well, and the rocker creaked rhythmically.

"Well," said Sarah, in a voice that was calm and sure, "it's gone, Jo."

"The plant," said Jo with a small smile.

Sarah nodded slowly.

"Ohhh," said Jo, with a tiny squeal. "You're a sight, Sarah! You go in and change them clothes!"

Sarah turned and looked at her mother-in-law. "You're pleased as punch, Jo! People were killed, Jo. People were killed at the plant this morning." Sarah spoke evenly, unemotionally.

"Good thing it happened in the morning," Jo adjudged. "That way you got home in time to fix me and Dean some dinner."

"Becca Blair was one of them that's dead," said Sarah quietly. She leaned against a pillar of bricks and stretched her legs out along one of the porch steps.

Jo rocked a few seconds more, and looked closely at Sarah. She was very puzzled, and couldn't make out Sarah's attitude. It was not possible that Sarah wasn't cut up by her best friend's death—but Sarah sat perfectly still, turning her head in the shade of a large azalea.

"Anybody told Margaret yet?" Jo asked in a few moments. "That phone's been ringing there the whole morning long. Nearly went and answered it myself." She realized that something was amiss, and that she must discover it as soon as possible. Sarah wasn't herself. She was acting resigned, and appeared to possess that strength that always rises out of a despairing resignation.

"Margaret's gone on a picnic," said Sarah, "and there'll be plenty of time when she gets back to tell her about her mother being dead and all."

They were silent a few minutes more. The smoke was denser and blacker now, and the sun disappeared behind it.

Still Jo could not make out Sarah's attitude. The fat woman was vastly uncomfortable and tried to think, for

335

her own comfort's sake, that the change signified nothing. Sarah was simply bowled over by the events of the morning, by the fire at the plant, by the death of Becca Blair. Jo decided that she must quickly regain the upper hand, and therefore said, in her accustomed tone, "Sarah, after you change them clothes, I want you to fix Dean some dinner. And give him some *meat*. He's got to have his strength up, 'cause I am gone cut his bandages off this afternoon! He'll heal faster now, I know he will . . ."

"Because of the plant, you mean," said Sarah, but did not look at Jo.

"I didn't say that," said Jo. "I just got tired of seeing all that tape. You know where my sewing scissors are, Sarah?"

The two women exchanged glances. Sarah's was hard and tired, but Jo's was unsure and timorous. Sarah rose and went on into the house. She did not even look at her husband.

Chapter 71

LESS than an hour later, just at noontime, Dean Howell had been moved to the breakfast table in the center of the kitchen. Sarah sat close beside him, methodically spooning soft food into his mouth. Jo sat across the table from them, nervously clacking a pair of scissors together, in the expectation of removing the bandages from her sons's head and neck.

Sarah had gone about silently complying with Jo's commands. She had changed her clothes and washed and had prepared dinner for Dean. There was a casserole already in the oven for her and Jo.

Jo decided that she had been correct. Sarah was only momentarily disconcerted, but now she was her usual compliant self. In fact, she seemed even more docile than before. She performed all her duties without a breath of recalcitrance or protest. Perhaps, Jo imagined, Sarah had given in completely now. Perhaps all the resistance had been drained out of her.

Jo smiled her most unpleasant smile, and snapped the scissors together again.

"I sure do wish we could hear some more news about the plant," said Jo. "How many's dead. Who's dead besides Becca. Maybe they're gone close the place down. Maybe they're gone take it somewhere else, down to Mobile or over to Jackson maybe."

Sarah did not reply.

"How'd Becca die?" said Jo. "She get shot with one of the rifles that you two was always putting together?"

Sarah replied shortly, "She got caught in some machinery."

"Did it hurt?" Jo demanded.

"Didn't take long," said Sarah.

"D'you see the body?"

Sarah nodded. "Closed coffin on Becca too."

Jo whistled and clacked the scissors again. But inwardly, she couldn't declare herself pleased that Sarah spoke so callously of her friend's death. It wasn't at all like Sarah. "Bad things happen to you when you work in a place like that," said Jo. She stared at her daughter-in-law, expecting some reply to all of this. But Sarah only sat very quietly, and continued to feed her husband.

"I waited a long time for this day," said Jo.

"You talking about the plant or the scissors—cutting off the bandages, I mean?" said Sarah expressionlessly, and reached for another bowl of food for her husband.

"Couldn't take off Dean's bandages before today," said Jo, in an ambiguous reply.

"You never was a patient woman," said Sarah, with a small noncommittal sigh.

Jo nodded acquiescence to this opinion. Then she leaned forward across the table. "How much of that you gone feed him, Sarah? I tell you, Dean must be anxious as I am to get them bandages off him."

"He gets all of it," said Sarah, and stuck the spoon again into her husband's mouth.

"It's not mashed-up okra is it?" said Jo doubtfully. "Dean hates okra."

Sarah shook her head.

"He's eating it," said Jo, with a little maternal pride.

At that moment, there was a slight jerk in Dean's body. His mother trembled to see it. "Dean," she whispered with alarm.

Sarah removed the spoon from her husband's mouth. Silently, she held it out for her mother-in-law's inspection. The bowl of the spoon was filled with thick, discolored blood.

More of the nauseous liquid spilled out of the corner of

Dean's mouth, dribbling slowly down the bandages on his chin and neck.

Jo was speechless with astonishment. She leaned forward in her chair, and reached helplessly out to her son. Her short fat arms could not touch him. The folds of flesh in her neck trembled, and her tiny black eyes shone moistly.

Sarah wiped a little of the blood away with a paper napkin, and continued to spoon-feed her husband.

"Sarah!" cried Jo, "what are you doing? What's wrong with Dean?"

Sarah made no reply. Dean's body moved again, more violently, shifting awkwardly in the chair. He would have fallen over on the floor, had not Sarah steadied him with her arm.

Jo began to drag her chair around the table to get nearer her son. She scraped across the floor crying, "What you *giving* him, Sarah?" Jo reached out to protect her son. Sarah pushed her husband's head back and poured the remaining contents of the bowl down his throat.

"What is it!" Jo screamed.

"Applesauce and lye," Sarah answered quietly, and pointed to the opened can of lye on the kitchen counter, sitting next to an empty jar of applesauce.

Jo's expression was horrified, but then a terrible enlightenment entered into it. Her breathing became labored and short.

"Give it to me," she hissed. The flesh closed in around her eyes.

"What?" said Sarah.

"Give it to me," Jo repeated. "The amulet. It was in the plant, and you got it out of there."

Dean's head was thrown over the back of the chair. Black blood poured out of his mouth, spilled down his cheeks, and dripped onto the floor underneath the chair. Jo stared at her son, and then turned her head away. "You got it and I want it back," said Jo. "You got it on under your dress."

Quietly, Sarah said to her mother-in-law, "I found it on the belt. Becca had it on when she fell into the machinery, and somehow it got off her and onto the belt.

339

That was what caused the factory to explode, just like you wanted, just like you planned. But I found it again and I took it off the belt and stuck it on the end of a rifle. Then I held the rifle over a fire until the thing got melted down. I nearly got caught myself then, 'cause the fire was spreading. I nearly got burned up myself, but the amulet is gone."

Jo stared at Sarah uncomprehendingly. She was not sure whether to believe her or not. It sounded like a story that Sarah was making up as she went along. "Then how come—"

Sarah smiled then.

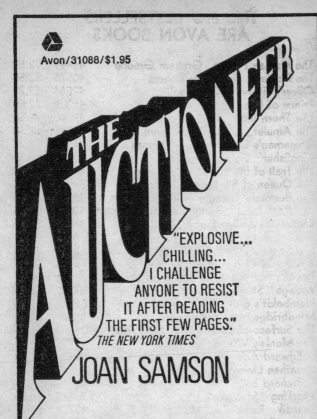

Avon/31088/$1.95

THE AUCTIONEER

"EXPLOSIVE...
CHILLING...
I CHALLENGE
ANYONE TO RESIST
IT AFTER READING
THE FIRST FEW PAGES."
THE NEW YORK TIMES

JOAN SAMSON

At first no one feared the smooth-talking outsider who ran the weekly auction. The slick, magnetic stranger was irresistible. The people of rural Harlowe, New Hampshire, willingly donated their antique junk for his auctions.

Then his quiet demands increased. Horrifying calamities befell those who refused him. What was behind his ever-growing power? After the heirlooms were gone, what would be next? The farm . . .? The children . . .?

SELECTED BY THE BOOK-OF-THE-MONTH CLUB
SOON TO BE A MAJOR MOTION PICTURE

EER 1-77

THE BIG BESTSELLERS
ARE AVON BOOKS

☐	**The Human Factor** Graham Greene	41491	$2.50
☐	**The Insiders** Rosemary Rogers	40576	$2.50
☐	**Oliver's Story** Erich Segal	42564	$2.25
☐	**Prince of Eden** Marilyn Harris	41905	$2.50
☐	**The Thorn Birds** Colleen McCullough	35741	$2.50
☐	**The Amulet** Michael McDowell	40584	$2.50
☐	**Chinaman's Chance** Ross Thomas	41517	$2.25
☐	**Kingfisher** Gerald Seymour	40592	$2.25
☐	**The Trail of the Fox** David Irving	40022	$2.50
☐	**The Queen of the Night** Marc Behm	39958	$1.95
☐	**The Bermuda Triangle** Charles Berlitz	38315	$2.25
☐	**The Real Jesus** Garner Ted Armstrong	40055	$2.25
☐	**Lancelot** Walker Percy	36582	$2.25
☐	**Snowblind** Robert Sabbag	44008	$2.50
☐	**Catch Me: Kill Me** William H. Hallahan	37986	$1.95
☐	**A Capitol Crime** Lawrence Meyer	37150	$1.95
☐	**Fletch's Fortune** Gregory Mcdonald	37978	$1.95
☐	**Voyage** Sterling Hayden	37200	$2.50
☐	**Humboldt's Gift** Saul Bellow	38810	$2.25
☐	**Mindbridge** Joe Haldeman	33605	$1.95
☐	**The Surface of Earth** Reynolds Price	29306	$1.95
☐	**The Monkey Wrench Gang** Edward Abbey	40857	$2.25
☐	**Jonathan Livingston Seagull** Richard Bach	34777	$1.75
☐	**Working** Studs Terkel	34660	$2.50
☐	**Shardik** Richard Adams	43752	$2.75
☐	**Anya** Susan Fromberg Schaeffer	25262	$1.95
☐	**Watership Down** Richard Adams	39586	$2.50

Available at better bookstores everywhere, or order direct from the publisher.

AVON BOOKS, Mail Order Dept., 224 W. 57th St., New York, N.Y. 10019

Please send me the books checked above. I enclose $_____ (please include 50¢ per copy for postage and handling). Please use check or money order—sorry, no cash or C.O.D.'s. Allow 4-6 weeks for delivery.

Mr/Mrs/Miss _____

Address _____

City _____ State/Zip _____

BB 4-79

IN HOLLYWOOD, WHERE DREAMS DIE QUICKLY, ONE LOVE LASTS FOREVER...

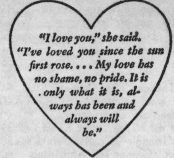

"I love you," she said. "I've loved you since the sun first rose. . . . My love has no shame, no pride. It is . only what it is, always has been and always will be."

The words are spoken by Brooke Ashley, a beautiful forties film star, in the last movie she ever made. She died in a tragic fire in 1947.

A young screenwriter in a theater in Los Angeles today hears those words, sees her face, and is moved to tears. Later he discovers that he wrote those words, long ago; that he has been born again—as she has.

What will she look like? Who could she be? He begins to look for her in every woman he sees . . .

A Romantic Thriller
by
TREVOR MELDAL-JOHNSEN

AVON

41897
$2.50